PENGUIN CLASSICS

HINDU MYTHS

ADVISORY EDITOR: BETTY RADICE

WENDY DONIGER O'FLAHERTY was born in New York in 1940 and trained as a dancer under George Balanchine and Martha Graham before beginning the study of Sanskrit at Radcliffe College in 1958. She holds doctoral degrees in Indian literature from Harvard and Oxford Universities, and is now the Mircea Eliade Professor of the History of Religions at the University of Chicago. Her publications include *Shiva: The Erotic Ascetic*; *The Origins of Evil in Hindu Mythology*; *Women, Androgynes and Other Mythical Beasts*; *Dreams, Illusion and Other Realities* and *Other Peoples' Myths: The Cave of Echoes*. She has also translated *The Rig Veda* and (with Brian K. Smith) *The Laws of Manu* for Penguin Classics.

HINDU MYTHS

A SOURCEBOOK
TRANSLATED FROM
THE SANSKRIT

WITH AN
INTRODUCTION BY
WENDY DONIGER O'FLAHERTY

PENGUIN BOOKS

PENGUIN BOOKS

Published by the Penguin Group
Penguin Books Ltd, 27 Wrights Lane, London W8 5TZ, England
Penguin Books USA Inc., 375 Hudson Street, New York, New York 10014, USA
Penguin Books Australia Ltd, Ringwood, Victoria, Australia
Penguin Books Canada Ltd, 10 Alcorn Avenue, Toronto, Ontario, Canada M4V 3B2
Penguin Books (NZ) Ltd, 182–190 Wairau Road, Auckland 10, New Zealand

Penguin Books Ltd, Registered Offices: Harmondsworth, Middlesex, England

First published 1975
15 17 19 20 18 16 14

Printed in England by Clays Ltd, St Ives plc
Set in Monotype Bembo

for Denny and Mike

CONTENTS

Guide to Pronunciation

Sanskrit vowels are pronounced very much like Italian vowels, with the exception of the short *a*, which is pronounced like the *u* in the English word 'but': long *ā* is pronounced like the *a* in 'father'.

As for the consonants a reasonable approximation will be obtained by pronouncing *c* as in 'church', *j* as in 'jungle', *ṣ* as in 'shun', *s* as in 'sun', *ś* as something halfway between the other two s's.

The aspirated consonants should be pronounced distinctly; *bh* as in 'cab-horse', *dh* as in 'mad-house', *gh* as in 'dog-house', *ph* as in 'top-hat', and *th* as in 'goat-herd'. *ṛ* is a vowel, pronounced midway between 'ri' as in 'rivet' and 'er' as in 'father'.

INTRODUCTION

Chaos out of Order

Turning and turning in the widening gyre
The falcon cannot hear the falconer;
Things fall apart; the centre cannot hold;
Mere anarchy is loosed upon the world,
The blood-dimmed tide is loosed . . .

WILLIAM BUTLER YEATS, *The Second Coming* (1921)

Nothing of him that doth fade
But doth suffer a sea-change
Into something rich and strange.

WILLIAM SHAKESPEARE, *The Tempest* (1611–12)

EVERY Hindu myth is different; all Hindu myths are alike. In spite of the deep-seated, totally compelling world-view that moulds every image and symbol, every word and idea of any Hindu myth, in spite of the stress placed upon traditional form at the expense of the individual artist, each myth celebrates the belief that the universe is boundlessly various, that everything occurs simultaneously, that all possibilities may exist without excluding each other. This concept is consciously expressed in at least one myth (myth 9 of this collection, p. 46): the creatures that the lord created were 'harmful or benign, gentle or cruel, full of *dharma* or *adharma*, truthful or false. And when they are created again, they will have these qualities; and this pleased him. The lord Creator himself diversified the variety and differentiation of all the objects of the senses, properties, and forms.'

In making the present selection, I have tried to give the reader as varied a taste of this delicious repast as possible: indeed, at times I fear the mixture may be a bit too rich and highly spiced for the unsuspecting browser, for Hindu mythology is a feast perhaps better suited to the gourmand than to the gourmet. Yet in spite of all attempts to preserve this essential variety, the pattern of the mythology has emerged and reasserted itself. The more myths one encounters, the more the basic themes seem to be reinforced; no matter what direction one sets out in, one is drawn back again and again to this centre of gravity, the still centre, the eye of the storm, just as Alice found herself always walking back in at the door of the Looking Glass House no matter what part of the magic garden she had hoped to reach.

The content of this pattern is merely another aspect of the form out of which it emerges, the tension between variety and pattern: the resolution of chaos into order, and its dissolution back into chaos. The reader will note that most of the myths in this collection are about birth or death, usually about both; this preponderance does not merely reflect the tastes of the translator, nor the peculiarities of Hinduism, but is basic to the concerns of mythology everywhere. The way that the Hindu myths deal with these basic concerns, however, is not so universal and merits closer scrutiny.

It is almost a truism in most mythologies that the act of creation is the process of developing order out of chaos. This traditionalist view that reveres order and fears chaos is mirrored in Yeats's famous description of a destructive anarchy: 'Things fall apart; the centre cannot hold.' One may even point out – recalling Yeats's love of Indian mythology – the Hindu symbolism of the falcon (myth 73, p. 281) and the blood-dimmed tide of the doomsday flood (myth 51, p. 183). Traditional Hindu philosophy accepted these values, which can be detected at the heart of several of the creation myths translated here; the Hindu universe is a closed system, a 'world-egg' with a rigid shell, so that nothing is ever 'created' *ex nihilo*; rather, things are constantly rearranged, each put in its proper place, and by doing this – propping apart heaven and earth, distinguishing male from female, separating the classes of mankind on earth – ordered life emerges out of lifeless chaos. Thus the disparate energies of the gods are combined and reintegrated in order to create the chariot of Śiva (myth 37, pp. 131–2) or the Goddess herself (myth 64, p. 241).

But against this Apollonian structure there flows another, Dionysian, current in Indian thought, which views the act of creation as the transformation of order into chaos. Only when living creatures are in conflict – the gentle against the cruel, the truthful against the false – only when the powers of evil are allowed to rise up against the powers of good (albeit only to be inevitably, if temporarily, quelled), only when death exists to threaten life, can life realize its full value. This philosophy is reflected in Freud's discussion of the pleasure and pain principle: the death instinct, Thanatos, seeks always to regress to an earlier stage when all was in perfect order, before disintegration and differentiation took place, but the life principle, Eros, strives forward into further chaos.

The orthodox, Apollonian, order-oriented Hindu view of time regards the Golden Age, the Kṛta Yuga, as having occurred in the distant past, and tries to recapture it. Similarly, classical Indian philosophy has always followed the Thanatos principle and rejected the principle of Eros; the ideal state, the goal, is the reintegration of the self into the perfect whole, the 'release' of the individual life force from the debasing influence of the senses so that it may be reabsorbed into the undifferentiated godhead. This is the 'blowing out of the flame' (*nirvāṇa*). But the force of mythology often goes directly against the grain of philosophy, revering the flame of life more than the ocean of release. Although the tenets of classical Indian philosophy often form the basis from which the Hindu myths depart, the myths do in fact depart and range far afield; myth carefully builds up the assumptions of philosophy only to tear them down with equal care, like Penelope unravelling at night what she had woven by day.

'Things fall apart' – this state of chaos in the myths is no longer a threat to life but the only premiss on which life can take place. Things fall apart when the primeval Man is dismembered – and the human race is created (myth 2, pp. 27–8); things fall apart when Satī's corpse is torn limb from limb – and her shrines appear on earth (myth 67, p. 251); things fall apart when Agni is distributed among plants and animals, giving fire to mankind (myths 30–32, pp. 99–104), or when Śiva's fever is dispersed so that it will not destroy the universe (myth 35, p. 122). Things fall apart when the seed of Agni is divided, or the Six Embryos are divided, in order to give birth to Skanda (myth 33, p. 110) or Kṛṣṇa (myth 57, pp. 207–11). The disintegration into primal elements which appears to signify death is in fact the first step of the life transformation; that which seems to 'fade' actually undergoes Shakespeare's 'sea-change into something rich and strange'. For the sea is the womb of the Hindu universe, and to return to the womb is to die. The cosmic waters are the ultimate undifferentiated form of order – death. But when the ocean is churned into chaos (myth 72, pp. 275–8), the life forces – good and evil, ambrosia and poison – undergo their sea-change and are set free.

Problems and Methods

Sources

The major sources of Hindu mythology in the ancient and medieval periods are a series of texts composed in Sanskrit, an

Indo-European language closely related to Greek and Latin. The earliest source – and, indeed, the earliest known Indo-European document – is the *Ṛg Veda*, a collection of more than a thousand sacrificial hymns dedicated to a pantheon of gods and handed down orally for many centuries before they were consigned to writing. The next important texts are the Brāhmaṇas, elaborate, often stupefyingly detailed priestly treatises which deal with mythology only in order to elucidate ritual. An entirely new corpus of legends is introduced in the *Mahābhārata*, the great Epic of India, a compendium of over 100,000 verses (ten times as long as the *Iliad* and *Odyssey* combined); here, interwoven with the main thread of the Epic battle between the Pāṇḍavas and their cousins the Kauravas, are numerous myths as well as dynastic histories of obscure kings, explicit recipes for ritual offerings, hair-splitting philosophical arguments, and tedious discussions of caste law. The *Rāmāyaṇa*, the other great Sanskrit Epic, is far more homogeneous than the *Mahābhārata*, shorter and more sophisticated in its literary style; the core of the poem narrates the adventures of Rāma, but the first and last books (later accretions) incorporate many important myths.

By far the most extensive sources of Hindu mythology, however, are the eighteen 'great' Purāṇas and the numerous 'minor' Purāṇas, veritable encyclopedias of Indian thought. Most Purāṇas have a strong sectarian bias, so that the same myths appear in very different versions in different Purāṇas. During the many centuries of the recension of the Sanskrit Epics and Purāṇas, a number of classical myths were retold – and other local South Indian texts composed – in Tamil; this large body of literature is as yet largely untranslated and untapped, a deficit which the present work is unfortunately not prepared to remedy.[1] The Purāṇas remain the basis of most 'modern' Hindu retellings of the myths, which seldom deviate far in any essential point from the spirit – or, indeed, from the letter – of the traditional texts. More significant divergences may be found in the mythologies of the isolated, primitive tribes of India, which often utilize Hindu motifs but transform them into different, sometimes almost unrecognizable tales when absorbing them into their non-Hindu ideological frameworks.[2]

Dates

The myths translated in this collection range in date from before the twelfth century B.C. (the *Ṛg Veda*) to after the sixteenth century A.D. (the late Purāṇas). In tracing the historical developments of the myths, it would be most useful to be able to compare the earlier and later versions of the stories; it is, however, impossible to arrive at any accurate estimate of their dates. The primary obstacle is inherent in the subject matter: the myths do not *have* dates; since the Epics and Purāṇas represent an oral tradition that was constantly revised over a period of several thousand years, a passage actually composed in the twelfth century A.D. may represent a surprisingly accurate preservation of a myth handed down since the twelfth century B.C. – or a completely original retelling of that myth. The second obstacle is a technical one: we cannot be certain of the dates of the various texts in which the myths occur. The ancient Indians did not care to include in their sacred works sufficient worldly references to historical events to allow us to date them; even in those rare instances where datable material is present, its value is greatly undercut by the realization that, since many of the works were subject to frequent interpolations over a period of many centuries, two adjacent passages may have been composed hundreds of years apart, and any 'date' we may have established applies only to the short passage where the factual data occur. The absence of critical editions of most of the Purāṇas greatly compounds this problem, but even the best critical editions cannot build a firm chronological structure upon the shifting sands of oral tradition.

The dating of the Purāṇas is thus an art – it can hardly be called a science – unto itself. Yet in spite of the seemingly insurmountable obstacles, many Indologists have undertaken this Heraclean – one might even say Augean – task. In addition to many articles in scholarly journals, the most useful sources for the study of the dates of the Epics and Purāṇas are the works of Farquhar, Gonda, Hazra, Kirfel, Pargiter, Pusalker, and Winternitz.[3] Their estimates vary widely, often to the extent of more than a thousand years, but in general they agree upon several broad areas of Indian mythology: *Ṛg Veda* (*c.* 1200 B.C.); *Atharva Veda* and Brāhmaṇas (*c.* 900 B.C.); Upaniṣads (*c.* 700 B.C.); *Mahābhārata* (300 B.C. to A.D. 300); *Rāmāyaṇa* (200 B.C. to A.D. 200); early Purāṇas (*Brahmāṇḍa, Harivaṃśa, Mārkaṇḍeya, Matsya, Vāyu, Viṣṇu*: A.D. 300–500); middle Purāṇas (*Agni, Bhāgavata, Devī, Garuḍa, Kūrma, Liṅga, Saura, Vāmana, Varāha*: A.D. 500–1000); and late Purāṇas (all others, A.D. 1000–1500).

One hesitates to spill yet more ink in this chimerical pursuit, but a broad outline of the most likely *approximate* dates of recension of the relevant sources may be of use to the general reader:

Ṛg Veda: 1200 B.C.; Sāyaṇa's commentary, A.D. 1350.
Atharva Veda: 900 B.C.
Brāhmaṇas: 900–700 B.C.
Upaniṣads: 700 B.C.
Nirukta of Yāska: 500 B.C.
Bṛhaddevatā of Śaunaka: 450 B.C.
Mahābhārata: 300 B.C.–A.D. 300.
Rāmāyaṇa: 200 B.C.–A.D. 200.
Purāṇas (in alphabetical order. All dates are A.D.): *Agni*: 850; *Bhāgavata*: 950; *Bhaviṣya*: 500–1200; *Brahma*, 900–1350; *Brahmāṇḍa*: 350–950; *Brahmavaivarta*: 750–1550; *Bṛhad-*

dharma: 1250; *Bṛhannaradīya*: 750–900; *Devī*: 550–650; *Devībhāgavata*: 850–1350; *Garuḍa*: 900; *Harivaṃśa*: 450; *Kālikā*: 1350; *Kalki*: 1500–1700; *Kūrma*: 550–850; *Liṅga*: 600–1000; *Mahābhāgavata*: 1100; *Mārkaṇḍeya*: 250 (but the *Devīmāhātmya* section, from which myth 66 is taken, is a later interpolation, *c.* 550); *Matsya*: 250–500; *Narasiṃha*: 400–500; *Padma*: 750 (except for the *Sṛṣṭi Khaṇḍa*, which is earlier, *c.* 600); *Sāmba*: 500–800; *Saura*: 950–1150; *Śiva*: 750–1350 (with great variation between individual *Khaṇḍas*); *Skanda*: 700–1150 (also with great variations); *Vāmana*: 450–900; *Varāha*: 750; *Vāyu*: 350; *Viṣṇu*: 450.

Selection

Any selection of texts from such a rich treasury of mythology is necessarily arbitrary, and I must confess to having chosen many myths simply because I like them. But I have tried to strike a balance between variety and pattern – to select myths of as many different types as possible while remaining within the mainstream of Hindu tradition, so that all the myths, however various, fit somewhere within the general pattern which underlies that tradition. I have included some myths from each major period of religious development: some fairly long (19, 25, 33, 37, 72, 75), some consisting of a single verse (13a, 14a, 21, 53) or a short passage (1, 17, 20, 47, 52); some famous and already anthologized (2, 58–61, 72), others obscure even to scholars (11, 12, 42, 69); some in 'critical editions' (26, 28, 35, 56), others with interpolations rejected by these editions (8, 25, 32–3, 37, 40, 72, 74); some – about two thirds – from works available in translation, the other third from untranslated works. (I have made my own translations of all of the myths in this collection, but the reader may use the existing translations, despite their occasional inaccuracies, to supply the full context of a myth or to indicate the main points of other variants.) I have also tried to choose myths of different types: some straightforward, almost primitive in their simplicity (1, 27, 50, 73), others more elaborate and sophisticated both in language and in concept (8, 18, 37, 56, 62, 68); some deeply devotional (39, 54, 59, 66), others almost satirical in their attitude toward the gods (12, 28, 40, 55, 68, 75).

In order to demonstrate how myths develop in the course of time, and how different changes can be rung upon a single theme, I have thought it best to translate groups of myths about a few of the most important Hindu gods, rather than to offer single myths about unrelated minor gods (though these figures do appear in supporting roles in the course of the collection). Implicit in this point is a rather arbitrary principle of selection that should be admitted at the outset: these myths are about gods, rather than about men or ideas. This is in part a practical rule of thumb which facilitates a greater focus on a pattern that might be obscured by the inclusion of some of the thousands of Indian legends and fables; but, more important, I think it can be well argued as a matter of principle that, just as 'biography is about chaps', so mythology is about gods. The range of texts upon which I have drawn for this collection is, in spite of its great extent in time and sheer volume, a coherent body of literature concerning an interrelated group of figures who, rather like a repertory theatre group, fill all the major parts in the cosmic drama, exchanging roles from time to time and sometimes undergoing significant character developments, but always remaining in character.

As the Hindu gods are 'immortal' only in a very particular sense – for they are born, and they die – they experience most of the great human dilemmas and often seem to differ from mortals only in a few trivial details (gods do not sweat or blink, for example) and from demons even less. Yet they are regarded by the Hindus as a class of beings *by definition* totally different from any other; they are symbols in a way that no human being, however 'archetypal' his life story, can ever be. They are actors playing parts that are real only for us; they are the masks behind which we see our own faces. For this reason, stories about gods – to which I would restrict the use of the term 'myths' – have an impact totally different from that of stories about men – which I would call 'legends', and I have limited my selection to the former.

This yardstick has necessarily excluded a number of famous and important Hindu stories about men which might otherwise have been considered myths: the story of Śunaḥśepha, who was offered as a human sacrificial victim until the gods themselves rescued him at the last minute;[4] the tale of Yayāti, whose infidelity to Devayānī brought upon him the curse of premature old age from her father Śukra (see myth 74, pp. 282–9), whereupon Yayāti – in order to make love to a nymph sent to seduce him – transferred his infirmity to one of his five sons, whom he later restored to youth;[5] the legend of Sagara, whose sacrificial horse was stolen and carried away to the subterranean regions, after which Sagara's sixty thousand sons dug down for it (creating the great chasm known as the ocean) and were burnt to ashes, to be revived later by the Ganges' descent from heaven;[6] the story of Ṛṣyaśṛṅga, who lived in the forest unaware of the existence of women until a courtesan (whom he mistook for an ascetic like himself) seduced him and brought him to court in order to put an end to a drought.[7] These stories do indeed shed considerable light upon the human condition, particularly upon the ideas of life and death encountered in the myths, but they do not explain the causes of the great events of life in terms of the function of divine powers as effectively as do the myths centring upon the gods. The Hindus themselves consigned the legends of Śunaḥśepha and the others to the parts of the Purāṇas dealing with 'history' – the histories of the solar and lunar dynasties – in contrast with the stories of the gods, which they grouped under the headings of cosmic creation and destruction.

Translation and Interpretation

In translating the myths, I have remained as literal as possible, allowing the texts to speak for themselves in their own idiom. I have added nothing but a few names or pronouns to clarify oblique references and occasional glosses on obscure epithets, and I have omitted nothing but long hymns of praise. Footnotes provide only the information necessary for an understanding of the myth; other terms and names, as well as glosses on repetitions of terms first explained in footnotes, will be found in the glossary (Appendix D). Introductory material has been kept to a minimum, merely supplying the essential factual background, establishing the context of each myth, and pointing out links with other myths; in this way, it is hoped that the reader will discover his own patterns and meanings directly from the texts.

There is no single 'basic' version of a Hindu myth; each is told and retold with a number of minor and major variations over the years. I have translated several variants of some myths where significant changes have taken place in the course of historical development (myths 10–11, 24–6, 29–33, 47–9, 52–5); in other instances I have chosen a typical variant (or, occasionally, an atypical variant, such as myths 11, 35, 36, 41, 55, 67, and 75). For those readers who wish to read other versions of the myths or to acquaint themselves with some of the interpretations offered by other scholars, a further bibliography is provided for each myth (Appendix C) as well as a general bibliography of Indian mythology (Appendix B).

Whether the reader chooses to accept the scattered hints of my own approach to the myths, or to consult the opinions of other scholars, or to seek in the myths the answers to his own questions, he would be well advised to remember that a myth, by its very nature, has no one single meaning. The elemental simplicity of its plot, the transparent innocence of its world-view, allows a good myth to function like a perfect prism through which are refracted simultaneously all the possible ways of regarding the problems encountered in the myth. The first level that we encounter is the narrative, usually quite a good story, though often with a rather predictable ending. Closely related is the divine level, which concerns mythology as it used to be understood by scholars of the classics: the metaphorical struggles of divine powers and personalities. Above this is the cosmic level of the myth, the expression of universal laws and processes, of metaphysical principles and symbolic truths. And below it, shading off into folklore, is the human level, the search for meaning in human life. Great myths are richly ambiguous and elusive; their truths cannot be filed away into the scholar's neat categories.[8] Moreover, myths are living organisms that change constantly; the tale of Indra and Vṛtra in the *Ṛg Veda* (myth 24, pp. 74–6) does not have the same 'meaning' as the tale of Indra and Vṛtra in the *Mahābhārata* (myth 26, pp. 86–90); nor do either of these myths mean to me today what they meant when I first read them some fifteen years ago.

In harnessing these myths, exotic and inspired creatures that they are, to the leaden yoke of the critical apparatus, having already lamed them with my own prosaic translation, I hope that I have not belaboured all the life out of them.[9] Indeed, I take heart from the words of Claude Lévi-Strauss, who has said that while poetry may be lost in translation, 'the mythical value of myths remains preserved through the worst translation'.[10]

Acknowledgements

It was my father who first suggested that I write this book; but it was not until my friend A. J. Sherman independently hit upon the idea, and cheered me on in the enterprise, that I decided to undertake it. Since then, Richard Gombrich, Raymond Allchin, Betty Radice, Susan Gorodetsky, David Shulman, and Audrey Hayley have made a number of extremely useful suggestions, and my husband has tirelessly feigned interest in the hundreds of oral variations on each theme to which I have subjected him. To all of them, my gratitude and thanks.

I

PRAJĀPATI AND BRAHMĀ

Creation in the *Ṛg Veda*

TO begin at the beginning of both the story and the telling of the story, one must begin with the mythology of creation as it appears in the *Ṛg Veda*. The creation hymns – and indeed most of the Ṛg Vedic hymns which allude directly to myths – appear in the two latest books (the first and the tenth), which already show the seeds of the philosophical speculation that was to emerge fully in the Brāhmaṇas and Upaniṣads within a few centuries. The most basic form of Vedic cosmogony is implicit in many early hymns, though never explicitly described: it is the formation of distinct elements out of the primeval cosmic flux, the evolution of order out of chaos, the propping apart of heaven and earth. This concept of creation as separation remains at the heart of much of later Hindu mythology (as well as Hindu social thought) and forms the animating spark of the conflict between gods and non-gods (demons or human beings).

INCEST: THE FATHER COMMITS INCEST WITH HIS DAUGHTER

One concept of creation which begins in the *Ṛg Veda* and persists through later Hindu mythology is the idea of primeval incest. No single hymn tells this story, but scattered references may be collected to give a summary of the Vedic myth, which never actually names the father or the daughter and may simply express in anthropomorphic terms the idea of the One who creates a Second with whom he unites as a pair.[1] Heaven and earth, once so carefully

1. In later mythology, the primeval incestuous act is attributed to the first man, Manu – himself also incestuously begotten by the creator.

and safely propped apart, meet here in an act which is creative but dangerous.

I. FROM THE *Ṛg Veda*

As his phallus was stretched out in eagerness for the act of a man, the manly one pulled back. He drew back again from the maiden, his daughter, that tireless phallus which had been thrust in. As they were in the midst of the very act of union, when the father was satisfying his desire for the young girl, the two of them left a little of the out-flowing seed shed upon the back of the earth in the womb of good deeds. When the father shed his seed in his own daughter, he spilt his seed on the earth as he united with her. The benevolent gods created sacred speech and fashioned Rudra Vāstoṣpati, the protector of sacred rites ... As Agni[2] made the seed for the great father, heaven, he entered into the womb, having noticed that she was inclined to him. The hunter shot an arrow at him boldly. The god satisfied his lust in his own daughter ... As the heat of passion came to the king for his enjoyment, heaven laid aside on the ground the bright seed that had been spilt. Agni caused to be born the blameless benevolent group of youths[3] and made them great ... Heaven is my father, the engenderer, the navel here. My mother is this wide earth, my close kin. Between these two outstretched bowls is the womb;[4] in it the father placed his daughter's embryo.

2. Agni (cognate with Latin *ignis*) is the god of fire. See below, myths 29–33, pp. 79–115.

3. These youths are the Aṅgirases, mediators between gods and men, sons of heaven and progenitors of men, who distribute among men the gifts of the gods (cf. Greek *angelos*). Agni is one of the Aṅgirases.

4. The word here translated as 'womb' is *yoni*, which originally designated the maternal womb, was later extended to any source, and, still later, denoted the sexual organ of the Goddess, worshipped with the phallus (*liṅga*) of Śiva.

DISMEMBERMENT: THE PRIMEVAL MAN IS SACRIFICED

One cosmogonic myth is the subject of an entire Ṛg Vedic hymn, which explains original creation as the result of a primeval sacrifice – not a true blood sacrifice, but a dismemberment and distribution; not an actual creation of something out of nothing, but rather a re-arrangement, another instance of order out of chaos. The primeval Man is not *changed* into the various forms of life; rather, he *is* those forms, always. It is worthy of note that creation produces not only the physical elements of the universe but also the social order, the basis of life in the Hindu view, as well as the seasons and the parts of the very sacrifice from which creation proceeds.

2. FROM THE *Ṛg Veda*

The Man [Puruṣa] has a thousand heads, a thousand eyes, a thousand feet. He pervades the earth everywhere and extends beyond for ten fingers' breadth. The Man himself is all this, whatever has been and whatever is to be. He is the lord of immortality and also lord of that which grows on food. Such is his greatness, and the Man is yet greater than this. All creatures make up a quarter of him; three quarters are the immortal in heaven. With three quarters the Man has risen above, and one quarter of him still remains here, whence he spread out everywhere, pervading that which eats and that which does not eat. From him Virāj[5] was born, and from Virāj came the Man, who, having been born, ranged beyond the earth before and behind. When the gods spread the sacrifice, using the Man as the offering, spring was the clarified butter, summer the fuel, autumn the oblation. They anointed the Man, the sacrifice, born at the beginning, upon the sacred grass. With him the gods, Sādhyas, and sages sacrificed. From that sacrifice in which everything was offered, the clarified butter was obtained, and they made it into those beasts who live in the air, in the forest, and in villages. From that sacrifice

5. 'He who Rules Afar', a primeval being.

in which everything was offered, the verses and the chants were born, the metres were born, and the formulas[6] were born. From it horses were born, and those other animals which have a double set of incisors; cows were born from it, and goats and sheep were born from it.

When they divided the Man, into how many parts did they disperse him? What became of his mouth, what of his arms, what were his two thighs and his two feet called? His mouth was the brahmin, his arms were made into the nobles, his two thighs were the populace, and from his feet the servants[7] were born. The moon was born from his mind; the sun was born from his eye. From his mouth came Indra[8] and Agni, and from his vital breath the wind [Vāyu] was born. From his navel the atmosphere was born; from his head the heaven appeared. From his two feet came the earth, and the regions of the sky from his ear. Thus they fashioned the worlds. There were seven enclosing fire-sticks for him, and thrice seven fire-sticks when the gods, spreading the sacrifice, bound down the Man as the sacrificial beast. With this sacrifice the gods sacrificed; these were the first *dharmas*.[9] And these powers reached the dome of heaven where dwell the ancient Sādhyas and gods.

Creation in the Brāhmaṇas and Upaniṣads

The Brāhmaṇas deal at great length with the question of cosmogony, utilizing the various strands of Ṛg Vedic belief. The incestuous father

6. The three Vedas consist of verses (*Ṛg Veda*), chants (*Sāma Veda*) and formulas (*Yajur Veda*).

7. The four classes (*varṇas*) of ancient Indian society were the priests (*brahmins*), nobles or warriors (*kṣatriyas*), the 'all' – i.e. the general populace (*viś* or *vaiśyas*), and servants (*śūdras*).

8. Indra is the king of the gods. See below, myths 13–28, pp. 56–96.

9. *Dharma* designates social order, the social norm, the ideal order of the world.

is now identified as Prajāpati, the lord of creatures, and his seed is cast into the fire in place of the usual liquid oblation – clarified butter or Soma juice – in a form of Vedic sacrifice more sophisticated than the dismemberment of a victim, an actual ritual symbolically re-enacting primeval creation.

Incest and Oblation

Prajāpati commits incest and Rudra is born

A series of Brāhmaṇa texts develops the full consequences of the incestuous act, particularly its iniquities and dangers. The astral symbolism which appears in these texts persists in later myths, as do the distinction between the mortal and immortal parts of man, the idea of the distribution of the seed into various life forms (concepts already present *in nuce* in the hymn of the dismemberment of the cosmic Man), and the use of false etymologies and word-play upon names.

3. FROM THE *Aitareya Brāhmaṇa*

Prajāpati approached his daughter; some say she was the sky, others that she was the dawn. He became a stag and approached her, as she had taken the form of a doe. The gods saw him and they said, 'Prajāpati is now doing what is not done.' They wished for one who would punish him, but they did not find him in one another. Then they assembled in one place the most fearful forms, and these, assembled, became the deity Rudra;[10] therefore his name contains the sound *Bhūta* [Bhūtapati, lord of ghosts]. The gods said to him, 'Prajāpati is now doing what is not done. Pierce him.' 'So be it', he replied, 'and let me choose a boon from you.' 'Choose.' He chose as his boon the overlordship of cattle; therefore his name contains the word cattle [Paśupati, lord of cattle]. And one who knows this name of his becomes rich in cattle. He took aim and pierced him; when he was pierced he flew upwards; they call him 'the Deer'. The piercer of the deer

10. A malevolent god associated with wildness and danger. See below, myths 34–6, pp. 117–25.

is called by that name, and the female deer is Rohiṇī. The arrow, made in three parts, became 'the Tripartite Arrow'.[11]

When the seed of Prajāpati had been spilt, it ran and became a lake. The gods said, 'Let not this seed of Prajāpati spoil.' Since they said, 'Let not this seed of Prajāpati spoil [*mā duṣaṃ*]', it became 'not to be spoilt' and its name was 'not to be spoilt'; that which is 'not to be spoilt' is connected with man; therefore they call that which is 'not to be spoilt' 'connected with man' [*mānuṣa*, 'mortal' or 'descended from Manu'],[12] with a mystery [a riddle], for the gods seem to love mystery.

They surrounded it with Agni; the Maruts blew upon it, but Agni did not cause it to flow. They surrounded it with Agni Vaiśvānara; the Maruts blew upon it and Agni Vaiśvānara caused it to flow. The first part of the seed that was ignited became Āditya; the second became Bhṛgu, whom Varuṇa took, and so Bhṛgu was adopted by Varuṇa. The third part, which was brilliant [*adīdet*], became the Ādityas. The coals [*aṅgārā*] became the Aṅgirases; and when the coals blazed forth again after they had been quenched, Bṛhaspati was born. The completely charred coals became the black cattle; the reddened earth became tawny cattle. The ash spread in various forms – the buffalo, the ox, the antelope, the camel, the ass, and the tawny cattle.

The god said to them, 'This is mine; what remains here is mine.' But they deprived him of his claim by reciting the verse addressed to Rudra:

11. The Deer (Mṛga) is the constellation Capricorn, also called Deer's Head (Mṛgaśiras). The Deer-piercer or Hunter is Sirius. Rohiṇī (literally denoting a female gazelle or red cow) is alpha in Taurus. The Tripartite Arrow is the belt of Orion, near Rohiṇī and the Deer, while Prajāpati is Orion. See below, myth 37, pp. 131–7, for the arrow.

12. Manu is the progenitor of the human race. See below, myths 15–19, pp. 60–70.

'Father of the Maruts, let your good will approach us.
Do not separate us from the sight of the sun.
Spare our swift horses, O hero.
Let us increase in offspring, O Rudra.'[13]

Prajāpati and his sons create, and Rudra is born

The *Kauṣītaki Brāhmaṇa* expands several elements of the myth (Prajāpati's sons, instead of the father, are involved in the incestuous act; the daughter becomes actively seductive) and reverses certain others (Rudra is here born from the seed for which he punishes Prajāpati in the *Aitareya Brāhmaṇa*). Motifs from the *Ṛg Veda* also reappear: the Ṛg Vedic arrow here becomes a thousand arrows, and Rudra has a thousand eyes and feet, like the cosmic Man.

4. FROM THE *Kauṣītaki Brāhmaṇa*

Prajāpati, wishing very much to have progeny, practised asceticism. As he became heated, five were born from him: Fire, Wind, Sun, Moon, and the fifth, a female, Dawn. He said to them, 'Practise asceticism,' and they consecrated themselves; when they had been consecrated and were practising asceticism, Dawn, the daughter of Prajāpati, took the form of a celestial nymph and appeared before them. Their hearts were moved by her and they poured out their seed. Then they went to Prajāpati, their father, and they said, 'We have poured out our seed. Let it not be lost.' Prajāpati made a golden bowl, an arrow's breadth in height and in width, and he poured the seed into it. Then the thousand-eyed god with a thousand feet and a thousand fitted arrows arose.

He grasped his father Prajāpati, who said to him, 'Why do you grasp me?' He replied, 'Give me a name, for without a name I will not eat food.' He answered, 'You are Bhava ["Existence"].' [He gave him seven more names.]

13. A reference to *Ṛg Veda* 2.33.1.

Oblation into Fire: Prajāpati Creates Agni and Sacrifices into Him

The concepts of the eater versus the non-eater (or the eaten) and the appeasing of a dangerous, hungry creature are further developed in another text. Prajāpati spills his seed into the fire as before, but now the seed takes the form of milk that is milked out of him or butter that is churned from him, the verb 'rubbed' implying either or both of these acts.

5. FROM THE *Śatapatha Brāhmaṇa*

In the beginning, Prajāpati existed alone. He reflected, 'How may I produce progeny?' He exhausted himself practising asceticism, and he generated Agni from his mouth. Since he generated him from his mouth, Agni is therefore an eater of food. And he who knows that Agni is an eater of food becomes an eater of food himself. As he generated him first [*agre*] of all the gods, therefore he is called Agni, for the name Agni is the same as the name Agri. When he was born, he went forth in front, for they say that one who goes in front goes first. This is his Agni-ness.

Prajāpati then reflected, 'I have created from myself a food-eater, Agni, but there is no food here other than me, whom he would not eat.' Now, the earth was bald at that time; there were no plants nor any trees. And this was in his mind. Then Agni turned toward him with an open mouth, and the greatness went out of the terrified Prajāpati. Speech is his own greatness; and speech went out of him. He desired an offering made in himself. He rubbed[14] his hands; and because he rubbed his hands, therefore this and this palm are without hair. Then he obtained an offering of clarified butter or an offering of milk; for both of these are made of milk. This offering did not

14. By 'rubbing' or 'churning' with his hands he produces sacrificial butter.

please him, for it was mixed with hair. He poured it away into the fire saying, 'Burn and drink this [*oṣa dhaya*].' From it the plants were born; therefore they are called plants [*oṣadhayas*]. A second time he rubbed his hands; then he obtained another offering, an offering of clarified butter or an offering of milk; for both of these are made of milk. This offering pleased him. He was uncertain whether to offer this offering or not. His own greatness said to him, 'Offer it.' Prajāpati realized that his own [*sva*] greatness had spoken [*āha*] to him. And so he said, 'Svāhā' as he offered it. Therefore one says 'Svāhā'[15] as an offering is made.

Then he [the sun] rose up and grew hot, and then he [the wind] became mighty and blew.[16] Then Agni turned away. Prajāpati performed the offering, produced progeny, and saved himself from Agni, who was death and who was about to devour him. And whoever knows this and offers the Agnihotra oblation, he produces progeny just as Prajāpati produced progeny. And in this way he saves himself from Agni, death, when he is about to devour him. And whenever one dies and is placed in the fire, he is reborn from the fire just as he is born from his mother and father, for the fire consumes only his body.

Incest, Oblation, and Dismemberment: Brahmā Commits Incest

All three of the major methods of creation in the Vedas and Brāhmaṇas are combined in the Upaniṣads: incest, oblation (a fire sacrifice), and dismemberment (the sacrifice of the androgynous Self into two pieces). The distinction between mortal and immortal is further extended, but now the false etymology for the human being is derived

15. 'Svāhā', the exclamation made when an oblation is offered to the gods, is the name of the oblation and of the wife of Agni. See below, myth 33, pp. 109–13.

16. Another possible translation would be: 'Then Agni arose and grew hot and became mighty and purified.'

not from the incestuous seed but from the androgynous primeval Man, the Puruṣa, here regarded as a mortal but also identified with Brahmā, the Creator, the god who supersedes the Prajāpati of the earlier Brāhmaṇas. Puruṣa's name in this text utilizes the 'preceding' etymology applied in the *Śatapatha Brāhmaṇa* to Agni, who is connected here, as usual, with food.

6. FROM THE *Bṛhadāraṇyaka Upaniṣad*

In the beginning, this universe was Soul [*ātman*] in the form of the Man [Puruṣa]. He looked around and saw nothing other than himself. Then, at first, he said, 'I am,' and thus the word 'I' was born. Therefore even now when one is addressed he first says, 'It is I,' and then he speaks whatever other name he has. Since he, preceding [*pūrva*] all this universe, burnt up [*uṣ*] all evils, he is the Man [Puruṣa]. He who knows this burns up anyone who would precede him.

He was afraid; therefore one who is all alone is afraid. He reflected, 'Since there is nothing other than me, of what am I afraid?' Then his fear vanished, for of what could he have been afraid? One becomes afraid of a second. He did not rejoice; therefore one who is all alone does not rejoice. He desired a second. He was of the same size and kind as a man and woman closely embracing. He caused himself to fall [*pat*] into two pieces, and from him a husband and a wife [*pati* and *patnī*] were born. Therefore Yājñavalkya has said, 'Oneself is like a half-fragment.' Therefore this space was filled by a woman. He united with her, and from this mankind was born.

She reflected, 'How can he unite with me after engendering me from himself? For shame! I will conceal myself.' She became a cow; he became a bull and united with her, and from this all the cattle were born. She became a mare; he became a stallion. She became a female ass; he became a male ass and united with her, and from this all whole-hooved animals were born. She became a she-goat; he became a billy-goat;

she became a ewe; he became a ram and united with her, and from this goats and sheep were born. Thus he created all the pairs, even down to the ants.

He knew that he was creation, for he created all of this. Thus creation arose. Whoever knows this is born in that creation of his. Then he churned.[17] From his mouth as the fire-hole [*yoni*] and from his two hands he created fire. Therefore both mouth and hands are without hair on the inside, for the fire-hole is without hair on the inside. When people speak of him, saying, 'Sacrifice to this god!' 'Sacrifice to this god!', speaking of one single god and then of another single god, it is his own creation, and he himself is all the gods. Now, whatever is moist he created from semen, and that is Soma.[18] All this universe is food and the eater of food. For Soma is food, and Agni is the eater of food. This was the surpassing creation of Brahmā, for he created the gods, who were better than him, when he, being mortal, created immortals. Therefore it was a surpassing creation. Whoever knows this is born in that surpassing creation of his.

Creation in the *Mahābhārata*

Prajāpati in the Epic is no longer the supreme, original god, the universal Soul, but merely that member of the extensive Hindu pantheon whose particular task or assignment it is to perform crea-

17. Or 'rubbed' – that is, he twirled the fire sticks, his two hands, or 'churned' as in the previous myth.

18. Soma is the ambrosia that the gods drink to make them immortal; it is an elixir, unlike the solid food called ambrosia eaten by the Greek gods. Soma is the expressed liquid from the Soma plant, offered during the Vedic sacrifice, probably some kind of hallucinogenic drink; it is the name of the moon, for the ambrosia is said to be stored in the moon; and it is the name of the god who is the incarnation of the Soma juice.

tion. Frequently he is called Brahmā (as he is in the Upaniṣads) or the Grandfather.

Although the creation myths of the Brāhmaṇas carefully explain the evolution of immortals from mortals, or the reverse, the main conflict is not between gods and men but between gods and demons. In the *Mahābhārata*, however, men as well as demons threaten the gods; unlike Greek mythology, where the gods continually descend to earth and interfere with the affairs of mankind, in Hindu mythology men frequently acquire sufficient ascetic or moral power to rise to heaven and challenge the gods. When this occurs, the gods must find a way to reduce the power of these men, even as they often have occasion to pervert virtuous demons.[19]

Brahmā and the Jealous Gods Create Evil Women

By far the most effective weapon used by the gods to corrupt virtuous mortals is a woman – usually a seductive celestial nymph, but sometimes just Woman, the root of all evil in the misogynist, ascetic-oriented view of the orthodox Hindu.

7. FROM THE *Mahābhārata*

I will tell you, my son,[20] how Brahmā created wanton women, and for what purpose. For there is nothing more evil than women; a wanton woman is a blazing fire; she is the illusion born of Maya;[21] she is the sharp edge of the razor; she is poison, a serpent, and death all in one.

These creatures were full of *dharma*; so we have heard. And since they would become gods by themselves, the gods be-

19. Battles between gods and demons are described below, myths 70–75, pp. 271–300. Virtuous demons are perverted in myths 62 (pp. 232–5), 65 (pp. 242–6), 72 (pp. 274–80), and 75 (pp. 290–300).

20. Bhīṣma tells this myth to Yudhiṣṭhira.

21. A pun may be intended here; Maya is the architect of the demons; the word for illusion (derived from the same verbal root as that of Maya's name – 'to make') is *māyā*, a feminine noun often personified as a goddess.

came alarmed. The gods went to Brahmā, the Grandfather, and informed him of what was on their minds, and they stood silent before him, with downcast faces. The lord Grandfather, learning what was in the hearts of the gods, created women by a magic ritual in order to delude mankind. Now, the women of former creation had been virtuous, but these sinful sorceresses arose out of the creation performed by Prajāpati. For the Grandfather gave them all the desires that can be desired, and those wanton women, lusting for sensual pleasures, began to stir men up. Then the lord of gods, the lord, created anger as the assistant of desire, and all creatures, falling into the power of desire and anger, began to be attached to women.

Brahmā Creates Death

In another Epic myth, the woman whom Brahmā creates to preserve the distinction between mortals and immortals is no mere seductress, but Death herself;[22] yet even here, as in the first *Mahābhārata* myth cited, her weapons are desire and anger. In many other Hindu myths, death is regarded as a necessary evil, a measure required to preserve the balance of good and evil and the hierarchy of the universe, to prevent overcrowding in heaven or on earth, or simply to give human life scale, value, and motivation. Immortality, in the Hindu view, usually denotes not an eternity of life (which no material entity can possess) but the enjoyment of the full allotted span of life; thus both gods and human beings, each in their own way, must welcome death 'at the proper time'. This kind cruelty is often associated with Rudra–Śiva, who periodically burns to ashes the whole universe, including the 'immortals', at the proper time; he appears in this text explicitly in his chaste aspect as the Pillar (Sthāṇu), as well as implicitly in the form of the tears which become diseases, for Rudra's name is often derived from the verb 'to weep [*rud*]'.[23]

22. Death is usually personified as male (Yama or simply Death – Mṛtyu – as a masculine noun), but nouns ending in 'u' may also be feminine, and occasionally, as here, Death is female.

23. See below, myth 36, p. 123.

8. FROM THE *Mahābhārata*

At the time of creation, the Grandfather, full of fiery energy, created living beings. These creatures increased in age and number to excess, but they did not die again. Then there was no space anywhere between creatures; there was no space to breathe, so congested was the triple universe. He began to worry about how he could destroy them, but though he kept thinking, he could not find a means of accomplishing this destruction. He became angry, and from all the apertures of his body a fire shot forth, and with that fire the Grandfather burnt all the regions of the sky. The fire born of the lord's anger burnt heaven and earth and the air, all the universe that moves or is still. All creatures, moving and still, were burnt by that great blast of anger when the Grandfather became angry.

Then Rudra the Pillar, the lord of Vedic sacrifices, the god who destroys the power of his enemies, the god with tawny matted locks, spoke to Brahmā about succour and refuge. When the Pillar had come there because of his desire for the welfare of all creatures, Brahmā, the god who grants boons, seemed to flare up as he said to Śiva, 'What wish shall I grant for you today? For you are worthy of a boon from me, and I will do whatever you choose, whatever is in your heart, Śambhu.' The Pillar said, 'Know that I am concerned about the creation of living beings. You have created these creatures; do not be angry with them, Grandfather. Creatures everywhere are being burnt by the fire of your energy, and when I see them, I am full of pity. Do not be angry with them, O god, lord of the universe.'

'I am not angry,' said Prajāpati, 'nor is it my wish that living creatures should cease to exist. But in order to lighten the earth I have sought this destruction. This goddess Earth, oppressed by the burden, has kept urging me to destroy them, for she is sinking into the waters under the burden,[24] great

24. See below, myths 52–5, pp. 185–97.

god. Though I pondered for a long time, I was unable to think of a way of destroying these beings that kept increasing; then anger entered me.' The Pillar said, 'Have mercy; forbear this final destruction. O lord of the thirty-three gods,[25] do not be angry. Do not destroy creatures moving and still, all the ponds and grasses, the four-fold[26] community of creatures moving and still. The universe has been reduced to ashes and flooded over.[27] Have mercy, kind lord; this is the boon that I have chosen. Once destroyed, these creatures will never return again in any way; therefore let this fiery energy be absorbed by your own energy. Through your desire for the welfare of all creatures, find some other means so that all of these living beings may return, O Heater of Enemies. If creatures cease to exist now, they will be cut off from any descendants. You have appointed me to be the presiding deity over people here, O lord, lord of the universe, for all of this universe, moving and still, is born of you. If I have pleased you, great god, I beg that all creatures may be subject to repetitions of birth and death.' When the god Brahmā heard this speech of the Pillar, he controlled his words and his heart and drew his own energy back within himself. Suppressing the fire, the blessed lord who is worshipped by all people fashioned periodic activity and quiescence.

But as the noble Brahmā suppressed the fire born of his

25. Although there are far more than thirty-three gods in the Hindu pantheon, they are traditionally numbered at thirty-three, the ancient Vedic groups: twelve Ādityas, eight Vasus, eleven Rudras, and two Aśvins.

26. There are several different traditional ways of dividing the 'community of creatures'. What is probably meant here is gods, men, animals, and inanimate objects; elsewhere, the division is into gods, demons, ancestors, and men (see below, myth 9, p. 44) or serpents, birds, plants, and insects (myth 10, p. 47).

27. At the end of each aeon or *kalpa*, the universe is burnt and flooded. See below, myths 38, pp. 138–9, and 50–51, pp. 180–84.

anger, from all the apertures of his body a dark woman appeared, wearing red garments, with red eyes and red palms and soles, adorned with divine ear-rings and ornaments. As she came forth from the apertures she went to Brahmā's right, and the two gods, lords of everything, looked at the maiden. Then the god, the first, the lord of people, summoned her and said, 'Death, kill these creatures. I thought of you when I was angrily devising a means of destruction; therefore, destroy all creatures, imbeciles and scholars. In your passionate anger, destroy creatures without exception, and by my command you will win great merit.' Then the young goddess Death began to brood in sorrow. Wearing garlands of lotuses, she wept copious tears, which she took in her hands as she prayed for the sake of the welfare of mankind.

The wide-eyed, fragile woman, suppressing her extreme grief, joined her palms[28] and bent like a vine, saying, 'How could you, the Foremost of Speakers, have created a woman like me, to carry out such a hideous task, terrifying all creatures that breathe? I am afraid of violating *dharma*; appoint for me some task in keeping with *dharma*. Look upon me with a compassionate gaze, O lord, for I am so frightened. I cannot carry off guiltless children and old men and those in their prime, creatures who breathe, O lord of those who breathe. I beg you; have mercy on me. The beloved sons, friends, brothers, mothers, and fathers of the dead will think evil of me, O god, and I fear the dead whom they mourn. The moisture of their pitiable tears will scorch me for eternal years; I am terribly afraid of them, and I seek refuge with you. Those who have committed sins go at the end to the house of Yama;[29] have mercy on me, O god, lord, giver of boons; show your grace to me. This is the boon that I wish from

28. To join the palms together in the '*añjali*' or 'handful of flowers' gesture is to demonstrate reverence and supplication.

29. Yama rules over the dead in hell. See below, myth 19, pp. 66–70.

you, Grandfather of all people, lord of gods; by your grace, I wish to practise asceticism.'

The Grandfather said, 'Death, I fashioned you in order to destroy creatures. Go and destroy all creatures, and do not delay. This must be, inevitably, and cannot be otherwise. Sinless one with faultless limbs, do as I have told you to do.' When Death heard this command, she did not utter a word, but she stood there bowing humbly and gazing up at the lord. Again and again he spoke to the angry woman, but she remained silent as if robbed of her life force. Then the god of gods, lord of lords, Brahmā himself deigned to be gratified. Smiling, the lord of people looked down upon all people, and the anger of the lord who is conquered by no enemy thus became calm. And the maiden went away from him; so we have heard.

As Death slipped away without having promised to destroy creatures, she hastened to Dhenuka. There the goddess practised the supreme asceticism that is hard to practise: for fifteen thousand million years she stood on one foot. As she was practising this most difficult asceticism there, Brahmā, whose energy was great, again spoke to her, saying, 'Death, obey my command.' But she disregarded him and immediately began to practise asceticism on one foot for another twenty thousand million years, and then for yet another ten million million years she dwelt with the wild animals. Then for twenty thousand years she ate nothing but air, and for another eight thousand years she stood in complete silence in water. Then the maiden went to the Kauśikī river and there she undertook another act of asceticism, living upon only air and water; and then the blessed one went to the Ganges, and then to Mount Meru, where she stood all alone, as immovable as a piece of wood, for she wished for the welfare of all beings. Then on a summit of Himālaya where the gods performed their sacrifice she stood on one big toe for another thousand million years, and by this effort she satisfied the Grandfather.

Then he who is the creation and destruction of all people said to her, 'My daughter, what is happening here? Do as I have told you.' But Death replied to the lord, the Grandfather, 'I will not carry off creatures. Again I beg you to have mercy, O god.' As she begged him again, terrified of the danger of *adharma*,[30] the god of gods rebuked her, saying, 'Righteous Death, you will commit no act of *adharma*; subdue these creatures. My words, kind lady, can never fail to come true. Eternal *dharma* will enter you for this, and I and the gods will act constantly for your welfare. And I will grant you this other wish which you desire in your heart: creatures afflicted by disease will not blame you. Among men, you will have the form of a man; among women, you will have the form of a woman, and among eunuchs, a eunuch.' When she heard this, she placed her palms together and said again to the noble, unperishing lord of gods, 'No.' Then the god said to her, 'Death, destroy mankind. There will be no *adharma* in you, righteous one, I promise. Those teardrops which I saw fall, and which you held before you in your hands, will become terrible diseases which will afflict mankind when the appointed time has come. When the time comes for the end of all creatures that breathe, you, Death, will employ desire and anger together; thus immeasurable *dharma* will come to you, and you will not incur *adharma*, for your action will be impartial. Thus you will protect *dharma* properly as commanded, and you will not cause yourself to sink into *adharma*. Therefore welcome desire; let the two of you join together and destroy creatures here.' Though she was afraid of being known by the name of Death, she was so frightened of a curse that she agreed to what he asked.

Then she began to destroy the life's breath of creatures that

30. *Adharma*, the violation of *dharma*, is behaviour which contradicts the natural law of social order.

breathe, at the time of their end, bewildering them with desire and anger. And the teardrops fallen from Death became diseases which injure the bodies of men . . . Thus Death was created by the god, and when the appointed time has come she destroys creatures as is proper; and the tears she shed are the diseases which destroy creatures when the proper time has come.

Creation in the Purāṇas

The Purāṇas reintroduce into Epic mythology some of the ritual and philosophical undercurrents of the Brāhmaṇa texts as well as new devotional ideas associated with the great sectarian deities – Viṣṇu, Śiva, and Devī. Cosmology and cosmogony are developed at great length in the Purāṇas: in addition to the three main levels of the triple universe there are numerous subterranean hells below and a hierarchy of heavens above the original triad. At the end of each aeon (*kalpa*), the universe is destroyed by fire to remain submerged in the cosmic waters while Brahmā sleeps, until the time when all is to be created anew. Each *kalpa* consists of four ages (*yugas*), named after four throws of the dice: the first, the Kṛta Age, is the best (often it is called the Satya Age, the Age of Truth); it is followed by the Tretā Age, the Dvāpara Age, and finally the Kali Age, the present age, when virtue is at its lowest ebb and the human life-span is shortest.

Cosmic Creation: Brahmā Creates Good and Evil from his Body

Brahmā creates the pairs of opposites, good and evil, light and dark, either of his own will or under compulsion, for by this time his stature has declined so much that he, like all the other gods, is powerless against fate and his own *karma* – the cumulative force of his past actions, good or bad, a force that predetermines the course of his present existence. Moreover, only a world composed of the full variety of qualities is desirable, let alone possible; the three 'strands' or qualities of matter (*guṇas*) – *sattva* (goodness or light), *rajas* (dust, passion, or activity), and *tamas* (darkness or inertia) – must always be balanced; indeed, they are called 'strands' because they are inextricably intertwined everywhere like the strands of a rope.

9. FROM THE *Viṣṇu Purāṇa*

Although all creatures are destroyed at each cosmic dissolution, they are not released from rebirth, but are reborn according to the reputation of their former good or bad *karma*.[31] Therefore when Brahmā performs creation mentally, from him are born the four-fold creatures, varying from gods to inanimate objects. When Brahmā desired to create the four types of 'waters' – gods, demons, ancestors, and men – he harnessed the forces within his own self. When he was thus concentrated, desiring to create, the quality of darkness became manifest in Prajāpati, and first the demons were born from his thigh. Brahmā then abandoned his own body which had the quality of darkness, and that body which he had abandoned became night. Still desiring to create, he took another body and found pleasure; then the gods, in whom the quality of goodness was predominant, were born from the mouth of Brahmā. He abandoned that body too, and it became the day, in which the quality of goodness is paramount; therefore at night the demons are powerful, and by day the gods. Then he took another body in which the quality of goodness formed the essence, and as he thought of himself as being like a father, the ancestors [*pitaras*, 'fathers'] were born from him. The lord then abandoned that body when he had created the ancestors, and that cast-off body became the evening twilight which stands between day and night. Then he took another body in which the quality of passion was the essence, and from him was born the race of men, in whom the quality of passion abounds. Prajāpati quickly abandoned that body too, and it became the light of the early twilight, the dawn.

31. That is, their status is determined by their past *karma*.

Therefore when this light arrives, men are powerful, and the ancestors become powerful at the time of evening twilight. The light of dawn, night, day, and evening twilight – these four are the bodies of the lord Brahmā which served as vessels for the three qualities.

Then he took another body in which the quality of passion was the essence, and from Brahmā hunger was born, and with hunger anger was born. The lord then created in darkness beings that were emaciated with hunger, deformed, bearded, and they ran to the lord. Those who said, 'No! Not like that! Protect him [*rakṣyatām*]!' – they became the Rākṣasas. And others, who said, 'Let us eat!' – they became the Yakṣas, because of eating [*jakṣaṇāt*]. When the Creator looked upon them with displeasure, the hairs fell from his head and grew upon his head again. They became snakes, called serpents [*sarpa*] because they had glided down [*sarpaṇa*] and snakes [*ahi*] because they had departed [*hīna*]. Then the Creator of the Universe became angry, and he created creatures who had anger as their essence; because of their tawny [*kapiśa*] colour, these fierce ones are eaters of flesh [*piśitāśanas* or Piśācas]. Then the Gandharvas were born from his body as he sang; they are drinkers of speech and are therefore called Gandharvas.[32]

The lord Brahmā, having created these creatures when he was impelled by their own capabilities and powers, then created others of his own will. He made the birds [*vayāṃsi*] from his own youthful energy [*vayas*]; he made sheep from his breast, goats from his mouth; Prajāpati created cows from his stomach and his two sides. From his feet he made horses, elephants, donkeys, oxen, deer, camels, mules, antelopes, and other species. Grasses, fruits, and roots were born from the hairs of his body ...

32. A false etymology based upon *gām dhayantas*, 'speech-drinking' or 'singing', according to the commentator.

Thus the lord Brahmā, the First Creator and lord, created; and whatever *karma* they had achieved in a former creation, they received this *karma* as they were created again and again, harmful or benign, gentle or cruel, full of *dharma* or *adharma*, truthful or false. And when they are created again, they will have these qualities; and this pleased him. The lord Creator himself diversified the variety and differentiation of all the objects of the senses, properties, and forms. By the authority of the Vedas, he fashioned in the very beginning the name and form of creatures, gods and others, the diversity of their functions, and the appellations of the sages in the Vedas. In this way he made other creatures with the properties appropriate to their purpose. Just as the various signs of the seasons appear as the year revolves, so the various qualities of creatures appear at the beginning of each age. And thus, at the beginning of each aeon, again and again he performs creation of this sort, for his power is the will to create and he is impelled by the powers of the things to be created.

Personal Creation: Brahmā Curses Nārada

Another cycle of creation myths expresses in more anthropomorphic terms some of the conflicts which appear symbolically in earlier myths – mental or ascetic creation versus sexual creation, asceticism versus married life, men versus women, parents versus children, sons versus daughters.

Nārada curses the sons of Dakṣa

In the first of two such myths, Dakṣa, a son of Brahmā, plays the role of the creator and is opposed by Nārada, a meddlesome sage and notorious trouble-maker who here appears as the ascetic enemy of the house-holder.

10. FROM THE *Vāyu Purāṇa*

The Self-created Brahmā instructed Dakṣa to create progeny, and then Dakṣa created all creatures that move and those that are still, during the era of Manu the son of Vivasvat.[33] Dakṣa set out to create the four types of progeny: those born of the sloughed skin, those born of eggs, those born of sprouts, and those born of sweat.[34] For ten thousand years he practised fierce asceticism, and by the powers of his yoga, such as the power to become infinitely small, he was able to produce them. Then he dispersed himself among men, serpents, Rākṣasas, gods, demons, and Gandharvas, all born of his compact celestial body, and he created the Lords who were his own equals in form, strength, and energy. Then, rejoicing and wishing to create various kinds of progeny, he made other creatures that move and that are still, all born from his mind, and he made the sages, gods, Gandharvas, men, serpents, Rākṣasas, Yakṣas, ghosts, Piśācas, birds, domestic cattle, and wild beasts.

But these progeny born of his mind did not increase, for they were cursed by the wise lord Śiva, the great god. Then Dakṣa wished to create various progeny by means of pairing and emotion, and he married a wife, Asiknī, the daughter of the Prajāpati Vīraṇa; she had great ascetic powers and was capable of supporting people, for indeed she supported this whole universe, moving and still . . .

The sons of Dakṣa, the Haryaśvas, who had great heroic powers, assembled, for they wished to increase progeny. But Nārada said to them, 'How childish you are. You do not know the surface of the earth, how far it extends, how high or low; then how will you create progeny?[35] What is the measure of the earth? What is to be created? Without under-

33. There are said to have been fourteen different Manus, each acting as progenitor in a different era. The seventh Manu, progenitor of our present era, was Manu the son of Vivasvat, the sun (see below, myth 19, pp. 66–70).

34. That is, serpents, birds, plants, and insects.

35. A pun may be intended, based upon the Sanskrit verb 'you know' (*prajānītha*) and the noun 'progeny' (*prajā*).

standing this, how will you create? You would create too little or too much, and this would be a fault.' When they heard his words they set out in all directions, following the wind, and they disappeared; even today they have not returned, but are wandering with the winds. Thus the great sages wander on the path of the wind.

When his sons had been destroyed, Dakṣa the son of Pracetas begat another thousand sons in the daughter of Vīraṇa. They, the Śabalāśvas, wishing to increase progeny, were again addressed by Nārada as he had spoken before. Heeding his words, all those youths of great vitality said to one another, 'The great sage speaks the truth. We must follow the footsteps of our brothers; there can be no doubt of this. When we have learned the measure of the earth, we will happily create progeny.' Then they too went forth on that path in all directions, and even today they have not returned, like people who have been shipwrecked at sea. From that time forth, a brother who delights in following his brother and sets forth is destroyed; and this should not be done by a wise man.

When the Śabalāśvas had been destroyed, the lord Dakṣa became angry, and he cursed Nārada, saying: 'You will be destroyed, and you will become an embryo.' When his noble sons had been destroyed, Dakṣa begat sixty famous daughters in the daughter of Vīraṇa. The lord Kaśyapa took one of them in marriage to be his wife, and so did Dharma,[36] Soma, the lord Śiva, and the other great sages. Whoever truly knows this whole creation by Dakṣa becomes long-lived, famous, wealthy, and rich in progeny.

Brahmā curses Nārada

A more elaborate version of this myth, in which Brahmā resumes the role of the Creator, reintroduces more abstract levels of creation –

36. Here incarnate as a god.

time and measurement, music and scripture – but suddenly reverts to human imagery with the statement that Brahmā's wife gave these entities her breast to suck; furthermore, Nārada himself is here regarded as one of Brahmā's sons. The creation of abstractions, like the mental creation of living beings, is relatively simple, but difficulties immediately arise when concrete, physiological processes are introduced. The all-pervasive Vaiṣṇava bias of this version presents yet another conflict – a sectarian opposition between the (Śaiva) father, creator of the Rudras, and the sons, worshippers of Kṛṣṇa (who were cursed by Śiva in the shorter version of the myth). This same sectarianism is used to account for the decline in the worship of Brahmā.

II. FROM THE *Brahmavaivarta Purāṇa*

When Brahmā had fashioned all this universe, he placed his seed in Sāvitrī, his best wife, as a man full of desire places his seed in a woman full of desire. For a hundred celestial years she held the embryo, which was difficult to bear, and then when she was ready to give birth she bore the four enchanting Vedas, the various branches of knowledge such as logic and grammar, the thirty-six celestial Rāgiṇīs that capture the heart and the six beautiful Rāgas with their various rhythms. And she brought forth the Satya, Tretā, and Dvāpara Ages, and the Kali Age which is rich in quarrels, and the year, the month, the season, the lunar day, the inch, the second, and other measurements. She brought forth day and night, the days of the week, twilight and dawn; the goddesses Nourishment, Army of the Gods, Memory, Conquest, and Victory, and the six Kṛttikās;[37] the yogas and religious acts which result in abundant asceticism. She brought forth the great Ṣaṣṭhī, the Army of the Gods, who is dear to Kārttikeya; she is the leader of the Mothers, and she is the chosen divinity of children. The trinity of aeons – that of Brahmā, that of the lotus, and that of the boar; the natural, two-fold division –

37. The myth of the Kṛttikās, Ṣaṣṭhī, and Kārttikeya appears below, myth 33, pp. 105–15.

that which is constant and that which is momentary; the four kinds of universal dissolution, and time, and the maiden Death, and all the groups of diseases – all these she brought forth, and she gave them all her breast to suck.

Then Adharma was born from the back of the Creator, and Misfortune [*alakṣmī*] arose, insatiably lustful, from his left side. From his navel were born Viśvakarman, the guru of all artists, and the eight great Vasus, powerful and aggressive. And then from the mind of the Creator four little boys appeared, five years old, blazing with the energy of religion. They were Ancient, Joyous, Eternal, and Eternally-young, the best of wise men.[38] From Brahmā's mouth there appeared a boy shining like gold, a handsome youth with a celestial form, accompanied by a wife. He was the seed of all noble warriors, and his name was Manu the son of the Self-created; and the woman was Śatarūpā, first in beauty, delicate as a lotus. Manu remained with his wife to uphold the command of the Creator.

Then the Creator said to his sons, who were exulting,[39] 'Illustrious ones, perform creation.' But they said, 'No,' and they went to practise asceticism, for they were devoted to Kṛṣṇa. Because of this, the Creator, lord of universes, became angry, and as he was filled with anger, blazing with the energy of religion, the eleven Rudras appeared from his forehead; the first among them is famed as the Destroyer, the Rudra of the Doomsday Fire; he is known as the Dark One throughout the universes, while Brahmā himself is the Passionate and the auspicious Viṣṇu is the One Made of Goodness. But Kṛṣṇa, the lord of the world of cows, is without qualities, beyond nature; only fools who do not know the Supreme speak of Śiva as the Dark One, for he is in the vanguard of all Vaiṣṇavas, spotless, and pure goodness is his own form. Now

38. Sanaka, Sānanda, Sanātana, and Sanatkumāra.

39. Or: who had erections.

hear the names of the Rudras as they are proclaimed in the Vedas: Great, Noble, Wise, Terrifying, Frightening, He-who-has-seasons-as-his-banner, He-whose-hair-stands-up, Tawny-eyed, Brightness, Purity (and Rudra-the-howler as the eleventh).

Then Pulastya was born from his right ear and Pulaha from his left ear; Atri from his right nostril and Kratu from his left nostril. Araṇi was born from within his nose, the shining Aṅgiras from within his mouth, Bhṛgu from his left side, and Dakṣa[40] from his right side. From his shadow, the ascetic named Mud was born, and from his navel the sage with five tufts of hair on his head. From his breast was born the sage Voḍhu, and from his neck Nārada. Marīci was born from his shoulder, and the sage named Darkness-within-the-waters from his throat. Vasiṣṭha was born from his tongue, and Pracetas from his lower lip. From the left side of his stomach the ascetic named the Goose was born, and from the right side was born the Ascetic himself.[41]

Then the Creator commanded his sons to continue with creation, but when Nārada heard his father's speech he said to him, 'Grandfather, lord of the universe, first fetch my older brothers, Ancient and the others, and then speak to us about taking wives. Their father allowed them to practise asceticism; then why should we become involved in the wheel of rebirth? . . . As the flickering flame bewitches insects, as a scrap of flesh on a fish-hook causes the fish to fling himself upon it for the pleasure he thinks it will give him – so, father, the objects of the senses bring death to those who are attached to sensual and material life, for they are as transitory

40. Dakṣa, whose name is cognate with the Latin *dexter*, is appropriately born from the *right* side. The other sons preceding Dakṣa form one group of the Seven Sages, and the four that follow (Kardama, Pañcaśikha, Voḍhu, and Nārada) are famous Prajāpatis.

41. The Goose (Haṃsa) and the Ascetic (Yati) are ancient sages.

as dreams, vain, unreal, and deadly.' When Nārada had said this, he stood before the Creator, bowing to him, blazing like the flame of a fire.

Then Brahmā was overcome by anger, and he cursed his son; his limbs shook, his eyes were red, and his lip trembled as he said, 'Your knowledge will be wiped out by my curse, Nārada; you will be enticed like a beast kept for pleasure, a wanton lusting after women. You will charm the hearts of beautiful women intent upon permanent youth, and you will be the husband of fifty lustful women, dear to them as their very life's breath. You will be a savant of the erotic textbooks, ardently longing for the great erotic pleasures, the guru of the guru of those who are adept in the various ways of making love. You will be the best of the Gandharvas, singing beautifully with a beautiful voice, proud of your skill in playing on the lute, and you will be permanently young. No doubt you will be intelligent, sweet-speaking, calm, artful, handsome, and crafty, and your name will be Upabarhaṇa ['the Pillow']. When you have sported with these women for two hundred thousand celestial years in a deserted forest, then by my curse you will be the son of a slave girl. But then, my child, because of your attachment to Vaiṣṇavas and because you will have eaten what is cast off and left by Vaiṣṇavas, by the grace of Kṛṣṇa you will again be my son, and then I will give you celestial, eternal knowledge once more. But now, my son, you will be destroyed and you will be forced to fall.'

When Brahmā, the lord of the universe, had said this to his son, Nārada wept and, folding his palms together, he said to his father, 'Restrain your anger, father, my father, Guru of the Universe, Restrainer. Alas, that the anger of the Creator, lord of ascetics, has fallen upon me without cause. A wise man should curse and abandon a son who embarks on the wrong path; but why should you, a learned man, curse your ascetic son? Let me be born in any wombs whatever, but do not cause me to abandon my devotion to Hari; grant me this boon, Brahmā. If the son of the Creator of the Universe is no longer devoted to the foot of Hari, he dies as the very lowest upon earth, surpassed even by a pig . . . Four-headed Brahmā, since you cursed me when I had committed no offence, you deserve to be cursed by me, for even learned men will harm one who harms them. By my curse, Manu will be injured by the sun[42] despite all his amulets and hymns in your praise and acts of worship for you. And you will not be worshipped among all men for three aeons, father, but when these three aeons have passed you will again be worshipped, for you are worthy of worship. Then you will have a portion of the sacrifice and you will be given one kind of worship in all religious vows and similar acts, and you will be honoured by the gods and others.' When Nārada had said this to his father, the Creator remained in the assembly with an aching heart. Then Nārada was reborn as Upabarhaṇa, the Gandharva, son of a slave girl, because of his father's curse, but afterwards Nārada became a great sage again and obtained knowledge from his father.

The Degradation of Brahmā: He tries to Rape Anasūyā and is Cursed

By the time of the later Purāṇas, Brahmā was no longer generally worshipped (just as Nārada had predicted), although he was allowed to maintain his old position as Creator in the mythology. Viṣṇu and Śiva are linked with him in the myth of Anasūyā, which exalts Brahmins even above the great sectarian gods, but it is Brahmā who speaks for the Trinity, and his speech is ironically reminiscent of the words that his more illustrious antecedent, the Prajāpati of the Brāhmaṇas, spoke in the course of his primeval incest.

42. See below, myth 19, pp. 66–70.

12. FROM THE *Bhaviṣya Purāṇa*

One day, the lord Atri was practising asceticism on the banks of the Ganges, together with his wife Anasūyā, and he was meditating intently upon the Godhead.[43] The eternal ones, Brahmā, Hari, and Śambhu, approached him, each mounted on his own vehicle,[44] and told him to choose a boon. The sage who was the son of the Self-created Prajāpati heard their speech but did not say anything in reply, for he was firmly immersed in the highest Self. Observing his emotion, the three eternal gods went to his wife Anasūyā and spoke to her. Rudra himself had a *liṅga*[45] in his hand; Viṣṇu was exhilarated with desire for her; Brahmā's godhead was annulled by lust, and he was entirely in the power of Kāma.[46] He said, 'Grant me sexual pleasure, or I will abandon my life's breath, for you have caused me to whirl about drunk with passion.' When Anasūyā, who was true to her vow to her husband, heard their improper speech she did not say anything in reply, for she feared the anger of the gods. But the gods, out of their minds, grabbed her by force and prepared to rape her, for they were deluded by the Goddess's magic power.

Then the sage's beloved and faithful wife became angry and cursed them, saying, 'You will be my sons, for you have been

43. The all-pervading godhead is *brahma* (neuter). A pun may be intended with the name of Brahmā (masculine), who here assumes a most un-metaphysical role.

44. Each god rides on an animal which is his 'vehicle' in the metaphorical sense as well – his symbol, an animal in whose every instance the god is implicitly present. Viṣṇu (Hari) rides on the Garuḍa bird (see below, myth 60, pp. 222–3), Śiva on a bull (see below, myth 69, pp. 266–9), Indra on the white elephant Airāvata (myth 69), Gaṇeśa on a bandycoot (myth 69), and the Goddess on a lion (myth 68, pp. 258–9).

45. The *liṅga* or phallus is the symbol of Śiva (see below, myths 38–40, pp. 138–54). It is unclear whether Śiva is here carrying this symbol or touching his own personal phallus; a pun may be intended.

46. Eros, god of desire.

infatuated by desire. The *liṅga* of the great god, the great head of Brahmā here, and the two feet of Vāsudeva will always be worshipped by men, and so the supreme gods will be the supreme laughing-stock.' When they heard this terrible speech, they bowed to the sage's beloved wife, bent low with reverence, and praised her with Vedic verses as recited by the gods. Then Anasūyā said, 'When you are my little sons, you will be freed from my curse and you will be content.' Then Brahmā became Candramas, Hari became Dattātreya, and the lord Hara became incarnate as Durvāsas. And they all became yogis in order to dispel that evil.

2

INDRA

The Vedic cycle of Indra and Vṛtra

THE mythology of the god Indra, king of the gods, warrior of the gods, god of rain, begins in the *Ṛg Veda*. Unfortunately for the student of mythology, none of the Ṛg Vedic hymns actually sets out to narrate a myth; rather, various myths are alluded to, often in enigmatic terms. To 'read' a Vedic myth about Indra, therefore, it is necessary to have recourse to later Indian commentaries, interpretations, and reworkings of the Vedic myths, and then to re-examine the Vedic hymns themselves in the light of this knowledge.

INDRA BEHEADS DADHYAÑC, WHO REVEALS TVAṢṬṚ'S MEAD TO THE AŚVINS

The obscure verse which alludes to this myth is somewhat clarified by the knowledge that 'honey' refers to the Soma juice, an intoxicant that was drunk by the priests and offered to the gods in the sacrifice, often mixed with milk; that the Vedic horse-sacrifice consisted in the beheading of a stallion; that the Aśvins had the heads of horses; that to 'know' the secret of the Soma was to have the power of the magic formula, the word; and that Tvaṣṭṛ, the father of Indra, is later killed by Indra.

13a. FROM THE *Ṛg Veda*

O Aśvins, you placed a horse-head upon Dadhyañc, the son of the Atharvan priest. He, being honest, told you about the honey of Tvaṣṭṛ that was hidden from you, who accomplish wondrous deeds.

The actual events of the story, and Indra's connection with it, only emerge after the reading of a Brāhmaṇa expansion of this text.

13b. FROM THE *Śatapatha Brāhmaṇa*

Now, Dadhyañc, the son of the Atharvan priest, knew this essence, this sacrifice – how this head of the sacrifice is put on again, how this sacrifice becomes complete. Indra said to him, 'If you teach this to anyone else, I will cut off your head.' Now, the Aśvins heard this: 'Dadhyañc, the son of the Atharvan priest, knows this essence, this sacrifice – how the head of the sacrifice is put on again, how the sacrifice becomes complete.' They went to him and said, 'Let us be your pupils.' He asked, 'What would you wish to learn?' 'This essence, this sacrifice – how the head of the sacrifice is put on again, how the sacrifice becomes complete,' they replied. He said, 'Indra said to me, "If you teach this to anyone else, I will cut off your head." Therefore, I fear that he might indeed cut off my head. I will not accept you as pupils.' They said, 'We two will protect you from him.' 'How will you protect me?' 'When you accept us as pupils, we will cut off your head and put it somewhere else; then we will bring a horse's head and place it upon you. With that you will teach us, and when you have taught us, then Indra will cut off that head of yours. Then we will bring your own head and place it upon you again.' He agreed and accepted them as pupils, and when he had received them as pupils they cut off his head and placed it somewhere else, and they brought the head of a horse and placed it on him. With that head he taught them, and when he had taught them, Indra cut off that head of his. Then they brought his own head and placed it on him again.

Indra Makes a Weapon of Dadhyañc's Bones

The story of Dadhyañc does not end there. Another cryptic Ṛg Vedic hymn refers to Dadhyañc's role in another, more important beheading performed by Indra.

14a. FROM THE *Ṛg Veda*

Indra, unopposable, slew ninety-nine Vṛtras[1] with the bones of Dadhyañc. As Indra sought the horse's head that was hidden in the mountains, he found it in Śaryaṇāvat. Then they knew the secret name of the cow of Tvaṣṭṛ, in the house of the moon.

Sāyaṇa, a great Vedic commentator of the fourteenth century A.D., explains the myth to which this hymn refers.

14b. FROM *Sāyaṇa's commentary*

The demons obtained supremacy merely by looking at Dadhyañc, the son of the Atharvan priest, while he was alive. And when he went to heaven, the earth was filled with demons. Indra, who could not fight with the demons, searched for that sage, and he was told that he had gone to heaven. Then Indra asked the people there, 'Is there no limb left of him here?' and they replied, 'There is the horse-head by which he told the Aśvins the secret of the honey. But we do not know where that head might be.' Then Indra said, 'Search for it,' and they searched for it. They discovered it in Śaryaṇāvat and brought it. Śaryaṇāvat is the name of a lake that flows in the western half of the Plain of Kuru. With the bones of that head, Indra slew the demons.

The link between this and the first Dadhyañc episode is provided by Śaunaka, a commentator of the fifth century B.C. He identifies Śaryaṇāvat not as a lake but as a mountain; yet he also mentions a lake, for the myth must provide a watery home for the fiery horse-head that emerges to destroy the universe at the end of the aeon.[2]

14c. FROM THE *Bṛhaddevatā of Śaunaka*

Because Dadhyañc had told the secret of the mead to the two

1. Vṛtra is the arch-enemy of Indra. See below, myths 24–6, pp. 74–90.

2. See below, myth 42, pp. 160–61.

Aśvins by means of the horse-head, Indra took away that head, and the two Aśvins then replaced Dadhyañc's own head upon him. The horse-head, cut off by the thunderbolt of Indra who bears the thunderbolt, fell into the middle of a lake on Mount Śaryaṇāvat. Rising up from those waters to grant various wishes to living beings, it lies submerged in the waters until the end of the aeon.

The search for the magic of resuscitation, and the destruction of a sage who revives demons, are themes which persist in later Hindu mythology.[3] The role of Tvaṣṭṛ (also called Viśvakarman, 'All-fashioner') in this particular episode, as well as in the first Dadhyañc hymn, is further explained by Sāyaṇa, who draws upon other bits of Vedic lore: Tvaṣṭṛ – the Architect, artisan of the gods – had a magic cow whose udder yielded Soma; he hid this cow from Indra, and only Dadhyañc knew this secret; Dadhyañc told this to the Aśvins, and Indra beheaded Dadhyañc and stole Tvaṣṭṛ's Soma. Sāyaṇa's exegesis also resolves the tension between the solar and lunar symbolism; Indra and Tvaṣṭṛ are sun gods, but Soma is said to be stored in the moon.

14d. FROM *Sāyaṇa's commentary*

The cow of Tvaṣṭṛ – who is the blazing sun – is a traveller in the house – that is, the orb – of the moon. Her own name – that is, the energy of the sun – is hidden – disappearing at night. But they recognize her by her rays, for the sun's rays are reflected in the clear circle of the moon, which is made of water, and these rays reflected there create an identical sign or image even when cast upon the moon – this is the meaning. When the solar energy that disappears at night enters the circle of the moon, then, dispelling the darkness of night, it illuminates everything as if it were day. The sun which has this kind of energy is Indra himself, for Indra is enumerated

3. See below, myths 73–5, pp. 281–300.

among the twelve suns.[4] Indra is the illuminator of day and night . . . The sun is called a cow.

TVAṢṬṚ GIVES HIS DAUGHTER SARAṆYŪ TO VIVASVAT

Just as the two episodes related above combine to tell the tale of Dadhyañc, so the Dadhyañc tale itself is merely an episode in yet another myth of Tvaṣṭṛ; and the story of Tvaṣṭṛ is, in turn, merely one episode in the myth of Indra, a myth which is never told in full in any one text but which was known in its entirety to many educated Indians.

The Aśvins, Yama and Yamī, and Manu are born

The myth of Tvaṣṭṛ and his daughter was told, directly though briefly, by the etymologist Yāska at the turn of the fifth century B.C.

15. FROM THE *Nirukta*

Saraṇyū, the daughter of Tvaṣṭṛ, bore a pair of twins to Vivasvat, the sun. Then she substituted for herself another, identical female, and she herself took the form of a mare and fled. Vivasvat, the sun, took the form of a horse in the same way and followed her. Thus the Aśvins were born, and Manu was born in the identical female.

Tvaṣṭṛ begets Triśiras and Saraṇyū

The 'identical female' in Yāska's cryptic tale is reminiscent of the 'image' of the sun placed in the moon, while the procreative sun god who becomes a stallion to cover the unwilling, chaste mare resembles the incestuous creator in another equine Vedic cycle.[5] The details of the episode are made somewhat clearer in the version told by Śaunaka in a work composed only shortly after that of Yāska.

16. FROM THE *Bṛhaddevatā*

Tvaṣṭṛ had twin children, Saraṇyū and Triśiras ['Three-

4. That is, the twelve Ādityas.
5. See above, myths 3–6, pp. 29–35, and below, myth 34, pp. 117–18.

headed']. He himself gave Saraṇyū in marriage to Vivasvat. Then Yama and Yamī were born of Saraṇyū and Vivasvat; these two also were twins, but Yama was the elder of the two. Without her husband's knowledge, Saraṇyū created a woman identical to herself; entrusting the twins to the latter, she became a mare and went away. But in ignorance of this, Vivasvat begat upon the woman a son, Manu, who became a royal sage with energy like that of Vivasvat. Then he became aware that Saraṇyū had departed in the form of a mare, and he went quickly after the daughter of Tvaṣṭṛ, having become a horse of the same qualities. And Saraṇyū, knowing that it was Vivasvat in the form of a horse, approached him for sexual intercourse, and he mounted her. But in their haste the semen fell on the ground, and the mare smelled that semen because she desired to become pregnant. From that semen that was inhaled two youths were born, called Nāsatya ['From-the-nose'] and Dasra ['Performing-wondrous-deeds'], famed as the Aśvins.

Tvaṣṭṛ gives his daughter to Vivasvat

Of the four sets of twins in the *Bṛhaddevatā* (the two Aśvins, the 'twin' wives, the twin children of Tvaṣṭṛ and the twins Yama and Yamī), only two are mentioned in the original Ṛg Vedic verse upon which the myth is based.

17. FROM THE *Ṛg Veda*

'Tvaṣṭṛ is giving a wedding for his daughter' – hearing this, the whole world assembles. The mother of Yama, the wedded wife of the great Vivasvat, disappeared. They[6] concealed the immortal woman from mortals. Making an identical woman, they gave her to Vivasvat. Saraṇyū bore the two Aśvins, and then she abandoned the two twins.

6. 'They' refers to the gods, according to Sāyaṇa.

Yama Rejects Yamī and Becomes King of the Dead

Yama, the first son of the sun, becomes the first mortal man and later god of the dead, while Manu, the sun's son in post-Vedic versions, is said to be the ancestor of the human race but is not deified. The myth of Yama and Yamī is connected with the Indra corpus in several ways, although Indra himself does not appear in the Ṛg Vedic hymn on which the myth is based: the Yama myth is not only a part of the Saraṇyū myth but a multiform of it; Tvaṣṭṛ is active in both myths as the architect *par excellence*; Vivasvat is the father of Yama and husband of Saraṇyū; Yama, like Indra, is one of the four guardians of the quarters (Lokapālas) in later Hindu mythology; and the messengers of Yama are two brindle dogs, the descendants of Saramā the bitch of Indra. Both the Yama myth and the Saraṇyū myth may be seen as examples of the theme of the union of a mortal man with an immortal woman, resulting in the birth of Agni. (The myth of primeval incest also relates the union of a heavenly father and chthonic daughter to produce a son in the fire sacrifice, and in later mythology the celestial god Rudra unites with Pārvatī, the chthonic daughter of the mountain, to produce a son who is the child of fire.[7]) In spite of many obscurities and confusions – contradictory statements about the identity of the mothers and of the children – it is clear that the idea of twinness and the correlated idea of the conjunction and interactions of opposites (male and female, night and day, earth and heaven, mortal and immortal, ascetic purity and desire for progeny) underlie both sets of myths.

Yama rejects Yamī

18. FROM THE *Ṛg Veda*

[Yamī says,] 'Would that I might bring a friend to intimate friendship, now that he[8] has crossed the vast ocean; let the

7. See above, myth 3, pp. 29–30, and below, myths 33, pp. 108–10, and 43, pp. 162–8.

8. 'He' may be Yama, the sun, or Rudra. If it is Yama, then the ocean may be the metaphorical ocean separating mortals from im-

sage receive the son of the father and gaze far over the earth.'

[Yama says,] 'Your friend does not desire this intimate friendship, that a woman of his kind should become alien.[9] The heroes, the sons of the great spirit,[10] supporters of the sky, see far in all directions.'

[Yamī:] 'The immortals desire this offspring left by the one mortal. Let your creative power of thought unite with mine; enter my body as the husband enters the body of the wife.'

[Yama:] 'Shall we do now what has not been done before? Shall we who speak righteously now speak unrighteously? The Gandharva in the waters and the wife of the waters[11] – such is our source, our highest birth.'

[Yamī:] 'The god Tvaṣṭṛ, the creator, the impeller, shaper of all forms, fashioned us as man and wife even when we were still in the womb. No-one can disobey his commands; earth and heaven witness this for us.'

[Yama:] 'Who has witnessed this first day? Who has seen it? Who can speak of it? The realm of Mitra and Varuṇa[12] is

---

mortals, crossed by Yama in this hymn; if 'he' is the sun, the ocean may be the actual ocean crossed by the sun every day; if he is Rudra, Yamī may be saying that Yama need not fear Rudra, the punisher of incest, since he is absent across the ocean.

9. This would imply that his kinswoman, his sister, does not wish to become 'alien' by becoming his wife; an alternative translation would be: 'that a woman of another kind should become like him' – that is, that an immortal woman should become mortal like him.

10. The great spirit may be Varuṇa (the god who punishes sinful mortals and who sends his thousand spies everywhere among mortals); or, as Sāyaṇa suggests, he may be Rudra, whose sons – the Maruts – Yama fears in spite of Yamī's reassurance that Rudra himself is far away.

11. This is the sun, born in the waters as Agni is born. The wife of the waters is Saraṇyū. Yama and Yamī are the children of Vivasvat (the sun) and Saraṇyū.

12. Mitra and Varuṇa together represent the Indo-European duality of fire and water and of earthly and spiritual power.

vast. Wanton woman, what will you say in your temptation towards men?'

[Yamī:] 'The desire for Yama has come upon me, Yamī, the desire to lie with him upon the same bed. Let me open my body to him as a wife to her husband. Let us whirl about together like the two wheels of a chariot.'

[Yama:] 'These spies of the gods who wander about here below do not stand still, nor do they blink their eyes. Wanton woman, go quickly with a man other than me. Whirl about like the two wheels of a chariot with him.'

[Yamī:] 'She would serve him night and day; she would deceive the eye of the sun for the moment of a blink of the eye. The twins are closely tied like heaven and earth. Let Yamī behave toward Yama as if she were not his kinswoman.'[13]

[Yama:] 'In later ages there will be races in which kinswomen will act with their kinsmen as if they were not kin. Make a pillow of your arm for a bull, fair woman. Desire a husband other than me.'[14]

[Yamī:] 'What good is a brother, when a woman has no protector? What good is a sister, when destruction comes down upon her? Overcome with desire, I beg you again and again: unite your body with my body.'

[Yama:] 'Never will I agree to unite my body with your body. They call a man who unites with his sister an evil man. Seek your pleasures with some other man than me. Your brother does not wish this, fair one.'

13. Or: Let Yamī take upon herself the incest of Yama.

14. An alternative interpretation of these last two verses might be: Let the priest tend Agni day and night, as the eye of the sun dies repeatedly. May the pair of twins, related as are heaven and earth, bear the non-paired Agni. In later ages there will be races which will kindle the non-paired Agni. Stretch out your arm to Agni; find another man than me to produce the sacrificial fire.

[Yamī:] 'Fie, fie, Yama, you are feeble; I see no creative power of thought nor any heart in you. Indeed, let some other woman embrace you like a girth embracing a stallion or a creeper embracing a tree.'

[Yama:] 'Yamī, you will indeed embrace another man, and he will embrace you, as a creeper embraces a tree. Desire his creative power of thought, and let him desire yours. Join with him in an auspicious union.'

Yama becomes king of the dead

The story of the union of Yama and Yamī, which is more fully developed in Iranian mythology, is almost never referred to again in Hindu mythology. But the role of Yama (and his sister Yamī, who becomes the river Yamunā) in the story of Saraṇyū is often told, usually in connection with his appointment as god of the dead. In these later versions, the 'identical woman' who replaces Saraṇyū is sometimes called Saṃjñā, 'the Image', probably for the reason suggested by Sāyaṇa: Tvaṣṭṛ's daughter, the energy of the sun, becomes a bright image reflected in the moon.[15] Sāyaṇa identifies her with the cow of the original Ṛg Vedic verse; in the later tradition she becomes a mare, probably because she is the mother of the equine Aśvins. But in most Purāṇic texts, the figure of Saraṇyū herself – the original wife of Vivasvat – is given the name of Saṃjñā, and it is this woman, the bright image, who then seeks a replacement – the dark shadow.

In one Purāṇic text, the twins of opposition are further proliferated: now there are two Manus, both claiming the sun as their father but only one born of the 'true' wife of the sun. Other conflicts arise within the family, all but one a conflict between male and female and all but one a conflict between parents and children: husband versus wife (Vivasvat and Saṃjñā), daughter versus father (Saṃjñā and Tvaṣṭṛ), son versus step-mother (Yama and the 'shadow' Saṃjñā), and husband versus father-in-law (Vivasvat and Tvaṣṭṛ). On the symbolic level, the opposition between light and dark forms the basis of a myth of the death and revival of the sun and a myth of the birth of death. The sin of partiality in the anthropomorphic mother is

15. See above, myths 14d, pp. 59–60, and 15, p. 60.

contrasted with the impartiality of the son, the god of the dead,[16] whose own mortality is emphasized by the image of carnal decay – worms bearing his flesh to the earth. The concept of the control and distribution of excess, so basic to Hindu cosmogony, is expressed in the episode of the trimming of the sun as well as in the image of the fiery-mouthed mare, the mother of the Aśvins, who later becomes the doomsday mare,[17] submerged in the ocean even as the horse-headed Dadhyañc hides in a lake and as the sun-stallion – the Gandharva in the water, the robber of waters – is said to be born out of the waters.

19. FROM THE *Mārkaṇḍeya Purāṇa*

The lord of creatures, Viśvakarman, propitiated Vivasvat, bowed before him, and gave his daughter Saṃjñā to him. The sun, lord of cattle, begat three children in her, two sons of great splendour and a daughter named Yamunā. Manu the son of Vivasvat was the eldest; he is the lord of creatures, the god who presides over the offerings to the dead. After him Yama and Yamī, the twins, were born. But the energy of Mārtaṇḍa Vivasvat was excessive, and with it he overheated the three worlds, with all that moves and is still. And when Saṃjñā saw the round form of Vivasvat, she was unable to bear his great energy, and she gazed at her own shadow and said to her, 'I am going away to my father's house. Please remain here unchanged, by my command, fair lady. Be kind to these two little boys of mine and my fair daughter, and do not speak of this to my lord.' The shadow said, 'Even if I am dragged by the hair, even if I am cursed, I will never speak of your intention, O goddess. Go where you wish.'

When the fair-eyed Saṃjñā heard this said by her shadow, she went to her father's house and dwelt there in the house of her father for some time. Though her father admonished her

16. Compare the impartiality of the maiden Death in myth 8, p. 42.

17. See below, myth 42, pp. 160–61.

again and again to go to her husband, she took the form of a mare and went to the northern Kurus. There the chaste woman practised asceticism and fasted.

When Saṃjñā had gone to her father, the shadow obeyed her command, took her form, and approached the sun. And the lord, the sun, thinking that this was Saṃjñā, begat in her two sons and a daughter. The first son of these two was the equal of the Manu who had been born before, and so he was called Manu Sāvarṇi ['Of-the-same-kind' or 'Born-of-the-look-alike']; and the second son became the planet Saturn, the slowly-moving. The daughter, Tapatī, was chosen in marriage by king Saṃvaraṇa.

But the shadow did not behave as affectionately to those first-born children as queen Saṃjñā had behaved to them, who were her own children. Manu put up with this in her, but Yama could not bear it. As his father's wife continued to trouble him frequently, he became very unhappy, and so, because of anger or childishness, or by the force of pre-determined fate, Yama threatened the shadow Saṃjñā with his foot, and then the shadow Saṃjñā, full of great resentment, cursed Yama, saying, 'Since you threaten with your foot the wife of your father, a woman who deserves your respect, therefore your foot will certainly fall off.' Now Yama was much grieved in his mind by this curse, and he, whose soul was *dharma*, went with Manu and reported it all to his father, saying, 'Mother does not treat us with equal affection, O lord. She shuns us, the older ones, and favours the two younger ones. I lifted my foot toward her, but I did not touch her body with it, and since I acted out of childishness or delusion, you should forgive me. Father, best of those who give heat, since mother cursed me, her own son, in anger, I do not consider her my mother. For a mother does not behave badly even toward badly behaved sons; father, how could she say to me, "Let your foot fall off, my son"? O lord of cattle, blessed one, think of some way by which, through your grace, my foot will not fall off today by my mother's curse.' The sun said, 'Without any doubt, my son, this curse will take effect, since anger entered into you who know *dharma* and speak the truth. For all curses there is some remedy; but there is nothing anywhere that can dispel the curse of those who have been cursed by a mother. It is impossible to make your mother's words fail to come true; but I will do something as a favour for you, my son, because of my affection for you. Worms will take flesh from your foot and go to the surface of the earth. Thus her words will come true, and you will be saved.'

Then the sun said to the shadow, 'Why are you more affectionate to one among my sons when all are equal? You certainly cannot be their mother, Saṃjñā, but you are someone else who has come here; for how could a mother curse a son even among badly behaved children?' She avoided that question and did not say anything to Vivasvat, and he meditated within himself and saw the truth. When the shadow Saṃjñā saw that the lord of the day was about to curse her, she trembled with fear and reported to him what had happened. Vivasvat became furious when he heard this, and he went to his father-in-law, who received the Maker of Day decorously and fittingly and honoured and pacified him who wished to burn him up in anger.

Viśvakarman said, 'Your form is hard to bear, for it has excessive energy. Therefore Saṃjñā is unable to bear it and is practising asceticism in the forest. You will see your well-behaved wife today practising great asceticism in the wilderness, because of your excessive form. I recall the speech of Brahmā, and if it please you, O lord, lord of the day, I will restrain your form and make it lovely.' 'So be it,' replied the lord sun to Tvaṣṭṛ, and Viśvakarman, having received permission from Vivasvat, placed his spherical form upon his lathe on the island of Śāka and began to cut down his energy . . .[18]

Thus Viśvakarman praised the sun, and he kept a sixteenth part of the energy of the lord of the day in a spherical form. When fifteen parts of his energy had been cut away, then the body of the sun was extremely lovely and charming. And with the energy that had been cut away was made the discus of Viṣṇu, the trident of Śarva, the palanquin of Kubera (the lord of wealth), the rod of the lord of the dead,[19] and the spear of the general of the gods.[20] And Viśvakarman made the brilliant weapons of the other gods, for the quelling of their enemies, out of the energy of the sun. When his energy had been thus cut away, Mārtaṇḍa had a body that was beautiful in every limb but did not shine with excessive energy.

Then he meditated and saw his wife in the form of a mare, unapproachable by all creatures because of her asceticism and self-control. And the sun went to the northern Kurus and took the form of a horse and approached her. When she saw him approaching she feared it might be another male, and so she turned to face him, determined to protect her hind quarters. Their noses joined as they touched, and the seed[21] of Vivasvat entered the nose of the mare. Two gods were born in that way, the Aśvins, the supreme physicians, called Nāsatya and Dasra, the sons who came forth out of the mare's mouth. These are the sons born of Mārtaṇḍa when he had the form of a horse. And when the seed ceased to flow [*retaso 'nte*, 'at the end of the seed'] Revanta was born, holding a sword and a bow and arrows and a quiver, clad in armour, mounted on

18. Here he sings a long hymn of praise to the sun.

19. The lord of the dead is Yama, who has not yet been given this office.

20. Skanda is the general of the gods. See below, myth 33, pp. 105–15.

21. The word used here for seed (*tejas*) also denotes energy; it is significant that the sun's energy has just been compressed, made globular like a seed.

a horse. Then the sun revealed his own spotless form, and when she saw that his form was peaceful she rejoiced. And then the sun, the Robber of Waters, led to his own home his loving wife Saṃjñā, who had resumed her own form.

Her first-born son was known as Manu the son of Vivasvat, but her second was called Yama ('Curb') because of the shadow's curse and Eye of *Dharma* because of his father's favour. Yama was greatly distressed in his mind because of that curse, but since he delights in *dharma* he is known as the King of *Dharma*. 'Worms will take flesh from your foot and fall to the surface of the earth': thus his father himself set an end to his curse. And because he has the Eye of *Dharma*, he is impartial both to the kindly and the harmful. Therefore the Dispeller of Darkness, his father, the lord, appointed him lord of the south and made him a World-protector,[22] the overlord of the ancestors. And the Maker of Day, well satisfied, made Yamunā a river which flows from inside Mount Kalinda. The two Aśvins were made the physicians of the gods by their noble father, and Revanta was made overlord of the Guhyakas.

Indra Beheads Triśiras

One other male twin related to Tvaṣṭṛ is Triśiras, who appears only in the *Bṛhaddevatā* version of the Saraṇyū myth but is an enemy of Indra elsewhere in the *Ṛg Veda*. The story is told briefly by Śaunaka.

20. FROM THE *Bṛhaddevatā*

Triśiras, who could assume all forms, being a son of the sister of the demons, became the domestic priest of the gods, from a

22. The World-protectors are the guardians of the quarters, the regions or directions of the sky: Indra, lord of the east; Yama, lord of the south; Kubera, lord of the north; and Varuṇa, lord of the west. In addition, there are four gods of the intermediary directions: Agni (south-east), the sun (south-west), the wind (north-west), and Soma (north-east).

desire to destroy them. But Indra found out that the sage had been sent among the gods by the demons, and with his thunderbolt he quickly cut off those three heads. The head which had drunk Soma became a heathcock; the head which had drunk wine became a sparrow; and that with which he had eaten food became a partridge.

Trita Āptya and Indra Behead Triśiras

The Ṛg Vedic verses which tell this tale ascribe the act to Trita Āptya (an ally of Indra) as well as to Indra himself and relate it to the other Tvaṣṭṛ myths.

21. from the *Ṛg Veda*

Āptya, sent by Indra, knew the weapons of the ancestors, and he waged war. Having slain Triśiras, who had seven rays [or seven reins], Trita released the cows of the son of Tvaṣṭṛ. Indra struck down the ruler whose strength was great. After he had driven home the cows of Tvaṣṭṛ's son, who could assume all forms, he cut off his three heads.

Indra Sends the Bitch Saramā to the Paṇis

The motifs of hiding and finding – applied to the sun, to cows, to horses, to wives, to water or rain, to the Soma – combine again with the motif of the slaying of demons in another episode of the Indra cycle, in which the mythical animal is not the 'sought' (the valuable and symbolic cow or horse) but the 'seeker', the hunter, Saramā, regarded in later mythology as a bitch.

Saramā drinks the milk of the Paṇis

The later, explicit version of the tale states clearly the three central plot elements: the use of a woman to seduce or trick one's enemies; the voyage, across water, to the other world, where one must not eat or drink; and the obtaining of the magic elixir.

22. FROM THE *Bṛhaddevatā*

There were demons named Paṇis who lived on the other side of the Rasā.[23] They carried away the cows of Indra and hid them carefully. Bṛhaspati saw this, and having seen it he told Indra. Then the Chastiser of Pāka[24] sent Saramā there as a messenger. The Paṇi demons interrogated her with the hymn that begins 'With what ...',[25] saying, 'Where do you come from? Whose are you, fair one? And what is your business here?' 'I wander as the messenger of Indra,' replied Saramā, 'seeking you and the cow-pen and the cows of Indra, who is asking for them.' When they learned that she was the messenger of Indra, the evil-minded demons said, 'Saramā, do not go. Be our sister here. Let us divide the share of the cows. Do not be unfriendly again.' Then with the last verse of this hymn, as well as with the alternate ones throughout, she said, 'I do not desire sisterhood or wealth, but I would drink the milk of those cows which you are hiding.' The demons agreed and brought the milk. She drank that demonic milk because of her nature and her inconstancy; the milk was excellent, charming, delightful, bringing strength and nourishment. Then she crossed back over the Rasā, which extended for a hundred leagues, on the farther bank of which was the Paṇis' fort, which was hard to overcome. Then Indra asked Saramā, 'Have you seen the cows?' But she, because of the influence of the demonic milk, replied to Indra, 'No.' Furious, he struck her with his foot, and she vomited the milk. Then, trembling with fear, she went back to the Paṇis. And Indra followed the path of her footsteps, driving bay

23. Rasā may here denote a river; in later Hinduism, it is the name of the subterranean watery hell, abode of the demons. Clearly it acts, like the Styx, to separate the other world from this world.

24. Pāka ('childish') is the name of a demon killed by Indra; the epithet may thus mean 'instructor of the childish' or 'chastiser of Pāka'.

25. A reference to *Ṛg Veda* 10.108 (below, myth 23, pp. 73–4).

horses in his chariot; he went and killed the Paṇis and took back the cows.

Saramā speaks with the Paṇis

The hymn to which this myth specifically refers is a dialogue between Saramā and the Paṇis which contains in its imagery the germ of the ideas which developed into the narrative of later texts. It is interesting to note that while Saramā vomits forth the actual milk in the *Bṛhaddevatā*, in the *Ṛg Veda* the Paṇis vomit back words – for here, as in the Dadhyañc episode, the magic formula *is* the elixir.

23. FROM THE *Ṛg Veda*

[The Paṇis say,] 'With what desire has Saramā come to this place? The way is long and weary. What is the intention of your visit? How did you wander here? And how did you cross the waters of the Rasā?'

[Saramā:] 'I have been sent as the messenger of Indra, and I desire your great treasures, O Paṇis. Through fear of being jumped across,[26] the waters helped me; thus I crossed the waters of the Rasā.'

[Paṇis:] 'What is Indra like, Saramā? What is the appearance of him as whose messenger you have come here from afar? If he comes here, we will make friends with him, and he will be the herdsman of our cattle.'

[Saramā:] 'I do not know him as one who can be tricked; he tricks others, he who sent me here as his messenger from afar. The deep streams do not hide *him*; you Paṇis will lie there slain by Indra.'

[Paṇis:] 'These are the cows which you desire, fair Saramā, having crossed beyond the ends of heaven. Who would give them to you without a fight? And our weapons are sharp.'

[Saramā:] 'Your words, O Paṇis, are no armies. Your evil bodies may be proof against arrows, the path to you may be

26. The Rasā would, apparently, be ashamed to have it known that a dog had jumped over it.

impregnable, but Bṛhaspati[27] will not spare you in either case.'

[Paṇis:] 'Saramā, this treasure full of cows, horses, and riches is kept secure in the mountains. Paṇis who are good sentinels guard it. You have come in vain on this fruitless journey.'

[Saramā:] 'The sages – Ayāsyas, Aṅgirases, and Navagvas – made eager by Soma will come here and share this wide expanse of cattle. Then you will spit back these words, O Paṇis.'

[Paṇis:] 'Saramā, since you have come here, compelled by the force of the gods, we will make you our sister. Do not go back; we will give you a share of the cattle, fair lady.'

[Saramā:] 'I know no brotherhood, nor sisterhood with you; Indra and the dreadful Aṅgirases are my kin. When I left them, they seemed to me to be desirous of cattle. Paṇis, run away from here; run far away from here, Paṇis. Let the lowing cattle come out by the right path, the cattle which Bṛhaspati, the inspired sages, the pressing-stones and Soma found when they had been hidden.'

Indra Slays Vṛtra

The symbolism inherent in all of the Indra episodes is drawn upon by the Vedic poet in praising Indra for the greatest of his deeds, the slaying of the dragon Vṛtra, an act which also symbolizes the releasing of the waters or rains which Vṛtra had held back, the conquest of the enemies of the Āryans, and the setting in order of heaven.

Indra slays Vṛtra and releases the waters

24. FROM THE *Ṛg Veda*

I will tell the heroic deeds of Indra, those which the Wielder

27. Here Bṛhaspati is an epithet, 'lord of sacred speech', applied to Indra. By the time of the *Bṛhaddevatā* version of the myth (above, myth 22, pp. 72–3), Bṛhaspati and Indra had already become separate figures. See below, myths 74–5, pp. 282–300.

of the Thunderbolt first accomplished. He slew the dragon and released the waters; he split open the bellies of the mountain. He slew the dragon who lay upon the mountain; Tvaṣṭṛ fashioned the roaring thunderbolt for him. Like lowing cows, the gliding waters have flowed straight down to the ocean. Rejoicing in his virility like a bull, he chose the Soma and drank the extract from the three bowls. The Generous One took up the thunderbolt as his weapon and killed the first-born of dragons. O Indra, when you killed the first-born of dragons and overcame the deluding lures of the wily, at that very moment you brought forth the sun, heaven, and dawn; since then you have found no overpowering enemy. Indra killed Vṛtra, the greater enemy, the shoulderless one, with his great and deadly thunderbolt. Like the branches of a tree felled by an axe, the dragon lies prostrate upon the ground. For like a non-warrior muddled by intoxication, Vṛtra challenged the great hero who had overcome the mighty and who drank Soma to the dregs. Unable to withstand the onslaught of his deadly weapons, he who found Indra an overpowering enemy was shattered, his nose crushed. Without feet or hands he fought against Indra, who struck him upon the back with his thunderbolt. The castrated steer who wished to become the equal of the virile bull, Vṛtra lay shattered in many places. Over him, as he lay like a broken reed, the swelling waters flowed for man.[28] Those waters that Vṛtra had enclosed with his might – the dragon now lay at their feet. The vital energy of Vṛtra's mother ebbed away, for Indra had hurled his deadly weapon at her. Above lay the mother, below lay the son; the demoness lay down like a cow with her calf. In the midst of the waters which never stood still or rested, the body lay. The waters flow over Vṛtra's secret place; he who found Indra an overpowering enemy lay in long darkness. The waters, who had the demon for their husband, the dragon

28. Or: for Manu.

for their protector, were enclosed like the cows imprisoned by the Paṇis. When Indra slew Vṛtra he split open the outlet of the waters that had been closed. O Indra, you became a hair of a horse's tail when Vṛtra struck at your thunderbolt. You, the one god, the brave one, you won the cows, you won the Soma; you released the seven rivers so that they could flow. The lightning and thunder, fog and hail which he had strewn about did not bring him success, when the dragon and Indra fought, for the generous one remained victorious for all future time. O Indra, what avenger of the dragon did you see, that fear entered your heart when you had killed him? Then, frightened, you crossed the ninety-nine rivers like a falcon crossing the skies. Indra, who wields the thunderbolt in his hand, is the king of that which moves and that which rests, of the tame and of the horned. He rules the people as their king, enclosing them as a rim encloses spokes.

Indra slays Triśiras and Vṛtra

In the Vedic hymn, Indra is clearly the supreme god. The one element that could possibly be to his discredit – that he fled across the rivers like a falcon when he feared an avenger of the dragon – is glossed over by the Vedic poet, but it is precisely this element which becomes the central pivot of the Vṛtra myth when it is retold more than a thousand years later in the *Mahābhārata*, at a time when Indra, the great warrior, was no longer an object of worship, as his position had been usurped by the Brahmins' sectarian gods, Viṣṇu and Śiva.

Several metaphors and images from the Vedic hymn are acted out in the Epic. Indra, who was expressly said *not* to lie hidden in the deep streams in the Saramā hymn, now conceals himself under water like the very 'writhing serpent' whom he formerly overpowered; the dragon who had fallen like a tree felled by an axe is now cut down by the axe of a woodsman; the mist which Vṛtra had strewn about now becomes the weapon which kills him. The episode of swallowing and vomiting forth appears here twice over: Triśiras would swallow the regions of the sky and the universe, and Vṛtra actually swallows all the worlds and Indra. The twilight, which plays such an important role in Hindu cosmogony, appears here as a moment of mediation and ambivalence, in conjunction with other oppositional pairs including Vṛtra, who, as the son of the god Tvaṣṭṛ and a demoness mother, is half brahmin and half anti-god. The celestial nymphs are not successful as Saramā was in helping Indra to trick the demons, and so brute force is needed. Indra no longer does the deed himself, but calls upon two assistants, one below him and one above him: to behead Triśiras he uses a wood-cutter, to whom he offers the head of the sacrificial animal just as the gods offer Rudra Paśupati a share; and to kill Vṛtra he invokes Viṣṇu.

25. FROM THE *Mahābhārata*

Tvaṣṭṛ was the foremost of gods, a Prajāpati with great ascetic powers. He created a three-headed son, Triśiras, because he hated Indra, and that glorious son, who was able to assume all forms, coveted the place of Indra. His three hideous heads were like the sun, the moon, and fire; with one he read the Vedas, with another he drank wine, and with the third he stared as if he would drink up the regions of the sky. He was an ascetic, gentle and controlled, devoted to *dharma* and firm in asceticism, and he practised severe, extremely difficult asceticism. When Śakra[29] saw the ascetic power and spirit of this god whose energy was boundless, he became anxious. 'Let him not become Indra himself!' he worried. 'How may he be made addicted to sensual pleasures, so that he will stop practising his great asceticism? If Triśiras becomes yet greater, he will swallow the entire triple universe.' Thus the wily one pondered various ways, and then he commanded the celestial nymphs to seduce the son of Tvaṣṭṛ. He said to them, 'Act quickly. Go and seduce Triśiras immediately, so that he becomes addicted to sensual pleasures. With erotic garments and charming gestures, O fair-hipped ones, seduce him, please, and set my fear at rest. I feel uneasy in myself, O superlative

29. Śakra is a common epithet of Indra.

women. Quickly, girls, allay this sickening fear.' The celestial nymphs said, 'We will try to seduce him, Śakra, so that you will have no fear of him. Destroyer of Armies, we will go together to seduce him as he sits there, hoarding his ascetic power, his eyes blazing. We will try to put him in our power and to dispel your fear.' Then, taking their leave of Indra those superlative women went to Triśiras and tempted him with various gestures, skilfully dancing and revealing their elegant bodies. They moved wantonly, but the great ascetic did not experience an erection. He controlled his senses, like a full ocean, and when they had tried their best, they returned to Śakra, king of the gods. They folded their palms together and said, 'We cannot shake that unapproachable sage from his firmness. Illustrious lord, you must do what you must, immediately.' The high-minded Śakra honoured the celestial nymphs and dismissed them, and then he began to think of a means of killing the noble Triśiras.

The splendid, heroic, wise king of the gods thought in silence, determining how to kill Triśiras: 'I will hurl my thunderbolt at him today, and he will quickly cease to be. "A strong man must not disregard even a weak enemy who is increasing in strength."' And thus reflecting upon the wisdom of the textbooks, he made a firm resolution to kill him. Then Śakra, enraged, hurled against Triśiras his thunderbolt that was terrifying and horrible as fire. He fell, struck hard by that thunderbolt, like the peak of a mountain thrown down on the surface of the earth. But when the king of the gods saw him lying there like a mountain, slain by the thunderbolt, he found no peace, for he was blinded and scorched by Triśiras's energy. Even when he was dead, Triśiras shone with energy as if he were still alive.

Then the husband of Śacī[30] saw a wood-cutter working nearby, and the Chastiser of Pāka quickly said to him, 'Cut

30. Śacī ('power') is the wife of Indra.

off his heads right away; do as I say.' The wood-cutter replied, 'He has very great shoulders. My axe will not go through them. Besides, I cannot perform an action that is condemned by good people.' 'Do not fear, but do what I command, quickly,' said Indra. 'By my grace, your weapon will be like a thunderbolt.' The wood-cutter said, 'Whom may I know you to be, who have done this terrible deed today? I wish to hear this; tell me truly.' Indra replied, 'I am Indra, king of the gods; let this be known to you, wood-cutter. Now do what I said, wood-cutter, and do not delay. Know that Triśiras lies here, slain by me.' Then the wood-cutter bowed humbly, folded his palms together before Indra and replied, 'How is it, Śakra, that you are not ashamed of this cruel deed? Are you not afraid of brahminicide, having slain this son of a sage?' Indra replied, 'I will perform some difficult religious act of repentance afterwards for the sake of purification. This was a very powerful enemy whom I killed with my thunderbolt. Even now, wood-cutter, I am alarmed and frightened of him. Quickly, cut off his heads and I will do a favour for you. Men will give you the head of the sacrificial beast as your share in the sacrifice; this is the favour I grant you, wood-cutter. But now do what I wish, quickly.'

Hearing what the great Indra said, the wood-cutter then cut off the heads of Triśiras with his axe. And when they were severed, from those heads of Triśiras there came forth heath-cocks, partridges, and sparrows, in all directions. From the head with which he studied the Vedas and drank Soma heath-cocks came forth immediately; from that with which he stared at the regions of the sky as if to drink them, partridges came forth; and from that head of Triśiras which used to drink wine, sparrows emerged. When the heads were cut off, the fever left the bountiful one, who went happily back to heaven, and the wood-cutter also went home.

When the wood-cutter had gone home, he said nothing to

anyone, and no one knew what had happened for a whole year. But when the year had passed, the ghosts of the bands of the god Śiva, the lord of cattle, cried out, 'The bountiful Indra, our lord, is a brahmin-slayer.' Then Indra, the Chastiser of Pāka, undertook a terrible vow, and he practised asceticism with the divine army of the Maruts. He divided his brahminicide and placed it in the ocean, earth, trees, and women, and he gave them all boons: he gave boons to the earth, ocean, trees, and women, and thus he dispelled his brahminicide. Then, purified and worshipped by all the gods and people, the lord, who was now fit to be worshipped by great sages, returned to Indra's place in heaven.

When Tvaṣṭṛ, the Prajāpati, heard that his son had been slain by Śakra, his eyes reddened with anger and he said, 'Since Indra has injured my son who was engaged in asceticism and had conquered his passions, who was always patient, self-controlled, and had committed no offence – since he injured my son, therefore I will create Vṛtra to slay Śakra. Let all people witness my power and the great force of my asceticism, and let the evil-minded, wicked Indra, king of the gods, see too.' Then the famous ascetic in a fury rinsed out his mouth with water,[31] made an oblation into the fire, created the horrible Vṛtra and said to him, 'You are the overpowering enemy of Indra[32]. Grow, by the power of my asceticism.' And he grew, towering up to heaven like the fiery sun, as if the sun of doomsday had arisen. Then he said, 'What shall I do?' and Tvaṣṭṛ said, 'Kill Śakra.'

When he had been instructed in this way, Vṛtra went to heaven, and a violent battle took place as the furious Vṛtra and Indra Vāsava, lord of the Vasus, engaged in combat. The noble Vṛtra swallowed all the worlds, for he had been ex-

31. Before uttering any imprecation, one would rinse his mouth.

32. This is what Tvaṣṭṛ intends to say; but by misplacing the accent he unwittingly creates one whom Indra will overpower.

panded by the energy of Tvaṣṭṛ. The noble Vṛtra stole away all odours and tastes of the senses, for he took away the entire five-fold material world: earth, air, space, water, and light. Then the heroic Vṛtra grabbed Indra, the Performer of a Hundred Sacrifices, and Vṛtra opened wide his mouth and swallowed him in fury. And when Vṛtra had swallowed Śakra, the courageous gods of the triple heaven were perplexed and they created Jṛmbhikā ('the Yawner') to destroy Vṛtra. As Vṛtra yawned, his mouth opened, and the Destroyer of Armies came out, making himself small. And from that time forth, yawning has been inherent in the life's breath of people.

All the gods rejoiced to see Śakra emerge, and then the long, fierce battle between Vṛtra and Vāsava resumed. When the mighty Vṛtra waxed great in the battle, by the power of Tvaṣṭṛ's asceticism, then Śakra wisely retreated, and when he had retreated the gods despaired and joined Indra, for they too were dazed by the energy of Tvaṣṭṛ. They all took counsel together with the sages, stunned by fear, worrying what to do. They all thought of the noble and imperishable Viṣṇu, as they sat there on the peak of Mount Mandara, wishing for the death of Vṛtra. The whole universe was pervaded by Vṛtra, so we have heard, and when Vṛtra had become all the worlds, fear entered Indra. Then Indra, whose energy was great, took counsel with the gods in order to kill Vṛtra. Indra said, 'The entire imperishable universe has been pervaded by Vṛtra, O gods. Nothing could combat anyone like him. Formerly I was able, but now I am unable. Please, how can I do it? I consider him impossible to assail. Shining with energy, noble and of unlimited prowess in battle, he would swallow up the triple universe with all the gods and demons and men. Therefore hear what I have resolved, O heaven-dwellers: let us go together to the home of the noble Viṣṇu, and when we have met and consulted him we will know a means of slaying the evil one.'

Then all the gods and the bands of sages went to seek refuge with the mighty god Viṣṇu. Suffering from their fear of Vṛtra, the gods said to Viṣṇu, the lord of gods, 'You have crossed the three worlds with three steps; you have seized the ambrosial Soma and slaughtered the demons in battle; you, Viṣṇu, have bound the great demon Bali[33] and made Śakra king of the gods. You are the lord of all people, and you are inherent in everything. You are the great god worshipped by all people; O god, foremost of immortals, subduer of demons, be the refuge of all the gods and Indra, for this whole universe has been pervaded by Vṛtra.' Viṣṇu said, 'Of course I will do what is best for you, and so I will tell you the means by which that demon will cease to exist. Go, with the sages and Gandharvas, to that demon who can assume all forms. Conciliate him, O gods, and then you will conquer him. My energy will serve Śakra, for I will enter invisibly into his thunderbolt, that supreme weapon. O best of gods, go now with the sages and Gandharvas and make a pact quickly between Vṛtra and Śakra.'

Heeding the words of the god, the thirty-three gods, whose vitality is great, went with the sages, preceded by Śakra, to the place where Vṛtra was blazing like the sun and moon, heating the regions of the sky with his energy as if he would swallow up the three worlds. The gods and Śakra saw Vṛtra there, and then the sages approached Vṛtra and spoke a pleasant speech to him, saying, 'This whole universe has been pervaded by your energy; you are hard to conquer, but you cannot conquer Vāsava, whose prowess in battle is abundant, though you two have been fighting here for a very long time. All creatures, gods and demons and men, are suffering; let there be eternal friendship between Śakra and you, Vṛtra. You will be

33. The myth of the three steps is told below, myths 47–9, pp. 176–9; the conquest of the demons in battle is told in myth 72, pp. 277–80; and the conquest of Bali in myth 49, pp. 178–9.

happy dwelling in the eternal worlds of Śakra.' When the mighty demon Vṛtra heard this speech of the sages, he bowed his head and said to all of them, 'I have heard all that you and the Gandharvas have said; now hear me, faultless and blessed ones. How can there be a pact between Śakra and me? How can there be friendship between two whose energy is so great?' 'A friendly alliance between good people is to be sought after,' said the sages, 'and after that, what is to be, will be. One should not neglect an opportunity for alliance with a good man; alliance with good men is to be sought after, for it is firm and constant. A wise man can give advice about money to those who are in difficulties because of money; therefore contact with a good man is like great wealth, and so a wise man would not injure a good man. Indra is honoured by good men and is the refuge of noble men; he tells the truth, is high-minded, knows *dharma* and has fine judgement. Let there be an eternal pact between you and Śakra; have confidence in this, and do not disagree.' The glorious Vṛtra replied to this speech of the great sages: 'Of course I will respect you, great ascetics, supreme brahmins. Let the gods do all that I say, and then I will do all that the brahmins have said to me. Let me not be killed by Śakra and the gods by anything dry or wet, by stone or by wood, by a weapon or a thunderbolt by day or by night. Such an eternal pact with Indra would be acceptable to me.' The sages agreed to this, and when this pact was made, Vṛtra was delighted. The sages blazing with energy, having made this false pact between Śakra and Vṛtra, returned whence they had come.

But Śakra was always on guard, trying to devise a means of killing Vṛtra, for he was jealous of him. Constantly uneasy, the great Indra looked for a loophole, for the Slayer of Armies and Slayer of Vṛtra remembered the treaty that the sages had urged upon him. Then one day Indra saw the great demon on the shore of the ocean at the moment when sunset had come, a moment both charming and poignant. The god then thought of the boon that had been given to the noble Vṛtra: 'It is now sunset, a dangerous time;[34] it is neither night nor day. And Vṛtra must certainly be killed, for he is my enemy who has taken everything away from me. But he has obtained a boon, that he cannot be slain even by the gods, so how can I devise a means of doing it here? If I do not kill Vṛtra now by deceiving the great demon, whose body and strength are great, I shall not prosper.' Thinking in this way, Śakra remembered Viṣṇu, and then he saw a mass of foam like a mountain in the ocean. 'This is neither dry nor wet, nor is it a weapon. I will throw this at Vṛtra and kill him in a moment.' And he hurled at Vṛtra that foam with a thunderbolt in it, and Viṣṇu entered into the foam and destroyed Vṛtra.

Now, when Vṛtra was slain, the skies were free of darkness; a pleasant breeze blew, and all creatures rejoiced. The gods and sages and all the Gandharvas, Yakṣas, Rākṣasas and snakes praised the great Indra with various laudations. Vāsava, thus honoured by all beings, comforted them and rejoiced with the gods, for he had killed his enemy; and, knowing *dharma*, he honoured Viṣṇu, the best in the three worlds. But when the mighty Vṛtra, who had terrified the gods, was dead, Śakra was overpowered by falsehood, and he became melancholy, for Śakra had been overpowered before by brahminicide because of Triśiras. Now the fearless ghosts of the great god called him 'Brahminslayer' again, and when the Slayer of Armies and Slayer of Vṛtra was thus reviled he became even more ashamed. Then he went to the end of the worlds, his consciousness destroyed, his wits gone. Overpowered by his own impurities, Indra, king of the gods, was unrecogniz-

34. Evening, when the sun is in the western realm of Varuṇa (god of morality as well as lord of the waters) is a time when truth must be spoken, a dangerous time for Indra to violate a treaty. It is also the time when demons become powerful. See above, myth 9, p. 44.

able, and he lived concealed in water like a writhing serpent.

When Indra, king of the gods, had vanished, suffering from his terror of brahminicide, the earth looked as if it had perished in treeless ruins; its forests withered away; the courses of the rivers were interrupted; the lakes were without water; all creatures were agitated because there was no rain.[35] The gods and all the great sages were terrified; the universe, without a king, was overrun by disasters ... Then the gods, with Agni at their head, took counsel together about Śakra. Those who were clever at speeches went in dismay to Viṣṇu, the powerful god of gods and said, 'Śakra, the lord of the bands of the gods, has been overpowered by brahminicide. You are our refuge, lord of gods, first-born lord of the universe. You became Viṣṇu in order to protect all creatures. When Vṛtra was killed by means of your energy, Vāsava was enveloped in brahminicide. O best of the bands of the gods, tell us how he may be set free.' In answer to the speech of the gods, Viṣṇu said, 'Let Śakra sacrifice to me and I will purify the Wielder of the Thunderbolt. When the Chastiser of Pāka has performed the meritorious horse sacrifice for me, he will again become Indra, king of the gods, fearing nothing ... For a certain time, you gods must remain patient and vigilant.'

Hearing Viṣṇu's auspicious and true words, as soothing and sweet as ambrosia, all the bands of the gods and sages and preceptors went to Śakra, who was agitated by fear. There a great horse sacrifice dispelling brahminicide was performed for the purification of the noble great Indra. Indra divided brahminicide among trees and rivers and mountains and the earth and women, and having thus dispersed it among beings, the lord of the gods was free of it. Free of fever, purified of sin, Vāsava became himself again.

35. Indra is the god of rain, Wielder of the Thunderbolt.

Indra slays Vṛtra and is afflicted by the Fury of Brahminicide

This myth is retold in another part of the *Mahābhārata*, where the emphasis is placed even more upon the expiation of brahminicide. This time Śiva is the one who helps Indra to kill Vṛtra, and it is Śiva who causes Indra to distribute his brahminicide even as Rudra punishes the sinful Prajāpati and Śiva himself must distribute his own Brahminicide[36]; even in the first *Mahābhārata* tale of Vṛtra, where Viṣṇu is supreme, the ghosts who are Śiva's servants force Indra to undergo expiation. The fever which is mentioned briefly in that version here becomes an affliction of Vṛtra rather than of Indra, and the yawning episode is transformed and compressed. Brahminicide now becomes a goddess incarnate, to replace the goddess of yawning, and a jackal, instead of Indra, comes out of Vṛtra's mouth. As the two demon-slayings are now compressed into one, awkward duplications arise: Indra must perform a double expiation – a horse sacrifice as well as a distribution of the sin – and the birds that were released from Triśiras's head in the other myth now appear first to circle over Vṛtra's head and then to pollute Vṛtra's blood. Indra hides in a lotus filament instead of in water; both are the hiding places of Agni,[37] who seeks Indra in the first version and accepts part of his sin here.

26. FROM THE *Mahābhārata*

[Vṛtra stupefied Indra by his powers of illusion.] But the divine Chastiser of Pāka, gathering his wits about him, engaged in great yoga and dispelled that illusion. When Bṛhaspati, the blessed son of Aṅgiras, and the great sages saw the great prowess of Vṛtra, they went to the great lord Śiva and spoke to him, for they desired the welfare of people and the destruction of Vṛtra. Then the energy of the lord, ruler of the universe, became a devastating fever, which entered Vṛtra, the best of demons. And the lord god Viṣṇu, who is worshipped

36. See above, myths 1, p. 26, and 3–4, pp. 29–31, and below, myth 34, pp. 117–18, for Prajāpati; and myth 35, pp. 121–2, for Śiva.

37. See below, myths 29–33, pp. 98–110.

by everyone and delights in protecting people, entered the thunderbolt of Indra . . .

Now I will tell you the symptoms that appeared in the body of Vṛtra when the fever had pervaded him. His hideous mouth began to blaze with fire, and he became extremely pale. His limbs trembled greatly and he began to breathe hard and fast. His hair stood on end and he emitted sharp sighs. A dreadful jackal of inauspicious appearance came out of his mouth: this was his memory. Burning, blazing meteors fell at his side; vultures, herons, and cranes emitted dreadful cries and circled over Vṛtra's head, shuddering with delight. Then Śakra mounted the chariot that the gods had made strong for battle, and he took his thunderbolt in his hand and looked carefully at the demon. The great demon emitted an inhuman roar, and as the sharp fever pervaded him he yawned. Śakra hurled the thunderbolt at him as he was yawning, and that thunderbolt of enormous energy, like the fire of doomsday, quickly struck down the demon Vṛtra whose body was so great.

Then another roar arose on all sides from the gods when they saw that Vṛtra had been slain. And when the enemy of demons, the lord whose fame is great, had slain Vṛtra with the thunderbolt permeated by Viṣṇu, he went back into heaven. But out of the body of Vṛtra the Fury of Brahminicide came forth; she was terrifying and hideous, striking fear into people, for she had enormous, sharp teeth and was frightfully deformed. She was dark and tawny; her hair was dishevelled and her eyes were gruesome. She wore a garland of skulls and she was emaciated, smeared with blood, clothed in rag garments. As she came forth in that terrifying form, she began to hunt the Wielder of the Thunderbolt. After a little while, when the Slayer of Vṛtra had set out for heaven, because of his desire for the welfare of people, she saw him, Indra, king of the gods, Śakra of great strength. She grabbed him around the neck and held fast as he came forth out of a lotus filament, for when he had become afraid of having committed brahminicide, he had entered the middle of the filament of a blue lotus and stayed there for many years. But Brahminicide had followed him carefully, and when she grabbed him he became paralysed. Śakra tried as hard as he could to dispel her, but the lord of the gods could not dispel Brahminicide. In her grasp, the lord of the gods went to the Grandfather and honoured him, bending his head, and when Brahmā realized that Śakra had been seized by the Fury of the slaughter of a superior brahmin, he began to deliberate.

Then the Grandfather said to Brahminicide, as if to conciliate her with honeyed words, 'Angry lady, release Indra, the lord of the thirty-three gods; do me a favour. Tell me what I can do for you today, what desire you wish for.' 'If the god who is worshipped throughout the triple world, the Maker of the Triple World, is pleased,' said Brahminicide, 'I consider my desires already accomplished. But appoint a dwelling-place for me. You made the moral law, for you wished to protect people, and so you established this great law and promulgated it. Now, lord god, ruler of all people, knower of *dharma*, I will go forth from Śakra if you are pleased; but appoint a dwelling-place for me.' The Grandfather agreed to this, and by this means he dispelled Brahminicide from Śakra.

But as the noble Self-created Brahmā was meditating there, Agni approached him[38] and said, 'I have come to you, lord god; tell me what I must do.' 'I will divide this Brahminicide into many parts,' said Brahmā. 'Accept a quarter of it from me in order to release Śakra now.' Agni replied, 'Devise the limit of time, when I will be released. This is what I wish to learn truly, O lord worshipped by all people.' Brahmā replied,

38. When a great god thinks of anyone, that person immediately appears before him, summoned and transported by telekinesis.

'Any man who is so enveloped in darkness that he ever fails to make a sacrifice of seeds, herbs, or juices into the blazing fire, into you, Agni – Brahminicide will quickly enter into him and dwell in him. Let this fever in your mind disappear, Oblation-bearer.'[39] Agni, who consumes the oblations offered to the gods and to the ancestors, accepted the command of the Grandfather, and it transpired in that way.

Then the Grandfather summoned the trees, herbs, and grasses, and he spoke to them to the same purpose. When the trees, herbs, and grasses had been addressed as Agni had been, they became agitated like him, and they asked Brahmā, 'Grandfather of all people, what limit will there be for our Brahminicide? You should not hurt us, for we are by our very nature injured: we must always bear fiery heat and frost and rains driven by the wind, and then there is the cutting and breaking, O god. By your command, we will take this Brahminicide today, but you should think of a release, O lord of the triple world.' Brahmā said, 'Any man who, through delusion or ignorance, cuts or breaks any of you on the day of the new or full moon – he will take upon himself this share.' When the trees, herbs, and grasses heard these words of the noble Brahmā, they honoured him and went quickly back whence they had come.

Then the god who is the Grandfather of all people summoned the celestial nymphs and spoke to them with honeyed words, as if conciliating them: 'Superlative women, this Brahminicide has been taken from Indra; accept a quarter of it, as I command you.' The celestial nymphs replied, 'Lord of gods, we have decided to take it, as you command; but think of a release from this agreement for us, Grandfather.' Brahmā said, 'This quarter of Brahminicide will quickly enter any

39. Or 'let it be diffused and scattered'. 'Fever' here may indicate either Agni's worry or the Fever of Brahminicide which will be diffused.

man who has intercourse with women during their menstrual period. Let this fever leave your minds.' The bands of celestial nymphs rejoiced and gladly assented, and they went to their own places and amused themselves.

Then the god of great ascetic power, Maker of the Triple World, thought of the waters, and as soon as he thought of them they arrived. They all assembled and bowed to Brahmā, the Grandfather, whose vitality was immeasurable, and said, 'We have come to you, Subduer of Enemies. Command and instruct us, lord god of gods, great lord.' Brahmā said, 'This terrifying Brahminicide has come upon Indra who is invoked by many, from Vṛtra. Accept a quarter of it.' 'So be it, even as you say, lord of all people,' said the waters. 'But you should devise a release from this agreement for us. You are the supreme guru of the whole universe, lord of the gods; who else could be a source of grace and mercy to lift us out of our distress?' Brahmā answered, 'Any man who, deluded in his wits, thinks that the waters need not be respected and casts phlegm, urine, or excrement into you – this part of Brahminicide will immediately come to him and dwell in him. This will be your release; I tell you the truth.'

Then Brahminicide left Indra, king of the gods, and went to each of the places that had been ordained by Brahmā's command. Thus Brahminicide afflicted Śakra, who performed a horse sacrifice at the behest of the Grandfather; for it has been heard that when Vāsava was afflicted by Brahminicide he obtained purification from it by means of a horse sacrifice. When he regained his prosperity and slew his foes by the thousand, the god Vāsava found a joy without equal. From the blood of Vṛtra cocks were born; therefore these are not to be eaten by twice-born brahmins or initiated ascetics ... Thus the great demon Vṛtra was slain by Śakra whose energy is immeasurable, slain by means of subtle intelligence and wily forethought.

The degradation of Indra in the later Epics

The statement that Indra slew Vṛtra 'by means of subtle intelligence and wily forethought' must carry at least a measure of sarcasm, in the context of the myth which has preceded it, a myth in which Indra is motivated by fear, stupidity, and dishonesty. Even in the *Ṛg Veda*, Indra's behaviour falls below even the permissive standards of the warrior, for he strikes Vṛtra in the back; in the *Mahābhārata* he openly violates his 'false' treaty with Vṛtra. By the time of the later Epics, when brahmin morality had almost totally superseded the warrior ethics of the Vedas, Indra is actually mocked, though an attempt is still made to rationalize and justify his immoralities.

Indra Destroys the Embryo in the Belly of Diti

The Maruts, who are Indra's companions in his most glorious exploits in the *Ṛg Veda*, are the occasion for one of his most dastardly deeds in the *Rāmāyaṇa*, a combination of fratricide, abortion, and incest at a single stroke. (Indra has already killed a father – Tvaṣṭṛ – and two half-brothers – Triśiras and Vṛtra.) In this myth, Indra uses his thunderbolt to tear open the belly of Diti, mother of demons and his own step-mother and aunt (wife of Kaśyapa and daughter of Dakṣa, like Indra's mother Aditi), just as he had used his thunderbolt in the *Ṛg Veda* to tear open the bellies of mountains and to kill the mother of the demon Vṛtra.

27. FROM THE *Rāmāyaṇa*

Diti grieved deeply when all her sons had been slain,[40] and she said to her husband Kāśyapa, the son of Marīci, 'My lord, your mighty sons have killed my sons. I wish to have a son who will slay Śakra, a son won by my long asceticism. I will

40. An important race of demons, called Daityas, are the sons of Diti. Most of them were slain at the time of the churning of the ocean (see below, myth 72, pp. 274–80).

practise asceticism; please grant me an embryo of this kind, a slayer of Śakra.' When Kāśyapa the son of Marīci, a sage of great energy, heard her words he replied to Diti, who was grieving deeply, 'So be it, good lady rich in asceticism. Be pure and you will bring forth a son who will slay Śakra in battle. If you are pure when a thousand years have passed, you will bring forth a son of mine who will slay the triple world.' When the sage of great energy had said this he stroked her with his hand, said, 'Farewell,' and went to practise asceticism.

When he had gone, Diti rejoiced greatly; she went to the Shrine of *Kuśa* Grass and began to practise fierce asceticism. As she was practising asceticism, the thousand-eyed god[41] served her most virtuously, supplying her with fire, sacred *kuśa* grass, fuel, water, fruits and roots, and whatever else she desired, massaging her limbs to relieve their exhaustion. Thus the thousand-eyed Śakra served Diti at all times. And when all but ten of the thousand years had passed, Diti was highly pleased, and she said to the thousand-eyed god, 'Only ten years remain for me to practise asceticism, and then you will see your brother, if it please you, O best of heroes. For your sake, my son, I will join him to you when he is eager for victory; with him, my son, you will enjoy the conquest of the triple world, and you will be without fever.'

When the goddess Diti had said this to Śakra, she lay down to sleep, for the sun, Maker of Day, had reached the zenith. But she put her feet where her head should have been,[42] and when Śakra saw that she was thus impure, that she had placed her hair where her feet should have been and put her feet in the place of her head, he laughed and rejoiced. Then the Shat-

41. In one version of the myth of Indra and Ahalyā (below, myth 28, pp. 94–6), Indra is branded with the marks of a thousand female organs (*yonis*), which are later changed into eyes.

42. That is, she lay with her head pointing to the north, an impure position.

terer of Citadels, possessor of the highest soul, entered the opening of her body and cut the embryo into seven pieces. As the embryo was cut up by the hundred-jointed thunderbolt, it cried out loudly, so that Diti woke up. Śakra said to the embryo, 'Do not cry! Do not cry! [*Mā rudas*]', and he, Vāsava whose energy is great, cut it up even though it continued to cry. 'Do not destroy it! Do not destroy it!' cried Diti, and then Śakra, respecting his mother's words, fell out. Folding his palms together, still holding the thunderbolt, Śakra said to Diti, 'Goddess, you were sleeping impurely, having put your hair where your feet should be. Taking advantage of this opportunity, I cut into seven parts the one who would have been a slayer of Śakra in battle. Forgive me for this, goddess.'

When the embryo had been cut into seven parts, Diti grieved deeply, but she humbly supplicated the thousand-eyed god, who is unassailable, and she said, 'It was my fault that this embryo was divided into seven and made fruitless. It was not your fault, lord of gods, Destroyer of Fortresses. I wish to have a favour done to please me: in exchange for the lost embryos, let them become the guardians of the regions of the seven winds; let my little sons be the seven kinds of breezes and waft over heaven. Let my children in celestial form be known as the Māruts, and let one wander in the world of Brahmā, another in the world of Indra, and the third in heaven, known and famed as the wind. My remaining four children will become gods, if it please you, O best of gods, and wander in all directions as you command. They will be known by the name of Māruts, which you gave them.'[43] When the thousand-eyed Shatterer of Cities and Destroyer of Fortresses heard what she said, he folded his palms and said to Diti, 'All will come about as you have said; do not doubt. If

43. By saying '*Mā rudas*'. Rudra obtains his name in the same way (below, myth 36, p. 123).

it please you, your children will wander as gods.' Thus the two of them, mother and son, made an agreement in the forest of asceticism, and both of them went back to the triple heaven, having achieved their ends; so we have heard.

Indra Seduces Ahalyā and is Castrated by Gautama

Another myth which exalts the power of a brahmin at the expense of Indra satirizes the widespread mythological belief that the gods must dispel the dangerous powers of an ascetic by stirring him to lust or anger. In the myth of Ahalyā, Indra's claim to do this is obviously a thin excuse to justify his own lust, just as Diti's trivial 'impurity' must be made to excuse Indra's slaughter of the unborn Indra-killer. Another bathetic falling-off from Vedic times may be seen in the ritual animal imagery of the Ahalyā myth: while Dadhyañc was given a horse-head to replace his own,[44] Indra must settle for the testicles of a ram.

28. FROM THE *Rāmāyaṇa*

The noble sage Gautama once lived in a hermitage that was like a heaven and was venerated even by the gods. There the famous sage practised asceticism with Ahalyā for many years. The thousand-eyed husband of Śacī, knowing that Gautama was absent, disguised himself as the sage and said to Ahalyā, 'Calm lady, men who are intent upon getting what they want do not wait for the fertile season.[45] I wish to unite with you, fair-waisted one.' Although she recognized the thousand-eyed god disguised as the sage, the foolish woman was swayed by her fascinated desire for the king of the gods and set her heart upon him. Then, when she was satisfied deep within herself, she said to the best of the gods, 'Best of the gods, you have

44. See above, myth 13, pp. 56–7.

45. It is the duty of a Hindu to impregnate his wife during her fertile season, and forest-dwellers who live with their wives are not supposed to have intercourse with them at any other time.

been satisfied. Now go quickly from here, my lord, proud lord of gods. Protect yourself and me.' Indra laughed and said to Ahalyā, 'Lady with lovely hips, I am well satisfied and I will return whence I came.' And when he had thus united with her, he went out of the hermitage in confused haste, for he was worried about Gautama.

But then he saw Gautama, the great sage, the bull among sages, entering the hermitage, unassailable by gods and demons, full of the might of his asceticism, still moist with the water from the sacred bathing place, shining like a fire, carrying fuel and sacred *kuśa* grass. When the lord of the gods saw him he became terrified and his face fell, and when the virtuous sage saw the villainous thousand-eyed god disguised as the sage he said to him angrily, 'Evil-minded one, by assuming my form you have done what is not to be done. Therefore you will be impotent.' And the moment that the noble Gautama said this, the two testicles of the thousand-eyed god fell to the ground. Having thus cursed Śakra, the angry sage cursed his own wife as well, saying, 'You will dwell here for many thousands of years, eating nothing but wind, with no food, lying on ashes, practising asceticism, invisible to all creatures; thus you will dwell in this hermitage. And when the unassailable Rāma, the son of Daśaratha, enters this dangerous forest, then you will be purified. Wicked woman, by offering hospitality to him you will become devoid of greed and delusion, and you will resume your own form and rejoice in my presence.' Having said this to the woman of evil behaviour, the sage Gautama of great energy and ascetic powers left that hermitage and practised asceticism on a delightful peak of Himālaya which was frequented by Siddhas and Cāraṇas.

When Śakra had been made impotent in this way, his face was full of terror, and he said to the bands of sages and Cāraṇas and Agni and the other gods, 'By causing an obstacle to the noble Gautama when he was practising asceticism, and by arousing his anger, I acted for the benefit of the gods, for I took away his ascetic power when he uttered his great curse. But in his anger he has made me impotent and he has transformed Ahalyā. Since I acted to help the gods, all of you, supreme gods and bands of sages and Cāraṇas, should make me virile again.' When Agni and the other gods heard the words of the God of a Hundred Sacrifices,[46] they went with all the bands of Maruts to the celestial ancestors, and they said, 'Here is a ram with testicles; but Śakra has been deprived of his testicles. Therefore take the two testicles of the ram and give them to Śakra. The ram, made impotent, will give you great satisfaction, for men will give castrated rams to you to give you joy.' When the assembled celestial ancestors heard the speech of Agni they tore out the two testicles of the ram and gave them to the thousand-eyed god. And from that time forth, the assembled celestial ancestors have eaten castrated rams, whose testicles have been used in this way. And Indra has had the testicles of a ram ever since then, because of the noble Gautama's power of asceticism.

46. Indra prides himself on having performed a hundred horse sacrifices, both in demonstration of his royal nature and to expiate his many sins.

3

AGNI

AGNI, the god of fire, is one of the most important Hindu gods, for it is he who carries the sacrificial offering to all of the gods, but his straightforward function somewhat circumscribes the range of his mythology. The great Indo-European myth of Agni is the myth of the bird that carries fire or the elixir of immortality from heaven to earth, a reversal of his daily sacrificial journey. This image reverberates throughout the later developments of the Agni myth in a series of episodes of hide-and-seek, with Agni sometimes seeking but more often hiding, moving sometimes from earth to heaven but more often from heaven to earth.

Agni flees from the gods and hides in the waters

The Ṛg Vedic source of the myth is, like so many mythological hymns, a dialogue between opposed figures: Varuṇa, god of the waters, and Agni, god of fire; Yama, god of the dead, and Agni, who wins a full life span. The waters and plants which Agni enters (and which serve elsewhere as the receptacles for Indra or for Indra's sin)[1] are the *locus classicus* of the protean fire-water: Agni carries Soma in a hollow reed just as the Indo-European falcon (or Indra)[2] carries fire in a hollow reed, as the Vedic sacrificial fire was thought to lie dormant in the fire-sticks from which it was kindled, and as, later, Skanda the son of fire was born in a forest of reeds beside a river.[3]

1. See above, myth 26, pp. 87–90.
2. See below, myth 73, p. 281.
3. See below, myth 43, pp. 166–8.

29. FROM THE *Ṛg Veda*

[Varuṇa:] 'Great was that membrane, firm was it, which enveloped you when you entered the waters. One god, O Agni Jātavedas, saw all your various bodies.'[4]

[Agni:] 'Who saw me? Which was the god who spied out my various bodies? O Mitra and Varuṇa, where lie all the fuel-sticks by which Agni goes to the gods?'

[Varuṇa:] 'We searched for you in your various forms, O Agni Jātavedas, when you had entered into the waters and the plants. It was Yama who discovered you with your bright light which shines beyond the distance of ten days' journey.'

[Agni:] 'It was because of my fear of the role of Hotṛ[5] that I fled, so that the gods could not harness me for this, O Varuṇa. My bodies entered into various plants and waters; I, Agni, have ceased to worry about this matter.'

[Varuṇa:] 'Come. Manu[6] who loves the gods wishes to sacrifice. When you have completed the ritual you will live in darkness, Agni. Make the paths which lead to the gods easy to go upon; carry the offerings with a benevolent heart.'

[Agni:] 'The brothers of Agni formerly ran back and forth on this business like a chariot horse upon a road. Out of fear of this I went far away, Varuṇa. I fled like a buffalo before the bow-string of a hunter.'

[Varuṇa and the other gods:] 'We will make a lifespan free of age for you, Agni Jātavedas, so that you will not be injured when you have once been harnessed. Then with a benevolent heart you will carry the portion of the offering to the gods, O well-born one.'

4. Agni assumes various forms in the sky (the sun), in the air (lightning, comets), and on earth (sacrificial fire, domestic fire, and the digestive fire within all men).

5. The Hotṛ is the priest who recites the *Ṛg Veda* at a sacrifice.

6. Or: a man.

[Agni:] 'Ordain for me alone the pre-sacrifices and the post-sacrifices, the nourishing part of the offering; and the clarified butter out of the waters and the Man out of the plants.[7] And may the life-span of Agni be long, O gods.'

[Varuṇa and the other gods:] 'The pre-sacrifices and the post-sacrifices will be for you alone, the nourishing parts of the offering. This whole sacrifice will be for you, Agni; the four quarters of the sky will bow to you.'

Agni hides in the waters and is distributed

The *Bṛhaddevatā* rearranges the Ṛg Vedic dialogue to form a connected narrative, but the motivations of the plot are already clear in the dialogue: like Rudra, Agni demands a share; and like all the gods, he seeks the immortality of a full life-span. This text then adds another motif from the corpus of cosmogonic myths and Indra myths; Agni is dismembered and distributed.

30. FROM THE *Bṛhaddevatā*

When the brothers Agni Within-all-men, Householder, Youngest, Purifier, and Son-of-strength had been broken by the *Vaṣaṭ*[8] call, Agni Sharp-as-a-needle went away from the gods; so a Vedic text relates. When he departed, he entered the seasons, the waters, and the trees. Then the demons appeared, when Agni the Oblation-bearer had disappeared. The gods slew the demons in battle and searched for Agni. Yama and Varuṇa spied him from a distance; the two of them took him and went to the gods . . . Agni said to the gods, 'Let my

7. Or: Make the clarified butter the share allotted to the waters, and make the sacrificial victim the share allotted to the plants.

8. 'Vaṣaṭ' is the exclamation used when making an offering of an oblation to a deity (in contrast with 'Svāhā', used in making an oblation to all of the gods together). See myths 5, pp. 32–3, and 33, pp. 109–13.

life-span be long, and let me have various oblations, and let my older brothers be without injury at sacrifice after sacrifice. And let the pre-sacrifice and the post-sacrifice, and the clarified butter and the sacrificial beast in the Soma sacrifice have me as their divinity, and let the sacrifice have me as its divinity.' This was granted with the verse 'This whole sacrifice will be for you, Agni', and he was made the offerer of good sacrifices, to whom the three thousand, three hundred and thirty-nine gods gave all these boons. Then Agni became benevolent in his heart and pleased with all the gods who had given him the foremost place. He shook his bodies off[9] and performed the office of Hotṛ tirelessly, together with his brothers, for the Oblation-bearer, whose soul was divine, was pleased. His bone became the pine tree; his fat and flesh became a fragrant resin; his sinew became sweet-smelling *tejana* grass; his seed became silver and gold. The hair of his body became *kāśa* grass; the hair on his head became *kuśa* grass; his nails became tortoises, his entrails the *avakā* plant,[10] his marrow sand and gravel; his blood and bile became various minerals such as red chalk. Thus Agni and the gods conversed with the three hymns beginning 'Great ...'

Agni hides in the waters and curses the fish

A Brāhmaṇa text relates another version of the myth which further expands the role of Yama, who merely spied in the *Ṛg Veda* and brought Agni back in the *Bṛhaddevatā*, but now gives his own immortality to Agni.

9. This may mean that he removed his bodies from their hiding places.

10. The fragrant resin is *guggulu*, or bdellium, used for perfume or medicine; *tejana* is a kind of bamboo; *avakā* is a grass growing in marshy land. *Kāśa* (*Saccharum spontaneum*) is used for mats and roofs; *kuśa* grass (*Poa cynosuroides*) is a long, pointed grass used in sacrificial rituals. Both Kāśa and Kuśa are personified as servants of Yama.

31. FROM THE *Taittirīya Saṃhitā*

Agni had three older brothers. They perished while carrying the oblation to the gods. Agni feared that he too would be destroyed, and so he disappeared. He entered the waters. The gods wished to find him. A fish reported him and was cursed by him: 'Since you reported me, they will slay you whenever they fancy.' Therefore they kill the fish whenever they fancy, for he is cursed. They found Agni and said to him, 'Come to us and carry the oblation for us.' He said, 'Let me choose the boon that when the offering is taken up, whatever is shed outside the enclosing sticks will be the share of my brothers.' . . . Agni was in that world; Yama was in this. The gods said, 'Let us exchange them'; the gods invited Agni by offering food, and they invited Yama by offering kingship over the ancestors; therefore Agni is the food-eater of the gods, while Yama is the king of the ancestors. He who knows this obtains kingship and food, for he who knew this obtained the share which they cut off for Agni, the offerer of good sacrifices. When the sacrificer cuts off a share for Agni, the offerer of good sacrifices, he gives a share to Rudra.

Agni curses the frogs and is distributed

In the *Mahābhārata*, Agni hides not because he is afraid to carry the oblation but because he is afraid to carry the seed of Śiva, which is a multiform of the oblation.[11] The fish who betrayed Agni in the *Taittirīya Saṃhitā* is now replaced by a frog and by other animals; all of these are cursed to have their speech distorted in some way, as a fitting punishment for having spoken out of turn, 'telling' Agni even as Dadhyañc 'told' Soma.

11. See below, myth 43, pp. 164–8.

32. FROM THE *Mahābhārata*

The gods and sages wandered over the triple world in search of Agni, for they all desired the sight of Agni and their hearts were set upon him. And all the blessed Siddhas, famed throughout the world and endowed with supreme ascetic powers, wandered over the worlds, but they did not find the Oblation-eater, for he had concealed himself by disappearing within himself.[12] But then a frog, who lived in the water and was scalded and wearied at heart by the energy of Agni, emerged from the subterranean waters. He said to the gods, who had become frightened and were eager to see Agni, 'Agni is living in the subterranean waters, O gods. I have come here because of the painful heat arising from the Purifier. The blessed Oblation-bearer is asleep in the water, O gods, but his energy that has mingled with the waters heats us. If you gods wish to see the lustrous one, or if you have any business with fire, then go to him there. Go, and we will flee, for we fear Agni, O gods.' When the frog had said this, he hurriedly entered the water. But when the Oblation-eater found out about the treachery of the frog, he cursed him: 'You will have no tongue, nor will you know the sensation of taste.'[13] Thus having cursed the frog, the lord Purifier went elsewhere to live; he did not reveal himself to the gods. But the gods did a favour for the frogs, saying, 'Although you have been made tongueless by the curse of Agni, and deprived of the knowledge of taste, you will utter many kinds of speech. Though you dwell in holes, without food, without consciousness, even without the breath of life itself, dried up, the earth will support you, and you will move about even at night when all is in darkness.'

When the gods had said this to them, they went again over the earth in search of fire; but they did not find the Oblation-

12. Agni had hidden within water or within the elemental fire.
13. *Rasa* can denote either 'tongue' or 'taste'.

eater. Then a certain elephant, who resembled the elephant of Indra, said to the gods, 'Agni is within an *aśvattha* tree.'[14] The blazing fire became swollen with anger and cursed all the elephants: 'Your tongues will be bent backwards.' When he had said this, Agni went out of the *aśvattha*, for he had been pointed out by the elephant. He entered the inside of bamboo, but even as he went in he was betrayed by the steam in the variegated reeds. He left them and entered a *śamī* tree;[15] he entered the interior of a *śamī*, for he wished to sleep. But the gods, whose prowess is truth, were pleased with the elephants, and so they did them this favour: the gods said, 'Although your tongue will be bent backwards, with it you will eat all foods and you will utter loud sounds with indistinct syllables.'

Having said this, the heaven-dwellers yet again went after Agni. A parrot reported that Agni had gone out of the *aśvattha* and had gone into the interior of a *śamī*. The gods ran after Agni, who cursed the parrot: 'You will be deprived of speech.' And the Oblation-eater then turned around the tongue of the parrot, too. But when the gods saw the blazing fire, they were filled with compassion for the parrot, and they said to him, 'Bird, you will not be entirely deprived of speech. Though your tongue will be turned around, you will have speech confined to "ka", sweet, indistinct, and wonderful, like the speech of a child or an old man.' When the gods had said this, they spied Agni in the interior of the *śamī*, and so they made that tree the sacred abode of fire, for all rituals. From that time forth, Agni is considered to be within the interiors of *śamī* trees, and men use it as a means of producing fire. And the waters of the subterranean regions, which had been in contact with the deity of bright lustre and heated by

14. The *aśvattha* is the sacred fig tree.

15. The *śamī* is the tree from which fire-sticks are made; the tree itself is said to contain fire in its interior (literally its womb [*garbha*] or perhaps its hollow), and this fire is kindled from the sticks.

the energy of the Purifier when he lay in them, they release their steam through the mountain streams.

When Agni, the Purifier, saw the gods he became agitated and he asked them why they had come. The gods all said to him, 'We would ask you to perform a task which you ought to do. When it is done, it will bring great merit to you.' Agni said, 'Tell me what you wish me to do and I will do it thoroughly, O gods. I will fulfil your command; do not worry about this.'[16]

Agni seduces the sages' wives and begets Skanda

Although in the *Mahābhārata* tale of Agni and the frogs Agni agrees to beget Skanda, in other versions of the myth Skanda is merely a fortunate by-product of Agni's adulterous encounter with the Kṛttikās, the Pleiades, wives of the Seven Sages who form the constellation Ursa Major. Astronomical factors are central to this myth, which may represent the birth of the year (Skanda) with its six seasons (six heads) during the new moon at the Spring equinox, when the sun is in the Pleiades (i.e. when Agni is 'in' the Kṛttikās). The Kṛttikās appear in two contrasting aspects: they are the loving nurses whose breasts flow with milk because of their love, and they are the hideous Mothers who try to kill him; his particular wet-nurse partakes of this latter aspect, for she is Kālī or Death, the dark side of the gracious Gaurī who is Skanda's other mother.[17] Other oppositional pairs (sun and moon, fire and water) unite to produce Skanda at a moment of dangerous astrological ambivalence, like the moment of Vṛtra's death,[18] and specific reversals of 'the pairs', including male and female, take place at Skanda's birth.

16. At this point the story of the birth of Skanda is narrated in somewhat different terms from the version which I have translated in myth 33, pp. 108–10.

17. See below, myth 68, pp. 252–9.

18. See above, myth 25, pp. 83–4.

Indra is ambivalent toward Skanda: he needs Skanda to lead his armies, but he fears that Skanda will overcome Indra himself. Skanda proceeds to justify these fears by shattering several mountains, including a son of Himālaya – just as Indra cuts the wings off all the mountains but Mainaka (another son of Himālaya), Śiva sets fire to Himālaya, Viṣṇu uproots Mandara, and Kṛṣṇa uproots Mount Govardhana (in a battle with Indra).

Agni appears not only in his anthropomorphic form but in several ancient symbolic forms. He is the Garuḍī bird who carries the seed, the Indo-European fire-bird carrying the ambrosia,[19] while the 'goat-headed merchant' is Agni the sacrificial animal, the goat being his 'vehicle' in later Hindu mythology. The goat-head is also associated with Dakṣa,[20] who is related to almost all the central characters of this myth: he is the brother of Army of the Gods, grandfather of Indra, father of Svāhā, and father of Satī the wife of Śiva (who elsewhere in this same text replaces Agni as the father of Skanda).

33. FROM THE *Mahābhārata*

Long ago, the gods and demons were striving to kill one another, and the demons, whose forms are dreadful, were always conquering the gods. Indra the Shatterer of Cities, seeing his army being slaughtered by many weapons, decided that he was in great need of a general to lead his own army. 'I must find a powerful man who, when he sees the army of the gods shattered by the demons, will be able to rescue it by his own manly powers.' He went to the Mānasa mountain and thought long and hard there about this matter, and then he heard a terror-stricken cry of distress uttered by a woman: 'Let some man come and save me! Let him find a husband for me or be my husband himself.' The Shatterer of Cities said to her, 'Do not fear; you are in no danger.' When he had

19. See below, myth 73, p. 281.
20. See below, myths 35–6, pp. 119–25.

said this, he saw Keśin[21] standing before him like a mountain of red ore, wearing a diadem and carrying a mace in his hand, holding that maiden by the hand. Then Vāsava said to him, 'How can you try to rape this lady, an act which is not seemly for an Aryan? Know that I am the Wielder of the Thunderbolt, and stop tormenting her.' 'Leave her alone, Śakra,' said Keśin, 'I desire to have her. Be satisfied if you can return to your own city alive, Chastiser of Pāka.' As he said this, Keśin hurled his mace to kill Indra, but as the mace fell Vāsava cut it in half with his thunderbolt. Then Keśin became furious and threw the peak of a mountain at him, and when the God of a Hundred Sacrifices saw that mountain peak falling he split it with his thunderbolt, and it fell to the ground. Keśin was struck by that peak as it fell, and he let go of the fortunate maiden and ran away, badly wounded.

When the demon had departed, Vāsava said to the maiden, 'Who are you? Whose[22] are you, and what are you doing here, O lady with a beautiful face?' The maiden replied, 'I am the daughter of Prajāpati, and I am known as Army of the Gods. My sister, Army of the Demons, has already been carried off by Keśin. We two sisters used to come to enjoy ourselves on Mānasa with our girl-friends, with the permission of Prajāpati, but the great demon Keśin tried constantly to carry us off. Army of the Demons desired him, but I did not, O Chastiser of Pāka; he carried her off, my Lord, but you set me free by your might. King of the Gods, I wish you to choose an invincible husband for me.' Indra said, 'You are my maternal cousin, for my mother, Aditi, was a daughter of Dakṣa. Now I wish to hear you tell me of your own power.' 'I am a girl without power, O great-armed one,' replied the

21. Keśin ('Long-haired') is the name of a demon here. In the *Ṛg Veda*, Keśin is a long-haired sage who drinks poison with Rudra; in the Purāṇas, Keśin is the name of a wild horse demon killed by Kṛṣṇa.

22. That is, whose wife or whose daughter.

maiden, 'but my husband will be powerful. Because of a boon given by my father, he will be respected by gods and demons.' 'Goddess,' said Indra, 'what sort of power will your husband have? This I wish to hear you tell, blameless one.' The maiden answered, 'He will have great heroic powers, great strength, and he will conquer the wicked gods, demons, Yakṣas, Kinnaras, serpents, and Rākṣasas. Together with you he will conquer all beings; such will be my husband, pious and widely famed.'

When Indra heard her pronouncement, he thought for a long time in sorrow, 'There is no husband for this goddess, such as she describes.' Then he who shone like the sun saw the sun on the Hill of Sunrise,[23] and he saw Soma, the illustrious moon, entering the sun, the Maker of the Day. On this day of the new moon, a dangerous moment, he saw the battle between gods and demons raging on the Hill of Sunrise. The God of a Hundred Sacrifices saw the dawn full of blood-red clouds, and the lord saw the ocean, the abode of Varuṇa, full of blood-red water. Then Agni entered the Maker of Day, carrying the oblation that had been offered with various hymns by the descendants of Bhṛgu and Aṅgiras. And the twenty-four *parvans*[24] approached the sun; such was the dangerous condition of the moon, which had united with the sun. Observing the union of the hare-marked moon[25] and the sun, a dangerous conjunction, Śakra reflected, 'A dreadful halo has appeared around the sun and the moon, boding a great battle at the dawn after this very night. The ocean is carrying great quantities of blood against her current, and the fire-faced jackals are howling at the sun. This danger-

23. The sun is said to rise from behind the Hill of Sunrise in the east and set behind the Hill of Sunset in the west; it rises out of the eastern ocean and sets into the western ocean.

24. The *parvans* are the days of full moon and new moon each month.

25. The Indians see a hare in the moon where Europeans see a man.

ous confluence is great and full of energy; this union of Soma with fire and the sun is marvellous, for a son begotten by Soma could be the husband of this goddess. Agni is endowed with all these qualities, and he is a divinity; a child begotten by him could be the husband of this goddess.'

As the lord pondered in this way, he came to the world of Brahmā, taking Army of the Gods with him, and he bowed to the Grandfather and said, 'Appoint a great hero to be the husband of this goddess.' Brahmā said, 'Subduer of Demons, let it be done just as you have been imagining. In this way a child will be born of great power and wide prowess. He will be the leader of the army with you, God of a Hundred Sacrifices, and he will be the heroic husband of this goddess.' When he heard this, the king of the gods bowed to him in respect and went with the maiden to the dwelling-place of Vasiṣṭha and the other celestial sages, supreme brahmins of very great vows. All the gods, following the God of a Hundred Sacrifices, came to the sacrifice of those sages, for they desired to drink the Soma acquired by asceticism and to receive a share of the offerings. When the noble sages had performed the sacrifice in the proper way, they offered the oblation into the Oblation-devourer kindled with good fuel for all the dwellers in heaven. The marvellous fire, the carrier of oblations, the lord, was summoned there; he came out from the orb of the sun, restraining his speech according to the ritual. When the Oblation-eater arrived there he took the various oblations that had been offered by those brahmins together with the hymns; he took them from the sages and gave them to the dwellers in heaven.

As he was returning, he saw the wives of those noble sages bathing happily in their own hermitages. They shone like golden altars, like spotless slivers of the moon, like rays of the oblation-devouring fire, like marvellous stars. As Agni saw the wives of the supreme brahmins, his heart went out to them, his senses were agitated, and he was in the power of desire. But he thought, 'It is not proper for me to be agitated. I desire the virtuous wives of the supreme brahmins, and they are without desire. I cannot look upon them or touch them without cause, but by entering into the household fire I will look at them constantly.' He entered into the household fire and rejoiced to look upon them and to touch, as it were, all those golden women with his flames. Agni lived there for a long time in their power, setting his heart on them, desiring those supreme women. But then, as his heart was still enflamed with desire, Agni went into the forest and resolved to abandon his body, for he could not obtain the wives of the brahmins.

Previously, Svāhā, the daughter of Dakṣa, had desired him, and for a long time the blameless and passionate woman had been searching for a weak spot in him, but she had not seen any in the careful god. But when she found out that Agni had gone into the forest and was thoroughly heated by desire, the angry goddess thought, 'I will take the forms of the wives of the Seven Sages, and when the Purifier, tortured by desire, is deceived by their forms I will satisfy his desire. In this way, he will have his pleasure and I will obtain my wish.' The goddess first assumed the form of Śivā, the wife of Aṅgiras, a woman of virtue, beauty, and merit. The superb woman went to the Purifier and said to him, 'Agni, Oblation-devourer, you should satisfy me, for I am heated by desire. If you will not do so, consider me to be as good as dead. I am Śivā, the wife of Aṅgiras; I decided to come here after consulting my girlfriends.' Agni asked, 'How could you know that I am tortured by desire, and how could all the other beloved wives of the Seven Sages, to whom you have referred, know this?' 'Though you have always been dear to us,' said Śivā, 'we have been afraid of you. But when we read your mind by the signs, I was sent to you. I have come here for intercourse;

take your pleasure quickly. The Mothers are awaiting me and I must go, Oblation-devourer.'

Then Agni was overcome with rapture, and he united[26] with the goddess 'Śivā', who was filled with pleasure and took his seed in her hand. Then she thought, 'Those who see me in this form in the forest will falsely say that the wives of the brahmins have committed a sin with the Purifier. Therefore I will become a Garuḍī bird in order to avoid this, and my exit from the forest will be easy.' She became a female bird and went out of the great forest, and she saw a white mountain covered with reed clusters, guarded by marvellous seven-headed serpents with poisonous gazes, and full of Rākṣasas and female Rākṣasas and Piśācas and the fierce armies of Rudra's ghosts and many kinds of birds and beasts. She went quickly to the high plateau of that mountain, which was difficult to reach, and she threw the seed hastily into a golden pot. Then the goddess assumed the forms of the wives of the remaining noble Seven Sages and satisfied the desire of the Purifier. But she could not take the divine form of Arundhatī because of Arundhatī's powerful asceticism and devotion to her husband. Six times the lustful Svāhā threw the seed of Agni into that pot on the first day of the lunar fortnight.

The seed shed there, full of energy, engendered a son who was honoured by the sages as Skanda because he had been shed [*skannam*]. The Youth had six heads, twice that many ears, and twelve eyes, hands, and feet; he had one neck and one body. On the second day he assumed a distinct form, on the third he became a child, and on the fourth day he became Guha,[27] with all his limbs developed. As he was enveloped in a great red cloud ablaze with lightning, he glowed like the rising sun in a great red cloud. He grasped the enormous bow

26. The verb used here may also refer to the kindling of a fire.
27. Guha, 'Reared in a secret place', is a name of Skanda.

which was used by the Destroyer of the Triple City[28] to cut down the enemies of the gods, a bow that made one's hair stand on end, and as he grasped that supreme bow he roared powerfully, as if stupefying these three worlds that move and are still. Hearing that roar, which was like the sound of a mass of great clouds, the great elephants Citra and Airāvata sprang up with a start; and when Skanda whose glory was like that of the newly risen sun saw them hastening toward him he grasped them with two hands, and with another hand he held his spear, and with a fourth hand the heir of Agni held in a tight embrace a powerful red-crested cock with a great body. Then the powerful one shouted terrifyingly and played on a splendid conch-shell in two hands, blowing upon it in a manner to frighten even powerful beings. With two arms he clove the air again and again, and the great general whose soul is immeasurable seemed to drink up the three worlds with his mouths as he played on the peak of the mountain like the sun with his rays on the Mountain of Rising. Seated on the tip of the mountain, he of marvellous prowess and unfathomable soul looked about in all directions with his various heads, and when he saw various objects he roared again, and when people heard his roar they fell down everywhere, frightened and disturbed in their minds. Then they went to him for refuge, and all those people of the various classes who sought refuge with the god are known to the brahmins as the powerful assembly of his followers.

The great-armed one arose and reassured those people, and then he drew his bow and shot arrows at the white mountain. His arrows pierced the mountain Krauñca, ('the Curlew'), the son of Himālaya, and therefore geese and vultures go to Mount Meru. The shattered mountain fell down, crying out

28. See below, myth 37, pp. 133–7.

with painful screams, and when it had fallen the other mountains roared with great fear. Even when the mightiest of the mighty, whose soul is infinite, heard that roar of the wounded mountains, he was not at all disturbed, but he took up his spear and roared. Then the noble one hurled his stout spear, which quickly split the awful peak of the white mountain. The miserable white mountain, frightened of the noble one who had wounded him, left the earth and flew up with the other mountains. Then the earth was hurt, wounded, and shattered on all sides, and she went to Skanda and became powerful again. The mountains bowed to him and returned to earth, and then the world adored Skanda, on the fifth day of the bright moon.

When the great general of great power and courage was born, various horrible omens arose. There was a reversal of male and female and similarly of all the pairs of opposites; the planets and the heavens and the regions of the sky blazed with light, and the earth resounded excessively. When the sages saw these various horrible omens, they were disturbed, and they restored peace among people, for they wished for their welfare. The people who lived in the Caitraratha Forest said, 'This great misfortune has been brought upon us by the Purifier's union with the six wives of the Seven Sages.' And others said to the Garuḍī, 'You have brought this misfortune,' for they had seen the goddess flying in the form of the Garuḍī and did not know that the deed had been done by Svāhā. But when the female bird heard it said that he was her son, she went slowly up to Skanda and said, 'I am your mother.' And when the Seven Sages heard that a son of great vitality had been born, they abandoned their six wives, all except for the goddess Arundhatī, for those who lived in that forest said that he had been born from those six. But Svāhā said to the Seven Sages, again and again, 'This is my son; I know it is not as you think.'

The great sage Viśvāmitra had performed a sacrifice for the Seven Sages and, unseen, had followed behind the Purifier when he was heated by desire; he had perceived everything as it had truly happened. Viśvāmitra first sought refuge with Skanda, the Youth, and he praised the great general with divine prayers, and the great sage performed for him all the thirteen rituals for a youth, beginning with the birth ritual. He sang the praises of the six-headed one, and he performed a ceremony for the cock, and a ceremony for his divine spear,[29] and one for his assembly of followers. And when Viśvāmitra performed this ritual for the sake of all people, the sage Viśvāmitra became dear to the Youth. Then the great sage revealed to all the sages that Svāhā had changed her form and that their own wives had committed no offence, but though they heard this told truly, they all abandoned their wives.

When the gods heard about Skanda they said to Vāsava, 'Śakra, you must quickly kill Skanda, whose power is unbearable, and do not delay. For if you do not kill him today, he will become Indra, and the all-powerful one will seize the triple world, and us, and you, Śakra.' He was disturbed and said to them, 'This boy has very great power. He could attack and destroy in battle even the Creator of Worlds. I cannot kill the boy.' When Śakra had said this, they replied, 'There is no manliness in you, since you can talk in this way. Let all the Mothers of the World approach Skanda today and kill him, for they can assume whatever heroic powers they wish.' 'So be it,' said the Mothers, and they went to him. But when they saw him, with his unassailable might, their faces fell and they thought, 'He is invincible,' and they went to him for refuge. They said, 'You are our son; we support the universe. Let us all rejoice in you as a son, for our breasts are flowing with milk and we are beside ourselves with love.' The great general

29. Or: for the goddess Śakti.

honoured them and granted their desires, for when the lord heard their speech he wished to drink from their breasts.

Then the mightiest of the mighty saw his father Agni approaching, and he honoured Agni, who remained there together with the group of Mothers who surrounded him, to protect the great general, the firm one. Skanda's wet-nurse was the woman, among all the Mothers, who was born of anger; she held her trident in her hand and protected him as if he were her own son. The cruel daughter of the ocean of blood, the drinker of blood,[30] embraced the great general and cared for him as if he were her own son. And Agni transformed himself into a goat-headed merchant with many children, and he played with the boy who dwelt in the mountains, delighting him with toys.

The planets with their satellites, and the sages and the Mothers, and all the shining bands of assembled followers, headed by the Oblation-eater, these and many other terrifying inhabitants of the three heavens surrounded the great general along with the hosts of Mothers. The lord of gods, desiring victory but seeing that victory was dubious, mounted the shoulder of Airāvata and went forth with the gods. Indra went faster and faster, wishing to kill the great general, and the army of the gods was terrible and swift, shining with its many-coloured banners and armour, with various vehicles and bows. When the Youth saw Śakra, dressed in his best clothes, adorned and enhanced by Prosperity, approaching him to kill him, he advanced to meet him. The powerful Śakra shouted to encourage the army of the gods in his path, and he rode swiftly towards the son of the Purifier, desiring to kill him. Praised by the thirty-three gods and by the supreme sages, Vāsava came into the presence of Kārttikeya. Then the lord of the gods, together with the gods, gave a lion roar, and when Guha heard that sound he roared back like the

30. The Mother born of anger, drinker of blood, is Kālī.

ocean. At that great noise the army of the gods wandered about in all directions, here and there, stunned and senseless, like an agitated ocean. When the son of the Purifier saw that the gods had come near him in order to kill him, he became angry, and he emitted from his mouth swollen flames of fire which burnt the armies of the gods as they struggled on the ground. Their heads and bodies aflame, their weapons and vehicles ablaze, the gods shone like bright multitudes of suddenly fallen stars. Burning, the gods sought refuge with the son of the Purifier; they abandoned the Wielder of the Thunderbolt and then they found peace.

When Śakra had been deserted by the gods, he hurled his thunderbolt at Skanda. That missile swiftly struck the right side of the noble Skanda and split his side. And from the blow of the thunderbolt another man was born from Skanda, a young man with golden armour, bearing a spear, wearing celestial ear-rings. Since he was born from the entrance [*viśana*] of the thunderbolt, he became known as Viśākha. When Indra saw that another had been born, blazing like the fire of doomsday, he became afraid; he joined the palms of his hands together and sought refuge with Skanda. Skanda gave him safety, together with his army, and then the thirty-three gods rejoiced and made their instruments resound.

4

RUDRA AND ŚIVA

The Vedic myth of Rudra

Śiva only became a great sectarian Hindu god at the time of the late Epic, a period in which his worship is characterized by many non-Vedic practices – notably the worship of the phallus (*liṅga*) and the cult of asceticism. Nevertheless, his mythology may be traced back to the Vedas, not only to the god Rudra (whose name remains an important epithet of Śiva) but to Prajāpati, Indra, and Agni. The earliest mythology of Rudra–Śiva reveals a process of assimilation well under way; the dark outsider is already beginning to be included in the Vedic ritual, but he is still regarded warily, worshipped more in fear than in the spirit of devotion which came to characterize the later cult of Śiva.

Rudra Punishes Prajāpati and Distributes the Seed

When Rudra punishes Prajāpati, as he does in the *Ṛg Veda*,[1] the gods must first appease Rudra (who is sometimes satisfied with a share in the sacrifice, just as Agni is) and then they must 'appease' or control the dangerous fiery seed. In the Brāhmaṇas, this seed is usually Prajāpati's, but already it becomes confounded with the part of Prajāpati wounded by Rudra's arrow; later it is the fire from Śiva's eye which injures Bhaga and Pūṣan, and, still later, the protean substance becomes the seed of Śiva himself, which, like the seed of

1. See above, myths 1, p. 26, 3, pp. 29–31, and 4, p. 31, for the myth of Prajāpati; below, myth 36, pp. 123–5, for Rudra's share; and above, myth 5, pp. 32–3, for Agni's appeasement.

Prajāpati, is shed prematurely and remains destructive until it gives birth at last.[2]

34. FROM THE *Śatapatha Brāhmaṇa*

Prajāpati desired his own daughter – either heaven or the dawn. Wishing to pair with her, he united with her. This was a sin in the eyes of the gods, who thought: 'He who does this to his own daughter, our sister, commits a sin.' The gods said to Rudra, the god who rules over beasts, 'This one commits a transgression, who does this to his own daughter, our sister. Pierce him.' Rudra took aim and pierced him. His incomplete seed[3] was shed immediately, prematurely. Therefore the sage has said, 'When the father shed his seed in his own daughter, he spilt his seed on the earth as he united with her.'[4] This is the chant to Agni and the Maruts, in which it is told how the gods caused that seed to give birth.

When the anger of the gods subsided, they cured Prajāpati and they cut Rudra's arrow out. For Prajāpati is the sacrifice. They said, 'Devise a way so that this [seed][5] will not be spoilt and so that it will be a small part of the offering. Take it to Bhaga, who sits to the south of the sacrifice. Bhaga will eat it as the pre-sacrifice, so that it will be as if offered as an oblation.' They took it to Bhaga who sat to the south. Bhaga looked at it and it burnt out his two eyes immediately. Therefore it is said, 'Bhaga is blind.' They said, 'It has not been

2. See below, myth 36, pp. 123–5, for Bhaga and Pūṣan, and myth 43, pp. 164–8, for Śiva's seed.

3. Or: half of his seed was shed. (In some versions of the Skanda myth, Agni sheds half of his seed in his wife and the other half elsewhere.)

4. A reference to *Ṛg Veda* 10.61.7. See above, myth 1, p. 26, and the expanded text, myth 3, pp. 29–31.

5. 'This' may perhaps refer to the part of Prajāpati injured by the arrow or even to the arrow itself, but in the context of other variants of the myth, 'this' probably refers to the seed.

quenched. Take it to Pūṣan.' They took it to Pūṣan. Pūṣan ate it as the pre-sacrifice, but it knocked out his teeth immediately. Therefore it is said, 'Pūṣan has no teeth,' and so when they prepare the offering for Pūṣan they make it from ground rice, as for one who has no teeth.

They said, 'It has not been quenched. Take it to Bṛhaspati.' They took it to Bṛhaspati. Bṛhaspati ran to Savitṛ to cause it to be born, for Savitṛ is the one among the gods who causes birth [*prasavitṛ*]. 'Cause this to be born for me,' he said to him. Savitṛ, who causes birth, caused it to be born, and when Savitṛ had caused it to be born it did not injure him, and therefore it was for ever after quenched.

Śiva Destroys Dakṣa's Sacrifice and Distributes Fever

Although Rudra is often given a name, or a task, or some other form of recognition in the Brāhmaṇas, he is also specifically denied a share in the Vedic sacrifice.[6] The *Mahābhārata* myth of Dakṣa's sacrifice is based upon this premiss and develops into a myth of Śiva's assimilation into the orthodox pantheon, for in the end he is at last given a share. Śiva's action in this myth is ambivalent from the standpoint of orthodoxy: by beheading the sacrifice, he simultaneously *destroys* it as demons were said to try to do (he even sprinkles it with blood to make it impure) and actually *completes* it as the sacrificial butcher would do; thus he restores it at the end, replacing the head even as the Aśvins replaced Dadhyañc's head and learned the secret of 'how this sacrifice becomes complete'.

This version is set in the context of the Indra–Vṛtra myth,[7] and although Śiva is now clearly a great god, he is still more to be pacified than to be adored, while Viṣṇu appears at the end as a more gracious god, who forgives the sinners when Śiva would destroy them. Later versions of this myth further expand this sectarian rivalry and state

6. See above, myth 3, pp. 30–31.

7. See above, myths 25–6, pp. 77–90. Both Indra and Rudra/Śiva are beheaders and parricides, and both are punished by the Fury of Brahminicide.

that it is because Dakṣa is a worshipper of Viṣṇu that he refuses to invite Śiva to the sacrifice. But here the opposition is rather that of Vedic versus non-Vedic cults.

35. FROM THE *Mahābhārata*

[The listener, Yudhiṣṭhira, asked,] You have told me that Vṛtra was deluded by Fever and slain by Vāsava with a thunderbolt. How did this Fever appear, and from whence? I would like to hear in detail the origin of Fever.

[The narrator, Bhīṣma, replied,] Hear the birth of Fever, as it is famed throughout the world. I will tell you about it at length.

There was once a peak of Mount Meru famed throughout the triple world. This peak was descended from the sun and was named 'Luminary'; it was adorned with all gems, immeasurable, unapproachable by all people. There on the mountain slope adorned with gold and minerals the god Śiva sat as if on a couch, shining intensely, while Pārvatī, the daughter of the king of mountains,[8] stayed at his side constantly. The noble gods; the Vasus of great vitality; the two noble Aśvins, the best of physicians; King Kubera Vaiśravana, the overlord of Yakṣas, the prosperous lord who lives on Kailāsa surrounded by the Guhyakas; the divine sages, with Aṅgiras at their head; the Gandharva, Viśvāvasu; Nārada and Parvata; and the massed bands of celestial nymphs – they all came there together. A clear and pleasant wind blew, wafting various perfumes; the great trees were in blossom, bearing flowers of all seasons. The Vidyādharas, Siddhas, and ascetics all came to serve the great god, lord of cattle. The ghosts of diverse forms, the hideous Rākṣasas and the powerful Piśācas

8. In most versions of this myth, Dakṣa's daughter Satī, Śiva's wife, drives Śiva to destroy her father's sacrifice (see below, myth 67, pp. 250–51). Here, the woman is Pārvatī, Śiva's second wife, daughter of the mountain Himālaya (see below, myth 41, pp. 157–9).

of many forms and various weapons – all the servants of the god stood there like fires, rejoicing. The lord Nandin stood there with the god's consent, holding the blazing trident that glowed with its own energy. The Ganges, best of rivers, born of all the sacred waters, incarnate served the god. Thus the lord, the great god, was worshipped there by the divine sages and by the gods of great good fortune.

Then, after some time, a Prajāpati named Dakṣa began a sacrifice according to the Vedic rites ordained in former times. All the gods, with Śakra at their head, assembled and decided to go to his sacrifice. Shining like fires, the noble gods in their blazing celestial chariots went to the Door of the Ganges with the permission of the god; so the tradition goes. Then the virtuous daughter of the king of mountains saw the gods setting out, and she said to the god her husband, the lord of cattle, 'My lord, where are all the gods going, with Śakra at their head? Tell me truly, for you know the truth. A great misgiving has come over me.' The great lord replied, 'Blessed lady, the supreme Prajāpati, named Dakṣa, is performing a horse sacrifice, and all the heaven-dwellers are going there.' 'Illustrious one, why are you not going to this sacrifice?' asked Umā. 'What could prevent you from going?' The great lord answered, 'All of this was decided by the gods themselves: in all sacrifices, no share is designated for me. Illustrious lady with a superb complexion, by the course sanctioned by this former agreement, in keeping with *dharma*, properly, the gods do not offer me a share of the sacrifice.' Umā said, 'Lord, among all beings you are supreme in power because of your qualities. You are invincible, unapproachable because of your energy, fame, and glory. Illustrious one, sinless one, great sorrow and trembling have come upon me because you have been denied a share.'

When the goddess had said this to the god her husband, the lord of cattle, she fell silent with a burning heart, and he knew what the goddess thought and longed for in her heart. 'Stay here,' he said to Nandin, and then the lord of all lords of yoga gathered his powers of yoga, and the god of gods, whose energy is great, took the Pināka bow and attacked that sacrifice by force with his terrifying servants. Some of them emitted roars; some laughed; others sprinkled the fire with blood. Some with deformed faces uprooted the sacrificial stakes and whirled them about; some swallowed up in their great mouths the priests performing the sacrifice. Then the sacrifice, attacked on all sides, took the form of a deer and flew up into the sky; but the Lord, seeing the sacrifice fleeing in that form, took up his bow and an arrow and followed it.

As the lord of gods, whose energy is infinite, became angry, a terrible drop of sweat came out of his forehead; and as soon as that drop of sweat had fallen on the earth, an enormous fire like the fire of doomsday appeared. In it was born a short man with extraordinarily red eyes and a tawny beard; he was gruesome and his hair stood on end; his body was extremely hairy like that of a hawk or an owl. He had a gaping mouth with monstrous teeth; he was hideous, dark-complexioned, and wore red garments.[9] That creature of great essence burnt the sacrifice as a fire burns dry wood, and all the terrified gods fled in all directions. As that man strode about, the earth trembled violently and a moan of woe arose, terrifying everyone. The Grandfather appeared before the great god and said, 'All the gods will give you too a share, O lord. Lord of all gods, Heater of Enemies, great god, withdraw this destruction. All the gods and sages can find no respite from your anger. Supreme god, Knower of *Dharma*, if this man named Fever born of your sweat wanders among people, the whole earth will not be able to bear his energy in one piece; let him be divided into many.' When the god had been addressed in

9. Men condemned to death, as well as Buddhists and other heretics, wore red clothes.

this way by Brahmā, and when he had also been given a share, he accepted the command of the lord Brahmā whose vitality is infinite. Bhava, holding the Pināka bow, was well pleased and began to smile, and he accepted the share that Brahmā had mentioned.

Then he who knows all *dharma* divided Fever into many parts, for the sake of the peace of all beings; hear how he did this. The headaches of elephants, hot exudations of mountains, moss in waters, slough of serpents, sore hooves of bulls, barren saline patches on the surface of the earth, blindness of cattle, constipation of horses, moulting of the crests of peacocks, eye-diseases of cuckoos – each was called Fever by the noble Śiva. And disturbances in all sheep's livers, and hiccups of all parrots, and fatigue among tigers are known as Fever; so we have heard. But among men, the name of Fever is indeed famous; it enters a man at death, at birth, and in the midst of life. This awful energy of the great god is called Fever, and the lord is to be bowed to and honoured by all creatures that breathe.

When Vṛtra, the best of those who uphold *dharma*, was pervaded by this Fever he yawned,[10] and then Śakra hurled the thunderbolt at him. The thunderbolt entered Vṛtra and split him, and when the great demon and great yogi had been split by the thunderbolt he went to the highest place of Viṣṇu, whose energy is infinite. It was because of his devotion to Viṣṇu that he had formerly pervaded the universe, and therefore when he was slain in battle he reached the place of Viṣṇu.

Śiva Destroys Dakṣa's Sacrifice and Restores it

Another early version of the Dakṣa myth combines three Vedic motifs: the shedding of Prajāpati's seed, the piercing of the sacrificial

10. See above, myth 25, p. 81.

deer (or of the incestuous Prajāpati in the form of a deer), and the destruction of the Prajāpati's sacrifice: Rudra shoots an arrow that pierces the testicles of Dakṣa's sacrifice (now personified as a man), just as (according to one reading) Rudra's dart (or the part of Prajāpati wounded by it) is treated like the dangerous seed. This myth incorporates motifs from the castration of Indra (who is 'restored' like Kratu), and it leads to the later myths in which Śiva castrates himself when he is superseded as a creator,[11] just as he is here.

36. FROM THE *Varāha Purāṇa*

As Rudra wept, Brahmā said to him, 'Do not weep [*mā ruda*],' and so the ancient one became known as Rudra.[12] Brahmā said to him, 'Perform creation and cause it to be diffused with your own form, for you are capable of this, as you have great splendour.' As soon as this was said Rudra plunged into the water, and while he was immersed, Dakṣa performed creation for his own welfare; while Rudra, the best of the gods, remained in the water, the offspring that Brahmā had created from his mind performed creation. And while this creation was being diffused by the overlord of the gods, Dakṣa enthusiastically began to perform the supreme sacrifice to the Grandfather.

Then Rudra, who had previously plunged into the water, emerged wishing to create the universe and the gods. When he found out that the sacrifice was being attended by gods, Siddhas, and Yakṣas, he was overcome by anger: 'What infatuated person has created this universe,' he cried out, 'thus insulting this shining maiden[13] and overreaching me?' Then the tawny god lamented, and out of his mouth there came blazing flames, from which were born the bands of low

11. See above, myth 28, pp. 94–6. Kratu is identified with the castrated Śiva in myth 39, pp. 143–5. See also below, myth 38, pp. 139–41.

12. Compare the derivation of the Maruts' name, above, myth 27, p. 93.

13. Satī, the daughter just created by Dakṣa.

Piśācas and vampires and ghosts, and the bands of yogis. The heavens were thickly permeated by them, and the earth, and all the regions of the sky and all the worlds.

Then in his omniscience he made a bow which measured twenty-four hands' breadths, and he made a three-fold string, and in fury he made two celestial quivers and placed his arrows in them. Then he knocked out the teeth of Pūṣan and the eyes of Bhaga and the two testicles of Kratu;[14] when Kratu's seed was pierced he disappeared from the sacrificial ground, taking the path of the wind. All the gods, who were reduced to the condition of beasts, went to Bhava and bowed to him, and the Grandfather came there and acknowledged Bhava and embraced the gods who were full of devotion, for he inspected them and discerned that the gods had been wronged by Rudra. Then the god of gods looked at Rudra and said, 'Father, do not let the sacrifice be destroyed by anger.' When Rudra heard Brahmā's speech he said angrily, 'You created me before these gods; then why have they not given me a share of the sacrifice? Because of this, I have deprived them of their knowledge and deformed them, O god of gods.'

Brahmā said, 'All of you, gods and demons, must sacrifice to Śambhu and praise him loudly, for the sake of your knowledge, so that the lord Rudra will be pleased, so that the omniscient one will be pleased.' When the gods heard his instructions, they praised the noble one ... When Śambhu, the eternal one, the god of gods with his fierce bow, was thus praised by the gods, he said, 'I am the god of gods. Tell me what I can do.' The gods said, 'Grant us knowledge of the Vedas and sacred books without delay, and let the sacrifice with its secret doctrines be restored, if you are pleased with us, lord Bhava.' The great god said, 'Let all of you together be

14. As Kratu is the sacrifice, he here replaces Prajāpati, for whose act of incest Kratu's punishment (castration) is set forth in ancient Indian law.

beasts [*paśavas*], and I will be your lord [*pati*], and then you will obtain release.' The gods agreed to this, and so he became lord of cattle [*Paśupati*]. Then Brahmā said to the lord of cattle, with a calm inner heart, 'Lord of gods, the fourteenth lunar day will certainly be yours. Those twice-born ones who, though worthy of being fed, fast and faithfully sacrifice cows and incense and food to you on that day will please you so that you will bring them to the highest place.' When Rudra was thus implored by Brahmā, whose birth is unperceived, he restored teeth to Pūṣan, eyes to Bhaga, and seed[15] to Kratu, and he gave full understanding to the immortals. Thus was the birth of Rudra formerly brought about by Brahmā, and because of this act Rudra became known as the lord of gods. And whatever man hears this and always arises at dawn, he is released from all sins and obtains the world of Rudra.

The Epic myth of the destruction of the triple city of the demons

This is a myth of cosmic destruction by means of combining disparate elements, the mirror image of the myth of cosmic creation by means of dismemberment.[16] To separate and put in order is to create, in this context; to cause oppositional pairs to unite, and thus to lose their separate identities, is to produce chaos and annihilation, just as the total fusion of positive and negative atomic particles (or of 'matter' and 'anti-matter') results in an atomic explosion. The chariot which the gods create in order for Śiva to destroy the triple cities (i.e. the triple worlds of the universe - heaven, sky, and earth) is made by reassembling all the elements, animate and inanimate, abstract and concrete, which were so carefully dispersed and labelled at the time of primeval creation.[17]

15. Literally, his fruit.
16. See above, myth 2, pp. 27–8.
17. See above, myth 9, pp. 44–6.

Although Śiva explicitly restrains his fire from reducing everything to ashes at the end of the myth, it is clear that this is merely a temporary postponement of the inevitable conflagration, for Śiva's weapon is Time, Doomsday. This destruction is regarded as a favour to the demons who explicitly ask to be killed by Rudra, even as Rudra brings periodic universal dissolution as a favour to all beings. The necessity of death is expressed in the sub-episode of the magic lake which revives the dead demons; this lake is against the rules of Hindu metaphysics (as Brahmā says to the demons, 'There is no complete immortality'), and it makes the virtuous demons become corrupt. These three related themes – that immortality corrupts, that virtuous enemies must be corrupted so that they can be killed, and that the gods must steal from the demons their secret revivifying magic – are at the heart of the mythology of the battle between gods and demons.[18]

The imagery of the myth of the triple cities is Vedic: the three demons are the descendants of the triple-headed son of Vṛtra; the bow and arrow are the weapons which Rudra used against Prajāpati; and the villain of the piece is Maya, the architect of the demons and thus the demonic counterpart of Tvaṣṭṛ, who constructs the chariot for the gods. The charioteer is the Sūta, a cross between warrior and priest, a combination of body-guard, panegyrist, and counsellor; he reappears often in Hindu mythology, notably in the *Bhagavad Gītā*, which is a conversation between the archer Arjuna and his charioteer, Kṛṣṇa.

37. FROM THE *Mahābhārata*

There was a great conflict between the gods and demons, in which the first battle destroyed the demon Tāraka;[19] the demons were then conquered by the gods, we have heard.

18. See below, myths 73–5, pp. 274–300.

19. In order to destroy Tāraka, the gods caused Kāma to excite Śiva (see below, myth 41, pp. 154–6) so that Skanda would be born to kill Tāraka (myth 43, p. 163).

But when the demons had been conquered, the three sons of Tāraka, who were Tārākṣa, Kamalākṣa, and Vidyunmālin,[20] undertook fierce asceticism, observing the highest vow, wasting away their bodies with asceticism. The Grandfather, giver of boons, was pleased by their self-restraint, asceticism, and vow, and he granted them boons. They all asked the Grandfather of all people to ordain that they could not be slain by any creatures, ever. The lord god, lord of the worlds, said to them, 'There is no complete immortality. Therefore, demons, withdraw this request and choose another boon that is pleasing to you.' When they had all deliberated together for a long time, over and over again, they bowed to the lord of all people and recited this speech to him: 'Grandfather, faultless god, grant us the boon that we may establish three cities upon the earth and wander over this world, by your grace. Then, after a thousand years, we will come together and these cities will become one, and the blessed lord, the best of gods, will destroy these united cities with a single arrow, and that will be our death.' The god agreed to this and entered heaven.

When they had obtained their wishes, they deliberated happily together and chose the great demon Maya to create their three cities, for Maya was the wise, unaging Viśvakarman worshipped by demons. By his own ascetic power he created three cities, one of gold, one of silver, and the third of black iron. The gold city was in heaven, the silver in the air, and the iron city was set on a disc on earth. Each one was a hundred leagues wide and a hundred leagues long, with houses and high mansions with terraces and roof gardens, with many walls and ornamental gates. Though closely packed with all kinds of houses, adorned with various palaces and gateways, each city was spacious and airy. There was a separate king in

20. The names mean 'Star-eyed', 'Lotus-eyed', and 'Garlanded-with-lightning'.

each separate city: the sparkling city of gold belonged to the noble Tārakākṣa; the silver was Kamalākṣa's, and the iron Vidyunmālin's. The three demon kings soon overwhelmed the three worlds with their energy and ruled for many years, by the grace of Prajāpati. Then millions, and tens of millions, and hundreds of millions of demon chiefs with invincible heroism, desiring great sovereignty, came together from all sides to take refuge in the fortified triple city. Maya supplied everything that they all needed, and, relying upon him, they all dwelt there fearing nothing. Whenever anyone living in the triple city thought of any wish, Maya immediately fulfilled that wish, by his magic powers.

Tārakākṣa had a powerful son named Hari, who satisfied the Grandfather with his extreme asceticism and asked the gratified god for a boon: 'Let there be in our city a lake, such that those who have been wounded by weapons become more powerful when they are thrown into it.' When the heroic Hari, son of Tārakākṣa, had obtained this boon, he created there a lake that revived the dead. In whatever form or clothing a demon died, when he had been thrown into the lake he came to life in the same form and clothing. When the inhabitants of the triple city had obtained that lake, achieving supernatural powers through their great asceticism, they oppressed all the worlds and augmented the fears of the gods, for they never suffered any loss in battle. Then they were overcome by greed and infatuation and they lost their wits; shamelessly they all plundered established civilization. Routing the gods and their attendants here and there, now and again, filled with pride because of the boon they had been given, they roamed at will over all the forests of the gods that were cherished by the inhabitants of heaven. They destroyed the sacred hermitages of the sages, and the sacrificial posts, and the countryside; the wicked demons violated all moral bounds.

When all the worlds were thus oppressed, Śakra, surrounded by the Maruts, attacked the cities on all sides by hurling his thunderbolts. But the Shatterer of Cities could not pierce those cities, which had been made impenetrable by the boon given by the Creator. Then the lord of the gods became afraid, and he left those cities, and all the gods went together to the Grandfather to tell him of the injury done by the enemies of the gods. They told him everything truly and bowed to him with their heads and asked the blessed lord, the Grandfather, for a means of slaughter. When the god heard this he said to the gods, 'These evil demons who hate the gods offend you constantly and oppress you. I am certainly impartial to all creatures, but I tell you these offenders against *dharma* must be killed. These fortresses can be pierced by a single arrow, but not otherwise; and no one but Sthāṇu can pierce the forts with a single arrow. Gods, choose as your warrior the lord Sthāṇu the Vanquisher, who is never wearied by any task, and he will kill the enemies of the gods.'

When the gods, led by Śakra, heard this speech, they went with Brahmā to seek refuge with the god Śiva whose symbol is the bull. The gods, who knew *dharma*, practised great asceticism and proclaimed the eternal Vedas, and together with the sages they went to Bhava with their whole souls. They praised with well-chosen words the one who grants safety from all dangers, the soul of all, the noble one who pervades everything with his self. They saw him who by many special acts of asceticism learned his yoga of the self, who knows the Sāṅkhya of the self, who holds the self in his power, who is the lord, a mass of energy, the husband of Umā, unlike any other in the world, the undefiled performer of vows. They had imagined the one lord to be of various forms, but when they saw in the noble one the forms and images of themselves and each other, they were all amazed. And when they saw the unborn lord, lord of the universe, the very substance of all creatures, the gods and priestly sages touched the ground with their heads.

The lord Śaṅkara welcomed them, arose, smiled and said, 'Tell me, tell me.' When they were thus encouraged by the three-eyed god, though their minds were uneasy they said to Bhava, 'Honour, honour to you; we bow to you, O lord ...' Then the Lord was pleased, and he welcomed them with salutation and said, 'Do not fear. Tell me, what can I do for you?' When the noble one had offered this boon to the throngs of ancestors, gods, and sages, Brahmā honoured Śaṅkara and said these words for the benefit of the world: 'By your permission, lord of gods, I was appointed to this position of Prajāpati, and when I was thus appointed I gave a great boon to the demons. No one but you, lord of all that has been and is to be, is able to destroy them now that they have transgressed all moral bounds; you can oppose them in the slaughter. O god, lord of gods, show your grace to the heaven-dwellers who have come to beg you: kill the demons, O Bearer of the Trident.' The blessed lord replied, 'All of your enemies are to be slain; this is my opinion. But I am not able, all alone, to slay those who hate the gods. All of you, together, must slay your enemies in battle, by means of a weapon made of my energy, for unity is great strength.' 'Their power and energy is double the strength of ours,' said the gods; 'this is what we think, and we have seen their power and energy.' The lord said, 'Those evil ones who have offended you must be slain altogether. Kill all of these enemies with a half of my power and energy.' The gods answered, 'Great lord, we will not be able to bear a half of your energy. But with a half of all of our power, *you* must slay the enemy.'

The lord of gods granted their request and took half of the energy from all of them and became greater. With that power the god became more powerful than all of them, and thenceforth Śaṅkara was known as the Great God. Then the Great

God said, 'I will take my bow and arrow and chariot and I will slay in combat those enemies of the inhabitants of heaven. You must see to my chariot and to my bow and arrow so that this very day I will cause the enemy to fall upon the surface of the earth.' 'We will gather all the forms in the triple world from here and there to make your chariot of great strength, O lord of gods,' said the gods, 'and Viśvakarman will make the auspicious chariot, designing it cunningly.' Then they who were like tigers among the gods fashioned that chariot, and they made his arrow out of Viṣṇu and Soma and the Oblation-eater: Agni became its shaft, Soma its head, and Viṣṇu the point of that supreme arrow.

They made the body of the chariot out of the goddess Earth, garlanded with spacious cities, the supporter of all creatures, with her mountains and forests and islands. Mount Mandara was its axle; the great rivers were made its shanks; the regions of the sky and the intermediary directions were its cover. The dynasty of constellations became its shaft; the Kṛta Age became its yoke.[21] The supreme snake Vāsuki became the pole to which the yoke is fixed. The mountains Himālaya and Vindhya became appendages to the wheels; the gods made the Hill of Rising and the Hill of Setting into the two wheels. They made the ocean, the supreme abode of demons, into the other axle, and they made the circle of the Seven Sages into the decoration of the chariot wheels. The Ganges, Sarasvatī, Sindhu, and the sky were its axle pins; and all the mountain streams were the ornaments of the chariot. Day and night, and all the minutes and seconds, and the seasons adorned it. The shining planets were its under-carriage, and the stars were its wooden fender. Dharma, Artha, and

21. The Sanskrit word for dynasty (*vaṃśa*) has the primary meaning of a bamboo reed; perhaps a pun is intended, if the shaft is made of bamboo. Moreover, as the primary meaning of *yuga* is a yoke, another pun may be intended.

Kāma[22] conjoined as its tripartite curved pole; the various herbs and all species of flowers, fruits, and shoots were its bells. The sun and moon they made into the two supreme wheels, and night and day were made into its two splendid wings in front and back. They made the ten lords of snakes, led by Dhṛtarāṣṭra, into its strong shaft; the sky was its yoke, and the two clouds of doomsday[23] were made into the leather thongs of the yoke. The pins of the yoke were Fortitude, Memory, Steadfastness, and Humility; the animal skin[24] was the firmament spangled with the planets and constellations and stars.

The World-protectors,[25] the rulers of the gods, water, the dead, and wealth, were made into the horses, and the snakes Kālapṛṣṭha, Nahuṣa, Karkoṭaka, Dhanañjaya and others became bands to bind the manes of the horses. The day preceding the new moon, the day after the full moon, the day of the new moon and the day of the full moon – these auspicious days they made the traces of the horses and the riders and the leather neck-strap. Action, truth, asceticism, and profit were made the reins; mind was the base, and speech the chariot's path. Banners of various hues and patterns fluttered in the wind, and the chariot shone forth brilliantly, as it was girded with lightning and rainbows.

The gods were amazed when they saw the chariot formed in this way, for they saw that the energies of all the world were

22. *Dharma* (social law), *artha* (success or wealth), and *kāma* (sensual pleasure) formed the triad of goals in ancient India, to which a fourth goal – *mokṣa*, release – was later added.

23. The two clouds are named Saṃvartaka ('Dissolution', also a name of the submarine doomsday mare) and Balāhaka ('the Crane'). Elsewhere, five more doomsday clouds are enumerated (see below, myth 51, p. 183).

24. A skin would be stretched over the frame of the chariot.

25. The Lokapālas: Indra ruler of the gods. Varuṇa ruler of waters, Yama king of the dead, and Kubera lord of wealth.

united, and they reported to the noble god that it was ready. When the supreme chariot had been thus fashioned by the gods to wipe out those who hated them, Śaṅkara placed his own superior weapons in the chariot. He made the sky his chariot staff and placed his bull upon its banner. The rod of Brahmā, the rod of death, the rod of Rudra, and Fever became the outriders of that chariot, watching in all directions. Atharvan[26] and Aṅgiras protected the wheels of the noble chariot, and the *Ṛg Veda*, *Sāma Veda*, and *Purāṇa* rode in front, while the *Itihāsa*[27] and the *Yajur Veda* protected the rear. Sacred words and sciences were made servants standing on all sides. The sound *Vaṣaṭ* was made into the whip, and the sound *Om* shone forth surpassingly at the head of the car. Having made the year embroidered with the six seasons his bow, he made his own shadow the bow string, unbreakable in battle. For the lord Rudra is Time and Death, and the year is his bow, and therefore the Night of Doomsday for men was made the unwithering string of that bow. Viṣṇu, the blazing Agni, and Soma were the arrow, for this whole universe is made of Agni and Soma, and the universe is said to be made of Viṣṇu, and Viṣṇu is the soul of the lord Bhava of infinite energy. Therefore they cannot bear it when Hara touches that bowstring. The lord cast onto that arrow his unbearable, sharp anger, the fire of anger, born of the anger of Bhṛgu and Aṅgiras, which is very hard to bear.

The red and blue one, the smoky one, the Wearer of Skins, the Terrifier blazed forth enveloped in flames of energy like ten thousand suns. He who hurls down those who are hard to

26. The Atharvan is the priest presiding over fire and Soma. Dadhyañc is the son of an Atharvan priest (see above, myths 13, pp. 56–7, and 14, pp. 58–9).

27. The term *Itihāsa* (literally, 'thus he spoke') refers to historical tradition, dynastic histories and legends, in contrast with sacred tradition.

hurl down, the conqueror and slayer of those who hate religion, Hara, the eternal saviour of those people who follow *dharma* and the eternal slaughterer of those who follow *adharma*, the lord Sthāṇu was surrounded by his hideous, terrifying, fierce and destructive bands of servants as if surrounded by his own qualities. This whole universe, moving and still, entered into his limbs and presented a marvellous sight. When he saw the divine chariot, he put on his armour and took up his bow and the celestial arrow born of Soma, Viṣṇu, and Agni, and the gods made the feathers of that arrow out of a fragrant, gentle breeze. The great god mounted the chariot and made ready, terrifying even the gods and causing heaven and earth to tremble.

The brilliant Giver of Boons, the god armed with his sword and bow and arrow, laughed and said, 'Who will be my charioteer?' The bands of gods replied, 'Whomever you appoint, he will certainly be your charioteer, O lord of gods.' Then the god spoke again to them, saying, 'Deliberate briefly and make him my charioteer who is better than me.' When the gods heard this speech uttered by the noble one, they went to the Grandfather and begged his favour: 'God, we have done precisely as you instructed regarding the annihilation of the enemies of the thirty-three gods. We have propitiated him whose banner is the bull and we have made the chariot and equipped it with various weapons. But we do not know who could be the charioteer for this supreme chariot. Therefore, O lord god, appoint someone to be charioteer; make fruitful the words that you spoke to us when you said, "I will do what is for your benefit." Now you should keep that promise. The supreme chariot is ready for us, O god; it is an unassailable router of enemies; and the god who holds the Pināka bow in his hand has been designated the warrior for it and is girded and eager, terrifying the demons. The four Vedas are its fine horses; the earth with her mountains is the noble chariot; the cluster of constellations is the wooden fender on which the warrior should be protected by the charioteer. A charioteer must be sought who excels all these, for upon him depend the chariot, the horses, the armour, weapons, bow, and even the warrior. O lord god, Grandfather, we can see no charioteer for this other than you, for you have all the qualities and are the foremost of gods. Mount the chariot quickly and rein in the supreme horses.' Then the gods bowed their heads to the lord of the triple world, the Grandfather, begging him to be their charioteer; so we have heard. Brahmā replied, 'There is not a word of falsehood in all that you have said, O dwellers in heaven. I will rein in the horses for Śiva, whose hair is braided, when he fights.' Then the lord god, Creator of the Worlds, the Grandfather, was appointed by the gods to be the charioteer for the noble lord Śiva.

When Brahmā mounted that chariot which was worshipped by all the world, the horses swift as the wind quickly bowed their heads, and when the great lord Śiva had mounted, they went down on their knees. Then the great Grandfather, the lord of the triple world, took up the reins and drove those horses that were as swift as thought or the wind. And when Brahmā, the giver of boons, had mounted and driven toward the demons, Śiva, the lord of all, smiled and said, 'Well done! Well done! Drive on, O lord; drive the horses tirelessly to the place where the demons are. Witness today the might of my two arms as I kill our enemies in battle.' Then he drove those horses swift as a blast of wind to the triple city that was protected by the demons. The lord went quickly to win victory for the dwellers in the triple heaven, driving the horses worshipped by all the world, horses which seemed to drink up the skies.

When Bhava set out toward the triple city in the chariot, the bull bellowed a great roar that filled the regions of the sky. Hearing that great and terrifying roar of the bull, some of the descendants of Tāraka, enemies of the gods, were destroyed on the spot; others stood there ready to face battle. Then Sthāṇu, bearing the trident, went mad with anger; all creatures were terrified, and the triple world trembled. Dreadful omens arose as he placed his arrow on the bow-string, for, because of the excitement of Soma, Agni, and Viṣṇu in it, as also of Brahmā and Rudra, and because of the vibration of the bow, the chariot sank down badly. Then Nārāyaṇa[28] came forth out of the arrow and assumed the form of a bull and raised up the great chariot. But while the chariot was sinking and the enemies were bellowing, in all the confusion, the mighty lord stood on the head of the bull and on the back of a horse and roared. The lord Rudra looked at the city of the demons and he cut off the breasts of the horse and clove in two the hooves of the bull. And from that time forth, the hooves of cattle are cloven, and from that time forth horses have had no breasts, for they were wounded by the mighty Rudra of marvellous deeds.

Then Śarva strung his bow and placed his arrow on it and strengthened it with the magic weapon of the lord of cattle, and he thought of the triple city. And as he stood there, angrily holding his bow, at that moment the three cities became one, and when the triple city had become one, a great hubbub of joy arose among the noble gods. Then all the bands of gods and the Siddhas and supreme sages shouted, 'Victory!', praising and rejoicing. The triple city then appeared before the slayer of demons, the god whose form was indescribably fierce, whose energy was unbearable. The lord of all the world drew his bow and released against the triple city the arrow which was the essence of the triple world. It burnt the band of demons and hurled them into the western

28. A name of Viṣṇu. See below, myths 54, p. 186, and 72, pp. 274–80.

ocean.[29] Thus the triple city was burnt, and all the demons without exception were burnt by the Great Lord in his anger, for he wished for the welfare of the triple world.

The three-eyed god restrained the fire which was born of his own anger, saying to it, 'Alas! Do not reduce the worlds to ashes.' Then all the gods and people and sages resumed their natural state and praised with significant words Sthāṇu whose vitality is incomparable. And then, having been given permission to leave by the lord, whom they had propitiated, all the gods, led by Prajāpati, went back whence they had come, for their desires were fulfilled.

The Purāṇic myths of *liṅga*-worship

The most important form of the cult of Śiva is the worship of the *liṅga* or phallus of Śiva, a practice which may be traced back to the pre-Vedic societies of the Indus Valley civilization (*c.* 2000 B.C.) but which first appears in Hindu iconography in the second century B.C. Myths explaining the origin of *liṅga*-worship occur in the latest layers of the Epics and are then widespread, probably because of the need to justify this non-Vedic aspect of the god, which had been only recently assimilated to orthodox Hinduism.

Śiva Castrates Himself

Like the story of Dakṣa's sacrifice, this is a myth of antagonism and competition between gods in which Śiva terrorizes the other gods into worshipping him, first with a share of the Vedic sacrifice and here with devotion to the *liṅga*. In the Dakṣa myth, Śiva and Dakṣa compete as creators; here, Viṣṇu gives Brahmā the same command which Brahmā had given to Rudra[30] ('Create progeny, for you are

29. As the sun sets in the western ocean, this is an appropriate place to dispose of the demon cities (or the universe itself) when they meet their fiery doom.

30. See above, myth 36, p. 123.

capable'), but, unlike Rudra, Brahmā obeys this command and 'overreaches' Śiva just as his son Dakṣa did. This conflict is then resolved into an opposition between Brahmā the creator and Śiva the destroyer, for Śiva's destructive aspect is emphasized from the very beginning of this myth. Just as Viṣṇu mediates between Śiva and Brahmā, so on the symbolic level wind mediates between fire and water during both destruction and creation.

38. FROM THE *Śiva Purāṇa, Dharmasaṃhitā*

Once in the past, when all the universe moving and still had been destroyed and had become a single ocean, Brahmā, Viṣṇu, and Rudra arose from the water. Their arrival was unwitnessed, and even wise men do not know it. The earth, which had been the domain of former beings, had been destroyed with its creatures moving and still, for a piercing wind had arisen and dried up the seven oceans, and when all the waters were dried up everywhere, all creatures moving and still were destroyed, dried up gradually in succession. A single sun appeared, rising in the east, and then a second in the south, just like the first, drying up the water on all sides with its rays and burning all that moved and was still. Then in the west a third sun arose, and in the north there arose a fourth, burning all that moved or was still; and later on eight more arose, and then there were twelve.

The one who is known here as Rudra, the Fire of Doomsday, arose from the subterranean hell and filled all the regions of the sky. The exalted one, as he is known everywhere, burnt all of the underworld above and sideways, without exception, and then he went to his own dwelling place which he had made before.[31] Then clouds arose and rained in all directions, flooding the whole earth and all the regions of the sky with waters; afterwards, they plunged into the single ocean which the universe had become. There was no earth, nor any

31. This dwelling, according to the commentator, is the subterranean watery hell, which is also the dwelling place of the demons.

regions of the sky, no space, no heaven; everything was like a giant cask filled to the brim.

Then the three eternal gods arose from the midst of the water – Brahmā, Viṣṇu, and Rudra, whose arrivals are unwitnessed. The two – Ka[32] and Viṣṇu – bowed and said to Śarva, who blazed with sharp energy and embraced the *śakti*[33] of Rudra, 'You are the lord of everything, our lord. Perform creation as you wish.' 'I will perform it,' he said to them, and then he plunged into the waters and remained immersed for a thousand celestial years. Then they said to one another, 'What will we do without him? How will creation take place?' Hari said to the Creator, 'Do as I tell you, Grandfather: let no more time elapse, but make an effort to create progeny. For you are capable of creating various creatures in the worlds; I will give you your own *śakti*, so that you will be the creator.' Thus encouraged by the words that Viṣṇu had spoken to him, he thought about creating, and then he created everything conducive to happiness – gods, demons, Gandharvas, Yakṣas, serpents, Rākṣasas. When that creation had been performed, Śambhu emerged from the water, desirous of creating and thinking about it in his mind. But when he saw the whole universe stretching above and below with the gods, demons, Gandharvas, Yakṣas, serpents, Rākṣasas and men, the great god's heart was filled with anger, and he thought, 'What shall I do? Since creation has been performed by Brahmā, I will therefore destroy, cutting off[34] my own seed.' When he had said this, he released from his mouth a flame which burnt everything.

32. Ka, a name of Brahmā, also means 'Who?'. An agnostic Vedic verse (10. 129.6) which asked, 'Who [*ka*] knows whence this creation was born?' was later interpreted as a statement: 'Who [the god Who?, Prajāpati] knows whence this creation was born.'

33. The creative power of the god, often personified as a goddess.

34. An alternative reading (*ucchādya* for *ucchidya*) would be translated, 'uncovering my own seed'.

When Brahmā saw that everything was on fire, he bowed to the great lord with devotion and praised the lord ... Śaṅkara was pleased by Brahmā's praise, and he told him, 'I am Śaṅkara. I will always accomplish everything that is to be done for anyone who seeks refuge with me, devotedly. I am pleased with you; tell me what wish you desire in your heart.' When Brahmā heard this he said, 'I created an extensive range of progeny; let that be as it was, O lord, if you are pleased with me.' When Rudra heard this he said to Ka, 'That energy which I gathered in excess in order to destroy your creation – tell me, what shall I do with it for you?' Brahmā thought carefully for the sake of the world, and then he said to Śaṅkara, 'Cause your own energy to enter the sun, since you are lord over the sun; for you are the creator, protector, and destroyer. Let us live together with all the immortals in the energy of the sun, and we will receive with devotion the sacred image of the three times[35] that was given by mankind. Then, great god, at the end of the aeon you will take the form of the sun and burn this universe, moving and still, at that moment.'

He agreed to this and laughed, for he was secretly amused, and he said to Brahmā, 'There is no good use for this *liṅga* except for the creation of progeny.' And as he said this he broke it off and threw it upon the surface of the earth. The *liṅga* broke through the earth[36] and went to the very sky. Viṣṇu sought the end of it below, and Brahmā flew upwards,[37] but they did not find the end of it, for all their vital effort. Then a voice arose out of the sky as the two of them sat there, and it said, 'If the *liṅga* of the god with braided hair is wor-

35. Past, present, and future are the three times; the *liṅga* is their image.

36. Down to the subterranean hell.

37. Viṣṇu assumes the form of a boar and Brahmā the form of a goose.

shipped, it will certainly grant all desires that are longed for in the heart.' When Brahmā and Viṣṇu heard this, they and all the divinities worshipped the *liṅga* with devotion, with their hearts set upon Rudra.

The Pine Forest Sages Castrate Śiva

The sages of the Pine Forest are the sons of Brahmā and are directly responsible for the castration of Śiva even as Brahmā is indirectly responsible; but they are sometimes particularly designated as the Seven Sages, whose wives are seduced by Agni–Śiva.[38] A third, later level of the myth appears in texts which state that the sages are heretics whom Śiva enlightens. Even in the present text, which is most closely related to the myth of Agni and the sages' wives, their 'opinion about *dharma*' wavers, and Śiva teaches the sages a lesson, a balance between their violent asceticism and their involvement in 'worldly ways', the balance of the system of four classes and stages of life. Finally, this is a myth of revelation and epiphany, for the sages fail to recognize Śiva and accuse him falsely (even as they accused their wives, the Kṛttikās, falsely) until they are taught to see him truly and to worship him as the *liṅga*.

39. FROM THE *Brahmāṇḍa Purāṇa*

The sages said: 'Bard of great intellect, tell us more about the noble great god; we are eager to hear of his greatness. How did he enter the Pine Forest in which the bands of divine sages lived, changing his guise so that the intelligent great sages, who knew the great god, were deceived and bereft of their wits? And how did they propitiate him to obtain his favour, when Bhava was not pleased with them? Tell us all of this as it really was enacted by the god of gods; for you are the foremost of intellectuals.' The bard replied, 'Listen carefully and I will tell you how the god of gods fashioned this *dharma* out of pity for those who were devoted to him.'

38. See above, myth 33, pp. 108–12.

Formerly, in the Kṛta Age, priests lived on an auspicious peak of Himālaya in a delightful pine forest full of various trees and vines. Many sages were practising asceticism there, having taken the vows of sages: some ate nothing but moss; some lay down immersed in water; some had clouds as their only shelter; others stood on the tip of the big toe; some used their teeth for mortars; others broke things on stones. Some sat in yogic posture on their hams; others took pleasure in living like wild animals. Thus these men of great minds spent some time in their keen asceticism.

Then the god came to that forest in order to show his grace to them. His body was pale with the ashes smeared on it; he was naked, and all his identifying marks were defaced; his hair was disordered and loose; he had enormous pointed teeth; his hands were busy with fire-brands, and his eyes were red and tawny. His penis and testicles were like red chalk, the tip ornamented with red and white chalk. Sometimes he laughed horribly; sometimes he sang, smiling; sometimes he danced erotically; sometimes he yelled again and again. As he was dancing, their wives became bewitched immediately and stood in his way as he came into the hermitage and begged for alms over and over again. His wife took a similar form, adorned with ornaments made of grass. He roared like a bull and bellowed like an ass. As he thus began to deceive all the embodied creatures there, laughing at them, the sages became angry and were sullied by anger.

Bewitched by his magic power of delusion, they all tried to curse him: 'Since you sing like an ass, therefore you will be an ass', or 'a Rākṣasa' or 'a Piśāca' or 'a demon' or whatever else. All the angry sages together cursed him with their various curses as each one wished, and they hurled all their ascetic powers at Śaṅkara, the god who is the lord of the universe. But just as the stars in the firmament do not shine when the sun shines, so their energies did not have any effect on Śaṅkara. It has been heard that the enriched sacrifice of the noble Brahmā, the source of all good things, was destroyed by a sage's curse; and Viṣṇu, of supreme heroic power, became incarnate ten times, always to be made miserable, because of the curse of Bhṛgu; and formerly the angry sage Gautama caused the penis and testicles of Indra to fall to the ground.[39] The Vasus were made to dwell as embryos in the womb because of a curse, and Nahuṣa became a serpent because of the curse of a sage. Brahmins made the ocean of milk undrinkable, and Dharma himself was cursed by the noble Māṇḍavya.[40] These and many others suffered thus from retaliatory curses, all except for the three-eyed god of gods, the great lord.

But since they were deluded by Śaṅkara so that they did not recognize him, all the sages said to one another, 'This is not the behaviour of householders like us, nor is it the conduct of those who delight in chastity, nor of those who live in the forest; nor is this the *dharma* of ascetics.[41] It has never been seen anywhere. This most evil conduct has deluded this man.' Then they said to him, 'Cause your *liṅga* to fall off. This is not the *dharma* of ascetics. Speak with honeyed words and put on a single garment,[42] and when your *liṅga* has been abandoned you will then be worshipped.' Then the lord Śaṅkara, the Destroyer of the Eyes of Bhaga, spoke to the sages with smooth words, seeming to smile, saying, 'Brahmā and all the other gods cannot make our *liṅga* fall off by force, let alone others who are rich in ascetic powers, but I will cause this

39. Bhṛgu's curse is described in myth 75, p. 293, below, Gautama's in myth 28, p. 95, above.

40. For the myths of Nahuṣa, the Vasus, and Māṇḍavya, see the glossary.

41. A reference to the four stages of life (*āśramas*): chaste student, householder, forest-dweller, and ascetic. Although the sages refer to themselves as householders, they practise extreme asceticism.

42. The loincloth of the ascetic.

liṅga to fall off, O best of twice-born ones.'[43] 'Stay in the hermitage or go,' they said to him, and when the great god was thus addressed all his senses and emotions were delighted, and, as they all watched, the lord vanished.

When the lord had vanished and the *liṅga* was cut off, there was no manifestation of the deity among all the beings in the triple world, and there was confusion everywhere. Nothing shone forth; the sun gave no heat, purifying fire had no lustre, and the constellations and planets were all topsy-turvy. The seasons did not come about for the sages of mighty souls who had become involved in worldly ways for the sake of offspring and who went to their wives during the fertile season.[44] They continued to practise *dharma*, free from egoism, free from possessiveness, but their virile powers were destroyed, and their energy was destroyed. Then their opinion about *dharma* wavered, and they all went together to the world of Brahmā; they went to the house of Brahmā and saw the lotus-born god, and they all fell at his feet and told him what Śiva had done:

'A hideous person – one with enormous pointed teeth, his hair standing on end, his hands busy with fire-brands, his eyes red and tawny, his penis and testicles adorned with red chalk – moved about amongst our daughters-in-law and daughters, and especially our young daughters, lusting for the "reversal".[45] We thought, "He is mad!" and so we treated him

43. The three upper classes (priests, nobles, and commoners) are technically twice-born, as they are 'reborn' at the time of their consecration; but 'twice-born' usually denotes only the brahmin class.

44. In this, the sages follow the practice of yet another stage of life, that of the forest-dwellers, combining the roles of householders and ascetics.

45. This term is used to denote a position of sexual intercourse in which the woman is on top of the man, but it may here imply nothing more specific than general unchastity or perversions. The words of the sages are contradictory and vague, betraying their lack of control or

with contempt; we abused him and beat him and tore out his *liṅga*. Now we have come to you for refuge, in order to allay his anger, for we do not know how to do this; tell us, Grandfather.'

When Brahmā heard the speech of the sages, he realized by meditation that it had been the Lord. Then he replied to them, very calmly, 'You should have recognized that god as the great lord, the great god Śiva. His highest place cannot be comprehended even by gods and sages and ancestors, for he is the lord. During the dissolution at the end of a thousand aeons, the blessed great lord destroys all embodied creatures, for then he becomes Doomsday. He alone creates all creatures by his own energy; he is the bearer of the discus, whose chest is marked by the Śrīvatsa sign.[46] In the Kṛta Age he is the yogi; in the Tretā Age he is known as Kratu; in the Dvāpara Age he is the Doomsday Fire, and in the Kali Age he is Dharmaketu.[47] Three forms of Rudra are recognized by learned men: his dark form is Agni, his passionate form Brahmā, and the form of goodness is known as Viṣṇu.[48] Digvāsas,[49] one of his forms, is known by the name of Śiva, and that form is full of the yoga of Brahmā. Therefore you should propitiate the god, the god of gods, the lord, the undying lord; and you must conquer your anger and your senses, O best of priests. You

---

understanding: they say that Śiva seduced their daughters, though in fact it was their wives who followed him; they say that they castrated him, though he himself did this, allowing them to think that this happened as the result of their curse upon him.

46. The Śrīvatsa is the twist of hair on Viṣṇu's chest, and the discus is Viṣṇu's weapon. Thus Śiva is here identified with Viṣṇu.

47. Dharmaketu ('Having the law as his banner') is an epithet of the Buddha. Again Śiva assumes Viṣṇu's role and becomes the Buddha in the Kali Age; see myth 62, pp. 232–5.

48. A reference to the three strands or *guṇas*; see myth 9, p. 44.

49. 'Clothed in the sky', that is, naked; a term applied to Śaiva or Jain beggars.

should make an image of the *liṅga* of the noble one as you saw it, and go to the god who has the trident in his hand. Then you will see the lord of gods who cannot be seen by those who have not mastered their selves, and when you have seen him all your ignorance and *adharma* will be destroyed.' They reverently walked around[50] Brahmā, whose vitality is immeasurable, and they stayed in the Pine Forest, for their sorrow had been removed. They began to propitiate Śiva as Brahmā had instructed, on altars measured out on the ground, and on undulating hills, and in caves, and on the sparkling, brilliant sand-banks of rivers, for a full year, until spring came again.

Then the god took the same form and came to the forest. The great lord entered that forest hermitage that was full of flowers and many trees and creepers, with swarms of bees humming around the sweet sap, and full of the lovely sound of cuckoos. All the sages praised him calmly, and with offerings of water and garlands of many kinds of flowers and incense and perfume the illustrious ones with their wives and sons and servants worshipped him. Then with gentle words they said to the lord of the mountain, 'Forgive all that we did in our ignorance of the god of gods, in act or mind or speech . . ' Then the lord god said, 'Those who delight in my ashes have their sins burnt away by ashes; they are self-controlled priests intent upon meditation, who act as they speak. A wise man will not censure them nor transgress against them, nor will he speak unpleasant things to them if he wishes to prosper here. Whatever fool blames them, he blames the great god; and whoever worships them, he constantly worships Śaṅkara. Behave in this way, if you please, and you will obtain fulfilment from me.'

When they learned from Śiva this supreme ritual that

50. It was a sign of reverence to walk around someone to the right, clockwise.

destroys great darkness and is without equal on earth, they all fell on the ground, touching it with their heads, for their fear and greed and delusion and worries had been removed. Then the priests rejoiced and they bathed the image[51] of the great lord with pure perfumed waters mixed with *kuśa* grass and flowers, and they bathed the great lord, the god, with great pots of water, and they sang various sweet-sounding secret spells . . . When the *liṅga* had been established again for the welfare of the worlds, those excellent sages became intent upon the *dharma*[52] of the classes.

Then the great lord was pleased, and he said to the sages, 'I am pleased with your asceticism. You have kept your vows well. Choose a boon.' All the sages then prostrated themselves before the great lord – Bhṛgu, Aṅgiras, Vasiṣṭha, Viśvāmitra, Gautama, Atri, Sukeśa, Pulastya, Pulaha, Kratu, Marīci, Kaśyapa, and Saṃvarta of great ascetic power. They all bowed to the great god and said, 'The bathing with ashes, nakedness, and "left-handedness" that goes against the grain,[53] and that which is to be used or not to be used – lord, we wish to know that.' The lord replied, 'I will proclaim this entire matter to you this very day. I am Agni joined with Soma, and I am Soma mingled with Agni. They say that Agni is "done and not done",[54] and yet people have often sought refuge with Agni; again and again the universe, moving and still, is burnt by Agni. The supreme purification of this entire universe is to be accomplished by ashes; I place my seed in ashes and sprinkle creatures with it. One who has done that which is to be done by fire will master the three

51. The *liṅga*.

52. The law of the four classes and four stages of life.

53. Literally, against the hair. A reference to unorthodox, perhaps Tantric, rites.

54. That is, made (kindled) but not completed (consumed), often said of gold.

times. By means of ashes, my seed, one is released from all sins. When ashes illuminate anything brightly and make it fragrant, from that moment it is called "ash" and ashes alone remain from all evils. The ancestors are known as drinkers of steam,[55] and the gods are born of Soma; for all this universe, moving and still, has Agni and Soma for its soul. I am Agni of great energy, and this woman, my wife Ambikā, is Soma; and I am both Agni and Soma, as I am myself the Man together with Nature.[56] Therefore, illustrious ones, ashes are known as my seed, and I bear my own seed upon my body as is my custom. Henceforth, ashes will be used for protection against inauspicious people, and in the houses where women give birth. And one who has purified his soul by bathing in ashes, conquered his anger, and subdued his senses will come into my presence and never be reborn again. The vow of the lord of cattle, and the yoga of the skull[57] – this vow performed by this yoga is the supreme vow, for it was made first and all the other orders were created afterwards by the self-created one. This creation was created by me and has shame, delusion, and fear as its soul; for the gods and sages are born naked, and all the other men in the world are born without clothing. People with unconquered senses are naked even if they are clothed in silk, for if one is enveloped in unconquered senses no garment can hide him. Patience, forbearance, non-injury, passionlessness, indifference to honour or dishonour – this is one's best garment. Let a man smear his body until it is pale with ashes and meditate upon Bhava in

55. That is, they are fires and drink fire, while the gods are Soma-drinkers.

56. According to Sāṅkhya philosophy, Man is inert spirit until he unites with the active female element, Nature (*prakṛti*), which is composed of the three strands or qualities.

57. A reference to the Kāpālikas or skull-bearers, who wander about holding a human skull in their hands, in imitation of Śiva's act of beheading Brahmā and carrying Brahmā's skull to Benares.

his heart, and then even if he does a thousand things that one ought not to do, by bathing in ashes he will cause all of that to be burnt to ashes as fire burns a forest with its energy. Therefore if anyone makes a great effort always, even throughout the three times, to bathe with ashes, then he becomes a leader of my hosts, receives all sacrifices, and grasps the supreme ambrosia.'

The Vaiṣṇava Version: Bhṛgu Curses Śiva to be Worshipped as a *liṅga*

In the pro-Śaiva versions of the Pine Forest myth, even where it is not clear whether Śiva's *liṅga* falls because of the sages' curse or as part of Śiva's plan, he establishes *liṅga*-worship himself, for the benefit of the sages and to magnify himself. In Vaiṣṇava versions of the myth, however, the *liṅga*-worship itself is a curse inflicted upon Śiva by Bhṛgu, the leader of the Pine Forest sages. This myth is the mirror image of the myth of Dakṣa: both begin with a great sacrificial gathering, but here Śiva becomes deprived of a share of the sacrifice, reduced back from orthodoxy to heterodoxy once more. Śiva and Brahmā receive the same curses which Anasūyā inflicts upon them elsewhere,[58] but Viṣṇu is now the supreme god, and he alone here escapes unscathed, for he allows the brahmin to treat him as contemptuously as the Pine Forest brahmins tried in vain to treat Śiva.

40. FROM THE *Padma Purāṇa*

Once, in the past, Manu the son of the Self-created Prajāpati[59] went to a special, lengthy sacrifice on the highest mountain Mandara, with all the pre-eminent sages of painful vows, sages who knew the various sacred books and had the lustre of the fire of the sun at dawn, brahmins who knew all the Vedas and were devoted to all *dharmas*, whose sins had been worn away. When the great sacrifice was taking place, the

58. See above, myth 12, pp. 54–5.

59. Manu Svāyambhūva, the first Manu, progenitor of mankind in the Kṛta Age.

sages rich in asceticism said to one another, in order to find out the true nature of the divinities, 'Who is the best of the divinities, worthy of being worshipped by brahmins who know the Vedas? Who, among Brahmā, Viṣṇu, and the Great Lord, should be praised as the one who gives release to men? The water left from washing his feet is to be sought; the leavings from his food are purifying; his favour would be a shrine to delight the spirits of the departed ancestors, for he is the undying, the highest abode, the eternal, supreme self.'

A great discussion arose among them as they sat together. Some of the great sages said, 'Rudra is the One'; other eminent sages said, 'Brahmā is to be worshipped.' Other worshippers said, 'The sun should be worshipped by all souls.' And some of the twice-born said, 'The blessed husband of Śrī, the highest Man, who is in everything, undying, whose eyes are like pale lotuses, the son of Vasudeva, beyond the beyond, without birth or death, Viṣṇu is the highest lord, the best of divinities, the one to be worshipped.' As they were disputing, Manu the son of the self-created one said, 'He who is made of pure goodness,[60] the lord endowed with the auspicious quality, with eyes like pale lotuses, the blessed lord of Śrī, the highest Man, he alone is the lord worshipped by brahmins who know the Vedas. The others should not be worshipped by brahmins, for they are tainted with passion and darkness.'

When all the great sages heard his speech, they folded their palms and said to the brahmin Bhṛgu, who was rich in ascetic power, 'You are able to dispel our doubt, for you have kept

60. Viṣṇu is here said to embody all of the third strand or quality, while Brahmā and Śiva are made of passion and darkness. Compare the Śaiva attitude, wherein Śiva embodies all three strands, though his antecedent Agni predominates in the quality of darkness, while Brahmā and Viṣṇu ('forms of Rudra') are still characterized by passion and goodness (see above, myth 39, p. 145), and myth 10, p. 50.

your vow well. Go to Brahmā, Viṣṇu, and the great lord Śiva, and observe their forms to find out in which one the quality of goodness is pure. That one is to be worshipped by brahmins, but never the others; the left-overs from his food are very purifying for gods and ancestors. Therefore, best of sages, go to the dwelling-places of the gods; act quickly for the welfare of all people, O lord.'

When that supreme sage heard this he went quickly on the path of the wind to Kailāsa, to the god whose banner bears a bull. The twice-born one went up to the door of the house of the noble Śaṅkara and said to the fierce Nandin, who held a trident in his hand, 'I am the brahmin Bhṛgu, and I have come to see Hara, the supreme god. Announce me quickly to the noble Śaṅkara.' When Nandin, the lord of all Śiva's hosts, heard his speech, he replied rudely to the great sage whose vitality was immeasurable: 'No one can enter the presence of the lord now, for Śaṅkara is making love to the goddess. Turn back, turn back, sage, if you wish to live.' When Nandin had thus turned him away, the great ascetic remained there for many days at the door of Śaṅkara's house. Then Bhṛgu was filled with anger, and the sage pronounced a curse: 'Śaṅkara, the fool, is immersed in darkness and does not recognize me. Since he is so intoxicated by union with a woman that he dishonours me, therefore he will have the form of the *yoni*[61] and the *liṅga*. He shows contempt for me, a brahmin, for he is overcome by darkness. Since he has behaved in a way unbefitting a brahmin, he is not to be worshipped by the twice-born. Therefore the food, water, flowers, and oblations given to him will all be what is left from offerings to other gods.'

When the sage of great energy had thus cursed Śaṅkara who is worshipped by all people, he said to the servant Nan-

61. The symbol of the female organ of generation, particularly that of the Goddess, worshipped in union with the *liṅga*.

din, who was very cruel and held a trident in his hand, 'Those who are devoted to Rudra in the world, who carry the *liṅga* and wear ashes and bones, they will be heretics beyond the pale of the Vedas.' When Rudra, the Destroyer of the Triple City, heard his speech, he set out to slay Bhṛgu, taking his trident in his hand, for he was immersed in total darkness. But Pārvatī, who had a sense of decorum, restrained the great god, folding her palms together and prostrating herself before him. As Śiva stood there, restrained by Gaurī, Bhṛgu of great energy saw the forehead eye blazing like the fire of ten million suns. But the sage, pointing out that Śiva's eye was looking at his own two feet, laughed and went away, saying, 'My curse is never in vain. You are certainly hideously deformed.' And thenceforth the water that has washed the feet of the Lord of Ghosts is not to be touched by priests, and Śiva in the form of the *liṅga* is to be worshipped only by heretics.

After the sage had thus cursed Rudra, the Destroyer of the Triple City, he went to the world of Brahmā, which is honoured by all people. There the great sage saw Brahmā, the supreme lord, seated with the gods, and the great ascetic folded his palms and bowed to the god and stood in silence before him. When the creator saw that the great sage, the tiger among sages, had arrived, he did not welcome him, for he was immersed in passion; the creator did not rise or make a pleasant speech to him, but he remained there majestically on his lotus seat. When the great sage of great energy saw him sitting on his lotus, full of passion, he spoke thus to the Grandfather of the world: 'Since you who abound in great passion have dishonoured me, therefore you will not be worshipped by anyone.'

When he had thus cursed the noble Brahmā, who had been worshipped by all people, the brahmin Bhṛgu went quickly to the palace of the lord Viṣṇu. And thereafter the Grandfather was not worshipped by gods, men, Rākṣasas or supreme sages. As Bhṛgu entered the world of Viṣṇu on the northern shore of the ocean of milk, he was worshipped as he deserved by the generous ones who dwelt there. Unhindered, the twice-born one entered the inner harem in the spotless palace that shone like the sun. There he saw Viṣṇu, the lord of the lotus goddess Lakṣmī, lying on his serpent couch[62] with his two feet being massaged by the lotus hands of Lakṣmī. When Bhṛgu, the tiger among sages, saw him he was filled with anger, and he stamped with his left foot upon the glorious breast of Viṣṇu. The lord arose quickly and said joyfully, 'I am grateful to you,' and he rejoiced and pressed the sage's foot with his two hands and rubbed his foot gently and spoke these honeyed words: 'I am fortunate today, O brahmin sage; I am fulfilled in every way, for the touch of your foot upon my body will be a blessing. May I be purified by the particles of dust from a brahmin's feet, particles which cause one to obtain all good fortune, fires to burn away whatever misfortunes may arise, bridges over the shoreless ocean of rebirth. Whenever the dust from a brahmin's feet touches one's body, all the shrines of the Ganges and the other rivers surely remain in him forever.'

When Viṣṇu, who excites men, had said this, he arose quickly with the goddess and welcomed him with devotion, with celestial garlands, sandalwood paste, and so forth. When the tiger among sages saw him, his eyes filled with tears of joy; he stood up from his fine seat and bowed to the Treasury of Compassion. Folding his palms together, the great ascetic spoke to him joyfully . . . Bhṛgu then bowed to the god again and again. The great and noble celestial sages honoured Bhṛgu to his soul's delight, and he went back to the place where the sages were gathered at the sacrifice. The great sages arose and bowed to the noble Bhṛgu and offered him worship in various ways. Then the bull among sages reported everything to them:

62. Viṣṇu sleeps on Ananta, the serpent of eternity.

'The creator and the lord, Brahmā and Śiva, the two supreme gods, abound in the qualities of passion and darkness. I cursed them, and they are not to be worshipped by priests, O best of sages. Śaṅkara, who is enveloped in darkness on a peak of Kailāsa, acted in a way unbefitting a brahmin, and so he has assumed a despicable form. But Viṣṇu is made of pure goodness, an ocean of the auspicious quality; Nārāyaṇa is the highest godhead; Hari is the divinity for brahmins. Viṣṇu, the husband of Śrī, the son of Vasudeva, the Exciter of Men, whose eyes are like pale lotuses, Govinda, the unfallen Hari acts as befits a brahmin. He alone, but no other bull among men, is to be worshipped by priests. Anyone so deluded that he worships another god will become a heretic, but by merely thinking of Kṛṣṇa sinners obtain release.'

The Purāṇic myths of Śiva and Pārvatī

Śiva Destroys Kāma and Revives Him

As the great ascetic, Śiva is opposed to Kāma, the god of desire; but as the god of the *liṅga*, Śiva competes with and 'overreaches' Kāma. The complex cycle of Śiva–Kāma myths begins, like so many myths, with a boon foolishly granted by Brahmā to a powerful demon.

41. FROM THE *Saura Purāṇa*

The demon Tāraka was born in the family of demons; he was a thorn in the world, a hero who was the very form of death for those who dwell in heaven. He propitiated Brahmā by means of his asceticism and obtained a boon from him; then Tāraka put the gods to flight, for he was more powerful than they, and he forcibly carried off the wives of the gods. Śakra and the other gods, so famous for their vitality, were heated by the fire of misery, and they sought refuge with Brahmā, the lord of the thirty-three gods. When the lotus-born god saw that the gods had arrived, he said, 'What are you frightened of, gods, to make you come here to me? Tell me all about it, and I will find a means of helping you.' The gods replied, 'Because we are as terrified of Tāraka as we are terrified of death, we have come to seek refuge with the god; therefore you should protect us, for we cannot find contentment even for a moment, O god, best of gods. For thirty thousand years, day and night, without respite, there has been a fierce battle between Hari and Tāraka, but the god of gods, armed with his discus, has not conquered Tāraka. Knowing that he cannot be killed, the mighty Viṣṇu, armed with his bow, has abandoned the fight and gone quickly to the great ocean, confused and worried. Therefore we are frightened and have come to you for refuge, lord; protect us; grant us comfort, lotus-born one.'

Brahmā said, 'Listen to my words, which will bring you all great comfort, immortals. This proud Tāraka practised supreme asceticism, and when I saw that the universe moving and still was being burnt by the ascetic heat of that demon, I went to Tāraka to grant him a boon. "My child," I said, "choose a boon," and the great demon, king of the demons, folded his palms and bowed to me and said, "Lotus-born one, grant me the boon that I may not be slain by any of the gods, Viṣṇu and the others." I granted him that boon, but then I added, for the sake of your welfare, supreme gods, "Tell me, by whom may you be slain?" Tāraka answered, "My death will come from one born when the gods, including Viṣṇu, become pregnant by drinking the seed of the god above all gods, the god with braided hair, the blue and red one; but not otherwise." I agreed to this and went to the top of Meru. Therefore seek refuge with him who is a refuge to all embodied creatures, the lord of all, the lover of Umā, Śaṅkara who gives peace to all people. Except for Hara, I see no god in the triple world, moving and still, who could kill Tāraka, O gods.'

When he heard the speech of Brahmā, the thousand-eyed lord of Śacī wondered how this could come about, and the king of the gods, together with the divinities and their guru, determined to think of a way to bring about the birth of a son of Hara. Then the gods went with Śakra and Brahmā to a peak on the tip of Meru where Mādhava[63] was hiding, for though his soul was immeasurable he was tortured by fear of Tāraka. When Mādhava saw the gods and Brahmā he was delighted, and he said, 'What means has been devised for the slaughter of Tāraka? If there is any, tell me, gods, so that we may have shelter and comfort.' When they heard the speech of Viṣṇu, Brahmā and the rest of the supreme gods told Viṣṇu what Brahmā had told them. Then the king of the gods considered what was to be done now, and he remembered Kāma, who could not be conquered by gods or demons. When Kāma, the husband of Rati, knew that Śakra had thought of him, he took up his flower-bow, went to the husband of Śacī, and said, 'What duty is there for me to perform, O best of the thirty-three gods? Who threatens your position with his keen asceticism? Or what woman does not wish to obey your command? I will make her full of desire, intent upon thoughts of you, this very day. There is no hero, no proud woman, no learned man too powerful for me. I pervade the whole universe, moving and still, beginning with Brahmā the Creator. But what need is there to say more? Even the great sage Durvāsas[64] would fall quickly when pierced by my arrows, O lord of the Maruts.'

'Lord of Rati,' said Indra, 'I know what you are capable of with your flower-bow. All things that are to be done are accomplished by you, and not otherwise. Go to the great lord Śiva, if you wish to do what is for the welfare of the gods;

63. A name of Viṣṇu, 'Descendant of Madhu' or 'Vernal'.

64. There is irony in this boast, for the irascible Durvāsas is an incarnation of Śiva – whom Kāma is about to attack in vain.

shake the mind of Hara and make him unite with Pārvatī. This is what must be done for me; this is my wish. For this reason I thought of you who bear the flower-bow.' When he heard what Śakra had said, the powerful god who is born in the heart, who has the crocodile on his banner, the god with five arrows, went with Rati and his friend Spring to the place where the lord Śambhu, the great lord, was concentrating with the gaze of trance, motionless, meditating upon the self within himself.

As he reached the abode of Śambhu, the god who has the crocodile on his banner saw Śailādi[65] at the door, standing as high as a peak of Meru, adorned with all ornaments, glowing like a thousand suns, holding a trident in his hand, three-eyed, adorned with a sliver of the moon, a thunderbolt in his hand, four-armed, like a second Śaṅkara. When Madana[66] saw him, he was filled with anxiety: 'How shall I be able to enter and wax strong inside Śambhu who is venerated by the thirty-three gods? How will I do what must be done to increase the pleasure of the gods?' As he was thinking of various ways to deceive Nandin, he took the form of a fragrant breeze, gentle and cool. Then Kāma entered from the southern direction; and for this reason, even today the breeze from the region of Yama, the south, is pleasant, fragrant, gentle and cool.

There Madana saw the lord, like ten million suns, with a thousand eyes and a thousand bodies, the tall god with a blue neck, shining like ambrosia, adorned with a shining crescent moon, shining like pure crystal, like a smokeless fire, the god whose favour is the cause of the birth, destruction, and maintenance of the universe ... When the god who bears the crocodile on his banner saw the great god, he rejoiced and

65. A name of Nandin, guardian of Śiva's door. See below, myth 68, pp. 254–61.

66. 'The Maddener', a name of Kāma.

stretched his bow and stood ready, watching the god who is the source of all existence; thus Kāma, who is born in the mind, stood for sixty million years. Then the lord god Śaṅkara, Śiva, the lord of all, who puts an end to the god of the flower-arrows, opened his two eyes and saw the goddess, the daughter of the mountain, shyly engaged in asceticism before him. A suspicion arose within him as he saw her, and he wondered, 'What is going on here?' Then Śarva decided, 'Kāma is here,' and when he realized this he looked about and saw him with his bow drawn, and Madana was burnt by the fire from his eye.

When the husband of Rati had been burnt, Śambhu said to the daughter of the mountain, 'What can I do for you, empress of the gods? What is in your heart? Tell me what boon you wish, great goddess, empress of the gods, and I will grant it today. Mistress of the gods, what is there that you cannot obtain when I am pleased?' 'Blue-necked god,' answered Pārvatī, 'now that Kāma has been killed, what can I do with a boon from you today? For without Kāma there can be between a man and a woman no emotion which is like ten million suns. When emotion is destroyed, how could happiness be attained? Tell me, you who are to be honoured by the lord of gods.'

Then he who had put an end to Madana replied, 'Lady with beautiful eyes, I did not burn Madana, but this very form of my eye which has fire as its essence burnt him by itself. Now tell me, what can I do?' 'Bhava, lord of ghosts,' said the goddess, 'you who are not to be blamed or excluded, why are you embarrassed when you think, "This is a girl!" Since you are under no one's control, then burn me too as I stand before you. You are the god Hara, Śiva, ruler of all the gods, Brahmā and the others. If you are determined to carry out a deception, who is capable of preventing you? But you should not deceive me, O lord god, for I have come to you for refuge, and

I have no one else to go to for shelter, and so you should protect me. You are the eye of the universe; you are the lord of worlds. You create the universe and put it in order; you face in all directions . . .'

Then Hara, the Destroyer of the Triple City, was propitiated, and he said to the goddess Kālī,[67] 'Choose a boon and I will grant it, goddess, for you have kept your vow well.' 'Great god,' replied the goddess, 'let Kāma live and heat the world. My lord, without Kāma I do not request anything at all.' The lord answered, 'Let Madana be without a body in order to please you, lady with beautiful eyes. In that form he will be able to shake the world.' And because of what Hara said when Umā urged him, the god with the crocodile banner arose in a disembodied form, impossible to delimit, going here and there like the wind with his bow and arrow, accompanied by Rati. Thus the great lord Hara himself happily gave a boon to Smara,[68] the god of five arrows, and then he vanished. Whoever reads this chapter with devotion, is released from all sins and grows great in the world of Brahmā, in the presence of the lord.

Śiva Engenders the Submarine Mare

In the myth of Śiva, Kāma, Pārvatī and Skanda, the episode of the submarine mare appears to be superfluous and digressive in terms of plot; most variants of the Skanda myth omit it entirely, while many other tales are told to explain the birth of the submarine mare. But the symbolism of the mare reveals an essential tie with the Skanda myth, for the fiery mare is placed in a delicate balance deep within the ocean, where her flames harmlessly devour the waters, holding in

67. The Black Goddess (or goddess of doomsday). See below, myth 68, p. 259.

68. 'Memory', an epithet of Kāma. His five arrows are made of the sun lotus, the *aśoka* flower, the mango, jasmine, and blue lotus, and they cause infatuation, excitement, parching or withering, heating, and paralysis (or stiffening).

check both their floods and her own destructive flame, until, at doomsday, she is released; like Śiva's seed in the Ganges, the mare is the immortal fire that – unlike common flames – is unquenched by waters and, on the contrary, burns them.

42. FROM THE *Śiva Purāṇa*

When the fire from the third eye of Śambhu had burnt Kāma to ashes, it blazed forth everywhere fruitlessly. A great cry of woe arose in the triple world, moving and still, and all the celestial sages ran quickly for refuge with Brahmā. Deeply upset, they all narrated their misery to Brahmā, and they folded their palms together and bent their heads and bowed low to him and praised him. When Brahmā heard this he pondered over the cause and, remembering Śiva, he went to him humbly in order to protect the three worlds. The fire which had burnt Kāma shone forth with a halo of flames, but it was paralysed by Brahmā who had obtained great energy by the grace of Śambhu. Then Brahmā took that fire of anger which wished to burn the triple universe, and he put it inside a mare with ambrosial[69] flames in her mouth. And then, by the wish of Śiva and for the sake of the world, Brahmā, the lord of universes, took that fire in the body of a mare to the ocean. When the ocean saw that Brahmā had come, he assumed the form of a man, folded his palms, and approached Brahmā. The ocean bowed low to the Grandfather of all people, praised him as was fitting, and said with pleasure, 'Why have you come here, Brahmā, lord of all? Command me freely, knowing that I am your servant.'

When Brahmā heard the words of the ocean spoken so gladly, he remembered Śaṅkara and spoke for the benefit of the world, saying, 'Wise one, you who bring about the welfare of the whole world, great ocean, listen and I will gladly

69. *Saumya* here could mean either 'gentle' or actually made of ambrosia.

tell you, for I am urged by Śiva's wish in my heart. This great power that has become a mare is the anger of the great lord, which, having burnt Kāma, desire, quickly became desirous of burning everything. At the wish of Śaṅkara and the importunity of the suffering gods, who came quickly to me, I paralysed the fire, gave it the form of a mare, and brought it here to show it to you, to beg you to show pity, O bearer of waters, lord of rivers. This anger of the great lord in the form of a mare with flames in her mouth must be held by you until the final flood, when I will come and dwell here and you will release this marvellous anger born of Śaṅkara. Your water will be its constant food, and you must control it with great care so that it does not reach inside you.'[70]

The ocean made a firm promise to Brahmā to hold the fierce mare-fire which could not be held by anyone else. Then the fire with the body of a mare entered the ocean, shining with its halo of flames, thoroughly burning the floods of water. Brahmā went home, satisfied in his mind, and the ocean in its celestial form bowed to Brahmā and vanished. All the universe became safe, freed by Bhava from that danger, and the gods and sages became content.

Śiva Engenders Skanda

In some versions of the myth of the mare, Brahmā seeks in vain the assistance of several rivers before he finds one that will agree to carry the fire to the ocean; in the same way, the burning seed of Śiva is handed on from one agent to another (all of them regarded as the 'parents' of Skanda) until it finds its final rest in the Ganges – and even then it is cast out once more, now in the form of the infant Skanda, to find its final elixir in the milk from the breasts of the Goddess.

In the myth of Skanda's birth, the gods and Agni interrupt the love-play of Śiva and Pārvatī just as Bhṛgu attempts to do and the

70. That is, so that it does not devour all the water and get loose again.

Pine Forest sages do in many variants of the myth; this interruption is necessary because, although the gods have gone to great pains to cause Śiva to marry – enlisting the aid of Kāma, begging Śiva to revive Kāma, sending the Seven Sages[71] to ask Himālaya for Pārvatī on Śiva's behalf – nevertheless, when Śiva does marry, his violent erotic activity causes new problems for the gods.

43. FROM THE *Śiva Purāṇa*

The earth with its serpent and tortoise[72] trembled, oppressed by the weight of the excessive amorous play of the two powerful deities, the god with his *śakti*. Because of the burden of the tortoise, the very air which supports everything was compressed solid, and the three worlds were agitated with fear. Then all the gods went with Brahmā to take refuge in Hari, and, dejected at heart, they reported everything that had happened: 'God of gods, husband of Lakṣmī, lord, saviour of everyone, protect us; we have come to you for refuge, for our minds are disturbed by fear. The breath of the triple world is compressed solid, and we do not know the cause; the triple world, moving and still, with all the sages and gods, is agitated.' Brahmā and all the gods then stood there before Viṣṇu, dejected, silent, and miserable, and when Hari heard this, he took all the gods quickly to Mount Kailāsa, the place dear to Śiva.

Hari, who is dear to the gods, came there with the gods and went to Śiva's favourite place, for he wished to see Śaṅkara. But when Viṣṇu failed to see Śiva there, he and the gods were surprised, and with great courtesy he asked the hosts of Śiva who were standing there, 'Servants of Śaṅkara the lord of all, where has Śiva gone? Be merciful and tell us kindly, for we are so unhappy.' Then the hosts of Śaṅkara said kindly to the

71. Compare their role in the other version of Skanda's birth, above, myth 33, pp. 108–12.

72. The earth is said to rest upon a great tortoise; this became one of the avatars of Viṣṇu. See below, myth 72, p. 275.

husband of Lakṣmī, 'Hari, if you and Brahmā and the ageless ones listen with love for Śiva, we will tell you accurately all that has happened. The great lord Śiva, the lord of all, has gone into the dwelling place of Pārvatī, the daughter of the mountain, after stationing us here; he is an expert in various forms of love-play. We do not know what the great lord Śambhu is doing in the inner apartments of her house, but many years have passed, O husband of Lakṣmī.'

When Viṣṇu and Brahmā and the immortals heard their speech they were most amazed, and they went to Śiva's door. Hari, who is dear to the gods, went there with the gods and Brahmā, and he spoke in a shrill, pained, frenzied voice; with great emotion Hari stood there with Brahmā and the gods and praised Śiva, Hara, the lord of all people: 'Great god, supreme lord, what are you doing inside there? All of us, the gods, have come to you for refuge, for we are tortured by Tāraka; protect us.' Thus Hari and Brahmā and the gods who were tortured by Tāraka praised Śambhu in many ways, and Hari wept copiously. A dismal uproar arose among the dwellers in heaven who were tortured by the demon, a moan which mingled with the sound of their praise of Śiva.

When the great god, expert in the knowledge of yoga, heard this, he lost his desire but still he did not cease his erotic play, for he was afraid of Pārvatī. Finally, after some time, Śiva came to the door of his house where the gods awaited, oppressed by the demon, for Śaṅkara is full of affection toward his devotees. When all the ageless gods saw the lord Śiva full of affection toward his devotees, they became extremely happy and bowed down and bent their shoulders and praised Śaṅkara with great emotion, saying, 'God of gods, great god, ocean of mercy, lord, you move within all creatures; Śaṅkara, you know everything. Do what must be done for the gods, O lord; protect the gods, great lord. Kill the demons, Tāraka and the others, and have pity on us.'

When the lord Bhava heard their words he was saddened, and he replied with a sorrowful heart, 'Viṣṇu, Brahmā, gods, my heart is the refuge for all of you. What will be comes to be, and no one can prevent it; what has been, has been. Now, immortals, listen to the matter at hand: who will now take my seed, the semen of Śiva, that has been shed? Let him take it.' And as he said this, he caused it to fall upon the ground. Then Agni, urged by all the ageless ones, became a dove and with his beak he ate all the seed of Śambhu.

At this moment the daughter of the mountain came there, when Śiva delayed in returning, and she saw them who were like bulls among the gods, and she knew all that had happened. Then Śivā[73] was filled with great anger, and she said to Hari and all the other thirty-three gods, 'All of you bands of gods are wicked, particularly eager to accomplish your own ends always, so that you cause great misery to others. For the sake of your own purposes you gods propitiated the highest lord, the great lord, and ruined my erotic pleasure, and so I have become barren. But no one, not even the ageless ones, can be happy after opposing me, and therefore you wicked ones who dwell in the triple heaven will become miserable.' When she had said this, Śivā the daughter of the king of mountains blazed forth with anger and cursed Viṣṇu and all the gods: 'From today forth, let all the wives of the gods be barren, and let all the gods who opposed me be miserable.'

Thus having cursed Viṣṇu and all the gods, the empress of everything spoke in fury to the Purifier, who had eaten the seed of Śiva: 'Fire, you will be omnivorous, constantly tortured in your soul. You do not know the true nature of Śiva; you are a fool, doing what the gods need to have done. You wicked wretch, who obey the foul counsel of the wicked, you should not have eaten the seed of Śiva, as it was neither proper nor beneficial.' When Śivā the daughter of the king of

73. Śivā, the wife of Śiva, is an epithet of Pārvatī.

mountains had thus cursed Fire, she went quickly to her own dwelling-place, unsatisfied. Śivā went to Śiva and reported to him accurately, and then she brought forth another son named Gaṇeśa. (I will tell that story, omitting nothing,[74] but first hear now as I gladly tell you about the birth of Guha.)

The ageless gods eat food and other offerings whenever these are placed in the Purifier according to Vedic custom; in this way, the seed made all the gods pregnant. The gods were painfully afflicted by that unbearable seed, and, moreover, Viṣṇu and all the others had lost their wits by the command of Śivā. Then all the gods, including Viṣṇu, were embarrassed and burnt, and they sought refuge immediately with the husband of Pārvatī. They all went to the door of Śiva's house and folded their palms together and bowed and warmly praised Śambhu and Śivā, saying, 'God of gods, lord, great god, lord of the daughter of the mountain, great ruler, what has happened now? Your magic power of illusion is impossible to fathom. We have become pregnant, and we are being burnt by your seed. Have pity, Śambhu; undo this condition.'

When the highest lord, husband of Śivā, heard this eulogy by the immortals, he went quickly to the door where the gods stood. Then all of the gods, including the unfallen Viṣṇu, bowed to Śaṅkara who had come to the door; they bent low and warmly praised the god who is affectionate to his devotees: 'Śambhu, Śiva, great lord, we bow particularly to you. Protect us who have come to you for refuge and who are burning with your seed. Hara, remove [*hara*] this misery, for we will certainly die otherwise. Who but you can remove this misery from the gods today?' When the lord, king of the gods, heard this rather miserable speech, he laughed, but as he was affectionate to his devotees he replied to the gods, 'Hari, Brahmā, and all you gods, listen to my speech. You will be relieved today, but you must attend carefully. All the

74. See below, myth 69, pp. 262–9.

gods must quickly vomit up my seed, and then, by my command, you will be content in this particular matter.'

Viṣṇu and all the other gods accepted this command, bowing their heads, and they quickly vomited, thinking of the unchanging Śiva. That shining golden seed of Śambhu fell upon the ground in the form of a marvellous mountain, touching the very sky. Then all the gods, including the unfallen Viṣṇu, were relieved, and they praised Śaṅkara, the highest lord, who is affectionate to his devotees.

But the Purifier was not content, for Śaṅkara, the supreme lord, had given him a command and injured him. Therefore Agni folded his palms together and bowed and praised Śiva, for his soul was not content, and he said: 'God of gods, great lord, I am your foolish servant. Master, forgive my offence and remove this feverish burning, for you are affectionate to the lowly.' Then Śambhu, the supreme lord, who is affectionate toward the lowly, was propitiated, and he replied to the Purifier, 'You committed an improper act when you ate my seed; therefore by my command the feverish burning has fallen upon you because of your surpassing sin. But now that you have come to me for refuge you will be relieved, Agni. I am pleased and will destroy all your misery. Leave that seed carefully in the womb of some good woman and you will be relieved, for, in particular, your soul will be free of the feverish burning.'

When Fire heard Śambhu's speech, he folded his palms together, bowed, and replied happily and gently to Śaṅkara who gives peace [*śaṅkara*] to his devotees, 'Your seed[75] is hard to bear, great lord and ruler. No woman in the three universes is capable of holding it in her womb, except Śakti.' When Fire spoke in this way, Nārada was prompted by Śaṅkara to help Agni, and he said, 'Agni, listen to my auspicious words which will remove your feverish burning, delight you, bring

75. Or energy (*tejas*).

you supreme bliss, and dispel all your sins. By using this expedient, your fire will be content and without any feverish burning. I will tell you this carefully and accurately as Śiva wishes: Fire, place this great seed of Śiva in the bodies of those women who bathe at dawn in the month of summer.'

Now, at this time the wives of the Seven Sages came there wishing to bathe at dawn in the month of summer, in accordance with their rites. When they had bathed, six of the women were pained by the intense cold, and they wished to go near the flames of the fire. Arundhatī, seeing them behaving so stupidly, tried to prevent them, by the command of the lord of the mountain, for she was of particularly good conduct and good counsel. But the six wives of the sages were so deluded by Śiva's magic power of illusion that they went there against her will in order to dispel their chill. All the tiny particles of his seed immediately entered their bodies through their hair follicles, and Agni was free of his feverish burning. Then Fire quickly vanished in the form of a flame and went happily back to his own world, thinking in his heart of Śaṅkara and Brahmā. All of the women but Arundhatī became pregnant and they went home, tortured by the feverish burning and suffering because of Agni. When the husbands saw the condition of their wives, they were quickly overcome by anger, and they all took counsel together and abandoned their wives. When all the six women realized their transgression, they were afflicted with great misery and their hearts were deeply troubled. The sages' wives left the seed of Śiva in the form of an embryo on a peak of Himālaya, and then they were free of the feverish burning.

But the mountain Himālaya could not bear that seed of Śiva; trembling and tortured by the feverish burning, he threw that unbearable seed into the Ganges. Even the Ganges could not bear that seed of the highest soul, and she threw it on her waves into a clump of reeds. When the seed fell there it immediately became a boy, handsome, well-endowed, blessed, full of energy, and a source of growing pleasure. On the sixth lunar day in the bright half of the month when the moon is in the constellation Deer's Head,[76] the son of Śiva appeared on the surface of the earth. At that moment, Pārvatī the daughter of the mountain Himālaya and Śiva the lord of the mountain became happy for no apparent reason, on their own mountain. Then milk flowed from the breasts of Śivā because of her joy, and everyone went there and became very happy. An auspicious event took place throughout the three worlds bringing happiness to the good and obstacles to the wicked, particularly to the demons. A great sound of drums was heard in the sky with no apparent cause, and a rain of flowers fell upon the little boy. Supreme joy came to Viṣṇu and all the gods, as if by a miracle, and there was great jubilation.

Śiva Fights Andhaka for Pārvatī

Skanda and Gaṇeśa[77] are sons of Śiva whose birth is desired by some of the gods but feared by others (notably Indra). This ambivalence is even more marked toward other sons of Śiva who actually become demons, enemies of the gods. Of all of these sons, Gaṇeśa alone is physically connected with Pārvatī (though even he is not born from her in the 'natural' manner); Jalandhara and Andhaka are demons engendered by the fire of Śiva's third eye (like the mare) and are thus only 'adopted' by Pārvatī (as Skanda is). Both demons seek, unsuccessfully, to win Pārvatī from Śiva, just as Gaṇeśa sometimes competes with Śiva for Pārvatī. In the myth of Jalandhara, this ambiguous relationship between Pārvatī and her 'son' is slurred over, but in the myth of Andhaka it is clearly emphasized. These myths, in which Śiva opposes an incestuous relationship between mother and 'son' by injuring his own 'son', may also be seen as inversions of the myth of Rudra and Prajāpati, in which Rudra opposes an incestuous

76. See above, myth 3, pp. 29–30.
77. See above, myth 33, pp. 105–15, and below, myth 69, pp. 262–9.

relationship between father and daughter by injuring his own father.[78]

Śiva engenders Andhaka

44. FROM THE *Śiva Purāṇa, Dharmasaṃhitā*

Once in the past, on Mount Mandara, Pārvatī closed the eyes of the god with braided hair, the god of fierce attack, and she did it in play, as a jest, closing his eyes with her two lotus hands that shone like newly sprouted coral and golden lotuses. When Hara's three eyes were shut, total darkness fell in a moment.[79] But from the touch of her hand, the great lord shed the liquid of passion. A drop of that copious water came forth and splashed on Śambhu's forehead, and it was heated.[80] It became an infant who terrified even Gaṇeśa, the elephant-headed god, ungrateful and full of anger, strange, deformed, disfigured, a dark, hairy man with matted locks and a beard. He sang and laughed and wept and danced; his tongue flickered and he roared fiercely and deeply. When this creature of marvellous aspect was born, Bhava smiled and said to Gaurī,[81] 'You closed my eyes as a jest; how can you be afraid of me, my darling?' When Gaurī heard what Hara had said, she laughed and released his three eyes, and light arose, but because the hideous creature had been born in darkness he had no eyes.

She asked, 'My lord, who is this deformed creature? Look at him, such as he is, and tell me truly: for what purpose was he created, and by whom, and whose son is he?' When Hara heard the words of his beloved, he replied, 'This child whose

78. See above, myths 3–6, pp. 29–35, and 34, pp. 117–18.

79. The commentator notes that darkness falls because Śiva's eyes are the moon, the sun, and fire.

80. The commentator points out that the drop is a drop of sweat, and that it is heated by the fire of the third eye in Śiva's forehead.

81. 'The golden one', an epithet of Pārvatī. See below, myth 68, pp. 252–9.

heroic power is marvellous and fierce was born when you closed my eyes; he was born of sweat and is named Andhaka ('Blind'). Therefore I am his maker, as is fitting, and you and your girl-friends must tenderly protect him from the other troops of Śiva for one half year; and you must consider intelligently and carefully how to do this, good lady.' Then Gaurī was filled with pity, and with her friends she protected her son by various methods and many means.

At the same time that Andhaka appeared on earth, Hiraṇyanetra ('Golden-eye'), the son of Kaśyapa, desired a son, and he went to the forest and practised asceticism for the sake of a son. He conquered the flaw of anger and remained motionless as a piece of wood, in order that the great lord Śiva should appear to him. Then the god who wields the Pināka bow was satisfied with his asceticism and went to give him a boon, and said to him whose senses were unmoved, 'For what purpose have you undertaken this vow? Tell me what you desire. I am Bhava, the Giver of Boons, and I will give you all that you wish.' 'God with the moon on your forehead,' replied the demon, 'since I have no heroic son worthy of the dynasty of demons, I have undertaken this vow. Lord of gods, give me a heroic son. My brother[82] has five sons of infinite heroism, Prahlāda and the others, but I have not, and so I have no descendants, no son to adorn my kingdom, to steal the kingdom of another by his own might and enjoy it or the kingdom allotted properly to him by his own father. He would be called my son, and the man who had such a son in this world would be a father. Wise men supreme among those who know *dharma* have said that those who have sons find an abode above, and for this reason all creatures are compelled by their very natures to act at the fertile season. But as there

82. Hiraṇyakaśipu, 'Golden-garments', twin brother of Hiraṇyākṣa, who persecuted his son Prahlāda for worshipping Viṣṇu; Viṣṇu then assumed his Man-lion incarnation and killed Hiraṇyakaśipu.

are no worlds for a man who is without descendants, they wish for sons in great abundance. There are eight kinds of son, bought and so forth;[83] and of these, I wish for one single son.'

When Bhava heard this speech he was full of pity, and as he was satisfied with the king of demons he said to him, 'Overlord of demons, there is no son fated to be born of your seed, but I will give you a son born of myself, named Andhaka; his heroic power is equal to yours, for he can be conquered by no enemy. Choose this son and lose all your misery; accept him, as he is your own happiness.' Then Hara, the noble overlord of the ghosts, the hideous one, enemy of the triple city, gave a son to Hiraṇyanetra, for he and Gaurī were pleased to grant his wish. When the noble demon had received the son from Hara, he walked around Rudra in reverence and worshipped him with various hymns of praise and then, exulting, he went to his own kingdom.

Śiva kills and transfigures Andhaka

The motif of the eye is central to the myth of Andhaka; just as he is born of Śiva's eye, and born blind, and given to a demon named Golden-eye, even so he is destroyed by Śiva's eye and finally purified and reborn through it.

45. FROM THE *Kūrma Purāṇa*

When he went to the Pine Forest, Śiva placed the goddess Pārvatī in the care of Nārāyaṇa, and he established as guards

83. Manu (9.158–160) enumerates twelve kinds of sons, only the first six kinsmen and legitimate heirs: the legitimate son of the body, the son begotten on a wife, the son adopted, the son made, the son secretly born, and the son cast off; the son of an unmarried girl, the son begotten on a remarried woman, the son of a servant woman, the son received with the wife (that is, born of a woman already pregnant at her marriage), the son bought, and the son who gives himself. The commentator on this myth considers the last three and the adopted son to be subsumed under one heading and disregarded as 'given' rather than 'begotten'.

Nandin, the joy of the family, and all the hosts and gods led by Indra. When the great god had set out, Viṣṇu, who is himself the form of everything, took the form of a woman and served the great empress, while Brahmā, the Oblation-eater, Śakra, Yama, and the others who were like bulls among the gods served the great goddess by assuming graceful female forms. The blessed lord Nandin, the overlord of hosts, who is especially dear to Śambhu, stood at the door as before.

At this time, an evil-minded demon named Andhaka, tortured and blinded by lust, came to Mount Mandara in order to carry off the goddess, daughter of the mountain . . . Then the lord, the Rudra of the doomsday fire, the refuge of the good, took Andhaka and placed him on the tip of his trident and began to dance . . . When Andhaka was fixed on the tip of the trident, all his sins were burnt away, and he obtained perfect knowledge and praised the highest lord . . . The highest lord was pleased with this praise and took Andhaka down from the tip of his trident and touched him with his two hands and said, 'Your praise has thoroughly pleased me, demon. You will become a leader of my hosts and dwell with me as a follower of the lord Nandin, honoured even by the gods, free from disease or misery, and all your doubts will be dispelled.' As soon as the god of gods had said this, the gods saw that the great demon Andhaka had become a leader of hosts in the presence of the god, shining like a thousand suns, three-eyed, bearing the moon, blue-necked, with matted locks, carrying a trident, with an enormous body . . .

Then Hara took the son of Hiraṇyalocana[84] by the hand and went to the place where the daughter of the mountain, the darling of the lord, was waiting. She saw her husband arrive to dispel the pain of her heart, and she received Andhaka pleasantly and graciously. When Andhaka saw the great empress at the side of the god, he prostrated himself on the

84. 'Golden-eye', another name of Hiraṇyākṣa.

ground and bowed to her lotus feet and praised her . . . The blessed goddess was pleased with the lord of demons as he praised her, bent low in devotion, and she accepted Andhaka as her own son.

The sage Maṅkaṇaka dances for Śiva

Śiva is the lord of the dance (Naṭarāja); he dances the dance of death (the Tāṇḍava) when he impales Andhaka, and he dances erotically in the Pine Forest. In the myth of Maṅkaṇaka, these two dances confront one another; the mortal ascetic uses his magic to transmute blood to plant sap, and he dances in erotic joy, disturbing the world just as Śiva does when he 'dances' with Pārvatī; but then Śiva uses his own far greater ascetic power to change blood to ashes[85] – the symbol of the seed of life transfixed in death.

46. FROM THE *Vāmana Purāṇa*

The twice-born sage Maṅkaṇaka, the mind-born son of Kaśyapa, set out to bathe in his bark garment, and the celestial nymphs, Rambhā and the others, who were pleasing to look upon, shining, affectionate, and flawless, bathed there with him. Then the sage, whose ascetic power was great, became excited and shed his seed in the water; he collected that seed in a pot, where it became divided into seven parts, from which were born seven sages who are known as the bands of the Maruts: Wind-speed, Wind-force, Wind-destroyer, Wind-circle, Wind-flame, Wind-seed, and Wind-disc, whose heroic power is great. These seven sons of the seer support the universe, moving and still.

Once, long ago, the Siddha Maṅkaṇaka was wounded in the hand by the tip of a blade of *kuśa* grass, and plant sap flowed from that wound – so I have heard. When he saw the plant sap, he was filled with joy, and he started to dance; and

85. See above, myth 43, p. 162, for the dance, and myth 39, pp. 147–9, for the symbolism of ashes.

then everything that was moving or still started to dance; the universe started to dance, for it was bewitched by his energy. When Brahmā and the other gods and the sages rich in ascetic power saw this, they reported to the great god Śiva about the sage: 'You should do something so that he does not dance, O god.' When the Great God saw that the sage was filled with joy to excess, he spoke to him for the sake of the welfare of the gods, saying, 'Best of twice-born sages, what is the reason that has occasioned this joy in you who are an ascetic stationed on the path of *dharma*?' 'Why, brahmin,' said the sage, 'do you not see the plant sap flowing from my hand? When I saw it I began to dance with joy.'

The god laughed at the sage who was deluded by passion, and he said to him, 'I am not amazed, priest. Look at this,' and when Bhava, the god of gods, of great lustre, had said this to the eminent sage, he struck his own thumb with the tip of his finger, and from that wound ashes shining like snow came forth. When the priest saw this he was ashamed, and he fell at Śiva's feet and said, 'I think that you are none other than the noble god who holds the trident in his hand, the best in the universe moving and still, the Trident-bearer. Brahmā and the other gods appear to be dependent upon you, faultless one. You are the first of the gods, the great one who acts and causes others to act. By your grace all the gods rejoice and fear nothing.' When the sage had thus praised the great god, he bowed and said, 'O lord, by your favour let my ascetic power not be destroyed.' Then the god was pleased, and he answered the sage, 'Your ascetic power will increase a thousand-fold by my favour, O priest, and I will dwell in this hermitage with you for ever. Any man who bathes in the Saptasārasvata and worships me will find nothing impossible to obtain in this world and in the other world, but he will certainly go to the Sārasvata world and, by the grace of Śiva, he will obtain the highest place.'

5

VIṢṆU

ALTHOUGH only a small proportion of the mythology of Viṣṇu can be traced back to the *Ṛg Veda* – hardly any more than that of Śiva – Viṣṇu is a far more straightforward, orthodox god; those elements of proto-Indian worship which were assimilated to his cult are generally more benevolent, human, and conventional that those of Śiva. Of his many avatars or incarnations[1], only three – Kṛṣṇa, the Buddha and Kalkin – bring moral or physical destruction to mankind, and even these are designed ultimately to bring about our well-being.

The Vedic avatar of Viṣṇu: the dwarf

VIṢṆU TAKES THREE STRIDES

By far the most important Vedic myth of Viṣṇu is the story of his three steps, a creation myth based upon the Vedic concept that to measure out, to spread, and to prop apart the elements of the universe is to create. The magic number three, which is woven into almost all of Hindu cosmology, appears here in Viṣṇu's three *padas*:

1. Viṣṇu is generally said to have had ten incarnations: the fish (myth 51, pp. 181–4), the tortoise (myth 72, p. 275), the boar (myth 54, pp. 186–7), the Man-lion (myth 55, p. 195), the dwarf (myth 48, pp. 177–8), Rāma (myth 56, pp. 198–204), Kṛṣṇa (myth 57, pp. 206–13), the Buddha (myth 62, pp. 232–5), and Kalkin (myth 63, pp. 236–7), as well as Paraśurāma ('Rāma with the axe'), the son of Jamadagni, who beheaded his unchaste mother and killed all the Kṣatriyas.

this word (cognate with other Indo-European words such as foot in English and *pes*, *pedis* in Latin) has many meanings which lend secondary overtones or resonances to this myth; besides 'step', *pada* denotes (primarily) foot, and it is significant that Viṣṇu's feet are the object of worship; *pada* may also be translated 'footprint', and the footprint of Viṣṇu (also the object of worship)[2] leads the worshipper to cattle just as Saramā's footprint led Indra to the cattle of the Paṇis; and, lastly, it may signify 'dwelling-place', the highest of the three *padas* being Viṣṇu's heaven.

47. FROM THE *Ṛg Veda*

I will proclaim the heroic deeds of Viṣṇu, who measured apart the earthly realms, who propped up the upper dwelling place, when the wide-striding one stepped forth three times. Viṣṇu is praised for his heroic deed, he who stayed in the mountain wandering cruelly like a wild beast. All creatures dwell in his three wide steps. Let the resounding prayer go forth to Viṣṇu who lives in the mountains, the wide-striding one, the bull who alone measured apart with three steps this far extended dwelling-place. His three footprints, inexhaustibly full of honey, intoxicate with their own power; he alone has supported three-fold the earth, and the sky, and all creatures. Would that I might reach his dear dwelling place, where men who love the gods become intoxicated; there one is joined with the wide-strider, Viṣṇu, in his highest place, the fountain of honey. We wish to go to the dwelling-places of both of you, Viṣṇu and Indra, where there are untiring, many-horned cattle. There the highest place of the wide-striding bull brightly shines down.

Viṣṇu Becomes a Dwarf

The Brāhmaṇas incorporated the myth of Viṣṇu's strides into the corpus of myths dealing with gods and demons. Motifs from other

2. See above, myth 12, pp. 54–5, for the worship of Viṣṇu's feet, and below, myth 60, pp. 224–5, for the footprint.

Vedic cycles are used to embellish the myth: hiding from the gods (in the roots of plants, where Indra and Agni hide)[3] and obtaining a share of the sacrifice.[4] The Vedic concept of Viṣṇu as one who expands and pervades is central to this myth; here he actually changes from a dwarf into a giant, but in more philosophical texts he is viewed as the microcosmic soul (*ātman*) who is simultaneously the macrocosmic godhead (*brahman*).[5]

48. FROM THE *Śatapatha Brāhmaṇa*

The gods and the demons, both born of Prajāpati, were striving against one another. Then the gods seemed to be left behind, and the demons thought, 'All this world is ours.' They said, 'Let us divide this earth, and when we have divided it let us live upon it.' Then they set out to divide it from west to east with hides of oxen. The gods heard about this and said, 'The demons are dividing this earth. Let us go where the demons are dividing it, for who would we be if we did not share in it?' They placed Viṣṇu, the sacrifice, at their head and went there and said, 'Let us also share in this earth; let a portion of it be ours.' The demons, rather jealously, replied, 'As much as this Viṣṇu lies on, so much we give to you.'

Now Viṣṇu was a dwarf, but the gods did not contest this offer, for they thought, 'They have given much to us, for they have given us a space as large as the sacrifice.' They placed Viṣṇu on the east and enclosed him all around with Vedic metres, saying, on the south, 'With the Gāyatrī metre I enclose you'; on the west, 'With the Triṣṭubh metre I enclose you'; on the north, 'With the Jagatī metre I enclose you.' Having enclosed him with metres all around, they placed Agni

3. See above, myth 26, p. 88, for Indra, and myths 29–32, pp. 98–104, for Agni. The soul in transmigration was said to 'hide' temporarily in plants and in water.

4. See above, myth 36, pp. 123–5.

5. Compare the simultaneously minute and enormous forms of Kṛṣṇa, below, myth 59, pp. 220–21.

on the east,[6] and they went on worshipping with him and exhausted themselves, and with him they obtained this whole earth; and since with him they obtained [*samavindanta*, from *vid*] this whole earth, therefore he is called the altar [*vedi*]. And so it is said, 'The altar is as great as the earth'; for with the altar they obtained this whole earth. He who knows this wrests this whole earth from his enemies and excludes his enemies from a share.

Viṣṇu was exhausted, but as he was enclosed all around by the Vedic metres and by Agni on the east, he could not get out, and so he went down into the roots of plants. The gods said, 'Where has Viṣṇu gone? Where has the sacrifice gone? He is enclosed by metres all around and by Agni on the east; he cannot have got out; let us search for him here.' By digging a little they searched for him and found him three fingers down. Therefore let the altar be three fingers high.

Viṣṇu Becomes a Dwarf to Trick the Demon Bali

The cosmology implicit in the Brāhmaṇa myth is stated explicitly in the Purāṇa version: the whole universe is in Viṣṇu's body. Another Vedic thread – Viṣṇu's role as a sun god whose three 'steps' are his rising, noon, and setting – is also made explicit here. The demons of the Brāhmaṇas are now replaced by the individual demon, Bali (whose name, significantly, denotes the offering of a portion of the daily meal); for Viṣṇu, who is closely associated with Indra in many Ṛg Vedic martial exploits (including the three strides), comes to replace Indra in later mythology as the demon-slayer *par excellence*.

49. FROM THE *Vāyu Purāṇa*

In the seventh Tretā Age, when all the worlds were controlled by Bali and the demons had occupied the triple world, the dwarf appeared, Viṣṇu's third avatar. Contracting himself in all his limbs, he went, preceded by Bṛhaspati, to the place where the lord of demons was performing a sacrifice. At this

6. That is, they made Agni the rising sun.

auspicious time, the lord, the joy of the family of Aditi, became a brahmin and said to Bali the son of Virocana, 'You are the king of the triple world. In you everything is firmly placed. O king, you should give me the space covered in three strides.' 'I grant this,' answered the king, Bali the son of Virocana, and since he thought him to be just a dwarf he himself was very pleased about it. But the dwarf, the lord, stepped over the heaven, the sky, and earth, this whole universe, in three strides; he, the famous one, the individual soul, surpassed the sun in his own energy, illuminating all the regions of the sky and the intermediate points of the compass. The great-armed Viṣṇu who excites men shone forth, illuminating all the worlds, and stole away the demons' prosperity as he stole away the three worlds. He sent the demons, with all their sons and grandsons, to hell; Namuci, Śambara, Prahlāda – these cruel ones were destroyed by Viṣṇu and scattered in all directions. Mādhava, the individual soul, is the essence of all the great elements, and time with all its parts; and he revealed this wonder to the brahmins there. He revealed that the whole universe was in his body; there is nothing in all the worlds that is not pervaded by the noble one. When the gods, demons, and men saw that form of the supreme ruler, they were all bewitched by Viṣṇu's energy over and over. Bali, with his friends and relations, was bound with great cords, and the whole family of Virocana was sent to hell. Then Viṣṇu gave the noble Indra kingship over all immortals.

The Brāhmaṇa avatars of Viṣṇu

The Fish

The fish saves Manu from the flood

Another ancient incarnation is that of the fish. The myth of the fish and the flood is not originally associated with Viṣṇu; indeed, it is likely that this myth is not only far older than the worship of Viṣṇu but even older than the Indo-European dispersal and the civilization of the Fertile Crescent, for the parallels with Semitic flood legends are striking.

50. FROM THE *Śatapatha Brāhmaṇa*

In the morning they brought Manu water for ablutions, just as they bring it for washing the hands. As he was washing, a fish came into his hands and said, 'Care for me and I will save you.' 'From what will you save me?' 'A flood will carry away all these creatures; I will save you from it.' 'How should you be cared for?' 'As long as we are tiny,' said the fish, 'our destruction is great, for fish swallows fish.[7] Care for me at first in a pot, and when I outgrow it, dig a trench and care for me in it. And when I outgrow that, then take me down to the ocean, for then I will be beyond destruction.'

The fish grew steadily into a *jhaṣa*,[8] for that grows largest. It said, 'In a certain year, the flood will come. Then you will build a ship and come to me, and when the flood has risen you will enter the ship and I will save you from the flood.' Manu cared for it in this way and carried it down to the ocean. And in the very year which the fish had indicated, he built a ship and came to him, and when the flood had risen he entered the ship. The fish swam up to him, and he fastened the rope of the ship to the horn of the fish, and with it he sailed through to the northern mountain. 'I have saved you,' said the fish. 'Fasten the ship to a tree, but do not let the water cut you off when you are on the mountain; as the water subsides, keep following it down.' And he kept following it down, in this way, and so that slope of the northern mountain

7. 'Fish swallows fish' was the basis of the Indian term for anarchy, the equivalent of our 'dog eats dog'.

8. The *jhaṣa*, a large fish of indefinite species, is the constellation Pisces.

is known as Manu's Descent. The flood swept away all other creatures, and Manu alone remained here.

Viṣṇu becomes a fish to save Manu from the universal dissolution

As the central motif of the earliest Indian version of the flood myth is one of expansion (from a minnow to a giant fish), the fish was later identified with Viṣṇu, the Expander, rather than with any of the other Hindu gods. Once the fish had become a god, his expansion frightened Manu just as Viṣṇu's cosmic form frightened Arjuna in the *Bhagavad Gītā* and Kṛṣṇa's cosmic form frightened his mother in the *Bhāgavata Purāṇa*;[9] in this way the fish becomes a fiery destructive force that must be disposed of like the seed of Śiva and the submarine mare, transferred from one body of water to another until it finds its rest in the ocean. In fact, although the earliest plot demands that the fish *save* Manu, the later Hindu imagery influences the text so that the fish appears to participate in doomsday: the submarine mare comes out of the ocean after the fish has entered it, and a detailed description of the final conflagration is inserted to balance the original motif of the final flood. In keeping with these elaborations, Manu saves not merely himself alone (which was the point of the earlier myth) but all living creatures; he requests not his own immortality (the usual boon) but the immortality of the human race.

51. FROM THE *Matsya Purāṇa*

In times past, a king named Manu, the child of the sun, practised extensive asceticism and patiently handed his kingdom over to his son. Endowed with all the qualities of the soul, equally indifferent to sorrow and joy, the hero achieved the highest yoga in a solitary place on the Malaya mountain range. When a million years had passed, Brahmā who sits on a lotus was pleased and came to give him a boon, saying, 'Choose a boon.' The king bowed to the Grandfather and

9. See below, myth 59, pp. 220–21.

said, 'There is only one unsurpassed boon that I wish from you: let me be able to protect the multitude of all beings, moving and still, when the dissolution takes place.' The soul of all agreed to this and vanished. Then a great rain of flowers fell from the sky, sent by the gods.

One day as he was performing in his hermitage the libation which delights the ancestors, a *śapharī*[10] fish came into his hands along with the water. When the king, who was full of compassion, saw that fish, he took care to protect it in a vessel of water for a day and a night, until it had the form of a fish sixteen fingers long. Then it cried, 'Save me! Save me!' and he threw the water-creature into a jar, and even within that jar it grew to three hands during one night. Again the fish said to the son of the thousand-rayed god, in a wail of distress, 'Save me! Save me! I have come to you for refuge.' Then the child of the sun threw the fish into a well, and when the fish could no longer fit even into that well, he threw it into a vast lake; but still it grew to the width of a league, and again it cried out there in distress, 'Save me! Save me! O best of kings.'

Then Manu threw it into the Ganges, and when it continued to grow, the lord of the earth threw it into the ocean. But when the fish had pervaded the whole ocean, Manu became frightened and said, 'Who are you? A lord of demons? Or are you Vāsudeva? Who else could there be like this? Whose body could be equal to twenty thousand leagues? I have recognized you in your fish form, Keśava; but you are wearing me out. Homage to you, Hṛṣīkeśa, lord of the universe, dwelling-place of the universe.'

Then the lord Viṣṇu who excites men, who had taken the form of a fish, said, 'Bravo, bravo! You have recognized me

10. First a bright little fish found in shallow water; later a large carp that preys on other fish, an interesting development in the light of the myth.

rightly, and have faultlessly kept your vow. In a short time, the earth will be submerged in water with all its mountains and trees and houses. This boat has been fashioned out of the assemblage of all the gods in order to protect the assemblage of great living souls, O lord of the earth. Those born of sweat, those born of eggs, or of water, and those living creatures which slough their skins – place them all in this boat and save them, for they have no protector. And when your ship is struck by the winds that blow at the end of the age, fasten the ship to this horn of mine, O king, lord of kings, lord of the earth. At the end of the dissolution, you will be the Prajāpati of the whole universe, moving and still. Thus at the beginning of the Kṛta Age you will be the omniscient, firm king, the overlord of the period of Manu, worshipped even by the gods.'

Then Manu asked the Chastiser of Madhu, 'O lord, for how many years will the interval of destruction last? And how shall I protect the creatures, O lord, Chastiser of Madhu? And how shall I be united with you again?' The fish replied, 'From today, there will be a drought upon the earth that will last for a hundred years, when food will be scarce and misfortune rife. Then seven cruel rays will destroy those few creatures still left, and seven times seven rays will rain down hot coals. The fire of the submarine mare will be transformed at the end of the Age, and a poisonous fire will shoot forth from her contracted[11] mouth, out of hell; and a fire will arise from the third eye in the forehead of Bhava, burning and agitating the triple universe, great sage. And when the whole earth has thus been burnt to ashes, the sky will be heated by steam. Then the universe, with its gods and constellations, will be totally destroyed. The seven clouds of doomsday – Whirlpool, Frightening-roar, Bucket, Fierce, Crane, Lightning-banner, and Blood-red – these clouds born of the sweat of Agni will

11. The mare's mouth is tightened to keep the fire inside her.

flood the earth; the oceans will be stirred and will all come together, and all of the three universes will be a single ocean. 'Then take this boat of the Vedas and place the essences and seeds of all living creatures upon it; and by attaching the rope as I have taught you, fasten the boat to my horn, and you will be protected by my majesty. You alone will remain, when even the gods have been burnt. The moon and the sun, Brahmā and I, together with the four World-protectors, the holy river Narmadā, the great sage Mārkaṇḍeya, Bhava, the Vedas and Purāṇas and subsidiary sciences – all of these will remain with you during the interval of destruction of the era of Manu Cākṣuṣa, when all is a single ocean. I will proclaim the Vedas to you at the beginning of creation, O lord of the earth, heater of enemies.' Then the lord vanished, and Manu practised the rope technique that Vāsudeva had favoured him with, and practised it until the final flood occurred as it had been foretold. When the time arrived as it had been foretold from the mouth of Vāsudeva, Viṣṇu, the Exciter of Men, appeared in the form of a horned fish, and a serpent in the form of a rope came to Manu's side. Then the sage who knew *dharma* gathered together all creatures and placed them on the boat, and by the technique of attachment he tied the boat to the horn of the fish with the rope that was a serpent; he approached Viṣṇu, the Exciter, upon it and prostrated himself before him.

The Boar

Like the avatar of the fish, the boar avatar was originally a part of the mythology of the Brāhmaṇas not associated with Viṣṇu, but the concepts underlying the symbolism of the boar were easily assimilated to Viṣṇu, who helps Indra to retrieve a sacrificial boar from the demons even in the literature of the Brāhmaṇas. The boar who saves the earth, however, is originally Prajāpati, who keeps her afloat by flattening and spreading her in a typical Vedic act of creation.

Prajāpati becomes a boar to create the earth

52. FROM THE *Taittirīya Saṃhitā*

In the beginning this universe was the waters, the ocean. Prajāpati became the wind and moved in the ocean. He saw the earth and became a boar and seized her; he became Viśvakarman and stroked her, spreading her out so that she became extended; she became the earth, and so the earth is called Pṛthivī ('the Extended'). Prajāpati exhausted himself in her, and he produced the gods, Vasus, Rudras, and Ādityas.

Prajāpati becomes a boar to save the earth

The idea of 'extending' the earth is easily connected with the expanding aspect of Viṣṇu; similarly, the idea of the 'saving' of the earth comes to Viṣṇu later, perhaps in association with the fish who saves the people of the earth from submersion even as the boar saves the earth herself.

53. FROM THE *Śatapatha Brāhmaṇa*

In the beginning, the earth was only the size of a hand-span. A boar raised her up, and he was called Emūṣa; he was Prajāpati, her husband, and she was his mate, his dear abode.

Viṣṇu becomes incarnate as the boar to save the earth

From these two brief myths, the two essential symbolic qualities of the boar are apparent: the boar is a sacrificial animal and it is ambivalent by virtue of its amphibious nature; the boar lives in water and on land, and in later mythology the cosmic boar dwells at the boundary of the universe and the non-universe, 'World-non-World', a ring of mountains forming the boundary between the visible world and the regions of darkness. As Viṣṇu in the Purāṇas takes this avatar from Brahmā, he is explicitly identified with Brahmā: he 'creates' the earth by finding it in the water as Prajāpati does. The water is thus both the birth-place and the hiding-place of the earth, for the ancient Indians believed in a closed universe in which matter could never increase, but the semblance of creation could be produced by re-ordering – by finding – already present elements, retrieving them over and over again from the cosmic flood.

54. FROM THE *Viṣṇu Purāṇa*

When the interval between aeons was past, the lord Brahma, endowed with the quality of goodness, arose from his night sleep and saw that the world was empty. The supreme Nārāyaṇa, incomprehensible, the lord of all others, the lord without a beginning, the source of everything, he who has the very form of Brahmā – he is called Nārāyaṇa for the reason explained in this verse about the god who has the very form of Brahmā and is the beginning and end of the universe: 'The waters are called Nārā, for the waters are the offspring of the Man [*nara*]; and as they were formerly his abode [*ayana*], therefore he is known as Nārāyaṇa.'[12] Realizing that the earth was within the waters when the universe had been made into a single ocean, Prajāpati wished to raise it. He made another body; as at the beginning of previous aeons he had made the fish, the tortoise, and others, so now the eternal, constant, supreme soul, the soul of the universe, Prajāpati took the body of a boar, a form composed of the Vedic sacrifice, in order to preserve the whole universe.

Then he who is the supporter of the earth, the support of the soul, was praised by Sanaka and the other Siddhas who had gone to the world of men, and he entered the water. When the goddess earth saw that he had entered the sub-terranean region of hell, she bowed to him in humble devotion, and she praised him . . . While the blessed supporter of the earth was being praised by the earth in this way, he murmured a resonant, low growl like the chanting of the *Sāma Veda*. Then the great boar, whose eyes were like full-blown lotuses, and whose body, as dark and smooth as blue

12. 'Having the waters for his abode', a quotation from Manu 1.8.

lotus petals, resembled the great Dark Blue Mountain, lifted the earth up from the regions of hell on his own tusk. As he rose up, the water that had touched him was driven by the wind from his mouth and washed Sananda and the other shining sages who had taken refuge in the world of men, so that they were purified of their sins. The roaring waters rushed down into hell, which had been torn open by the tips of his hooves; and the winds of his breath scattered all about the Siddhas who dwelt in the world of men.

As the great boar arose, holding the earth, his belly dripping with water, shaking his great body that was made of the Vedas, the sages who had gone between his bristles praised him . . . As the supreme soul, supporter of the earth, was praised in this way, he lifted the earth up quickly and placed her upon the great ocean. The earth stayed like a great ship on the top of the flood of water and did not sink, because her body was so spread out. Then, when he had made the earth level, the lord who has no beginning, the highest lord, piled up mountains on the earth in order to divide it. By means of his power which is never in vain, he whose wish is never in vain created on the surface of the earth all those mountains which had been burnt in the previous creation. He divided the earth into seven continents as it had been, and he created the four worlds, earth and the others,[13] as before.

The Śaiva version: Śiva chastises the boar

Even in the Vaiṣṇava story of the boar avatar there are hints of incidental destruction caused by the boar; these hints are made the central point of the Śaiva version of the myth, which exaggerates the erotic element (which is already present, albeit sketchily, in the *Śatapatha Brāmaṇa*) and explains the boar's fatal flaw in social, ritual, and cosmic terms: he becomes too attached to his family, makes love to a polluted woman (as Agni makes love to the Kṛttikās when they are menstruous, according to some versions), and is unable

13. Earth, aether, heaven, and the underworld.

to control his destructive fire once it has been loosed. On the first level, the earth herself shares his ambivalence: both of them know what should be done, but they are unable to do it without the help of Śiva. On the ritual level, the polluting 'blood' is expiated by a blood sacrifice of the boar.[14] And on the cosmic level, there are three multiforms of the postponement of doomsday: first the playful boars dive into the ocean, then they all fall into the ocean during the battle, and finally they are killed and thrown into the ocean. Doomsday is imminent; Viṣṇu takes the form of a fish and saves the Vedas, as he does at the final flood.

55. FROM THE *Kālikā Purāṇa*

When Viṣṇu had become incarnate as the boar in the primeval creation, Śaṅkara said to the boar, the lord of all, lord of the universes, 'O lord, you have now fulfilled the purpose for which you fashioned the boar form, for you have re-established the earth properly as she was, and settled the oceans and the rivers of the earth. And Brahmā has performed creation by your grace, for you are the substance of everything, substance of the sacrifice, and substance of energy itself. You are the guru of all gurus; you are beyond the beyond. The earth cannot bear you, O lord of the universe, and she is almost shattered, though formerly you bound her fast by placing the mountains firmly upon her. Therefore, lord of the universes, you should abandon this body of a boar which is the substance of the universe, the form of the universe, the cause of the cause of the universe. Who else could bear your boar form, except you yourself, O lord? The earth, in the water, is full of desire and behaving like a woman; she has been violated and has conceived a cruel embryo from your fiery seed; she is menstruating, however, and therefore unfit for the embryo with which you impregnated her, O lord of the universe. Therefore the son who will be born will also carry off un-

14. Compare the blood sacrifice of the buffalo, below, myth 66, pp. 248–9.

restrained women; he will develop a demonic nature and harm the gods and Gandharvas.'[15]

Thus the lord of the world spoke to Viṣṇu, who had a shameful look, about the vicious son begotten by sexual pleasure with a menstruating woman, a son who would do unpleasant things: 'Abandon this lustful boar-body, lord of the world; you alone are the cause of creation, preservation, and destruction; you are the cause of the world. At the proper time, you will bring about preservation, creation, and destruction; therefore, for the sake of the welfare of the world, abandon this body, mighty one. At the proper time, you will make another boar-body again.' When the lord who had the form of a boar heard this speech of the noble Śaṅkara, he said to the great god, 'I will do precisely as you say, great lord. I will certainly abandon this body of the sacrificial boar, and at the proper time I will again make another marvellous body of a boar, one that is hard to strike against, in order to create the worlds.' And when he had said this, the great-bodied one, guru of the universe, creator of the universe, supporter of the universe, lord of the universe, disappeared. When that god had disappeared, the great lord god Śiva went to his own place, with all the bands of gods and his own hosts.

But the boar went to his own mountain, named World-non-World, and he made love with the earth, who had the form of a lovely female boar, and though he made love with her for a very long time on that supreme mountain the lord of the world was still unsatisfied, as his lust for the female boar was so strong. Three excellent brahmin sons were born of the earth when she made love in the form of a female boar; their names were Suvṛtta, Kanaka, and Ghora,[16] and they were all

15. In early versions of this myth, Viṣṇu begets in the earth one son, Naraka ('Little Man') or Bhaumya ('Born of Earth'), a troublesome demon. Here Naraka remains an embryo, but his mischief is predicted.

16. 'Well-rounded', 'Golden', and 'Horrible'.

very powerful. These children played affectionately together in the caverns and lakes on the various levels of the tablelands of the golden mountain Meru. The boar, surrounded by these sons, made love with his wife and did not consider giving up his body. Sometimes the powerful boar embraced his children and played games in the mud with his wife; when the boar, tawny as honey, was smeared with mud he shone forth like a cloud at sunset, and he splashed his family with water just like a cloud. He was so delighted with his sons and with his wife, the earth, that he played until he shattered the earth so that she bent in the middle. The serpent Ananta was also tortured by the pressure, for he carried Hari; his head was broken and he trod upon the tortoise on the surface of the earth. Suvṛtta, Ghora, and Kanaka split open the golden tablelands with their boarish blows, and when the gold was broken the tablelands became flat, and all those golden things which the gods had carefully wrought on the tablelands of Meru were broken by the boar's sons. Then the boarish blows of the children made Mānasa and the other lakes of the gods turbid everywhere.

The earth in the form of a woman played with the boar, but in her stable form she was intensely unhappy. Suvṛtta and the others plunged into the ocean on all sides, and all the oceans were whipped up as their gems were strewn about by the inundations of boars. As the young boars played here and there, the universes with their rivers and wishing-trees[17] were broken. Even though the boar himself, supporter of the universe, knew that the universe was tortured in this way, his love for his sons kept him from restraining them. When Suvṛtta, Kanaka, and Ghora went to heaven, the bands of gods were frightened and ran away in all directions. As the sacrificial boar thus played with his sons and his wife, he never became sated, but his desire grew ever and ever greater and he

17. Wishing-trees produce all things desired, on their branches, as wishing-cows are 'milked' of what one wants.

did not want to abandon his body as he had been instructed to do.

Then all the bands of gods took counsel together with the offspring of the gods and with Śakra, for the welfare of the universe. And they all came to a decision with Śakra and the sages and went to the refuge of all refuges, Nārāyaṇa the unborn lord. When the thirty-three gods reached Govinda, the son of Vasudeva, lord of the universe, they bowed and praised the god who has Garuḍa on his banner: '. . . In fear and devotion we have come to you for refuge; protect us, Viṣṇu.' When the god of gods, cause of the welfare of all beings, was praised in this way, he said to all the bands of gods and Indra, in a voice deep as a thundercloud, 'Tell me quickly why you have come or what you are afraid of or what I can do.' 'The earth is crushed by the constant play of the sacrificial boar,' said the gods. 'All the worlds are shaken and find no peace. As a dry gourd is shattered by blows, so the earth is shattered by the blows of the boar's hooves. And the three sons of the boar, Suvṛtta, Kanaka, and Ghora – they too assail the universe, O lord of the universes, for their energy is like the doomsday fire. Mānasa and the other lakes are so muddied and torn up by their mud games that they now do not return to their natural state. The powerful boars have broken the trees of the gods, the coral trees in Indra's paradise and the others, and they have blocked the rivers of the gods with bits of fruit and flowers. When Suvṛtta and the other two mounted the Triple Peak, they made such a deluge as they fell into the ocean of salt that they stirred up inundations of water that flooded the whole earth. All the people were flooded and ran away in all directions, O great-armed one; trying to save their lives, they ran away in all directions. When the little sons of the sacrificial boar went to Indra's heaven, the gods were routed on one side and another, and found no peace. The peaks of all the mountains where the sons of the boar play have been smashed and brought down. O lord of the universe, lord, Vaikuṇṭha, the whole universe is being destroyed by them as they play their games; therefore you must protect the universe.'

When the god who causes men to prosper heard the speech of the gods as they complained in this way, he said to Śaṅkara and Brahmā, 'Because of the boar's body, all the gods and all these creatures are suffering greatly, and the whole universe is shattered. Śaṅkara, I wish to abandon that boar-body which is still capable of atonement, but I cannot abandon it by my own will; you, Śaṅkara, must now make an effort to cause me to abandon that body. Brahmā, you must fill the destroyer of Smara with your own energies, again and again, and let all the gods fill him, and let Śaṅkara slay the boar. Because it had intercourse with a menstruating woman, and because it murdered brahmins, the body has become a source of evil, and it is proper to abandon it now. I will perform a great expiation, and my offspring will perform acts of expiation; for the sake of that, subdue my body quickly. I should always protect creatures, but now they are steadily sinking to ruin because of me every day; therefore I will abandon this body for the sake of all creatures.'

Brahmā and Śaṅkara replied to Govinda, the son of Vasudeva, 'We will do as you say.' The son of Vasudeva then dismissed all of the thirty-three gods and became intent upon meditating so that he himself might withdraw the energy of the boar. As Mādhava withdrew the energy little by little, the body of the boar became drained of its vital essence. And when all the immortals knew that the body was devoid of energy, the god Śiva approached the marvellous sacrificial boar. All of the thirty-three gods, led by Brahmā, followed the great god, husband of Umā, in order to give their energy to the Chastiser of Smara: all of the bands of gods gave their own energy to Śiva whose banner bears the bull, and by this means he became extremely powerful. At that moment, Śiva the lord of the mountain took the form of the *śarabha* beast, a terrifying form with eight legs, some on top and some on the bottom. He was two hundred thousand leagues tall, one hundred and fifty thousand leagues wide; the body of the boar was one hundred thousand leagues high and fifty thousand leagues wide. Then the sacrificial boar saw the great god, husband of Umā, in the terrifying form of the *śarabha*, the colour of black coals, touching the moon with his head, with a very long nose and long claws, with a long mouth and a giant body, with eight tusks and a mane and a tail, with long ears. He had four legs on his back and four on his stomach; he roared and leapt up again and again.

When Suvṛtta, Kanaka, and Ghora saw him coming, running swiftly and angrily, they were beside themselves with anger, and the three mighty brothers attacked that *śarabha* whose body was so great and tossed him up all together with the blows of their tusks. As great as was the measure of the *śarabha*, so great a measure did the three boars assume by means of their magical powers as they tossed up the *śarabha*. When the *śarabha* was tossed up by the blows of those boars, he fell to the farthest edge of the earth, into the deep ocean of water, and when he had fallen into the ocean that was the abode of sharks and sea-monsters, the three flew up and plunged furiously into the great ocean. When Suvṛtta, Kanaka, and Ghora had plunged into the water of the ocean, the boar also flew up suddenly in fury and plunged into that mass of water because of his love of his sons.

When all the boars and the *śarabha* had flown up, they had shattered the gods in heaven, and the constellations and planets. Some of the gods were wounded and some fell to the earth; some wise gods sought refuge in the Mahar world.[18] The

18. The fourth of the seven worlds above the earth.

constellations fell from their heavenly cars[19] to the surface of the earth, where they appeared garlanded with flames. The violent blast that arose when they fell gave rise to a violent storm of wind which raised the mountains up one after the other off the surface of the earth. Some of the peaks fell back down among the mountains, smashing the trees and living creatures, falling down again and again. Other mountains danced upon the surface of the earth, and with each blow the mountains shattered many creatures as they moved, and as the mountains rubbed against one another in the blast of the wind they seemed to be walking along on the surface of the earth.

As the boars and the *śarabha* and the mountains with their great peaks fell into the ocean, masses of water were hurled up. By the blast of the impacts that caused such masses of water to be hurled up, all the oceans became emptied of their water in a moment, and when all those waters were cast upon the surface of the earth all creatures were flooded in a moment and destroyed. As the creatures were drowning in the water everywhere, they moaned piteously, terrified and tortured as they were about to die: 'Alas, father!' 'Alas, my little one!' 'Alas, mother!' 'Alas, my child!' The earth sank down in the place where the *śarabha* and the boars had fallen, split open by the blast of their feet, and the other edge of the earth rose up with all of its mountains . . . When all the universe was thus flooded by the oceans and dissolved, the Grandfather, eldest of the gods, became worried and said to Hari, 'My lord, this whole universe with its gods, demons and men is in ruins; the earth is shattered, and all that moves and is still is destroyed. Gods, demons, Gandharvas, sages, ascetics, and even the reptiles that crawl – all are ruined, O lord of the universe. You are the protector of all; you are the lord of the universe; therefore, protect all of us and the earth. You yourself must

19. The constellations are floating palaces drawn by chariots.

withdraw and absorb this boar's body and restore the earth with all that moves and is still, great-armed one.'

When the god who brings prosperity to people, the unfallen one, heard this speech of Brahmā, he made every effort to restore the earth. Hari assumed the form of a red fish[20] who took up the Vedas and the seven sages, those excellent sages well versed in all the Vedas, for he was determined that the Vedas should not be destroyed and he wished for the welfare of the universe. He took them all: Vasiṣṭha, Atri, Kaśyapa, Viśvāmitra, Gautama, Jamadagni, and Bharadvāja, sages rich in asceticism, and he placed them on his back as he stood in the middle of the water, and he built a great ship so that those supreme sages could preserve their lines of descent.

Then the god who brings prosperity to people went to win Śiva's pardon, where Śiva, fighting with the boars, was exhausted by them, wounded by the boars' blows, his mouth open as he breathed hard. When the boar saw that Hari had arrived, he remembered his former shape as the Man-lion,[21] and as soon as he remembered the Man-lion the latter came there for the sake of his friend the boar. And when the boar saw that the Man-lion had arrived, he took the energy from that body, and the boars and the *śarabha* saw that energy which was the equal of the sun as it entered into Viṣṇu. The boar emitted many sighs when he realized that the Man-lion was devoid of energy, and the sighs became many boars of great proportions, with sharp tusks . . . The divine Hari, the boar,

20. *Cyprinus rohitaka.* Compare the earlier versions of Viṣṇu's fish incarnation, above, myths 50–51, pp. 180–184.

21. In actual historical development, mirrored in the time sequence of the myth, Viṣṇu's Man-lion incarnation preceded, and perhaps inspired, Śiva's *śarabha* form. The way in which the Man-lion appears, emerging from within a stone pillar, to save his devotee from a murderous demon may also have inspired the famous image of Śiva appearing from within the stone *liṅga* to save his devotee from the god of death.

approached the *śarabha* and said again, 'I must certainly abandon this body for the sake of the universe. This is what I promised before, and it was because of that promise that Hari, Śambhu, and Brahmā have undertaken this great enterprise.' The supreme lord, the hog, continued to deliberate about this and then said to the great god, the powerful *śarabha*, 'Kill me, great god, and I will certainly abandon this body for the welfare of all universes and the gods and even their enemies. And with the collection of the limbs of my body you must perform a sacrifice with an animal slaughter, and a ritual ladle and the other requisites, each of you receiving a great portion of the animal. Perform three sacrifices with my three sons, Kanaka, Suvṛtta, and Ghora, for the sake of the three universes. Gods and creatures arise out of the sacrifice, for the sacrifice is their appointed food. Everything will always arise from the sacrifice; this whole universe is made of the sacrifice. And the embryo which the earth received when she was menstruating – the goddess earth herself will care for him secretly for a long time after his birth, and when the proper time has come the goddess, suffering under her extreme burden, will announce to you the time for his slaughter, and then you will kill him. When the earth, suffering under the burden, has sunk down for a hundred leagues, I will take the form of a tusked boar and raise her up. But your son who will be the general of the army of the gods, born of Rudra but said to have six mothers,[22] will then cause me to abandon that body when it has accomplished its purpose.'

As the mighty sacrificial boar said this, the great energy came out of the boar's body, shining with its garland of flames like the light of ten million suns, and this most miraculous energy entered into the body of the lord Hari. And when that energy of the boar had entered Viṣṇu, Hari himself took the energy from Suvṛtta, Kanaka, and Ghora. A portion of

22. See above, myth 33, pp. 108–12.

energy came out from each of their bodies separately, shining with its garland of flames, and entered the body of Hari as their father's had done. Then Hari and Brahmā and the great god replied to the boar's speech, saying, 'Om',[23] again and again, and they tried as hard as they could to cause the boars to abandon their bodies. The *śarabha* struck his beak upon the middle of the neck of the boar and broke it and hurled that form into the water. When he had caused him to fall first of all, he then broke Suvṛtta's neck and killed him, then Kanaka's, and then Ghora's, and they all gave up their life's breath and fell into the water of the great ocean, causing the water to echo with the noise and to blaze like the doomsday fire when the boars fell.

The Epic avatars of Viṣṇu

Rāma: Rāma Rejects Sītā and is Enlightened by the Gods

The story of Rāma the mortal king was certainly known in India for centuries before Rāma was elevated to the status of an avatar of Viṣṇu; even in the *Rāmāyaṇa*, the *locus classicus* (and by far the earliest extensive text) for the Rāma myth, only the two latest books (the first and seventh, accretions framing the earlier six books) refer to him consistently as a god. This ambivalence is apparent in the episode of Sītā's ordeal, which is placed in the sixth book in the critical edition, though earlier tradition placed it in the seventh. In fact, another version of this episode occurs in the seventh book, where Sītā enters the earth, her mother, instead of the fire, and is not restored to Rāma.

This is a myth of revelation and epiphany, unusual in that it is to the god-mortal himself that his divinity is revealed. Rāma's delusion is evident from his cruel, selfish, pompous treatment of Sītā (though elsewhere in the Epic he betrays an even greater lack of chivalry, particularly in his unprovoked mockery and mutilation of Śūr-

23. A sacred syllable indicating assent and approval, like 'Amen'.

panakhā); and he unwittingly supplies proof of his 'blindness' when he remarks that Sītā is offensive to him 'as a lamp to one whose eyes are diseased' and that he regards her 'with a jaundiced eye'. The basis of his boastful rejection of Sītā – that he, a mortal man, has accomplished such prodigies in battle for the sake of his illustrious (mortal) family, and that he cares more about appearances and public opinion than about the happiness of himself and his wife – is totally undercut and dwarfed by the revelation that he is not a mortal at all.

This episode takes place when, after Sītā has been carried off by the demon Rāvaṇa and won back, after many years of battle, by Rāma, she is summoned to come to him at court.

56. FROM THE *Rāmāyaṇa*

When Rāma saw Maithilī[24] standing humbly by his side, he spoke with anger deep in his heart: 'I have won you, fair lady, by conquering my enemy in battle; I have accomplished what was to be done through manliness. Now I have satisfied my jealousy and wiped out the insult; I have simultaneously obliterated both the dishonour and my enemy. Today my manliness has been demonstrated; today my efforts have borne fruit. Today, by fulfilling my promise, I have become master of myself. The stain brought about by fate, when you were separated from me and carried off by the fickle-minded demon – that has been overcome by me, a mortal man. He who is dishonoured and does not wipe out the insult by means of his own energy – what good is the manliness of a man of so little energy? The great deeds of Hanūmat – the leaping over the ocean, the destruction of Laṅkā, the trick that he played – all these have now borne fruit. The great effort of Sugrīva and his army – his valour when attacking, his cunning when giving me advice – today that has borne fruit. And the great assistance of the devoted Vibhīṣaṇa, who abandoned his worth-

24. Sītā ('the Furrow') is said to have been born out of a furrow in a field ploughed by Janaka, king of Videha. As Mithilā is the capital of Videha, Sītā is known as Maithilī.

less brother and came to me of himself – today that has borne fruit.'

When Sītā heard Rāma speak in this way, her eyes which were as wide open as those of a doe filled with tears. But as Rāma looked at her, his anger grew great once again, and he blazed like a fire into which great quantities of butter have been offered. He frowned and looked askance, and he spoke harshly to Sītā in the midst of the monkeys and the Rākṣasas, saying, 'I have done all that a man should do to wipe out an intolerable insult at the hands of an enemy. I won you, Sītā, just as the great-souled sage Agastya[25] won the unassailable southern realm for the world of living creatures, by means of his asceticism. But let it be known, if you please, that this great battle effort accomplished by means of the heroism of my friends was not undertaken by me for your sake. I protected my own reputation and expunged completely the scandal and degradation which had been cast upon my own famous family line.

'But as you stand before me, doubts have arisen about your behaviour, so that you are as deeply offensive to me as a lamp to one whose eyes are diseased. Go then wherever you wish, in any direction, with my permission, daughter of Janaka. I can have nothing to do with you, good lady. What man of energy, born into a good family, could take back a woman who had lived in the house of another man, simply because his mind was so tortured by longing for her? Looking with a jaundiced eye upon you who have been degraded upon the lap of Rāvaṇa, how can I take you back when I boast of such an exalted family line? The purpose for which I won you back was to regain my own fame, since I have no attachment to you, and you may go from here as you wish. This is my pro-

25. Agastya dwelt in a hermitage south of the Vindhya mountains' and was chief of the sages of the south, using his ascetic powers to conquer and control the Rākṣasas who infested the south.

nouncement, now that I have applied my intelligence to the matter, good lady. Set your mind on Lakṣmaṇa or Bharata or wherever you will be happy; set your heart on Sugrīva the king of the monkeys or Vibhīṣaṇa the king of the Rākṣasas, or wherever you will be happy, Sītā. For when Rāvaṇa saw your captivating, divine body, he would not have held back for long when you were dwelling in his own house.'

When Maithilī, who deserved to hear pleasant words, heard this unpleasant speech from her beloved after such a long time, she burst into tears and trembled violently like a clinging vine torn down by the trunk of a great elephant. As Rāghava spoke to her so angrily and harshly that her hair stood on end, the daughter of the king of Videha was greatly agitated. When Maithilī heard the rough words of her husband, such as she had never heard before, spoken in the midst of a great crowd, she was deeply ashamed and embarrassed. The daughter of Janaka shed torrents of tears which seemed to cause her limbs to shrink, as she was pierced by his words that were like arrows. Then she wiped her face that was wet with tears and spoke to her husband in gentle and faltering words, saying, 'Why do you speak such rough words, cruel to the ears, inappropriate to me, O hero, like a common man to a common woman? I am not such as you believe, great-armed one. Have confidence in me; I swear to you that I have behaved properly. Because of the conduct of other individual women, you distrust the whole sex; but abandon this doubt, since you have tested me. If my limbs were touched, it was by force, my lord; I did not desire to do it, but fate brought about this offence. My heart, which is under my control, is ever attached to you; not being mistress of the situation, what could I do about my limbs which were in the control of someone else? If you who have given me honour still do not know me by the constantly growing affection of our intimate contact, then I am destroyed for ever. O hero, why did you not discard me when you sent the hero Hanūmat to look for me when I was on Laṅkā? I would have abandoned my life as soon as I heard the monkey deliver your message that you had discarded me. Then you would not have wasted all this effort, risking your life, nor would your friends have exhausted themselves fruitlessly like this. Tiger among men, by giving way to anger like a trivial man you have made womankind preferable. Though I derive my name from Janaka, my birth was from the surface of the earth; you who understand conduct have not honoured my great conduct. You have not had faith in the chastity of my hand which you pressed[26] as a young boy, when I was just a young girl; and my devotion, and my nature – all this you have cast behind you.'

As she spoke and wept, stammering in her tears, Sītā said to Lakṣmaṇa, who was standing there deep in sad thought, 'Build a pyre for me; that is the medicine for this calamity. Destroyed by false accusations, I cannot live; abandoned in an assembly of people by my husband, who is no longer pleased by my virtues, the only possible thing for me to do is to enter the Oblation-bearer.' When Lakṣmaṇa, the slayer of hostile enemies, heard what the daughter of Videha said, he was overcome by indignation, and he looked at Rāghava's face. But when he understood the wish of Rāma's heart as revealed by his gestures, the heroic Lakṣmaṇa built the pyre as Rāma indicated. Then the daughter of Videha quietly and reverently walked around Rāma, who stood with his head down, and she approached the blazing Oblation-eater. Maithilī bowed to the divinities and to the brahmins, folded her palms, stood before the fire, and said, 'As my heart never wavered from Rāghava, so may the fire, the witness of all people, protect me.' As the daughter of Videha said this, she walked around the Oblation-eater and entered the blazing fire, her inner soul totally de-

26. 'To take a woman's hand' (in the marriage ritual) signifies 'to marry'.

tached. The great throng of people there, children and old people, saw Maithilī enter the Oblation-eater, and as she entered the fire a loud, horrified cry of mourning arose from the Rākṣasas and monkeys.

Then king Kubera the wide-famed, and Yama who wears away those who are hostile, and the thousand-eyed great Indra and Varuṇa who heats his enemies and the blessed three-eyed great god Śiva who has the bull on his banner and Brahmā the best of those who know the Vedas, maker of all people – all of these, the best of the thirty-three gods, came together in their celestial chariots that shone like the sun, and they came to the city of Laṅkā and approached Rāghava and stretched forth their massive arms adorned with rings and said to Rāma, who stood before them with his palms joined, 'Maker of all people, best of the wise, how can you disregard Sītā as she falls into the Oblation-bearer? How is it that you do not recognize yourself as the best of the bands of gods? Formerly you were the Vasu Ṛtadhāman, the progenitor of the Vasus; you are the Self-created, the first cause of the three worlds, the eighth Rudra of the Rudras, the fifth of the Sādhyas. Your two ears are the Aśvins, your two eyes the sun and the moon. Heater of enemies, you are seen by all people at the beginning and at the end; yet you disregard the daughter of Videha as if you were a common man.'

When Rāghava, Rāma, the best of upholders of *dharma*, the master of the world, was thus addressed by the World-protectors, the best of the thirty-three gods, he said to them, 'I consider myself to be a man, Rāma, the son of Daśaratha. O lord, tell me who I am, whose son, and where I come from.' Then Brahmā, the best of those who know the Vedas, said to Kākutstha, 'Hear the truth from me, Rāma, you who have truth as your valour. You are the god Nārāyaṇa, the blessed lord who carries four weapons;[27] you are the boar with one

27. Conch shell, discus, mace, and lotus, held in his four hands.

tusk, the conquerer of all forces in the past and in the future... Sītā is Lakṣmī, and you are the god Viṣṇu, Kṛṣṇa, Prajāpati. In order to slay Rāvaṇa, you entered into a mortal man's body here, and you have completed this task for us, O best of those who uphold *dharma*. Rāvaṇa has been slain; now rejoice, Rāma, and enter heaven...' When the shining fire heard these auspicious words uttered by the Grandfather, he rose up with the daughter of Videha in his lap and placed in the lap of Rāma the wise young daughter of Videha, who shone like the young sun,[28] her hair dark and wavy, adorned with gold that had been purified by fire, wearing red garments, and garlands that did not wither.[29]

Then the purifying fire, the witness of the world, said to Rāma, 'Here is your Sītā, daughter of Videha, and there is no evil in her. Neither in speech nor in mind, nor in thought nor in glance, has this woman of good conduct, of exalted conduct, transgressed against you. When you left her alone in the deserted forest, and she was miserable and powerless, she was carried away by the Rākṣasa Rāvaṇa, who was proud of his virility. Though imprisoned and hidden away in the inner apartments of the women, she set her thoughts on you and was intent upon you; guarded by throngs of deformed, hideous Rākṣasa women, Maithilī was tempted and threatened in various ways, but she never gave a thought to that Rākṣasa, for her inner soul had gone to you. Accept her, Rāghava, for she is pure in her whole essence and without evil. And she is not to be struck at all; this I command you.'

When Rāma, of great energy, forbearance, and firm valour, the best of the upholders of *dharma*, heard this, he said

28. The sun at dawn.

29. Certain signs are said to distinguish gods from mortals, with whom they may be otherwise identical: gods do not blink, their garlands do not wither, they do not perspire, no dust settles on them, and their feet do not quite touch the ground.

to the best of the thirty-three gods, 'It was necessary that the lovely Sītā should enter the purifying fire in the presence of all people in the triple world, for she had lived for a long time in the inner chambers of Rāvaṇa. Had I not purified the daughter of Janaka, good people would say of me, "That Rāma, the son of Daśaratha, is certainly lustful and childish." I know full well that Maithilī, the daughter of Janaka, has given her heart to no other, that she is devoted and has kept her thoughts always upon me, but in order to convince the people of the triple world that she spoke the truth, I spurned the daughter of Videha when she entered the Oblation-eater. Just as the great ocean cannot violate the seashore, so Rāvaṇa was unable to violate this wide-eyed lady, for she was protected by her own energy. The evil-minded one could not rape Maithilī even in his mind, for she was unattainable as the blazing flame of a fire. This lovely woman could not have presided over the inner apartments of Rāvaṇa, for she belongs to no one but me, just as light belongs to the sun. Maithilī, the daughter of Janaka, has been purified in the presence of all people in the three worlds. I could not abandon her, any more than one who is master of himself can forsake fame. Certainly I will do what all of you, affectionate ones who are revered by all people, have said for my welfare.'

When he had said this speech and was praised by the mighty because of the deeds that he himself had done, the mighty Rāma, descendant of Raghu, was united with his beloved and experienced the happiness which he deserved.

Kṛṣṇa

Like Rāma, Kṛṣṇa is an 'Epic' figure in two senses of the word: he appears in one of the two great Sanskrit Epics (the *Mahābhārata*), and he is a hero of the Epic type, a warrior and a king. But unlike Rāma, Kṛṣṇa is not the central figure in his Epic; he is (like Rāma) a mortal warrior, but merely one among many, and his identification with

Viṣṇu only begins to take place in the latest parts of the Epic. The myth of the child Kṛṣṇa is only dimly foreshadowed in Vedic and Epic texts, though it may have been a very old folk legend in the non-Sanskrit tradition (as yet unconnected with the god Viṣṇu), and this part of the Kṛṣṇa cycle is first told in full in the *Harivaṃśa*, the Purāṇic appendage to the *Mahābhārata*.

Kṛṣṇa and Balarāma are conceived by Devakī and transferred to other mothers

Two motifs in the myth of the birth of Kṛṣṇa have long been noted as being strikingly similar to Christian, Greek, and other widespread myths: the slaughter of the innocents and the royal or divine child raised by foster-parents ignorant of his true majesty. Yet the particularly *Indian* elements of this myth by far outweigh the more universal themes and place the Kṛṣṇa story securely in the midst of the great patterns of Hindu mythology.

The embryo that threatens and must be divided is reminiscent of the stories of Indra and the Maruts and of Skanda and the Kṛttikās.[30] Moreover, there are stronger reverberations of the Skanda myth in the complicated incidence of multiple wombs and multiple mothers: both Kṛṣṇa and Balarāma originate in the waters of hell, which is the womb of Kālī; they are then placed in Devakī's womb, whence Balarāma is transferred before birth to the womb of Rohiṇī and both are transferred after birth to the home of Yaśodā. (This multiplicity of wombs and children is further complicated by the fact that one Sanskrit word – *garbha* – may refer to womb, mother, embryo, or offspring, depending upon the context.) Thus Kṛṣṇa is a king disguised as a commoner, as well as a god masquerading as a mortal.

Another tie with the Śiva corpus may be seen in the third child, Sleep, an aspect of Kālī who appears as Night in the Skanda myth; she colours the embryo of Pārvatī black so that, years later, Pārvatī quarrels with Śiva and goes away to obtain a golden skin.[31] In the Kṛṣṇa myth, Kālī appears first as Sleep (a manifestation of Viṣṇu's

30. See above, myths 27, pp. 91–4, and 33, pp. 108–12.
31. See below, myth 68, pp. 252–9.

magic power of illusion),[32] then as Night and as a dream, and finally as Death herself.

Finally, the astral symbolism of the Skanda birth myth is present, in a veiled form, here as well, for Rohiṇī[33] is the constellation who is the favourite wife of the moon, and the constellation 'Victorious' under which Kṛṣṇa is born is at the meridional of the sky, the point marked by the mountain Kumeru ('Bad Meru'), which is the demons' equivalent of the gods' Sumeru ('Good Meru'); when the sun is there, in the equinox, the demons are 'victorious'. Furthermore, it has been suggested that the Six Embryos may be symbolic of the six months of winter, with Kṛṣṇa and Balarāma representing the first months of spring, an identification which brings to mind the possible association of the six-headed Skanda with the six seasons and his birth with the birth of the year.

57. FROM THE *Harivaṃśa*

[The wicked Kaṃsa, king of the Bhojas and Sātvatas, heard a prophecy that the eighth child born of his cousin Devakī would kill him. His first impulse was to kill Devakī, but Devakī's husband, Vasudeva, begged Kaṃsa to let her live on condition that Vasudeva would deliver to Kaṃsa every child born of her womb, and Kaṃsa agreed to this.]

Kaṃsa was greatly disturbed, and he reported to his ministers, who strove always for his welfare, 'You must all see to it that the offspring of Devakī are cut off. All of her offspring are to be slain at the first moment, for a person with harmful intentions must be cut down at the very root, if there is any doubt. Devakī must be concealed within the house and guarded secretly; let her wander about, believing herself to be free, but with my armies placed carefully around her. My women will count the months beginning with the month of conception, so that we will know the time that remains before the embryo is fully developed. Let Vasudeva and his wife be

32. See below, myth 62, pp. 232–5.
33. See above, myth 3, p. 30.

guarded everywhere, day and night, and let there be no carelessness on the part of the guards, nor let the women and eunuchs talk about our affair. This is a matter that concerns mere humans, and so it can be accomplished by us though we are humans. It is known that people like me can overcome fate;[34] even fate can be turned to one's advantage by the right combinations of spells, and by herbal medicines well prescribed, and by constant effort.' Thus Kaṃsa took precautions to cut off the offspring of Devakī, for he was warned by Nārada and frightened, and so be began to hold counsels.

When the heroic Viṣṇu heard what Kaṃsa planned to do about the lying-in chamber, he vanished and began to think: 'The son of a Bhoja will kill seven offspring of Devakī, but I will place myself in the eighth embryo.' As he was thinking in this way, his thoughts went to the subterranean hell, where six demons named the Six Embryos were lying in embryonic form. Their valiant forms blazed like the fire that eats the ambrosia; they were the very image of immortals in battle, for they were the sons of Kālanemi.[35]

Once, long ago, these demons had served the Grandfather of the world by practising keen asceticism, wearing their hair in matted piles on their heads. Brahmā was pleased with the Six Embryos and offered them a boon, saying, 'Tell me what you desire. What boon can I give to each of you?' All the demons agreed upon their goal, and they said to Brahmā, 'If you are pleased with us, hear the boon that we choose. Let us not be slain by the gods or the great serpents, nor by the restrained supreme sages armed with curses, nor by Yakṣas or

34. Kaṃsa refers to the prophecy that he will be killed by Devakī's son.

35. Kālanemi was a great demon, son of Virocana, grandson of Hiraṇyakaśipu. He was killed by Viṣṇu but became incarnate again in Kaṃsa and in Kāliya. As Kaṃsa is thus identified with the father of the embryos who become reborn as Balarāma and Kṛṣṇa, he is himself in a sense the father of Kṛṣṇa.

lordly Gandharvas or Siddhas or Cāraṇas or men. Let us not be slain, if you wish to give us a boon, O lord.' Then Brahmā was pleased at heart, and he said to them, 'All will take place just as you have declared.' And having given this boon to the Six Embryos, the self-created one went to the triple heaven. Then Hiraṇyakaśipu[36] became angry and said, 'Since you rejected me when you chose a boon from the lotus-born god, I will renounce my affection for you and abandon you, for you have become my enemies. And your father[37] who called you the Six Embryos and raised you will kill you all when you have become embryos. Although you are great demons named the Six Embryos, you will become the six embryos of Devakī, and Kaṃsa will kill you when you are within the womb.'

Therefore Viṣṇu went to the subterranean watery hell where the demons were living in the form of six embryos bound together, lying in their home, the womb of water. He saw the Six Embryos asleep there in the water, as if hidden in the womb of Sleep who had taken a black form. Then Viṣṇu, whose weapon is truth, entered into their bodies in the form of a dream and drew out their vital breaths and gave them to Sleep, saying, 'Goddess of sleep, go within the house of Devakī, as I command you, and take these Six Embryos into whom I have infused my vital breath, and place them one after another in the six embryos in the body of Devakī. Then, when these offspring have been born and brought to the house of Yama,[38] and Kaṃsa's effort has been fruitless, while Devakī's labour has borne fruit, then, goddess, I will do a favour for you to make your glory on earth equal to mine: you will be goddess of the whole world. The seventh offspring of

36. Hiraṇyakaśipu is the great-grandfather of the Six Embryos.

37. That is, Kālanemi divided them and Kālanemi's reincarnation, Kaṃsa, will kill them.

38. That is, when they are dead.

Devakī, my gentle older brother, this part you will transfer to Rohiṇī in the seventh month; and because the embryo will be drawn out [*saṃkarṣaṇāt*], the young man will be called Saṃkarṣaṇa,[39] my older brother with a face like the cool-rayed moon.

'When I am the eighth embryo in her womb, Kaṃsa will be very careful, thinking, "Devakī's seventh embryo miscarried,[40] because of her fear." Then you will become the ninth embryo in our family, born of Yaśodā, the dear wife of Nanda the cow-herd of Kaṃsa, and you will be born on the ninth day of the dark half of the month. I will arrive at midnight when the youth of night is gone, at the moment of the constellation "Victorious", and I will come out of the womb painlessly. Then we two will be born together in the eighth month, and we offspring will be exchanged because of the command of Kaṃsa. I will go to Yaśodā, and you, goddess, will go to Devakī. And when we two children have been exchanged, Kaṃsa will be fooled ; he will take you by the foot and throw you down on the stone, and when you have been thrown down you will obtain an eternal place in the sky. You will be dark like my own skin, and you will have a face like that of Saṃkarṣaṇa; you will have four stout arms like my arms, in which you will hold a trident and a sword with a golden handle and a pot full of honey and a flawless lotus. You will wear a delicate, dark skirt, with a golden bodice, and on your breast will shine a string of pearls like a mass of moonbeams. Your ears will be adorned by large celestial earrings, and your shining face will be the rival of the moon. A triple diadem will bind your shining hair, and your arms like iron clubs will resound with snakes and serpents.

39. 'He who draws or ploughs', an epithet of Balarāma, brother of Kṛṣṇa.

40. When the embryo is taken from Devakī's body to be placed in Rohiṇī, it is thought that Devakī has miscarried.

Your high banner will be made of a peacock's tail, and your shining bracelets and anklets will be made of peacock's feathers. You will be attended by throngs of grotesque ghosts, and by my command you will take a vow of eternal virginity and dwell in the triple heaven. There the hundred-eyed Śakra and the gods will anoint you and install you in your office by the divine ritual of consecration that I have appointed for you, and Vāsava will take you for his sister. As you will be born in the family of Kuśika, you will be called Kauśikī,[41] and Indra will give you an eternal dwelling place on the superb mountain Vindhya, where you will adorn the earth with thousands of residences.[42]

'Then you will place me in your heart and destroy the two demons Sumbha and Nisumbha as they wander with their followers in the mountains. Wandering over the triple world, restrained by truth, you will assume any form at will and grant boons generously. With your retinue of ghosts you will receive an offering of sacrificial beasts on the ninth day of each month, for you will always be fond of sacrifices of flesh. Mortals who bow to you when they remember my majesty will receive all that they desire, children or riches. Men who are lost in dense forests or sunk in the great ocean or opposed by thieves will have recourse to you. You will be Perfection, Prosperity, Firmness, Fame, Modesty, Knowledge, Restraint, Intelligence, Dawn, Night, Light, Sleep, and the Night of Doomsday. When men worship you you will protect them from capture, painful slaughter, the death of sons, loss of wealth, and danger of disease or death. You alone will bewitch Kaṃsa and you will devour the universe; and for the sake of my own enlargement, I will kill Kaṃsa.' When the lord had instructed her in this way, he vanished; she bowed to him and assented and went away.

41. See below, myth 68, p. 259, for another explanation of this name.
42. Her 'residences' are the shrines dedicated to Kālī.

When Devakī, who was like a great divinity, was impregnated, she received all seven embryos in the way that has been described. Kaṃsa killed the six embryos as soon as they were born, smashing them upon the stone ground, but Sleep brought to Rohiṇī the seventh embryo that Devakī had received. At midnight, the pregnant Rohiṇī let her embryo fall from her womb; then she was overcome by Sleep, and she fell to the ground. As if in a dream, she saw the embryo slip out of her and when she could not see the embryo inside she became confused and distressed for a moment. Then Sleep spoke in the dark night to the terrified Rohiṇī, who was as dear to Vasudeva as the constellation Rohiṇī is dear to the moon.[43] Sleep said, 'Since this embryo was drawn out and placed in your womb, fair lady, he will be your son, named Saṃkarṣaṇa.' Rohiṇī rejoiced to receive that son, and she lowered her face and entered the house, shining like the constellation Rohiṇī. Devakī then received another embryo in the same way, and this was the one for whose sake Kaṃsa had destroyed the seven other embryos. Kaṃsa's guards guarded that embryo carefully, but Hari himself, by his own wish, dwelt within that womb. Now, Yaśodā also received an embryo on that very day, and that embryo was Sleep herself, the servant of Viṣṇu, born of the body of Viṣṇu.

When the time of the pregnancy was still incomplete, after eight months, the two women, Devakī and Yaśodā, brought forth children together. On the night when the lord Kṛṣṇa was born to Devakī, wife of Vasudeva, in the family of the Vṛṣṇis, on that same night Yaśodā, wife of the cow-herd

43. Twenty-seven of Dakṣa's daughters were given in marriage to Soma, the moon, and are regarded as the twenty-seven lunar asterisms. The fourth, Rohiṇī, was favoured by Soma to the exclusion of all the others until Dakṣa cursed Soma to be childless and to suffer from consumption (the cause of the moon's waning). Soma's wives interceded on his behalf, and Dakṣa modified his curse so that the waning would be periodical.

Nanda, brought forth a daughter. Yaśodā and Devakī had become pregnant at the same time, and so when Devakī gave birth to Viṣṇu, Yaśodā gave birth to a daughter. At that moment, in the very middle of the night, when the moon was in 'Victorious', the oceans shook and the mountains trembled, and fires blazed peacefully, when the Exciter of Men was born. Gentle winds blew, and the dust lay undisturbed, and the stars shone brightly, when the Exciter was born. Drums which had not been struck resounded in the heaven of the gods, and the lord of the triple heaven sent down a rain of flowers from the sky. The great sages and Gandharvas and celestial nymphs approached the Chastiser of Madhu and praised him with auspicious and sacred words.

Then Vasudeva took up the little boy immediately, for he was frightened and full of tenderness toward his son, and he brought him to the house of Yaśodā. He gave the little boy, unrecognized, to Yaśodā and took her little girl and placed her on Devakī's bed. When the two children had been exchanged, Vasudeva was terrified, but he had done what he had to do. Then he went out of the house and reported to Kaṃsa, the son of Ugrasena, that a daughter of fair complexion had been born. When the mighty Kaṃsa heard this he hastened immediately with his guards and came to the door of Vasudeva's house, and at the door he said with brusque and menacing words, 'What has been born? Give it to me instantly!' Then all the women around Devakī cried out in alarm, and Devakī, stammering in her tears, said to Kaṃsa, 'A little girl has been born. My lord, you have killed my seven fine infant boys; this little daughter is already as good as dead. Look, if you don't believe me.' When Kaṃsa saw the girl he rejoiced and said, twisting her words with wicked intent, 'A daughter is indeed dead when she is born.' The infant girl was lying exhausted upon the bed of childbirth, her hair still moist from the water of the womb. Kaṃsa placed her on the ground before him, and the man took her by the foot and whirled her around vigorously and dashed her violently to the stone floor.

When she had been hurled down upon the stone floor, she flew up to heaven, unbruised, leaving behind the body of the infant. She entered the sky, wearing heavenly garlands and unguents, her hair loosened. She became an eternal, divine maiden, praised by the gods, four-armed. She wore dark blue and golden garments, and her breasts were like the swelling temples of elephants, her hips as broad as chariots, her face like the moon. Her complexion was like a flash of lightning; her eyes were like young suns; with her full breasts and her voice like thundering clouds, she was like a cloudy sunset.[44] When the night was swallowed by darkness and swarmed with bands of ghosts, she danced and laughed and shone against the darkness. This dreadful female in the sky drank from an enormous cup and laughed a great laugh and spoke in fury to Kaṃsa: 'Kaṃsa, Kaṃsa, since you attacked me to destroy me, hurling me down upon the stone, therefore at your death, when you are overpowered by your enemy, I will smash your body with my own hands and drink your warm blood.' When she had uttered this gruesome speech, the goddess wandered away with her bands of attendants, wandering wherever she pleased through the sky, the dwelling place of the gods.

When she had gone, Kaṃsa realized that she was his own death.

Four episodes from the Bhāgavata Purāṇa

The Kṛṣṇa of the *Bhāgavata Purāṇa* is a cow-herd (*gopa*), and the Vedic cow imagery is given a new dimension in this text: where the cows of Indra and Saramā were symbolic of wealth and battle spoils, and

44. This verse depends upon a play on words. *Payodhara*, 'liquid-bearing', may refer either to clouds (rain-bearing) or breasts (milk-bearing).

the cows of the Brāhmaṇas were sacrificial animals, the cows of the *Bhāgavata Purāṇa* are distinctly *not* to be killed – they are symbolic of maternal love (*vātsalya*, literally 'calf love'), the spirit of devotion which the worshipper should feel toward Kṛṣṇa, just as the cowherd women (*gopīs*) express through their erotic love for Kṛṣṇa another facet of this devotion.

Infancy: Kṛṣṇa kills the ogress Pūtanā

The mythology of Kṛṣṇa the baby, like the myth of Viṣṇu the dwarf, plays constantly upon the contrast between appearance and reality – the apparently tiny mortal (the dwarf, the infant, the individual soul) which occasionally reveals its true nature as the infinite immortal (the giant, the god, the universal godhead). Images of concealment abound in descriptions of the god: the sword in the sheath, the spark in ashes. A parallel masquerade takes place in the forces of evil, the hideous, putrid ogress disguised as a charming woman, the virulent poison which appears to be nourishing milk. The ambivalence of milk–poison is a central motif of Hindu mythology; the sweet milk of the Paṇis drugs Saramā, and Skanda's wet-nurse is the goddess of death, while the gods who churn the ocean of milk in order to obtain ambrosia also obtain poison.[45] In the present myth, this reversal (poison substituting for milk in Pūtanā's breasts) is reversed yet again, for the babe uses the act of sucking to kill *her* as she intended to kill him; and, finally, this reversal is in turn reversed, for it is said that by killing her when drinking her milk he purified her and made her sweet-smelling – i.e. he made the virtue which she had falsely assumed become real. As the present episode begins, Nanda has been to see Vasudeva and has been warned that Kṛṣṇa might be in danger.

58. FROM THE *Bhāgavata Purāṇa*

When Nanda heard the speech of Vasudeva he thought, as he went on the road homewards, that this could not be false, and he sought refuge with Hari, for he feared some misfortune.

The horrible Pūtanā ('Stinking'), a devourer of children,

45. For Saramā, see myth 22, pp. 72–3; for Skanda, myth 33, p. 114; for the churning, myth 72, p. 277.

was sent by Kaṃsa. She wandered through cities, villages, and pastures, killing infants. Wherever men do not recite the deeds of Kṛṣṇa the Lord of the Sātvatas, a recitation which destroys Rākṣasas, there evil demons work their sorcery. One day Pūtanā came to Nanda's village, wandering at will, flying through the sky,[46] and by her magic powers she assumed the form of a beautiful woman. Jasmine was bound into her hair; her hips and breasts were full, her waist slender. She wore fine garments, and her face was framed by hair that shone with the lustre from her shimmering, quivering earrings. She cast sidelong glances and smiled sweetly, and she carried a lotus in her hand. When the wives of the cow-herds saw the woman, who stole their hearts, they thought that she must be Śrī[47] incarnate, come to see her husband. The infant-swallower, searching for children, happened to come to the house of Nanda, and she saw there on the bed the infant Kṛṣṇa, whose true energy was concealed, like a fire covered with ashes. Though he kept his eyes closed, he who is the very soul of all that moves and all that is still knew her to be an ogress who killed children, and she took the infinite one onto her lap, as one might pick up a sleeping deadly viper, mistaking it for a rope. Seeing her, whose wicked heart was concealed by sweet actions like a sharp sword encased in a scabbard, his mother was overcome by her splendour, and, thinking her to be a good woman, stood looking on.

Then the horrible one, taking him on her lap, gave the baby her breast, which had been smeared with a virulent poison. But the lord, pressing her breast hard with his hands, angrily drank out her life's breath with the milk. She cried out,

46. In the *Harivaṃśa*, Pūtanā is a bird, who defies the distinction between the species of aves and mammals by giving Kṛṣṇa her poisonous breast to suck.

47. Śrī, 'Prosperity', is Lakṣmī, the wife of Viṣṇu and thus the wife of Kṛṣṇa. She carries a lotus, as Pūtanā does here.

'Let go! Let go! Enough!' as she was squeezed in all her vital parts. She rolled her eyes and thrashed her arms and legs and screamed again and again, and all her limbs were bathed in sweat. At the sound of her deep roar, the earth with its mountains and the sky with its planets shook; the subterranean waters and the regions of the sky resounded, and people fell to the ground fearing that lightning had struck. The night-wandering ogress, with agonizing pain in her breasts, opened her mouth, stretched out her arms and legs, tore her hair, and fell lifeless on the ground in the cow-pen, like the serpent Vṛtra struck down by Indra's thunderbolt. Then she resumed her true form, and as her body fell it crushed all the trees for twelve miles around; this was a great marvel. Her mouth was full of terrible teeth as large as plough-shafts; her nostrils were like mountain caves; her breasts were like boulders, and her hideous red hair was strewn about. Her eyes were like deep, dark wells; her buttocks were terrifying, large as beaches; her stomach was like a great dry lake emptied of water, her arms like dams. When the cow-herds and their wives saw her corpse they were terrified, and their hearts, ears, and skulls had already been split by her terrible roar.

When they saw the little boy playing on her breast fearlessly, the wives of the cow-herds were frightened and quickly took him away, and Yaśodā and Rohiṇī and the others protected the boy by waving a cow's tail on him and performing similar rites. They bathed the baby in cow's urine and cow-dust, and with cow-dung they wrote the names of Viṣṇu on his twelve limbs, to protect him . . .[48] Thus the loving wives of the cow-herds protected him, and then his mother gave her son her breast to suck and put him to bed.

Meanwhile, Nanda and the other cow-herds returned to the village from Mathurā, and when they saw the body of

48. Here they chant a series of spells protecting him from various ogresses and diseases.

Pūtanā they were astonished. 'Indeed, Anakadundubhi[49] has become a seer or a master of yoga,' they said, 'for he foresaw and foretold this whole calamity.' Then the villagers cut up the corpse with axes and threw the limbs far away, and they surrounded them with wood and burnt them. The smoke that arose from Pūtanā's body as it burnt was as sweet-smelling as aloe-wood, for her sins had been destroyed when she fed Kṛṣṇa. Pūtanā, a slayer of people and infants, a female Rākṣasa, a drinker of blood, reached the heaven of good people because she had given her breast to Viṣṇu – even though she did it because she wished to kill him. How much greater, then, is the reward of those who offer what is dearest to the highest Soul, Kṛṣṇa, with faith and devotion, like his doting mothers? She gave her breast to Kṛṣṇa to suck, and he touched her body with his two feet which remain in the hearts of his devotees and which are adored by those who are adored by the world, and so, though an evil sorceress, she obtained the heaven which is the reward of mothers. What then is the reward of those cows and mothers whose breasts' milk Kṛṣṇa drank? The lord, son of Devakī, giver of beatitude and all else, drank their milk as their breasts flowed because of their love for their son. Since they always looked upon Kṛṣṇa as their son, they will never again be doomed to rebirth that arises from ignorance.

When the inhabitants of the village smelled the sweet smoke from the pyre they asked, 'What is this? What has caused it?', and they returned to the village. There they heard the cowherds describe the arrival of Pūtanā and the subsequent events, and when they learned of the death of Pūtanā and the safety of the baby, they were amazed. The noble Nanda lovingly took his son on his lap like one who had returned from the

49. Vasudeva was called Anakadundubhi because at his birth the gods, foreseeing the birth of Kṛṣṇa, caused drums (*anaka* and *dundubhi*) to resound in heaven.

dead, and kissed his head and rejoiced. Whatever mortal faithfully hears this tale of the marvellous deed of the baby Kṛṣṇa, the liberation of Pūtanā, he finds his joy in Govinda.

Childhood: Kṛṣṇa's mother looks inside his mouth

The motif of concealment, of the big inside the little, of banal detail obscuring sacred majesty, assumes more metaphysical dimensions in the episode of Kṛṣṇa's open mouth, a motif based upon a much earlier myth from the *Mahābhārata*: the sage Mārkaṇḍeya was floating in the cosmic ocean after the dissolution of the universe, when he came upon a young boy sleeping under a banyan tree. He entered the mouth of the boy – who was Viṣṇu – and saw within him the entire universe, whereupon he came back out of Viṣṇu's mouth.[50] Through this link, the story of Kṛṣṇa and Yaśodā may be seen as part of the corpus of myths of rebirth through being swallowed.[51] Another masquerade typical of the *Bhāgavata Purāṇa* is the description of Kṛṣṇa's mischief: he pretends to be a good boy but does naughty things; yet his naughtiness is a source of pleasure to his mother, just as the apparent evils wrought by the gods – death, heresy, all the oppositional pairs[52] – are ultimately conducive to our welfare.

59. FROM THE *Bhāgavata Purāṇa*

After a little while, Rāma[53] and Keśava began to play in the village, crawling on their hands and knees. They slithered about quickly, dragging their feet in the muddy pastures, delighting in the tinkling sound.[54] They would follow some-

50. See *Mahābhārata* 3.183–190 and *Matsya* 167.

51. See myths 25, p. 81, and 73–4, pp. 281–7.

52. For death, see myth 8, pp. 38–43; for heresy, myth 62, pp. 232–5; for the pairs, myth 9, pp. 44–6.

53. Rāma in the *Bhāgavata Purāṇa* stories of Kṛṣṇa always refers to Balarāma, Saṃkarṣaṇa, the brother of Kṛṣṇa, and has nothing to do with the Rāma of the *Rāmāyaṇa*.

54. The commentator says that this is the sound of their own anklets and bangles.

one and then, suddenly bewildered and frightened, they would hasten back to their mothers. Their mothers' breasts would flow with milk out of tenderness for their own sons, whose bodies were beautifully covered with mud, and they would embrace them in their arms and give them their breasts to suck, and as they gazed at the faces with their innocent smiles and tiny teeth they would rejoice. Then the children began to play in the village at those boyish games that women love to see. They would grab hold of the tails of calves and be dragged back and forth in the pasture, and the women would look at them and forget their housework and laugh merrily. But the mothers, trying to keep the two very active and playful little boys from horned animals, fire, animals with teeth and tusks, and knives, water, birds, and thorns, were unable to do their housework, and they were rather uneasy.

After a little while, Rāma and Kṛṣṇa stopped crawling on their hands and knees and began to walk about the pastures quickly on their feet. Then the lord Kṛṣṇa began to play with Rāma and with the village boys of their age, giving great pleasure to the village women. When the wives of the cowherds saw the charming boyish pranks of Kṛṣṇa, they would go in a group to tell his mother, saying, 'Kṛṣṇa unties the calves when it is not the proper time, and he laughs at everyone's angry shouts. He devises ways to steal and eat curds and milk and thinks food sweet only if he steals it. He distributes the food among the monkeys; if he doesn't eat the food, he breaks the pot. If he cannot find anything, he becomes angry at the house and makes the children cry before he runs away. If something is beyond his reach, he fashions some expedient by piling up pillows, mortars, and so on; or if he knows that the milk and curds have been placed in pots suspended in netting, he makes holes in the pots. When the wives of the cow-herds are busy with household duties, he will steal things in a dark room, making his own body with its masses of jewels serve as a lamp. This is the sort of impudent act which he commits; and he pees and so forth in clean houses. These are the thieving tricks that he contrives, but he behaves in the opposite way and is good when you are near.' When his mother heard this report from the women who were looking at Kṛṣṇa's frightened eyes and beautiful face, she laughed and did not wish to scold him.

One day when Rāma and the other little sons of the cowherds were playing, they reported to his mother, 'Kṛṣṇa has eaten dirt.' Yaśodā took Kṛṣṇa by the hand and scolded him, for his own good, and she said to him, seeing that his eyes were bewildered with fear, 'Naughty boy, why have you secretly eaten dirt? These boys, your friends, and your elder brother say so.' Kṛṣṇa said, 'Mother, I have not eaten. They are all lying. If you think they speak the truth, look at my mouth yourself.' 'If that is the case, then open your mouth,' she said to the lord Hari, the god of unchallenged sovereignty who had in sport taken the form of a human child, and he opened his mouth.

She then saw in his mouth the whole eternal universe, and heaven, and the regions of the sky, and the orb of the earth with its mountains, islands, and oceans; she saw the wind, and lightning, and the moon and stars, and the zodiac; and water and fire and air and space itself; she saw the vacillating senses, the mind, the elements, and the three strands of matter. She saw within the body of her son, in his gaping mouth, the whole universe in all its variety, with all the forms of life and time and nature and action and hopes, and her own village, and herself. Then she became afraid and confused, thinking, 'Is this a dream or an illusion wrought by a god? Or is it a delusion of my own perception? Or is it some portent of the natural powers of this little boy, my son? I bow down to the feet of the god, whose nature cannot be imagined or grasped by mind, heart, acts, or speech; he in whom all of this universe is inherent, impossible to fathom. The god is my refuge, he through whose power of delusion there arise in me such false beliefs as "I", "This is my husband", "This is my son", "I am the wife of the village chieftain and all his wealth is mine, including these cow-herds and their wives and their wealth of cattle."'

When the cow-herd's wife had come to understand the true essence in this way, the lord spread his magic illusion in the form of maternal affection. Instantly the cow-herd's wife lost her memory of what had occurred and took her son on her lap. She was as she had been before, her heart flooded with even greater love. She considered Hari – whose greatness is extolled by the three Vedas and the Upaniṣads and the philosophies of Sāṅkhya and yoga and all the Sātvata texts – she considered him to be her son.

Adolescence: Kṛṣṇa subdues the serpent Kāliya

The story of Kṛṣṇa and Kāliya further expands the contrast between poison and ambrosia: the snake poisons the pool, while Kṛṣṇa makes its water 'like ambrosia' by churning it with his feet, just as the gods churn the ocean to obtain ambrosia and poison (and the ocean is the final resting-place for Kāliya, as it is for all other destructive forces). The snake has poison in his gaze, while Kṛṣṇa has ambrosia in his. Kāliya is the enemy of the Garuḍa bird, for snakes are symbolic of death, poison, and the underworld, while birds are symbolic of birth (the egg being a visible symbol of the world-egg, the golden egg in the cosmic waters), ambrosia (for the bird carries seed or Soma in his beak),[55] and heaven. Viṣṇu combines these symbols within himself, for he sleeps on the serpent of eternity (Ananta or Śeṣa – the good *alter ego* of the evil Kāliya) and then awakens to ride on the Garuḍa bird; but in this myth he is a dragon-killer, slaying Kāliya as Indra slays Vṛtra, purifying the pool as Indra releases the trapped waters.

55. See above, myth 33, pp. 110–12, and below, myth 73, p. 281.

60. FROM THE *Bhāgavata Purāṇa*

At the beginning of each month, all the serpents used to receive an offering under a tree, to prevent unpleasantness; this was agreed long ago by the people in the realm of the snakes. And each of the serpents, to protect himself, would give a portion of this offering to the noble Suparṇa[56] at the beginning of each lunar fortnight. But Kāliya, the son of Kadrū,[57] was full of pride because of the virulence of his poison, and he disregarded Garuḍa and himself ate that offering. When the lord Garuḍa who is loved by the lord Viṣṇu learned of this he became angry and flew swiftly after Kāliya to kill him; and when the serpent, whose weapons were poison and fangs, saw him approaching swiftly he raised his many heads with their hideous tongues and hisses and fierce eyes and began to bite Suparṇa with his fangs. But Garuḍa the son of Tārkṣya, the mount of the Chastiser of Madhu, became furious and swooped down upon him with a fierce attack and a great blast of speed, and struck the son of Kadrū with his left wing, which shone like gold. When Kāliya was struck by the wing of Suparṇa he was greatly afflicted, and he entered a pool in the river Kālindī which Garuḍa could not enter or reach.

For in that very place Garuḍa had once eaten a fish that he wanted; even though the sage Saubhari had forbidden him to

56. 'He who has beautiful feathers', an epithet of Garuḍa. Garuḍa is also called Tārkṣya, an epithet originally designating a horse.

57. Kadrū, daughter of Dakṣa, wife of Kaśyapa, was the progenitor of the race of *nāgas* or snakes. She once made a bet with Vinatā, mother of Garuḍa and the birds, that the horse Uccaiḥśravas had a black tail. Winning this bet by a ruse, she made Vinatā her slave, promising her freedom only if Garuḍa brought the ambrosia to the snakes. Garuḍa stole the ambrosia from the gods and placed it before the snakes on a bed of sharp *kuśa* grass. The snakes freed Vinatā and licked the grass, making their tongues forked, but Indra then stole back the ambrosia.

eat it, Garuḍa was so hungry that he ate it by force. And when Saubhari saw the poor fishes so miserable, their lord having been slain, he was overcome with pity and wished to protect and preserve the creatures there. 'If Garuḍa enters here to eat the fishes,' he said, 'he will immediately part with his life's breath; this I swear.' Kāliya knew of this, but no other serpent knew it; and so, because he feared Garuḍa, he dwelt there, until he was expelled by Kṛṣṇa . . .

One day as the lord Kṛṣṇa was wandering about in Vṛndāvana without Rāma, he went with his friends to the river Kālindī. The cows and cow-herds were oppressed by the heat of summer and suffering from thirst, and they drank the polluted and poisoned water of the river. Their wits were overwhelmed by fate so that they touched that poisoned water, and they all fell lifeless on the bank. When Kṛṣṇa, the lord of the lords of yoga, saw them in that condition, he revived his followers with a glance that rained ambrosia. They arose from the bank, their memories restored, and they looked at one another in amazement as they realized that their revival from death after drinking poison had been brought about by the favour of a glance from Govinda . . .

There was a certain pool in the Kālindī into whose waters, which boiled with the fire of Kāliya's poison, fell birds which were passing overhead and struck by blasts of air laden with drops from its poisonous waves; and breathing creatures, moving and still, who came to its banks died. When Kṛṣṇa, who had become incarnate to restrain the wicked, perceived that the river had been polluted by that serpent whose poison was so virulent and swiftly active, he climbed a very high Kadamba tree, clapped his hands, girded his loins tightly, and plunged into the poisoned water. The mass of water in that pool of serpents was swelled by the poison emitted by serpents who were shaken by the blast caused by the vigorous dive of the Man, and it overflowed for a hundred bow-lengths on all sides with terrible waves tawny with poison, but this was nothing to him of infinite might.

When Kāliya heard the noise of the whirling of the club-like arms of Kṛṣṇa, who was playing in the pool like a rogue elephant, and saw his own residence overwhelmed, he was unable to bear the sight and sound, and he slithered out. He enveloped angrily with his coils and bit in his vital spots that boy whose feet were like the inside of a lotus, who was bright as a cloud, beautiful to see in his youth, adorned with the Śrīvatsa, wearing yellow garments, with a beautiful smile on his face, playing fearlessly. When Kṛṣṇa's dear friends the cattle-tenders saw him caught up in the coils of the serpent, apparently motionless, they were greatly distressed; since they had consigned themselves, their friends, their wealth, their families, and all their desires to Kṛṣṇa, their minds were stupefied with grief, sorrow, and fear, and they fell down. The cows and bulls and calves lowed in their misery; gazing at Kṛṣṇa in fear, they stood and seemed to weep.

Then there appeared in the village three kinds of violent great portent boding danger nearby: there were calamities on earth, in heaven, and in the body. When Nanda and the other cow-herds noted them they were terrified, knowing that Kṛṣṇa had gone to tend the cows without Rāma. Not knowing who he really was, they thought that his death had come, because of the evil portents; and since he was their very life's breath, and their hearts were set upon him, they were tortured by grief, sorrow, and fear. All the cow-herds, the young, the old, and the women, went miserably out of the village, hoping to see Kṛṣṇa. When the lord Bala saw them so discouraged he laughed, but he did not say a word, for he knew the powers of his younger brother.

As they searched for their beloved Kṛṣṇa by following the path indicated by the footprints with the signs of the lord, they all came to the banks of the Yamunā. Hastening along on the path, they distinguished between the footprints of the cows and the footprints of the lord of all, for these were marked by the lotus, barley shoot, elephant goad, thunderbolt, and banner. When from a distance they saw Kṛṣṇa in the pool, the watery abode, wrapped in the serpent's coils, and they saw the cow-herds stupefied and the cattle scattered and lowing, they became deeply alarmed and unhappy. The hearts of the cow-herds' wives were passionately devoted to the infinite lord, and they remembered his friendship, his smiles and glances and words; and when their dearest one was swallowed by the serpent they were burnt by great sorrow and saw the triple world as empty, for it was devoid of their beloved. They went to Kṛṣṇa's mother, who was sorrowing for her child, and they sympathized with her and wept, for they shared their grief, and they told their favourite village stories, and fixed their gazes upon Kṛṣṇa's face and seemed as if dead. When the lord Rāma, who knew the true majesty of Kṛṣṇa, saw that Nanda and the others, whose very life's breath was Kṛṣṇa, were about to enter the pool, he prevented them.

Kṛṣṇa, seeing that his own village, with its women and children, was so miserable because of him, and knowing that it had no refuge other than him, conformed to the way of mortals and, staying for a moment, rose up from the serpent's grip. The serpent's hoods were tortured by the expanding body of Kṛṣṇa, and he released him; he raised his hoods angrily and stood spitting venom through his hissing nostrils; he stared at Hari with his unblinking eyes that were like frying pans, and he licked the two corners of his mouth with his forked tongue, and his very gaze was full of the fire of a virulent poison. Playfully, Kṛṣṇa circled about him, like Garuḍa, the lord of birds, and Kāliya also moved about, watching for an opportunity. When the serpent's strength was exhausted by moving about in this way, the First bent down the snake's raised shoulder and mounted upon his broad heads.

Then the master of all musical arts danced, his lotus feet made bright red by their contact with the multitude of jewels on the serpent's head.[58] When the wives of the Gandharvas, Siddhas, divine Cāraṇas, and gods saw that he was preparing to dance, they approached him joyfully with offerings of Mṛdaṅga, Paṇava, and Anaka drums, and musical instruments, and songs and flowers and praise.

He who bears a cruel rod of punishment trampled with his feet whatever head of the hundred-headed one was yet unbent, and the serpent, his life-span spent but still writhing, vomited clotted blood from his mouth and fell, suffering horribly. The Ancient Man danced on the serpent who still spewed poison from his eyes and hissed loudly in his anger, and he trampled down with his feet whatever head the serpent raised, subduing him as calmly as if he were being worshipped with flowers. Kāliya, his umbrella of hoods shattered by the gay dance of death, his limbs broken, vomiting blood copiously from his mouths, remembered the guru of all who move and are still, the Ancient Man, Nārāyaṇa, and he surrendered to him in his heart.

When Kāliya's wives saw that the serpent was sinking down under the burden of Kṛṣṇa who is the very womb of the universe, and that his umbrella of hoods was crushed by the blows of Kṛṣṇa's heels, then they were distressed, and their garments, ornaments, and hair-bindings became loose, and they sought refuge with the Primary One. Their hearts aching, the good women placed their children in front of them, prostrated their bodies on the ground, folded their palms together, bowed to the lord of creatures and sought refuge with him who gives refuge, for they wished to save their husband from harm and release him from sin.

The serpent's wives said, 'Your punishment of this man who has sinned is proper, for you became incarnate to restrain

58. Great cobras are said to have rubies imbedded in their hoods.

the wicked. Viewing with an indifferent gaze your enemy or your own sons, considering only the fruit of actions, you mete out punishment. You have favoured us, for your punishment of the wicked removes their impurity. Even your anger should be considered an act of grace, because our husband is embodied as a venomous reptile[59] . . . You should endure the offence committed by our husband, committed by your own creature. As you have a peaceful soul, you should forgive the fool who did not know you. Lord, be gracious; the serpent is giving up his life's breaths. Grant life's breath to our husband, for we are women for whom good people will sorrow. Command us, your servants, for one who obeys your commands with faith is released from all danger.'

When the lord was thus praised by the wives of the serpent, he released the unconscious Kāliya whose head had been smashed by the pounding of his feet. The wretched Kāliya gradually regained his senses and his life's breath, and breathing with difficulty he folded his palms together and said to Hari, Kṛṣṇa, 'We are evil from our birth, dark creatures whose anger endures. O lord, one's own nature is difficult to abandon, for it possesses people like an evil demon. Creator, this whole universe was created by you out of the three strands, with various natures, powers, strengths, sources, seeds, hopes, and forms. And in it are we, O lord, serpents whose anger is far-reaching from birth. How can we ourselves, deluded creatures, abandon your delusion which is hard to abandon? You are the cause of this, omniscient one, lord of the universe; ordain for us grace or punishment, as you think best.'

Then the lord, who had taken human form, answered, 'You must not stay here, serpent; go quickly to the ocean with your abundant kinsmen, children, and wives. Let this river be enjoyed by cows and men. Whatever mortal remembers my

59. That is, he is in a form from which your anger will soon release him, or a form which justifies your anger.

chastisement of you and recites it at dawn and sunset, he will have no fear of you. And whoever bathes in this pool where I have played and offers its waters to the gods and others, and fasts and remembers me and worships me, he will be released from all sins. Leave this pool and take shelter in the island Ramaṇaka. Suparṇa, whom you feared, will not eat you now that you have been marked by my foot.' When Kāliya heard the words of the lord Kṛṣṇa whose deeds are marvellous, he worshipped him in joy and ceremony, with his wives. He worshipped the lord of the universe, whose banner bears the Garuḍa, and propitiated him with excellent celestial garments, garlands, and jewels, with rich ornaments and with celestial perfumes and unguents, and with a great garland of lotuses; and he walked around him in reverence and bowed to him and happily received permission to leave. Then, with his wives, friends, and sons he went to the island in the ocean, and at that moment the Yamunā became free from poison, its water like ambrosia, by the grace of the lord who had taken human form for his sport.

Manhood: Kṛṣṇa steals the clothes of the girls of the village

In the battle with Kāliya, the concept of the devotee longing for god is expressed through the image of three groups of women bereft of their protectors – the fish-women whose lord is killed, the wives of Kāliya, and the cow-herd women who long for the child Kṛṣṇa. This image is further developed in later chapters, where Kṛṣṇa dances erotically in the moonlight with the cow-herd women (just as he danced the dance of death on Kāliya), only to vanish from their midst.

In another episode of this cycle, the stealing of the girls' clothes, the childish pranks of the little Kṛṣṇa are replaced by a well-worn bit of erotic strategy, yet the metaphysical overtones of this mischief are profound; by forcing the girls to reveal their nakedness, he forces them into a direct encounter with their god, and although the mortal Kṛṣṇa tricks them into clasping their hands over their heads so that he can get a full view of their bodies, the immortal Kṛṣṇa thus places them in an attitude of reverent devotion before him.

61. FROM THE *Bhāgavata Purāṇa*

In the first month of winter, the girls of Nanda's village performed a certain vow to the goddess Kātyāyanī. They ate rice cooked with clarified butter; they bathed in the water of the Kālindī river at sunrise; they made an image of the goddess out of sand and worshipped it with fragrant perfumes and garlands, with offerings and incense and lamps, and with bouquets of flowers, fresh sprigs of leaves, fruits, and rice. And they prayed: 'Goddess Kātyāyanī, great mistress of yoga, empress of great deluding magic, make the son of the cow-herd Nanda my husband. I bow to you.' Saying this prayer, the girls would worship her, and having set their hearts on Kṛṣṇa, the girls performed this vow for a month; they worshipped Bhadrakālī so that the son of Nanda would be their husband. Arising at dawn, calling one another by name, they would join hands and go to bathe in the Kālindī every day, singing loudly about Kṛṣṇa as they went.

One day, when they had gone to the river and taken off their clothes on the bank as usual, they were playing joyfully in the water, singing about Kṛṣṇa. The lord Kṛṣṇa, lord of all masters of yoga, came there with his friends of the same age in order to grant them the object of their rites. He took their clothes and quickly climbed a Nīpa tree, and laughing with the laughing boys he told what the joke was: 'Girls, let each one of you come here and take her own clothes as she wishes. I promise you, this is no jest, for you have been exhausted by your vows. I have never before told an untruth, and these boys know this. Slender-waisted ones, come one by one or all together and take your clothes.' When the cow-herd girls saw what his game was, they were overwhelmed with love, but they looked at one another in shame, and they smiled, but they did not come out. Flustered and embarrassed by Govinda's words and by his jest, they sank down up to their necks in the icy water, and, shivering, they said to him, 'You should not have played such a wicked trick. We know you as our beloved, son of the cow-herd Nanda, the pride of the village. Give us our clothes, for we are trembling. O darkly handsome one, we are your slaves and will do as you command, but you know *dharma*: give us our clothes or we will tell your father, the chieftain.'

The lord said to them, 'If you are my slaves and will do as I command, then come here and take back your clothes, O brightly smiling ones.' Then all the girls, shivering and smarting with cold, came out of the water, covering their crotches with their hands. The lord was pleased and gratified by their chaste actions, and he looked at them and placed their clothes on his shoulder and smiled and said, 'Since you swam in the water without clothes while you were under a vow, this was an insult to the divinity.[60] Therefore you must fold your hands and place them on your heads and bow low in expiation of your sin, and then you may take your clothes.' When the village girls heard what the infallible one said, they thought that bathing naked had been a violation of their vows, and they bowed down to Kṛṣṇa, the very embodiment of all their rituals, who had thus fulfilled their desires and wiped out their disgrace and sin. Then the lord, the son of Devakī, gave their clothes to them, for he felt pity when he saw them bowed down in this way and he was satisfied with them.

Though they were greatly deceived and robbed of their modesty, though they were mocked and treated like toys and stripped of their clothes, yet they held no grudge against him, for they were happy to be together with their beloved. Re-

60. Because they had exposed their naked bodies to Varuṇa, god of the waters. Compare the sin of the Kṛttikās in exposing themselves to Agni by bathing naked, above, myth 43, p. 167.

joicing in the closeness of their lover, they put on their clothes; their bashful glances, in the thrall of their hearts, did not move from him. Knowing that the girls had taken a vow because they desired to touch his feet, the lord with a rope around his waist said to the girls, 'Good ladies, I know that your desire is to worship me. I rejoice in this vow, which deserves to be fulfilled. The desire of those whose hearts have been placed in me does not give rise to further desire, just as seed corn that has been boiled or fried does not give rise to seed. You have achieved your aim. Now, girls, go back to the village and you will enjoy your nights with me, for it was for this that you fine ladies undertook your vow and worship.' When the girls heard this from Kṛṣṇa, they had obtained what they desired; and, meditating upon his lotus feet, they forced themselves to go away from him to the village.

The Purāṇic avatars of Viṣṇu

Viṣṇu Becomes the Buddha to Delude the Demons

The Buddha avatar is not, as it might seem at first glance, a true attempt to assimilate the teachings of the Buddha into Hinduism (though this was certainly done in many other ways); on the contrary, although it is Viṣṇu who expresses (most cogently) the anti-Vedic sentiments attributed by Hindus to Buddhists, Jains, Materialists, and other heretics, he does this in order to destroy the demons with an *evil* doctrine – Buddhism – on the principle that one cannot destroy a virtuous person unless one corrupts him first. That mankind is also converted to Buddhism (and Jainism) is merely an unfortunate by-product of Viṣṇu's act, in the Hindu view; and the fact that the doctrine is directed to the demons indicates the fanatic degree of anti-Buddhist sentiment that motivated the author of this myth.

62. FROM THE *Viṣṇu Purāṇa*

There was once a battle between the gods and the demons that lasted for a hundred celestial years, in which the gods were conquered by the demons commanded by Hrāda. The gods went to the northern shore of the ocean of milk and practised asceticism in order to propitiate Viṣṇu, and they sang a hymn of praise to him . . . When they had finished praising him, the gods saw the supreme lord Hari mounted on the Garuḍa bird, with his conch and discus and mace in his hands. All the gods prostrated themselves before him and said, 'Have mercy, lord; protect us from the demons, as we have come for refuge. The demons under the command of Hrāda have stolen away our portions of the sacrifices in the triple world, but they have not violated the command of Brahmā, O supreme lord. Even though we and they are both born of portions of you, who are the essence of all creatures, nevertheless we see the universe as divided, a distinction caused by ignorance. They take pleasure in the duties of their own class, and they follow the path of the Vedas and are full of ascetic powers. Therefore we cannot kill them, although they are our enemies, and so you should devise some means by which we will be able to kill the demons, O lord, soul of everything without exception.'

When the lord Viṣṇu heard their request, he emitted from his body a deluding form of his magic power of illusion,[61] and he gave it to the supreme gods and said, 'This magic deluder will bewitch all the demons so that they will be excluded from the path of the Vedas, and thus they will be susceptible to slaughter. For no matter how many gods, demons, or others obstruct the way of the authority of Brahmā, I will slaughter them all in order to establish order. Therefore go

61. *Māyāmoha*, literally, delusion (*moha*) caused by magic illusion (*māyā*).

away and do not fear; this magic deluder will go before you today and assist you, gods.' When the gods heard this they prostrated themselves before him and went back whence they had come, and the magic deluder went with the great gods to the place where the great demons were.

When the magic deluder, naked, bald, carrying a bunch of peacock feathers,[62] saw that the great demons had gone to the banks of the Narmadā river and were practising asceticism, he spoke to the demons with smooth words, saying, 'Lord of demons! Tell me why you are practising asceticism – do you wish for the fruits of asceticism in this world or in the world beyond?' The demons replied, 'Noble one, we have undertaken this practice of asceticism in order to obtain the fruits of the world beyond. What is there here for you to dispute?' He said, 'Do as I say, if you wish for release,[63] for you are worthy of this *dharma* which is the open door to release. This is the *dharma* worthy of release, and there is none better than this; by following it you will obtain heaven or release. All of you, mighty ones, are worthy of this *dharma*.' With many deductions, examples, and arguments of this sort, the magic deluder led the demons from the path of the Vedas: 'This would be *dharma*, but it would not be *dharma*; this is, but it is not; this would give release, but it would not give release; this is the supreme object, but it is also not the supreme object; this is effect, but it is not effect; this is not crystal clear. This is the *dharma* of those who are naked; this is the *dharma* of those who wear many clothes.' Thus the magic deluder taught a varying doctrine of more than one conclusion to the demons, who abandoned their own *dharma*. And they who took refuge in

62. Jains would go about naked and carry a small broom made of peacock feathers, which they used to brush their paths clean lest they should inadvertently tread on insects or other small living creatures.

63. The fourth goal, *mokṣa*. A Buddhist would more likely have referred to *nirvāṇa*.

this dharma became Ārhatas,[64] because the magic deluder said to them, 'You are worthy [*arhata*] of this great *dharma*.'

When the magic deluder had caused the demons to abandon the *dharma* of the triple Vedas, they themselves became his disciples and persuaded others; and yet others were persuaded by these, and still others by those, and so in a few days most of the demons abandoned the three Vedas. Then the magic deluder, who had subdued his senses, put on a red garment and went and spoke to other demons in soft, short, and honeyed words: 'If you demons wish for heaven or for Nirvāṇa, then realize that you must stop these evil rites such as killing animals. Comprehend that all this universe is perceived only by means of knowledge; understand my speech properly, for it has been said by wise men. All this universe is without support and is intent upon achieving what it mistakenly believes to be knowledge; it wanders in the straits of existence, corrupted by passion and the other emotions.' As he said to them over and over, 'Understand! [*budhyata*],' the magic deluder caused the demons to abandon their own *dharma*, and with various speeches employing logic he made them gradually abandon the *dharma* of the triple Vedas. Then they spoke in this way to others, who addressed yet others in this way, so that they abandoned the highest *dharma* which is taught in the Vedas and lawbooks.

Then the magic deluder, capable of producing total delusion, corrupted other demons with many other sorts of heresy, and in a very short time the demons were corrupted by the magic deluder and abandoned the entire teaching of the triple path of the Vedas. Some reviled the Vedas; others the gods; and others the collection of sacrificial rituals and the twice-born. 'This speech is not logical, that "injury is con-

64. Ārhata here clearly designates Jains, in contrast with the Buddhists who are about to appear; but Ārhata could also have meant a Buddhist monk.

ducive to *dharma*".'[65] 'It is the babbling of a child, to say that butter burnt as an oblation in the fire is productive of reward.' 'If the *śamī* fire-sticks and other wood are consumed by Indra, who has become a god by means of many sacrifices, then a beast who eats leaves is better than Indra.' 'If an animal slaughtered in the sacrifice is thus promised entry into heaven, why does not the sacrificer kill his own father?' 'If the oblation to the ancestors which is eaten by one man satisfies another, then people travelling abroad need not take the trouble to carry food.'[66] 'When you have understood what contemptible people will believe in, then the words I have uttered will please you. The words of authority do not fall from the sky, great demons; only the speech based upon logic should be accepted by men and by others like you.'

When the magic deluder had made the demons free-thinkers with many speeches like this, not one of them took pleasure in the triple Vedas. And when the demons were thus set upon the wrong path, the immortals made the supreme effort and prepared for battle. Then the battle between the gods and demons was resumed, and the gods slew the demons, who now stood in opposition to the right path. The armour of their own *dharma* which had at first been theirs had formerly protected them, and when it was destroyed, they were destroyed.

Viṣṇu Becomes Incarnate as Kalkin to End the Kali Age

Kalkin, Viṣṇu's final avatar, is the only one yet to come in the future, the messiah who will appear at the end of the present age, the Kali

65. Or: This speech is not proper, for injury (the sacrificial ritual) is not conducive to *dharma*.

66. Because their sons and others could eat it for them at home in the village, just as the living son nourishes his dead and absent ancestors – so the commentator explains.

Age. It is probable that this idea entered India with the Parthian invasions of the first centuries of the Christian era, a time when millennial ideas were rampant in Europe. Kalkin himself has the form of an invader: he comes riding on a white horse, like the Scythian and Parthian invaders of India. But his purpose is to destroy the invaders, to raze the wicked cities of the plain which have been polluted by foreign kings – these same horsemen – as well as to exterminate all heretics, including the Buddhists that he had himself just produced in his penultimate incarnation.

In reversing the Kali Age in this manner, Viṣṇu challenges the force of time itself, for the Kali Age was *meant* to be evil. Yet the dice of fate are not loaded, for the tide of evil civilization seems to turn even before Viṣṇu appears: people leave the wicked cities and eat roots and wear bark garments, just like virtuous sages; the seeds of the new Kṛta Age, the golden age, are already sown in the Kali Age, and Viṣṇu merely acts as a catalyst, a cog in the wheel of time.

63. FROM THE *Viṣṇu Purāṇa*

Unable to support their avaricious kings, the people of the Kali Age will take refuge in the chasms between mountains, and they will eat honey, vegetables, roots, fruits, leaves, and flowers. They will wear ragged garments made of leaves and the bark of trees, and they will have too many children, and they will be forced to bear cold, wind, sun, and rain. No-one's age-span will reach twenty-three years, and thus without respite the entire race will become destroyed in this Kali Age.

When Vedic religion and the *dharma* of the lawbooks have undergone total confusion and reversal and the Kali Age is almost exhausted, then a part of the creator of the entire universe, of the guru of all that moves and is still, without beginning, middle, or end, who is made of Brahmā and has the form of the soul, the blessed lord Vāsudeva – he will become incarnate here in the universe in the form of Kalkin, endowed with the eight supernatural powers, in the house of Viṣṇuyaśas,[67] the chief brahmin of the village of Śambala. His power and glory will be unlimited, and he will destroy all the barbarians and Dasyus[68] and men of evil acts and thoughts, and he will re-establish everything, each in its own *dharma*. Immediately at the conclusion of the exhausted Kali Age, the minds of the people will become pure as flawless crystal, and they will be as if awakened at the conclusion of a night. And these men, the residue of mankind, will thus be transformed, and they will be the seeds of creatures and will give birth to offspring conceived at that very time. And these offspring will follow the ways of the Kṛta Age.[69]

67. 'Fame of Viṣṇu'. In the *Mahābhārata*, the only indication that Kalkin is an avatar of Viṣṇu is the statement that Kalkin himself is 'Viṣṇuyaśas'.

68. Literally, slaves, a term used in the *Ṛg Veda* to designate non-Aryan aborigines, but here probably denoting any non-Hindus.

69. 'Because of the very nature of time itself,' explains the commentator.

6

DEVĪ, THE GODDESS

THE Goddess has been worshipped in India from prehistoric times, for strong evidence of a cult of the Mother has been unearthed at the pre-Vedic civilization of the Indus Valley (*c.* 2000 B.C.). Her assimilation into the Hindu pantheon, however, took place long after Śiva and Viṣṇu had been accepted, and in two distinct phases: first the Indo-Aryan male gods were given wives, and then, under the influence of Tantric and Śāktic movements which had been gaining momentum outside orthodox Hinduism for many centuries, these shadowy female figures emerged as supreme powers in their own right, and merged into the great Goddess. Abstract nouns, grammatically feminine, had occasionally been personified and 'wedded' to the great gods; thus Śrī (Prosperity) 'belonged' to Viṣṇu, and Śiva had his Śakti or Power, but these personifications merely expressed the qualities of the god to whom they were attached. Similarly, female divinities had served as the objects or instruments of divine struggles from the earliest times; thus Saramā was used to win the cattle from the Paṇis, and Pārvatī was used first to cause Śiva to beget a son and then to tempt Andhaka to his doom. But when the Goddess came into her element in the medieval period, these early myths were retold in a new light, with the Goddess using the gods to serve her higher purposes.

Devī slays the buffalo demon

The myth of the slaughter of the buffalo demon (Mahiṣa) falls clearly into the corpus of sacrificial myths which includes the beheading of Dakṣa (the goat) and the dissolution of the cosmic boar. As this is the most famous myth of the Goddess, it is usually the occasion for a description of her birth, which takes place in a manner similar to the creation of Rudra and of Śiva's chariot;[1] parts of all the gods combine to form a deity more powerful than all of them, the whole that is greater than the sum of its parts.

Devī and the Buffalo Demon are Born

64. FROM THE *Skanda Purāṇa*

In times past, in the battle between gods and demons, the sons of Diti were destroyed by the gods. Then Diti was distraught by grief, and she said to her daughter, 'Go, my daughter, and practise asceticism in a grove of asceticism for the sake of a son, so that because of that son Indra and the other gods, who have restrained their senses and are self-controlled, will no longer remain, O fair-hipped one.' When the daughter heard her mother's words, she bowed to her and took the form of a buffalo; she went to the forest and sat between five fires.[2] She practised asceticism so dreadful that the worlds trembled and the triple world was agitated by fear of her asceticism, and Indra and the other bands of gods and the supreme twice-born ones were stupefied. The sage Supārśva was shaken by her asceticism and said to her, 'Fair-hipped one, I am satisfied. You will have a son with the head of a buffalo and the body of a man, and your son's name will be Mahiṣa ['Buffalo']. He will have heroic energy in excess, and he will oppress heaven and Indra and his army.' When Supārśva had thus spoken to her to cause her to desist from her asceticism, he went back to his own world, taking the ascetic woman with him. Then the buffalo was born as Brahmā had formerly predicted, and he grew up and increased in heroic power as the great ocean grows during a lunar fortnight.

1. See above, myth 3, p. 29, and 37, pp. 130–33.

2. That is, she built four fires, one on each side of her, and sat beneath the sun as the fifth.

Then Vidyunmālin, the general of the demons, the son of Vipracitti, and other demon chiefs who live on the surface of the earth all heard of the boon that had been given to the buffalo, and they assembled joyously and said to the buffalo demon, 'Formerly we were kings in heaven, O clever one, but our kingdom was forcibly stolen by the gods when they sought refuge with Viṣṇu.[3] Bring that kingdom back to us by force; display your heroic power and your majesty today, buffalo demon. Your strength and heroism are unparalleled, and you have been elevated by the boon given by Brahmā. Conquer the husband of Śacī and the hosts of the gods in battle.' When the buffalo of great heroic power heard what the demons said, he began to wish to fight with the immortals, and he set out for Amarāvatī, the city of the gods.

A fierce, hair-raising battle between the gods and demons then took place for a hundred years, and at first the multitude of gods was put to flight in all directions; placing the Shatterer of Cities before them, they went to Brahmā in terror. Then Brahmā took all the immortals back to Nārāyaṇa and Śiva, the protectors of everything, and he arrived and bowed and praised them with many hymns of praise, and he reported to the two gods, Śambhu and Kṛṣṇa, what the buffalo demon had done and how the demons had oppressed the gods: 'He has thrown Indra, Agni, Yama, the sun, the moon, Kubera, Varuṇa and the others out of their positions of authority and assumed these positions himself; and he has usurped the positions of others among the multitude of gods as well. The gods have been thrown out of the world of heaven down to the surface of the earth and are wandering like men, hard pressed by the buffalo demon. I have come here with the bands of gods to report this to you two gods; protect those who have come here.'

3. Viṣṇu, incarnate as the dwarf, stole heaven from Bali. See above, myth 49, pp. 178–9.

When Viṣṇu, the husband of Lakṣmī, and the great lord Śiva heard the speech of Brahmā, their angry faces became so monstrous that one could not look upon them. From Viṣṇu's mouth, that blazed with extreme anger, his great energy came forth, and similarly from Śambhu and from the Creator, and from the bodies of Indra and all the other gods the cruel energies came forth and they all became one. The great mass of their united energies seemed to all the multitudes of gods like a blazing mountain that pervaded all the regions of the sky with flames. Then from the combination of these energies a certain woman appeared: her head appeared from the energy of Śiva, her two arms from the energy of Viṣṇu, her two feet from the energy of Brahmā, and her waist from the energy of Indra; her hair was made from Yama's energy, her two breasts from the moon's energy, her thighs from the energy of Varuṇa, her hips from the earth's energy, her toes from the sun's energy; her fingers were formed by the energy of the Vasus, her nose by Kubera's energy, her rows of teeth from the energy of the nine Prajāpatis; her two eyes arose from the energy of the Oblation-bearer; the two twilights became her two brows, and her ears were made from the energy of the wind; and from the incredibly fierce energies of the other gods other limbs were made for the woman who was the supremely radiant Durgā, more dangerous than all the gods and demons.

Devī Entices the Buffalo Demon

In another version of this myth the Goddess is not created expressly in order to kill the buffalo demon but is considered to exist already; now the gods give her not their energies but their weapons. The gods beg her to assume the role of a celestial nymph, to seduce and thus weaken the demon; but, unlike the conventional nymph, she is to kill him herself. This motif of the *Liebestod* appears in other myths of the Goddess; the demons Śumbha and Niśumbha, who were originally seduced by the most famous of celestial nymphs, Tilottamā, meet their death when they are overcome by desire for the Goddess, as does the demon Andhaka;[4] and later, under Tantric influence, Śiva himself, her husband, is slain by Devī.

A number of motifs are taken from the myth of Śiva and Pārvatī with the roles reversed and distributed between Devī and the buffalo: Devī places four guards at her door, just as she stations Vīraka when she goes to win a golden skin, and as Śiva stations guards to prevent the intrusions of Kāma, Bhṛgu, and Agni;[5] and the servants of the buffalo elude those guards in the same form that Agni assumes for this purpose, that of a bird. The buffalo then approaches the ascetic girl in disguise, just as Śiva approaches Gaurī; and he tries to lure her from Śiva as Jalandhara and Andhaka attempt to do. In this particular variant, it is Śiva, rather than Brahmā, who grants a boon to the demon: he will meet his death at the hands of the Goddess, a death which is considered to be a boon, releasing him from his sins (and from the buffalo form in which his soul is imprisoned) just as Śiva releases Andhaka and the boar and Kṛṣṇa releases Pūtanā.[6]

65. FROM THE *Skanda Purāṇa*

The gods were so oppressed by the buffalo demon that they left the earth and went in distress to seek refuge with Gaurī, who was practising asceticism. They bowed to her and said, 'Grant us safety, O Goddess,' and when the Goddess saw how alarmed and frightened the immortals were she asked, 'What is to be done?' Then Indra and the other gods cupped their palms and reported to the Goddess the danger that had been caused them by the demon king: 'He plays happily in the Nandana garden, surrounded by celestial nymphs,' said the gods. 'For his amusement, he has brought Airāvata and all the other elephants of the regions of the sky,[7] together with their

4. For Sumbha and Nisumbha, see above, myth 57, p. 210; for Andhaka, myths 44, pp. 169–71, and 45, pp. 171–3.

5. For Vīraka, see myth 68, pp. 254–61; for Kāma, myth 41, p. 157; for Bhṛgu, myth 40, pp. 151–2; for Agni, myth 43, pp. 162–4.

6. For Andhaka, see above, myths 44–5, pp. 169–73; for the boar, myth 55, pp. 188–97; for Pūtanā, myth 58, pp. 214–18.

7. According to ancient Indian cosmology, eight celestial elephants protect the eight points of the compass or regions of the sky.

elephant cows, to live in his own palace. He uses a hundred thousand times ten million horses, headed by Uccaiḥśravas, in his elegant stables; he has let his sons ride on the ram that is the vehicle of the Oblation-eater, and he has hitched the buffalo of Yama to a cart. He has dragged off all the goddesses of perfection and instructed them to do housework, and he has brought the entire group of celestial nymphs for his own service. Whatever other precious thing or gem there is in the triple universe that he has not already carried off he will not hesitate to carry off in fury. We have become his servants and are in constant terror; we honour all his commands, for we see no other way open to us.

'The protection of those who have come for refuge is said to be the fruit of asceticism; this supreme demon is hard for even all the mighty gods and demons to conquer, for he has been elevated by the boon obtained from Śiva. He has struck the ocean with his horn and made it totally destitute, for he demands that gems[8] be given to him constantly as peace offerings, and the ocean wishes to please him. The haughty one has uprooted the mountains with the tip of his horn, and he playfully dusts himself with the powder which he has made by pounding to dust all the minerals. His matchless strength cannot be challenged by anyone other than you; but you yourself know this by means of your own energy. The *śakti* of Śambhu appeared long ago in the form of a woman,[9] and the demon has obtained from Śiva the boon that he can only be slain by that woman, you. We know nothing about Śambhu's foolish misdeeds, Goddess; but we are to be protected by you alone, always, mother of the universe.'

When the Goddess heard this fine speech from those who were tortured by fear, her soul was undisturbed and she spoke

8. The ocean is the source of all gems, as the mountains are the source of all minerals and of the magic herbs that glow in the dark.

9. That is, in the form of the female half of the androgyne.

to them, giving them reassurance: 'While I am engaged in asceticism I will protect those who come to me for refuge, immortals. In a while, your enemy will be worn out; I will draw him in by some wily means and kill the great demon. But it is not proper for me to kill one who has not yet committed any offence, for those who violate *dharma* go the way of moths, O followers of *dharma*.' When the gods heard this speech they bowed to the daughter of the mountain and they all returned whence they had come, free from fear, rejoicing in their hearts. When the gods had gone, the lotus-eyed Gaurī became an enchantress, full of loveliness, with a rounded belly. The Goddess stationed four fine young boys on the four peaks of the Tawny Mountain[10] to protect it on the north, south, east, and west. The daughter of the mountain went away from the peak of Kailāsa, followed by the four mothers, her four servants, Kettle-drum, Truthful, Exalted, and Beautiful,[11] who followed her to serve her. She said to the four boys, 'No one is to see this Tawny Mountain except a traveller who is exhausted and suffering from hunger and thirst.'

When she had thus instructed the fine heroic boys and stationed them at the boundary peaks, the daughter of the mountain practised asceticism near the hermitage of Gautama. While the slender woman was practising asceticism, there were no calamities at all: the clouds sent rain at the proper time, the trees bore fruit, and all opposed creatures gave up their former ill-will. The hermitage became a refuge for all creatures, protecting them from all dangers, and the Tawny Mountain was guarded for a distance of two leagues on all sides by the four heroic young boys who were stationed at the boundary peaks. There was no alarm, no fear; no one was

10. The Tawny Mountain, sometimes called the Blood-red Mountain, is the name of a Himalayan peak sacred to the Goddess and of a sacred mountain (Aruṇācala) in South Arcot district.

11. Dundubhi, Satyavatī, Anavamī, Sundarī.

tortured by disease, nor was there any erection excited by a woman. All the sages achieved their goals and praised the daughter of the mountain; and some praised that hermitage as being the site of the world of Śiva. Gaurī practised her fearful asceticism day and night, but the girl was not content, for she wished to satisfy Śiva.

The heroic buffalo set out to go hunting and wandered through the whole forest far from the Blood-red Mountain, attended by his demon army. He killed many herds of wild animals in the forests and ate them as he wandered about swiftly. Some of the wild animals who fled in terror, pursued by the mighty archers, entered that hermitage. The demons pursued the wild beasts, determined to kill them, but they were prevented by the heroic young boys who said quickly, 'Do not come here.' The evil demons asked the boys, 'What is this?' and the boys answered promptly, 'The maiden who has excellent hips is practising asceticism here. No mighty one[12] can enter this place that is used by sages, the Goddess's place of asceticism, which offers protection to those who come for refuge.' When the mighty and evil demons heard this speech, they agreed and turned back quickly, debating what to do. By means of their magic power of illusion they took the form of birds and carefully entered the hermitage and settled on the branches of the trees in the grove in order to look for food.

Then the generals of the demon magician saw the Goddess practising asceticism in that graceful forest full of the flowers of all seasons, and when they saw the loveliness of her form as she remained firm in her asceticism, they were so astonished that they went and reported to him what they had seen. He was tortured with desire, and he took the form of an old man and entered the hermitage and was received respectfully by her girl-friends. As the old man stood there, his exhaustion seemed to be removed, and he asked them, 'What is the rea-

12. Mighty (*balin*) is also a word for a buffalo; a pun may be intended.

son for her asceticism?' 'The girl has been practising asceticism here for a long time in order to propitiate her beloved,' they replied, 'but her mighty beloved, the lord without precedent, has not yet been sufficiently propitiated to fulfil her wish with the customary ritual of the great nine-fold ceremony of marriage. To please him, she will offer a new-born wild cock, with newly picked ripe fruits, pots of freshly cooked rice, all means such as these, quantities of valuable things and riches such as have never been seen before, and when her offerings have met with success she will immediately choose her husband.'

When the buffalo heard their speech he laughed and replied, 'I have arrived and stand here, the true fruit of her asceticism. Ascetic girl,[13] hear of my full grandeur. I am the heroic buffalo, king of the demons, respected by the gods; I hold this entire triple universe by the prowess of my own arms, and there is really no other hero. Young girl, I am able to assume any form I desire, and I can supply all sensual enjoyments. Choose me as your husband, the fruit of the asceticism of creatures that have breath. I will accomplish everything by means of the magic wishing-trees that I have stolen, and by my ascetic power I will create the primeval Viśvakarman and I will create a thousand wishing-cows in a moment. Through the resources of my nine treasure-houses and my constant attendants, I will obtain immediately the absolute possession of any object I wish for.'

When she heard his speech, she remembered the gods, and she slowly abandoned her silence and smiled gently and said to him, 'I have practised asceticism for a long time in order to be the wife of a mighty man. If you are mighty, then show me your own might. Demonstrate your own true womanish nature.' When he heard that speech, the buffalo demon bellowed furiously, 'What! Who is this?', and when the maiden

13. Here he addresses the Goddess.

Durgā saw the buffalo demon coming at her to kill her, she took the unassailable form of a fire. But when the demon in the form of a buffalo saw her standing before him, blazing with her great magic power of illusion, he himself grew great as Mount Meru. He tossed up all the mountain peaks with his two horns again and again and summoned his own army, who filled all the corners of the sky.

Then Brahmā and the gods came there and bowed to Durgā, who had the form of the doomsday fire, and worshipped her by giving her all their own various weapons. Hari gave her five weapons, and the eternal Śiva gave her ten. Brahmā gave her four that were invisible because of their magic power of illusion; the Protectors of the Regions of the Sky and the other gods and the mountains and the clouds all gave her offerings of their own ornaments and weapons. The magic Goddess, Durgā, filled her many hands with blazing weapons, and she put on her armour and quickly mounted her lion.[14] The terrible energy of Durgā filled the very circumference of the skies, and when the buffalo saw it he fled, for he was unable to bear it. When she saw that the buffalo was fleeing, unable to bear her own violent energy, she reflected, 'This wicked buffalo demon must be killed by some wily means; wild animals, when they are in rut, are caught by hunters in the forest. I will send my envoys to attract him with persuasive speeches, to tell him of my vital weak spots and to stir his anger, and thus I will make him attack me in a moment ...'

Devī Slays the Buffalo Demon

The original core of the buffalo myth is the climax, the bloody slaughter, to which the episodes of birth and enticement were later added to build up the tension. In the oldest version of this battle, as it

14. The lion is the vehicle of the Goddess, particularly in her warlike aspect as Durgā.

appears in the *Mārkaṇḍeya Purāṇa*, there is little trace of the seductive aspect of Devī, though in her orgiastic drinking of wine and blood one may perhaps detect another, darker side of her erotic nature.

66. FROM THE *Mārkaṇḍeya Purāṇa*

When his own army was totally destroyed, the buffalo demon assumed his own buffalo form and terrified the troops of the Goddess. Some he struck with his muzzle; others he trampled with his hooves. Some he lashed with his tail and pierced with his two horns; others he rushed at and roared at and whirled around; and still others he hurled down upon the surface of the earth by means of the hurricane of his breath. When he had thus felled the vanguard of the Goddess's army, the great demon attacked her lion in order to kill him, and then the Mother became angry. The great hero was angry too, and he pounded the surface of the earth with his hooves and tossed the mountains high with his two horns, and he roared. The earth was shattered by the poundings of his swift turns; the ocean, lashed by his tail, overflowed on all sides; the clouds, pierced by his swaying horns, were broken into fragments; and mountains fell from the sky by the hundreds, cast down by the blast of his breath.

When the fierce Goddess saw the great demon attacking, swollen thus with anger, she became frantic to slay him. She hurled her noose over him and bound the great demon; but when he was thus bound in the great struggle he abandoned his buffalo form and became a lion. When the Mother cut off his head, he appeared as a man with a sword in his hand and a shield made of hide, but the Goddess took her arrows and quickly pierced the man. Then he became a great elephant, who pulled at the great lion with his trunk and trumpeted, but the Goddess took her sword and cut off his trunk as he pulled. Then the great demon once more assumed his buffalo shape and shook the triple world, moving and still. Enraged by this, the furious mother of the universe drank the supreme wine[15] again and again; her eyes became red, and she laughed. The demon roared, puffed up and intoxicated with his own strength and courage, and with his two horns he hurled mountains at the furious Goddess, but she pulverized his missiles with a hail of arrows.

Then she spoke to him, her syllables confused with passion as they tumbled from her mouth which was loosened by intoxication. The Goddess said, 'Roar and roar for a moment, you fool, while I drink this honeyed wine. The gods will soon roar when I have slain you here.' Then she leaped up and mounted that great demon and kicked him in the neck with her foot and pierced him with her trident. When he was struck by her foot he[16] came half way out of his own mouth, for he was enveloped in the Goddess's heroic power. And as the great demon came half way out, fighting, the Goddess cut off his head with his great sword, and he fell. Thus the demon named Buffalo was destroyed by the Goddess, together with his army and her band of friends, when he had bewitched the triple world. And when the buffalo had fallen, all creatures in the triple world, along with all the gods and demons and men, shouted, 'Victory!' A cry of lamentation arose from the entire demon army as it was destroyed, and all the bands of gods rejoiced. Then the gods and the heavenly great sages praised the Goddess, the Gandharva leaders sang, and the bands of celestial nymphs danced.

The corpse of Satī is dismembered

The Goddess herself is the subject of a *Liebestod* in a myth strongly reminiscent of the tale of Isis and Osiris. In this late variation on the

15. The Goddess becomes intoxicated by drinking celestial wine during her orgiastic rampages, but the essence of this wine is the blood of victims sacrificed to her.

16. That is, the demon spirit came out of the buffalo body.

Dakṣa myth, Satī's body is reduced back to the component parts from which it was originally fashioned, just as the universe itself is dismembered at doomsday; both of these dismemberments lead to new forms of creation and salvation. Here, Śiva dances erotically with her corpse just as (in still later Tantric myths) she unites sexually with the corpse of Śiva. This myth is also derived in part from the cycle of myths of the castration of Śiva, for when she is mutilated (as he is), it is sometimes stated that Śiva takes the form of a *liṅga* to remain with each part of her body, particularly with the female organ (*yoni*) that falls into Assam.

67. FROM THE *Devībhāgavata Purāṇa*

One day the sage Durvāsas saw the Goddess, the empress of gold, and he murmured the prayer of magic illusion. Then the empress of the gods was pleased with him, and took from her own neck a garland rich in sweet nectar around which humming bees hovered. She gave this to him as a favour, and the ascetic sage received it upon his head and flew away quickly through the sky. He came to the place where Dakṣa, the father of Satī, lived, and he bowed at the feet of Satī in order to have a sight of the Mother. Then Dakṣa asked the sage, 'Whose is this garland that is not of this world? How did you, my lord, obtain what is hard for men in the world to obtain?' Durvāsas replied with tears in his eyes, stammering because of the love in his heart, 'This was a matchless favour from the Goddess.' The father of Satī asked the sage for that garland, and the sage thought, 'Nothing in the orb of the triple world should be denied to one who is devoted to the Śakti.' And so he gave the garland to that man, Dakṣa, who received the garland upon his head and placed it upon the exquisite marital bed in his own palace. At night, the man was so delighted by the perfume of the garland that he made love in the manner of a mere beast; and because of this evil, the king conceived in his mind a hatred for Śiva, Śaṅkara, and even for the Goddess Satī. Because of this offence, Satī burnt that body, which the man had begotten, in the fire of her yoga, with a desire to demonstrate the *dharma* of 'suttee'[17] . . .

Then the triple world was totally destroyed by the fire of Śiva's anger, and Śiva engendered Vīrabhadra and the army of Bhadrakālī. When Vīrabhadra set out to destroy the triple world, Brahmā and the other gods sought refuge with Śaṅkara. And even when everything had been destroyed, the noble lord who is an ocean of pity granted them safety, and gave the head of a goat to the man Dakṣa and revived him. Then the great lord was exhausted, went to the sacrificial ground and wept in great sorrow. When he saw Satī being burnt in the fire, he placed her on his shoulder and cried out over and over again, 'Alas, Satī!' Then Śaṅkara wandered in confusion through various places, and Brahmā and the other gods became extremely worried, and Viṣṇu quickly took up his bow and arrows and cut away the limbs of Satī, which fell in several places. In each place, Hara assumed a different form, and he said to the gods, 'Whoever worships Śivā with great devotion in these places will find nothing unattainable, for the great Mother is constantly present in her own limbs there. And whoever among mortals performs the rituals in these places will have their prayers answered, especially the prayer of magic illusion.' When Śaṅkara had said this, he remained in those places forever, meditating and praying, tortured by separation.

Kālī obtains a golden skin and Śiva slays the demon Āḍi in her form

The antagonistic aspect of love which is implicit in the *Liebestod* appears on two levels in the myth of Kālī and Āḍi. First Śiva and Pārvatī quarrel in an apparently human way, squabbling and pouting

17. That is, the act of self-immolation as Satī performed it; see myths 35–6, pp. 120–25.

(with their sons supplying the usual focus for their conflict and separation); but their quarrels play upon their divine attributes, revealing the opposition which heightens and strengthens their ultimate union, their re-fusion into the primeval androgyne. Then Āḍi seeks and finds a literal death-in-love, even as he seeks to kill Śiva by a literally sexual means. These ambivalences of love and death are evident within the Goddess herself, who here divides herself into her two contrasting aspects – the golden, erotic Gaurī and the black goddess of death, Kālī. Āḍi's name designates an aquatic bird, which may have been his original form and is a form assumed by other gods who wish to elude door-keepers;[18] his transformation into a serpent is therefore yet another instance of symbolic opposition.[19]

68. FROM THE *Skanda Purāṇa*

One day, the great lord Śiva tossed his arm around the neck of the daughter of the mountain, the Goddess, and spoke in jest to her in order to bring about a particular act of asceticism. Now, Śarva had a pale body, made particularly pale because of the crescent moon[20] upon him, while the Goddess gleamed with skin like the petal of a blue lotus at night. Śarva said, 'Your slender body, shining darkly upon my white body, looks like a black female serpent coiled around a white sandalwood tree. You look like a dark night touched by the light of the moon, like the night during the dark half of the lunar month; indeed, you offend my sight.' When the daughter of the mountain heard this from him, she released her neck from Śarva's embrace, her eyes grew red with anger, her face was distorted in a frown, and she said, 'Everyone blames someone else for his own deeds, and when anyone seeks something he is inevitably disappointed. I sought to win you, who wear a fragment of the moon, with shining acts of asceticism, and the reward for all my careful vow is that I am dishonoured

18. See myths 43, p. 164, and 73, p. 281.
19. See myth 60, pp. 222–3.
20. Śiva wears the crescent moon as his diadem.

thus at every step. I am not crooked,[21] Śarva with the matted locks, nor am I irregular. You are patient enough with your own faults – and you are richly endowed with a veritable mine of faults. It is not I who knocked out eyes, Bhava; you are the eye-destroyer, and Bhaga and indeed the whole triple universe knows you well. You would place a trident on my head, casting your own faults upon me. You called me 'Black', but you are famous as the great black one.[22] I will go to the mountain to abandon my body by means of asceticism; there is no use in my living just to be insulted by a rogue.'

When Bhava heard her speech, in which every syllable was sharpened by anger, he was upset, and Hara, whose actions are hard to comprehend, said, 'Daughter of the mountain, you do not know the true state of affairs. I did not mean to blame you; it was with the intention of flattering that I spoke in jest. I was thinking, "My darling, the daughter of the mountain, has a mind pellucid as rock-crystal," but people like us, whose dark bodies are smeared with white ashes, have one sort of thought in the heart, but our words express the opposite thought. But if you are angry at this, I will not speak to you in jest again, terrifying lady, brightly smiling one. Control your anger. I bow to you with my head, and I fold my palms in reverence to you ...'

With many such words of flattery and hymns of praise the god sought to change her mind, but the virtuous woman did not let go of her anger, for she had been touched on a sore spot. Snatching away her two feet which had been propped up by the hand of Śaṅkara, the daughter of the mountain prepared to leave quickly, her hair in disarray. As she set out, the destroyer of the cities said to her angrily, 'Truly, the daughter

21. He is 'uneven' because he has three eyes.

22. Mahākāla may mean 'the Great Death', or 'Doomsday', or 'the Great Black One'.

is like her father in all her ways. Your heart is as hard to fathom as a cavern of Himālaya, in which many sharp blades have accumulated, fallen from his cloud-garlanded peaks; your cruelty comes from his rock; your inconsistency from his various trees; your crookedness from his winding rivers; and you are as difficult to enjoy carnally as snow. All of this has been transferred to you, Goddess, from the snowy mountain, Himālaya.'

When the daughter of the mountain was addressed in this way, her dark red mouth shook with anger, her lips trembled, and she said to the lord of the mountain, 'Śarva, do not blame virtuous people by comparing them with yourself, for all these faults have been transferred to you in the same way by your association with the wicked. You speak with many tongues because of your serpents; and you are devoid of affection[23] because of your ashes. Your heart is defiled by the moon which is stained with a hare, and you get your stupidity from your bull. But what is the use of all this talk, which is merely tiresome to me? You are frightening because you live in the burning-ground, and you have no modesty, because you are naked. You are disgusting, because you carry a skull; who could bear you thus?'

When the daughter of Himālaya had said this, she went out of the palace, and as she left the hosts of Śiva raised an uproar and ran after her, crying, 'Mother, where are you going?' Vīraka[24] grasped the feet of the Goddess and stammered tearfully, 'Mother, what is this? Where are you hastening so angrily? I will come with you and follow my mother who is full of affection to her child. If you abandon me, I shall not be able to bear the cruelty of the lord of the mountain; for a son is a vessel to receive his father's cruelty in the absence of his

23. This sentence depends upon a pun: *sneha* can mean either 'affection' or 'oil', the latter the opposite of ashes.

24. 'The little hero', a name of Nandin, the guardian of Śiva's door.

mother.' Vīraka's mother lifted up his face with her right hand and said to him, 'Do not grieve, my son. It is not proper for you to go with me, for you might fall off the tip of a mountain, but I will tell you what is right for you to do. Hara reviled me and treated me as if I were a blade of grass. Since he called me "Black", I will practise asceticism in order to become golden [*gaurī*]. But this Hara who has a pale golden body is a woman-chaser when I am absent, and so you must constantly guard his door, and peep through the keyhole, so that no woman enters his presence. If you see another woman here, report to me quickly, my little son, and I will immediately do what is proper.' 'So be it,' said Vīraka to the Goddess, and when he had received his mother's command his whole body was flooded with joy and he was no longer worried. He prostrated himself before his mother and went to watch the three-eyed one.

Then the elephant-headed Gaṇeśa bowed to her and begged her, with tears in his throat, 'Take me too, Pārvatī,' and she answered, 'He will laugh at you because you are elephant-headed, my son, just as he laughs at me. Therefore come with me; go where I go, for death is good when it results from the humiliation of rogues, my little son.' And so she took him with her and set out for Himālaya.

As the daughter of the mountain set out, she saw a friend of her mother, a glorious divinity of the mountain, named Kusumāmodinī. When this lady saw the daughter of the mountain, her heart was filled with affectionate concern, and she embraced her and asked where she was going. The daughter of the mountain told her mother's intimate friend everything that had caused her to become angry with Śaṅkara, and then she continued, 'Blameless lady, you are the eternal divinity of the supreme king of mountains, and you have always treated me most affectionately, like your own child. Therefore I will tell you what I would have you do now:

if another woman enters the presence of the god who wields the Pināka bow, tell me and I will then do what is proper, fair lady.' The goddess of the mountain assented, and the Goddess Pārvatī went to the mountain and laid aside her ornaments and put on garments made of the bark of trees. There, on a delightful high peak shining with various wonders, the daughter of the mountain practised asceticism, while her son guarded her. In summer she heated herself with the five fires, and in the monsoon she lived in the water; in the winter she slept on the bare ground and went without food.

At this time, Āḍi, the mighty son of the demon Andhaka, brother of Baka, found out that the daughter of the mountain had gone away, and he sought a secret entrance, for he remembered the enmity between his father and Śiva. For when the demon Andhaka, hater of the gods, had been conquered by Śiva the lord of the mountain, Āḍi had practised extensive asceticism because he wished to conquer Hara. Brahmā had been satisfied by his asceticism and had come to him and said, 'Tell me what it is that you wish to accomplish by this asceticism, O best of demons.' The demon had said to Brahmā, 'I choose immortality,' but Brahmā replied, 'No living creature can exist without death. An embodied creature obtains death from one source or another, O demon, lord of demons.' On hearing this, the lion among demons replied to the lotus-born god, 'When I have changed my form, then let my death come about, but otherwise let me be immortal, O lotus-born god.' The lotus-born god agreed to this, for he was satisfied. And when the demon had received this promise, he considered himself immortal, and he established the kingdom of the demons.

Then he went to the dwelling-place of the slayer of the triple city, and when he arrived he saw Vīraka stationed at the door. In order to deceive him, Āḍi took the form of a serpent and entered Hara's presence unhindered by Vīraka. The great demon then abandoned the form of a serpent and took the form of Umā, thinking stupidly that he could thus trick the lord of the mountain. The demon took the form of Umā, more charming than can be imagined, perfect in all her limbs, complete with all the signs of identity, and he placed hard teeth like thunderbolts with sharp tips inside the vagina, for his wits were so deluded that he intended to kill the lord of the mountain. The demon stood in Hara's presence in the form of Umā, and when the lord of the mountain saw 'her' he was satisfied, and he embraced the great demon, thinking him to be the daughter of the mountain because of the perfect detail of 'her' limbs.

Then he asked, 'Is it truly you, and not some imitation daughter of the mountain? Did you come here because you knew my hopes, O lady with a superb complexion? I find this triple universe empty when I am separated from you, and so it is good that you have relented and come to me in this way.' The demon in the form of Umā concealed his true feelings and said, 'I went to practise matchless asceticism because you called me "Black", but there was no sexual pleasure for me there, and so I have come to you.' When Śaṅkara heard this, he began to feel somewhat doubtful, thinking, 'The slender woman was angry with me, and she is obviously one who keeps her vow. How can she have come back without having obtained her desire? This is my secret doubt.' As he pondered in this way, he searched for signs of identity, and he did not see the mark of a lotus made with a twist of hair on her left side. Then the god who wields the Pināka bow realized that this was the demon's magic power of illusion, and he laughed a little and placed a dangerous weapon upon his phallus and satisfied the demon's desire. The demon screamed terrible screams and died.

Vīraka did not know about the slaughter of the king of demons, but the mountain goddess, who had not uncovered the true event, reported to the daughter of the mountain by means of a swift breeze, when the demon was killed. When the goddess heard this from the mouth of the wind, her eyes grew very red with anger, and in her tortured mind she pictured her son Vīraka, and said, 'Since you abandoned me, your mother who is besotted with affection for you, and gave an opportunity for women to enjoy the privacy of Śaṅkara, therefore your mother will be a stone marked with the syllable of Gaṇeśa,[25] rough, harsh, cold, heartless.' When the daughter of the mountain had uttered this curse, her anger immediately came forth out of her mouth in the form of a mighty lion. That lion which had been emitted from the Goddess when she had amassed ascetic power had a monstrous mouth like a cave filled with teeth, a great mane, and an enormous tail. His hungry tongue hung out of his gaping mouth, and his waist was slender.

The Goddess determined to enter his mouth as a good wife,[26] but Brahmā, the four-headed lord, knew what was in her mind and came to her hermitage which was the home of all good things; he spoke to the daughter of the mountain with soothing words, saying, 'What do you wish to achieve, O Goddess? What is unobtainable? I will give it to you.' When the daughter of the mountain heard that, she spoke words pregnant with respect for Brahmā, her guru, saying, 'I won Śaṅkara for my husband by practising difficult asceticism, but since Bhava now often calls me "Dark-skinned", I would have a golden form and be his beloved and enter into unity with the body of my husband, the lord of ghosts.' Then the

25. This may be a reference to one South Indian myth of Gaṇeśa's birth: one day Pārvatī saw the sacred syllable 'Om', and her glance transformed it into two coupling elephants, who gave birth to Gaṇeśa and then resumed the form of the syllable 'Om'. Thus 'Om' is Gaṇeśa's syllable, and the rock might be marked with this sign.

26. That is, to commit suicide or 'suttee'.

god who sits on a lotus replied, 'So be it. You will share half[27] of your husband's body.'

Then a woman whose skin was the colour of a dark blue lotus came out of her body, terrifying, three-eyed, holding a bell in her hand.[28] Her body was densely adorned with various ornaments, and she wore yellow and red garments. Brahmā then said to the goddess whose skin was the colour of a blue lotus, 'By contact with the body of the daughter of the mountain when your form was a part of her, and by my command, you have been perfected. You alone are her entire original form, not merely a part of her.

'This mighty lion which was born from the anger of the Goddess will be your vehicle and he will be on your banner, O Goddess. Go to the Vindhya mountains and there do the work of the gods, killing Śumbha and Niśumbha, Tāraka's generals. This Yakṣa, known as Pāñcāla, is given to you as your servant, endowed with hundreds of feats of magic illusion and attended by one hundred thousand Yakṣas, O Goddess.' The goddess Kauśikī[29] assented, and when Kauśikī had gone away, Umā became endowed with all those qualities which she had earned in her previous existence and which she herself had obtained in her present incarnation.

But although she had obtained her desire, Umā was full of remorse and blamed herself over and over again as she went back to the lord of the mountain. When Vīraka saw her returning, he held up his golden rod and stopped her steadfastly at the door, shouting angrily at the Goddess, 'Stay there! Stand! Where are you going? You have no business

27. A reference to the androgynous form of Śiva–Pārvatī.

28. Untouchables carry bells to warn approaching members of the higher castes to avoid them. Śiva as the beggar who wanders through the Pine Forest often has a bell tied to his leg (see above, myth 39, pp. 141–4).

29. 'The Sheath' – that is, the outer layer of the Goddess.

here. Go away so that you will not be threatened. A demon in the form of the Goddess entered here unseen in order to deceive the god, who slew him. And when he had been slain, the wise blue-necked god reprimanded me, saying, "Be careful not to let any woman get past you, my son." Therefore you will not be able to enter here even if you remain here at the door for many years, so go away. The only one who can enter here is my mother, the daughter of the king of mountains, Pārvatī, the darling of Rudra, who loves her child dearly.'

When the Goddess heard this, she thought to herself, 'It wasn't a woman; it was a demon. It was not as the wind said. I cursed Vīraka falsely when I was overcome by anger; fools who are filled with anger often do what should not be done. Anger destroys fame; anger destroys established wealth; and people whose perception of their goals is perverted easily find misfortune. Without uncovering all the truth, I cursed my son.' Then the daughter of the mountain lowered her face which had skin like a lotus and was contorted with shame, and she said to Vīraka, 'Vīraka, I am your mother; do not be confused or mistaken in your mind. I am the beloved of Śaṅkara, daughter of the mountain Himālaya. Do not doubt me, my son, or be misled by the appearance of my limbs: the lotus-born god was satisfied with me and gave me this goldenness. I cursed you when I did not know what had occurred with the demon, for I knew only that a woman had entered into the private apartments of Śaṅkara. I cannot turn back my curse, Vīraka, but I will say that you will be reborn in a human female named "Rock", engendered by a man named Śilāda,[30] in the sacred Arbuda forest which gives men release for heaven. There is situated the *liṅga* of the lord of mountains

30. As Nandin is called Śailādi, two etymologies are offered here: that his mother was a stone (*śilā*), or that his father was a man named Śilāda (from which Śailādi would be the patronymic).

whose rewards for men are equal to those of the Viśvanātha in Benares ... When you have propitiated the lord Bhava there, you will obtain from him the name of Nandin, and you will soon come here and become the guardian of the door.'

When Vīraka heard this, his hair stood on end with delight, and he prostrated himself before her and praised her, his mother, with various speeches: 'O Goddess, I am fortunate to have obtained the state of being a man, which is very hard to obtain. Your curse is a favour, especially as it will take place on the Arbuda mountain at the holy confluence of the earth and the ocean, above the earth, between the mountain and the ocean. I will go there and find great merit by my devotion to Bhava and then I will come back here, mother.' And when he said this, he became the son of 'Rock'.

The Goddess then entered the palace of the god who bears the moon as his diadem. When the three-eyed god saw her he said, 'Damn women,' and she bowed to him and said, 'You have spoken truly, and not falsely. This portion of Nature is senseless; women deserve to be reviled. It is the grace of men which brings release from the ocean of existence.' Then Hara rejoiced and said to her, 'Now you are worthy, and I will give you a son who will bring renown to you who are fair and glorious.' Hara, the abode of various wonders, then made love with the Goddess ... [and Skanda was born.]

Devī persuades Śiva to let her create a son, Gaṇeśa

Śiva and Pārvatī frequently quarrel about their children, who serve to separate rather than to unite the couple; just as Skanda is born of Śiva's seed without any true participation on the part of Pārvatī, so Gaṇeśa is born of Pārvatī alone; and just as she stations Vīraka at

Śiva's door to prevent Śiva from making love to other women, so she often stations Gaṇeśa at her own bedroom door to keep Śiva out. The sexual antagonism between Śiva and Gaṇeśa is thinly veiled in the present myth, but the pattern indicates clearly that Śiva treats his 'son' as he treats his other sexual opponents – Kāma (by burning him with his eye), Brahmā (by beheading him with a touch of his hand) and Dakṣa (by replacing his head with that of an animal).

This antagonism is explicit in other myths, when Śiva mutilates Gaṇeśa (because Pārvatī has admired Gaṇeśa's handsome body) or actually castrates him, and it gains momentum from another corpus of myths in which Śiva slaughters an elephant demon and drapes the skin around his own shoulders. Here it is Nandin (sometimes represented as a bull, or with the head of a bull) who kills the elephant, by fighting with Indra just as Skanda does, and the more basic competition between Indra and Śiva himself is evident from the fact that the two gods share the emblem of the bull.

Another level of sexual antagonism exists between Śiva and Pārvatī: as he is the god of ascetics he is free of passion and wants no attachment to children, yet as the god of the phallus, and as her husband, he is forced to make love to her and, ultimately, to produce a child – though he does so unwillingly and by unnatural means.

69. FROM THE *Bṛhaddharma Purāṇa*

[Jaimini[31] said,] This whole universe is filled everywhere with the descendants of Brahmā and Viṣṇu; tell me about the descendants of Śiva. [The sage replied,] Śiva is man and Pārvatī is woman; they are the causes of creation. All men have Śiva as their soul, and all women are Pārvatī. Śiva has the form of the male sign [*liṅga*], and the Goddess has the form of the female sign [*yoni*]; the universe, moving and still, has the form of the sign of Śiva and the Goddess. Thus this whole universe consists of Śiva's descendants and has Śiva for its soul, but Śiva has no separate descendants such as you are asking about, Jaimini . . .

31. The name of a narrator of this Purāṇa.

Once, long ago, the daughter of the mountain made a request of Śaṅkara, who gives peace to the world; for she wished to have progeny even though, being the Goddess, she dwells in all progeny. She said, 'No rituals are performed for a man who has no descendants;[32] therefore you should have descendants to follow you. Unite with me this very day and beget a natural son.' When Śaṅkara, who gives peace to the world, heard what the daughter of the king of the mountains said, he murmured honeyed words to her, saying, 'Daughter of the mountain, I am not a householder, and I have no use for a son. The wicked circle of the gods presented you to me as a wife, but a wife is certainly the greatest fetter for a man who is free of passion; moreover, dear lady, progeny are described as a noose and a stake. Now, householders have need of a son and of wealth, and a wife is useful for a son, and sons are useful to give oblations to the ancestors. But I have no death, Goddess, and so I have no use for a son. Where there is no disease, what need is there for medicinal herbs? You are woman, and I am man; let us enjoy being the two causes from which progeny arise and rejoice in the pleasures of men and women; without progeny, let us always sport, taking pleasure in ourselves.'

Pārvatī said, 'Lord god of gods, blue-necked, three-eyed, what you have said is indeed true, but nevertheless I do wish for a little child. When you have begotten a child, you can do your yoga, great lord; I will bring up the son and you can be a yogi quite properly. An excessive yearning for the kiss of a son's mouth has arisen in me, and since you took me as your wife then you should beget a child in me. If you wish, your son will be averse to marriage, so that you will not have a son and grandson and subsequent descendants.' When he heard this, the god became angry; he arose from his seat and went away. Then the Goddess became sad and brooded unhappily

32. The oblations to the ancestors must be offered by a male heir.

for a long time. Her two friends, Jayā and Vijayā, who had been staying with her, went to assuage Śiva's anger, and they won him over.

When Śaṅkara saw how sad the Goddess was, he said to her, 'How can you be so sad just because you lack a son, beautiful goddess? If you want to kiss the face of a son all over, I will make a son for you; kiss him if you yearn to do so.' As he said this, Śiva pulled at the gown of the daughter of the mountain and made a son with that fabric, and then Śaṅkara said, 'Daughter of the mountain, take your son and kiss him as much as you wish.' Pārvatī said, 'How can this piece of cloth be the source of a son for me? This is my red dress. Stop teasing me, great lord Śiva; I do not have the mentality of a common beast. How shall I rejoice in a son obtained by means of a piece of cloth?' But when she had said this, the Goddess born of the mountain made the cloth into the shape of a son, and she held him to her breast, brooding upon the teasing words of her husband.

And when that cloth in the form of a son had touched the breast of the Goddess, it came to life and fell from her breast, and it quivered and quickened more and more. As she saw it quickening, Pārvatī cried out, 'Live, live!', and she caressed it with the two lotuses which she held in her hands as she spoke before Śiva. Then the boy came to life, getting his life's breath at that very moment, and he made Pārvatī rejoice as he cried out indistinctly, 'Mama! Mama!' The Goddess took the little boy and was filled with maternal love; she held him to her breast and gave him her breasts to suck, and milk flowed from her breasts. As the boy drank the milk, his lotus face broke into a smile, and he gazed up at his mother's face and she kissed his face all over.

When she had embraced him for a moment, she gave the beautiful little boy to her husband, the great lord, and said, 'Husband, take my son. You gave me this son when your heart was softened by pity, and I want you too, Śaṅkara, to know how great is the happiness of having a son.' When Śaṅkara heard what the Goddess had said, he smiled a little and said to the daughter of the mountain, who was now dearer to him, 'Goddess, I gave you a son made out of cloth to tease you, but he became a true son by your good fortune. What is this miracle? Give him to me and let me see; he has indeed become a real son, but his body was made out of cloth; whence did life enter it?' As he said this, Śambhu, the lord of the mountain, took his son in his hands and laid him down; he looked at him carefully and minutely,[33] inspecting all his limbs with an acute scrutiny. But then, remembering the flaw in his birth, Śaṅkara said to the goddess Pārvatī, 'This son of yours was born with an injury wrought by the planet of suicides,[34] and therefore your son will not live for a long time, but in a very short time an auspicious death will come to this short-lived son. The death of one who has acquired virtues causes the greatest sorrow.' As Śambhu, the maker of the child, said this, the boy's head, which was pointing toward the north, fell from Śiva's hand.

When the little boy's head had fallen to the ground from her husband's hand, Pārvatī was overcome with grief; she took up the boy whose head had been cut off, and she wept copiously, crying out over and over, 'My little baby, my baby.' Śiva, astonished, took his son's head in his hand and spoke to the goddess Pārvatī with honeyed words, saying,

33. It is traditional to inspect a new born child to discover auspicious or inauspicious signs indicative of his horoscope and fate.

34. The planet of suicides is Saturn, Śanaiścara ('He who moves slowly'). In other versions of the myth of Gaṇeśa's birth, all of the gods but Saturn look at the child until, at Pārvatī's importunity, Saturn allows his gaze to fall upon Gaṇeśa, who is thereby beheaded. In this version, however, it is obviously Śiva's evil eye that beheads Gaṇeśa, though the story-teller is unwilling to state this bluntly and makes an awkward attempt to place the blame upon Saturn.

'Do not cry, lovely Pārvatī, though you grieve for your son. There is no grief greater than the grief for a son, nothing that so withers the soul. Therefore stop sorrowing for your son; I will bring your son to life. Goddess, join this head onto his shoulders.' The goddess Pārvatī joined that head on as he had told her to do, but it did not join firmly. Then Śiva thought about this, and at that very moment a disembodied voice in the sky said, 'Śambhu, this head of your boy has been injured by a harmful glance, and therefore your little boy will not live with this head. Put the head of someone else upon his shoulders and revive him. Since the boy was held in your hand with his head facing north, therefore bring here the head of someone facing north and join it to him.' When Śaṅkara heard this voice from the sky, he consoled the Goddess and summoned Nandin and sent him on this mission.

Nandin wandered over the triple universe and came to Amarāvatī, where he saw Airāvata, the elephant of Indra, with his head facing north. When the mighty Nandin saw Airāvata lying down facing north,[35] he started to cut off his head, but the elephant began to trumpet and roar, and Śakra came there with the other gods and said, 'Who are you who have come in this extraordinary form to kill the elephant? Who sent you, and why do you carry a sword in your hand?' Nandin said, 'I am Nandin, the servant of Śiva, and I have come at Śiva's command. I will take the head of Airāvata and give it to Śambhu. The head of Śiva's son, who was facing north, fell from Śiva's hand because of his harmful fate, and a voice from the sky said, "When the head of someone lying down facing north is fastened to his body, I will give the son of Śiva a head and bring him to life." Therefore I will definitely cut off the head of your king of elephants. If you wish to keep your own life's breath, abandon your hope for

35. This impure position makes him susceptible, as it makes Diti (myth 27, pp. 92–3).

Airāvata and go away, for no one is better suited than your Airāvata to give life's breath to the son of Śiva.'

When the great Indra heard this speech of Nandin, he became angry; he summoned all the gods and replied to Nandin, 'How can you, the minion of Śambhu who lives in the wilderness, intend to cut up my elephant by force when I, the king of the gods, am alive?' And as he said this, Śakra took up a trident to kill Nandin, but Nandin attacked and reduced that trident to ashes with a roar. Then Indra took up a mace and hurled it violently, but Nandin took the mace playfully in his left hand, saying, 'Take your own mace, Indra,' and threw it at him. The mace fell on Indra's chest, fracturing it painfully, and Indra reeled in agony. He picked up another trident and hurled it at Nandin, but Nandin cut it into three pieces with his sword. Then Indra took up his thunderbolt and rushed again like the wind, and Nandin became even more horrible, unbearably frightening.

At this moment, the powerful driver of Śakra's elephant brought Airāvata, who was in rut, to Indra. The mighty Indra mounted the elephant and took his thunderbolt in his hand; aided by the army of the Maruts, he fought with Nandin. All the armies of the gods surrounded him, with their bows in their hands, and they sent a rain of arrows down upon the dreadful Nandin as clouds send rain down upon a great mountain in the violent time of the monsoon. But Nandin, whose monstrous body was as hard as a rock and marvellous to behold, withstood that rain of arrows, repelling them with parries of his left hand, with his sharp sword, and with fierce roaring snorts, stupefying them with his terrifying body. Then, while the gods looked on, he cut off the head of Airāvata, and the severed head of Airāvata fell to the ground when Nandin had struck it off. The gods were bewildered by this marvel; they cried out 'Alas!' and did not move.

When Śiva heard of Nandin's deed of valour he embraced

him joyfully, and he placed the elephant head on his son's shoulders, and the moment that the head was joined on, the boy became surpassingly beautiful. The god was rather short and fat, with the lotus face of a king of elephants; his face was bright as the moon, red as a China rose. He had four arms and was adorned by bees attracted by the perfume of his flowing ichor, and with his marvellous three eyes he shone in Śiva's presence. All the gods came there and saw the son of Śiva who had the auspicious head of the king of elephants, and Śambhu held the boy to his breast. Then Brahmā and the other gods anointed him, and Brahmā gave him names, calling him 'Pot-bellied'. The marvellous child shone [*rarāja*] in the midst of all the gods, and so they said, 'Let him be king [*rājā*] of the gods, worshipped before all the gods.' Then Sarasvatī gave him a writing pen with coloured inks, and Brahmā gave him a rosary of beads, and Indra gave him an elephant goad. Padmavatī gave him a lotus, and Śiva gave him a tiger skin. Bṛhaspati gave him a sacrificial thread, and the goddess Earth gave him a rat for his vehicle.

Then all the sages praised the red son of Śiva, and Brahmā said, 'Śambhu, this is your son; you are he, there is no doubt, and he will be worshipped before all the gods except you, great lord, for you, great lord, are to be honoured first and last. The great-armed one has become the ruler of all the hosts [*gaṇas*] of the gods, and he is ruler of your hosts, too, and so let him be called Ruler-of-the-hosts [Gaṇādhipa or Gaṇeśa]. Since he has the head of an elephant, let him be called Elephant-headed [Gajānana]; and since, when Nandin performed his marvellous deed and conquered Indra and struck the elephant, the tusk of his head was broken, let him be called One-tusk [Ekadantaka]. Let him be called Heramba[36]

36. Heramba is a Dravidian loan-word meaning 'buffalo'. It is unclear how this can be connected with the Sanskrit word for one with the form of a seed (*bījarūpa*).

and always have the form of a seed, and because of his corpulence, Śiva, let this son of yours be called Pot-bellied [Lambodara]. By merely thinking of him, all those who would create obstacles become afraid, and so, Śaṅkara, let this son of yours be called Lord-of-obstacles [Vighneśa]. Anyone undertaking a journey or a worthy project should remember Gaṇādhipa and his journey will be fruitful, his undertaking successful in its outcome. Gaṇādhipa is to be honoured in all auspicious affairs, for when Gaṇeśa is honoured, the gods are honoured, and they will accomplish the affair.'

Brahmā said this and stopped, but Indra, grieving at the absence of Airāvata, said to Śiva, 'Greatest of gods, great god, three-eyed lord of Pārvatī, lord of the triple universe, I bow to you. Your powerful servant, Nandin, slew my elephant and in my ignorance I fought with him. Forgive me, O god, great lord. It is said, "You should give even your own head to one who begs", but I did not wish to give my elephant's head to him. Forgive me for that.' Then Śiva said, 'Throw Airāvata, headless, into the ocean, and you will obtain your king of elephants again when he arises from the churning of the ocean.[37] And since you gave Airāvata's head to my son, therefore I will also give you an immortal bull.' When the god Indra, the son of Kaśyapa, heard this, he went to heaven, and Brahmā and the other gods received the veneration due to them and went to their own homes. Then the goddess Pārvatī, rejoicing, cared for Gaṇeśa, and Gaṇeśa became a great yogi, averse to worldly attachments, and all the sages assembled and praised Gaṇeśa . . . and went away again.

This, O Jaimini, is the meritorious story of the birth of Gaṇeśa. But there are no descendants of Śambhu, who is the very form of final universal destruction. His other son, mentioned first, is Kārttikeya, the youth [Kumāra]; he did not marry either, but kept his vow of chastity [*kaumāra*].

37. See below, myth 72, p. 277.

7

GODS AND DEMONS

The battle between gods and demons, the central theme of Hindu mythology, sets the stage upon which all of the gods, from Indra to Devī, play their roles. But many important myths depict the battle directly, as a whole, the confrontation of massed forces, rather than isolated episodes in which a supreme god conquers the supreme demon of the moment. The battle lines are blurred by the lack of distinction between gods and demons, who share not only their superhuman powers (together with such tell-tale signs as an absence of sweating or blinking) but also their anthropomorphic moral ambivalences. In terms of cosmic symbolism, the battle may represent the conflict between light and darkness, but in actual myths there is little to distinguish between the two opposed forces. By definition, by status and official function, the gods are 'right' and right must triumph, but the nature of this 'right' and the method of the triumph underwent major transformations in the three broad periods of Hindu mythology. The heroic measures which the Vedic gods employ came gradually to be superceded by treacherous stratagems in the Epic period and finally, in the Purāṇas, by outright and elaborate deceptions which had been originally categorized as 'demonic'.

Vedic mythology: the battle for immortality

Gods and Demons are Created and the Battle Begins

The arbitrary nature of the distinction between gods and demons is emphasized by the circular logic of one early myth: Prajāpati makes the demons evil because they *are* evil, and he creates them out of darkness, but he then makes their substance into night.[1] Moreover, it is said that – presumably because the gods and demons are in fact the same – the battle between them – particularly between individuals – is mere illusion, for all that they do is preordained.

70. FROM THE *Śatapatha Brāhmaṇa*

Prajāpati was born to live for a thousand years. Just as one might see in the distance the far shore of a river, so he saw the far shore of his own life. He desired progeny, and so he sang hymns and exhausted himself, and he placed the power to produce progeny in himself. From his mouth he created the gods, and when the gods were created they entered the sky [*divam*]; and this is why the gods are gods [*devas*], because when they were created they entered the sky. And there was daylight [*divā*] for him when he had created them, and this is why the gods are gods, because there was daylight for him when he had created them. Then with his downward breath he created the demons; when they were created they entered this earth, and there was darkness for him when he had created them. Then he knew that he had created evil, since darkness appeared to him when he had created them. Then he pierced them with evil, and it was because of this that they were overcome.

Therefore it is said, 'The battle between gods and demons did not happen as it is told in the narratives and histories, for Prajāpati pierced them with evil and it was because of this that they were overcome.' And so the sage has said, 'You have not fought with anyone for a single day, nor do you have any enemy, O bountiful one. Your battles which they tell about are all magic illusion; you have fought no enemy today, nor in the past.'[2] The daylight which had appeared for him

1. See above, myth 9, p. 44.
2. A quotation from *Ṛg Veda* 10.54.2.

when he had created the gods he made into day; and the darkness which had appeared for him when he had created the demons he made into night. And they are day and night.

THE GODS TRICK THE DEMONS INTO LEAVING THE SACRIFICE

The problem of differentiation between 'hateful fraternal enemies' and the conflict which arises out of the separation of truth from falsehood lead to certain logical circles in a myth in which the gods use deceit as their weapon – after renouncing falsehood. The strategy of deceit is recommended by the earliest Indian textbook of political science – the *Arthaśāstra* – a source noted for the same cynical realism which appears here: those who speak the truth grow weak and poor, while the cunning flourish like a green bay tree . . . for a while.

71. FROM THE *Śatapatha Brāhmaṇa*

The gods and the demons were both born from Prajāpati, and they both wished to possess the inheritance from their father Prajāpati which consisted of speech – both truth and falsehood. Both of them spoke the truth, and both of them spoke falsehood; and as they spoke alike, they were alike. The gods then gave up falsehood and kept truth, and the demons gave up truth and kept falsehood. Then truth which had been in the demons saw this and said: 'The gods have given up falsehood and continued to keep truth. Very well, I will go there,' and it went to the gods. And falsehood which had been in the gods saw this and said: 'The demons have given up truth and continued to keep falsehood. Very well, I will go there,' and it went to the demons. The gods then spoke only truth, and the demons spoke only falsehood. The gods, speaking truth steadfastly, became weaker and poorer; and therefore whoever speaks truth steadfastly becomes weaker and poorer, but in the end he overcomes, as the gods overcame in the end. Then the demons, speaking falsehood steadfastly, grew strong and rich like salt soil;[3] therefore one who speaks falsehood steadfastly grows strong and rich as salt soil, but in the end he is overcome, for in the end the demons were overcome . . .

The gods performed the animal sacrifice, and the demons learned about this and arrived when the gods had performed part of it. When the gods saw the demons they snatched up the sacrifice and did something else, and the demons thought that the gods were doing something else and went away again. When they had gone away, the gods spread out the third sacrifice and completed it, and when they had completed it they obtained the whole truth. Therefore the demons fell and therefore the gods overcame and the demons were overcome. And whoever knows this overcomes his own enemy, and his hateful fraternal enemy is overcome.

Epic mythology: the gods and demons churn the ocean to obtain ambrosia

The churning of the ocean is the classic image of creation by means of chaos – the disruption of the serene primeval waters in order that all the oppositional pairs may emerge and meet in creative conflict. In the course of this process, the agents of the churning (the gods and demons) become differentiated, for at first they are united in their task, but then they are opposed. The basic symbolic dialectic is that of liquids, the neutral water which is transmuted into various elixirs – human (milk), ritual (butter) and divine (mead, ambrosia, or Soma)[4] – as well as into the reversal of all elixirs – poison. According to Hindu cosmology, the earth is ringed by several concentric oceans – first the salt ocean, then oceans of sugar-cane juice, wine, clarified butter, milk, whey, and fresh water. The gods here churn the first, the salt

3. Salt soil is valued in a pastoral society, for cattle thrive on it.

4. For milk, see above, myths 22–3, pp. 72–4, and 58, pp. 215–18; for butter, myth 5, pp. 32–3; for ambrosia, myth 13, pp. 56–7.

ocean, and produce from it first milk, then butter, then wine, then poison, and finally Soma. The ambrosia is trapped in the neck of a beheaded demon, while the poison is kept in the neck of Śiva – who is so often associated with beheadings. The structural force of this dialectic is so powerful that almost every essential element of the myth is duplicated: the ambrosia itself is obtained twice, and there are two snakes, two mountains, two eclipses, and two rains – one creative and one destructive.

72. FROM THE *Mahābhārata*

There is a shining mountain named Meru, an unsurpassed mass of energy; its blazing golden peaks outshine even the light of the sun. The gods and Gandharvas frequent its glittering, gold-adorned slopes, but men who abound in *adharma* cannot approach that immeasurable mountain. Dreadful beasts of prey wander over it and divine herbs[5] illuminate it. The great mountain stands piercing the firmament with its peak, and it is graced by trees and streams. It resounds with the charming songs of various flocks of birds, but others cannot approach it even in thought. Its magnificent slopes are studded with many gems, and an infinity of magic wishing-trees grow there. The gods, who dwell in heaven and are of great vigour, rich in ascetic powers, came together, mounted its plateau, and sat there to take counsel in order to obtain the ambrosia. While the gods were thinking and conferring together, the god Nārāyaṇa said to Brahmā, 'Let the gods and demons churn the ocean which is like a churning pot, and when the great ocean is churned there will be ambrosia, and you will also obtain all the herbs and gems. Churn the ocean, O gods, and you will find ambrosia in it.'

The tremendous mountain named Mandara is adorned with mountain peaks like pointed clouds; it is covered with a net of vines, it rings with the song of many birds, and it is crowded with tusked animals. Celestial nymphs and gods and

5. Magic herbs on great mountains shine in the dark.

Kinnaras frequent it, and it extends for eleven thousand leagues above the earth and as many leagues below. All the bands of gods were unable to uproot it, and so they came to Viṣṇu and Brahmā and said, 'Think of some perfect and effective plan to uproot Mount Mandara for our welfare.' Viṣṇu and Brahmā agreed, and the potent serpent Ananta arose at Brahmā's behest and was instructed by Nārāyaṇa in the task. Then the mighty Ananta forcibly uprooted that king of mountains with all its forests and forest-dwellers, and the gods went with the mountain to the ocean and said to him, 'We will churn your water to obtain ambrosia.' The lord of waters said, 'Let me also have a share of it. I will bear the intense agitation from the whirling of Mandara.' The gods and demons then said to the king of tortoises, the supreme tortoise, 'You are the one suited to be the resting-place for this mountain.' The tortoise agreed, and Indra placed the tip of the mountain on his back, fastening it tightly. They made Mandara the churning-stick and the serpent Vāsuki the cord, and they began to churn the ocean, the treasure of waters, for ambrosia. The gods acted together with the demons, for they all wished for the ambrosia.

The great demons grasped one end of the king of serpents, and all the gods held him by the tail. Ananta and the blessed god Nārāyaṇa would lift the head of the serpent first from one side and then from the other and throw it down again and again. As the gods vigorously hurled the snake Vāsuki about, winds full of smoke and flame came out of his mouth repeatedly, and these masses of smoke became clusters of clouds with lightning, and they rained down upon the bands of gods who were exhausted and over-heated from their exertions. Showers of flowers fell down from the tip of the mountain peak, strewing garlands everywhere on the gods and demons. Then a great roar, like the thunder of a great cloud, came forth from the ocean as it was churned by the gods and demons with Mount Mandara; for various water creatures, crushed by the great mountain, were dying by the hundreds in the salt water, and the mountain destroyed many kinds of aquatic beings living in the subterranean levels of hell. The mountain whirled about so that great trees filled with birds spun off and fell from the mountain peak. As the trees were crushed against one another, a fire born of their friction blazed forth into flames and enveloped Mount Mandara, which looked like a dark cloud charged with lightning. The fire burnt the elephants and lions who were driven out, and all the various creatures there lost their life's breath. Then Indra, the best of immortals, put out that burning fire everywhere with water from his clouds. But the various saps exuded from the great trees and the juices from many herbs flowed into the water of the ocean. And from these juices, which had the essence of ambrosia, and from the exudation of liquid gold mixed with the water, the gods obtained immortality. Then the water of the ocean turned to milk as it became mixed with those supreme juices, and from that milk there arose clarified butter.

The gods then said to Brahmā, the giver of boons, 'We are terribly tired, O Brahmā, all of us, and all the demons and supreme snakes, all except for the god Nārāyaṇa, but no ambrosia has come forth. We have been churning this ocean for a long time.' Then Brahmā said to the god Nārāyaṇa, 'Give them the strength, Viṣṇu. You are our last resort.' Viṣṇu replied, 'I grant strength to all who are engaged in this action. Churn the ocean-pot all together; twirl Mount Mandara.' When they heard the words of Nārāyaṇa they became strong, and all together violently stirred the milk of the great ocean once more. Then from the ocean there arose Soma, the calm moon, with its cool rays, and the sun of a hundred thousand rays. And immediately after this the goddess Śrī, dressed in white, appeared from the clarified butter; then the goddess of wine; then Uccaiḥśravas, the white horse of the sun; and then came the divine, shining Kaustubha gem for the chest of the blessed Nārāyaṇa, blooming with rays, born of the ambrosia. And the great elephant Airāvata, with his enormous body and his four white tusks, came forth and was taken by the Wielder of the Thunderbolt.

But as they continued to churn excessively, the terrible Kālakūṭa poison came forth and immediately enveloped the universe, blazing like a smoky fire; the poison paralysed the triple world with the smell of its fumes. The lord Śiva took the form of a sacred chant and held that poison in his throat, and from that time forth he has been known as Blue-throated; thus it is traditionally told. At the request of Brahmā and for the sake of protecting all people, Śiva swallowed the poison, and from it there arose the Eldest,[6] her dark form adorned with every kind of gem.

When, Śrī, Wine, the moon, and the horse swift as thought had come forth, the gods went on the path of the sun, the path that leads to immortality. And then the magic tree and magic cow that grant the fruits of all desires were born. At last, the god Dhanvantari[7] came forth incarnate, holding a white pot in which the ambrosia was contained. When the demons saw this marvel they let out a great roar for the ambrosia, each crying, 'It is mine!' Then the lord Nārāyaṇa took the form of Mohinī[8], a magic illusion of the marvellous body of a woman, and he went to the demons. As their minds were bewitched, they gave the ambrosia to him in his female form, for all the demons had their hearts set on her. The goddess who was made of the illusion wrought by Nārāyaṇa held the bowl and gave it to the gods to drink, but although the demons were seated in a row she did not give it to them to drink.

6. Jyeṣṭhā, the Eldest, is the goddess of misfortune.
7. The physician of the gods.
8. 'The Enchantress', the supreme celestial nymph.

Then the demons began to scream and, arming themselves with superb armour and various weapons, they attacked all the gods together; it was then that the mighty Viṣṇu, accompanied by Nara, took the ambrosia from the demon chiefs. When all the bands of the gods had obtained the ambrosia from Viṣṇu, they drank it amid great excitement and tumult. As the gods were drinking the ambrosia which they so desired, a demon named Rāhu took the form of a god and began to drink, but when the ambrosia had reached his throat, the moon and the sun reported it, for they wished to help the gods, and the lord Viṣṇu took his discus and cut off the well-adorned head of that demon who was drinking the ambrosia he had obtained by force. The great head of the demon, which was like the peak of a mountain, fell to the earth as it was cut off by the discus, and it shook the earth. The severed head rose up to the sky, roaring terribly, but the headless torso of the demon fell and split open the surface of the earth, causing a tremor throughout the earth with its mountains, forests, and islands. Since then there has been a deadly enmity between the head of Rāhu and the moon and sun, and the immortal head swallows them up even today.

The lord Hari then gave up his incomparable female form and routed the demons with various frightening weapons. Then a great battle began on the shore of the salt ocean, the most terrible of all battles between gods and demons. Sturdy, sharp darts, sharp-pointed javelins, and various weapons fell by the thousands. Demons pierced by the discus vomited forth quantities of blood; those wounded by knives, spears, and maces fell to the ground. Heads adorned with burnished gold were cut off by swords in the terrible battle and fell ceaselessly; great demons were struck down, their bodies smeared with blood, and they lay like mountain peaks crimson with mineral ores. Everywhere thousands of cries of distress were heard, and the sun grew red with the blood of those who were hacking at each other. As they struck at one another in the battle with clubs of iron or gold, or fought at close quarters with their fists, the noise seemed to touch the very heavens: 'Cut!' 'Break!' 'Attack!' 'Put them to flight!' 'Advance!' These terrible sounds were heard everywhere.

As the fierce, tumultuous battle raged, the two gods Nara and Nārāyaṇa entered the field. The lord Viṣṇu looked at the divine bow of Nara and thought of the discus that subdues demons. As soon as it was remembered, the shining discus called Sudarśana ('Beautiful') came from the sky; its glory was immeasurable; it shone like the sun; its curved edge was unblunted; it was terrifying, invincible, supreme, blazing like a fire devouring the oblation, frightening, nimble, glorious, a destroyer of hostile cities. The unfallen Viṣṇu, whose arms were like elephant trunks, threw it abruptly with great force; blazing like the fire of doomsday, it fell swiftly again and again, hurled from the hand of the best of men, piercing the demons by the thousands in battle. Sometimes it blazed like fire, licking the demon armies with its tongues; sometimes it cut them up violently as it was hurled through the sky; then it would fall on the battleground and drink their blood as if it were a flesh-eating Piśāca. But the mighty demons, still undaunted, continued to harass the bands of the gods again and again by hurling mountains, mounting to the sky by the thousands like clouds whose rain has dispersed. And from the sky would fall terrifying great mountains like clouds of various shapes, still bearing trees, the tips of their peaks having broken off, roaring as they struck with great force against one another. The earth with all its forests trembled as it was struck on all sides by the fall of the great mountains, and on the battle-field the warriors roared loudly and incessantly at one another.

Then Nara took his celestial bow and covered the heavens with his great, gold-tipped, feathered arrows, shattering the mountain peaks among the terrible bands of demons. The great demons, hard pressed by the gods, entered the earth and the salt ocean, for they saw Sudarśana raging angrily through the sky like a blazing fire devouring oblations. Then the gods, who were victorious, honoured Mount Mandara and placed it in its proper place, and they returned home like water-bearing clouds, making the air and the heavens resound on all sides with their thunderous shouts as they rejoiced greatly and loudly. Then Indra the Shatterer of Armies and the immortals gave the treasure of ambrosia to the diademed Viṣṇu to guard and keep very safe.

Purāṇic mythology: the gods win the secret of immortality from the demons

The Vedic Source: Indra Tricks Śuṣṇa into Giving up the Ambrosia

The myth of the theft of the ambrosia is an old Indo-European one; in one of the earliest Indian instances of it, Indra himself becomes the fire-bird[9] to steal the elixir. The demon from whom he steals it – Śuṣṇa, 'the Scorcher' – appears in the *Ṛg Veda* as a horned demon who lays eggs and who releases the heavenly waters when Indra kills him. This is a myth of conflict between two kinds of immortality: the demons pose a threat to the gods, as well as to the normal flow of time and fate itself, by reviving their dead, as they often do in Hindu mythology;[10] the gods take the ambrosia from them and use it for the only immortality which is natural and in order, even for the gods – 'a full life-span'.

The method which the gods use is one which arises naturally out of the image of ambrosia as food: Indra tricks his enemy into swallowing him. This episode is a reversal of the usual Indo-European stratagem of eating a potentially immortal enemy, as Chronos tries to

9. Even in the *Ṛg Veda*, Indra is said to be 'like a falcon' (see above, myth 24, p. 76).

10. See above, myths 14, pp. 58–9, and 37, p. 128.

eat Zeus and Śiva swallows Śukra. Yet the reversal also has precedent: for Atreus is tricked into swallowing his children, and Indra (though swallowed against his will) conquers Vṛtra by causing him to yawn him out of his mouth.[11] As the vomiting forth is almost always an immediate result of the swallowing in all the Indian variants of the myth, the episode becomes not a battle but a rite of passage; the initiate obtains immortality by being swallowed, returning to the womb, gaining the secret of immortality (or the substance, ambrosia), and being reborn from the mouth of his enemy.

73. FROM THE *Kāṭhaka Saṃhitā*

The gods and demons were prepared for war, but the ambrosia was among the demons, in the demon Śuṣṇa, who carried it within his mouth. Those among the gods whom the demons killed remained dead but those among the demons whom the gods killed Śuṣṇa breathed upon with the ambrosia and restored their life's breath. Indra learned that the ambrosia was among the demons, in the demon Śuṣṇa. He became a globule of honey and lay upon the path, and Śuṣṇa ate it up. Then Indra became a falcon and stole the ambrosia out of his mouth. Therefore this is the most heroic of birds, for he is one form of Indra. Whoever knows this bears the ambrosia, and whomever he desires to make live, free of disease, him he should swallow and breathe upon, for he breathes upon him with ambrosia. And thus he lives for his full life-span and does not die before his life-span is complete.

THE EPIC EXPANSION: THE GODS SEND KACA, THE SON OF BṚHASPATI, TO LEARN THE SECRET OF REVIVAL FROM ŚUKRA, GURU OF THE DEMONS

In the *Mahābhārata*, the two antagonists are no longer warriors but brahmins, the preceptors of the two opposed teams. Śuṣṇa is replaced by Śukra (also called Kāvya), guru of the demons, while Indra (who,

11. See above, myth 25, p. 81.

in the *Ṛg Veda*, is assisted by Aṅgiras and his descendants[12] and is given the epithet Bṛhaspati, 'Lord of Sacred Speech') is replaced by Bṛhaspati, now a separate figure, the guru of the gods. Indeed, the bond which joins the two priests proves far stronger than the gulf which separates the demons from the gods.[13] In this expanded version, the victim is killed not once but several times; here the secret of immortality is not the Vedic Soma of Indra but the Brāhmaṇa ritual formula of Bṛhaspati; nevertheless, Kaca is still swallowed (in wine, a form of elixir like the honey or mead of the earlier myth). The familiar expedient of sending a woman to steal the Soma[14] is given a twist here, for the gods send a man to bewitch the demon's daughter. As he wins the secret of immortality from her, the myth follows the pattern of other tales of a mortal man and an immortal woman;[15] and just as Jason rejects Medea when he has won the golden fleece, so Kaca rejects Devayānī after achieving his purpose.

74. FROM THE *Mahābhārata*

Strife arose between the gods and the demons for the sovereignty of the triple world, moving and still. In their desire for victory, the gods chose the sage Bṛhaspati, the son of Aṅgiras, for their family priest in the sacrifice, while the others chose Śukra, Kāvya Uśanas, and these two brahmins were constantly in fierce competition with one another. Now those demons whom the gods killed in battle Kāvya brought to life again by using his magic power, and then they arose again and fought with the gods. But those gods whom the demons killed in the vanguard Bṛhaspati could not bring back to life, for, although he had a noble mind, he did not know the magic of resuscitation which the heroic Kāvya knew.

12. See above, myth 23, p. 74.

13. Similarly, in an early myth which already incorporates the motifs of eating and transformation into birds, the demon Triśiras becomes the priest of the gods to trick them (see above, myth 20, pp. 70–71).

14. See above, myths 22–3, pp. 72–4, 65, pp. 242–7, and 72, pp. 277–8. Viṣṇu appears as Mohinī, Indra as the female fire-bird.

15. See above, myth 18, pp. 62–5.

Then the gods became very discouraged and alarmed by fear of Kāvya Uśanas, and they approached Kaca, the eldest son of Bṛhaspati, and said, 'Be kind to us, who honour and love you. Grant us your excellent assistance. Quickly steal away that magic which dwells in the brahmin Śukra of immeasurable energy and you will share the sacrifice with us. You can see, in the presence of the demon king Vṛṣaparvan, the brahmin who protects the demons there and does not protect those who are not demons. You, being young, can propitiate the noble seer as well as his beloved daughter, Devayānī, by your character, dexterity, and sweetness, and by your good behaviour and self-control, but no one else knows how. And when Devayānī has been satisfied, you will certainly obtain the magic knowledge.' Kaca, the son of Bṛhaspati, agreed to this, and when he had been honoured by the gods and was hastened by them on his way, he went to Vṛṣaparvan.

There in the city of the king of the demons Kaca saw Śukra, and he said to him, 'I am the grandson of the sage Aṅgiras and the son of Bṛhaspati. I am called Kaca; accept me as your pupil. I will practise the supreme vow of a chaste student with you as my guru for a thousand years; permit me, O brahmin.' Śukra said, 'Kaca, you are welcome. I grant your request. I will honour you who are worthy of honour, and let Bṛhaspati be honoured thus.'[16] Kaca agreed and accepted that vow as instructed by Śukra Uśanas, the seer's son. He accepted the period of the vow as it had been mentioned, and he propitiated his teacher and Devayānī. The young man in the bloom of youth tried constantly to win her over by singing and dancing and playing music before her, and by meeting her frequently he satisfied Devayānī. Thus he satisfied Devayānī, a young woman in the bloom of youth,

16. That is, when Bṛhaspati's son is honoured, honour will reflect upon the father.

and he gave her flowers and fruits and gifts, and the wanton Devayānī sang with him and secretly flirted with the brahmin who was under a vow of chastity.

Five hundred years passed while Kaca was performing this vow in this way, and then the demons found out about Kaca. They saw him guarding the cows in a forest, all alone in seclusion, and spitefully they killed him because they hated Bṛhaspati and because they wished to protect their magic knowledge. When they had killed him, they cut him into pieces the size of sesame seeds and gave him to the jackals. Then the cows returned to their own home without their cow-herd, and when Devayānī saw the cows returning from the forest without Kaca she said, at an appropriate moment, 'Father, you have not yet offered the oblation into the fire, but the sun has set. My lord, the cows have returned without the cow-herd, and Kaca is not to be seen. Evidently Kaca has been killed or he has died, and I will not live without Kaca; I tell you truly, father.' 'I will revive the dead man with the words "Come here",' said Śukra. Then, using the magic of resuscitation, he summoned Kaca, and when Kaca was summoned he appeared unharmed, because of the magic. When the brahmin's daughter questioned him, he told her, 'I had been killed.'

Then the demons pulverized Kaca and mixed him with the water of the ocean, but when he had been gone for a long time the maiden reported this to her father, and Kaca the son of the guru Bṛhaspati was summoned again by the brahmin Śukra with his magic formula, and he returned again and reported accurately all that had happened. Then he happened to go again to fetch flowers, as Devayānī requested, and when the brahmin Kaca went into the forest the demons saw him and killed him yet again and burnt him to a powder, which the demons gave to the brahmin Śukra in wine. The descendant of Bhṛgu drank the ashes of Kaca together with the wine, but when the cows returned at sunset without the cow-herd, Devayānī again said to her father, 'Father, I sent Kaca to fetch flowers, but he is not to be seen.' 'My daughter,' said Śukra, 'Kaca the son of Bṛhaspati has become a ghost. Even when I revived him with my magic he was killed. What can I do? Do not grieve, Devayānī; do not weep. A woman like you should not grieve for a mortal. All the gods and the entire universe bow before the inevitable transformation when it comes to them.'

Devayānī said, 'His grandfather was the ancient Aṅgiras, and his father was Bṛhaspati, rich in ascetic power – how could I not grieve and weep for the son and grandson of such sages? He is a chaste student, rich in ascetic power, always upright and dextrous in the rituals. I will follow the path of Kaca, father, and I will not eat, for the handsome Kaca is dear to me.' Śukra answered, 'Surely the demons hate me, for they are destroying my unoffending student. By this undertaking the fierce demons wish to make me cease to be a brahmin. But what end would there be for this evil? For brahminicide would burn anyone, even Indra.' At the urging of Devayānī, the great sage Kāvya again summoned Bṛhaspati's son Kaca with a great effort. When Kaca was summoned by the magic formula he answered his guru carefully, from within Śukra's stomach, for he was afraid for him. Then Śukra asked Kaca, 'By what path did you enter my stomach? Tell me, O brahmin.'

Kaca replied, 'By your favour, my memory has not left me, and I can remember all that happened. I am able to bear this hideous anguish by thinking, "Let not my ascetic power be destroyed in this way." The demons killed me and burnt me and pulverized me and gave me to you in the wine, Kāvya. How can the magic power of illusion of the demons surpass that of brahmins, as long as you remain?'

Śukra said, 'Devayānī, my child, what can I do to please

you now? Kaca could live only through my death, for only by breaking through my belly, and in no other way, would he be seen again.' 'Both of these sorrows burn me like fire,' said Devayānī, 'Kaca's destruction and your slaughter. If Kaca is destroyed there is no peace for me, and if you are slaughtered I cannot live.' 'Son of Bṛhaspati,' said Śukra to Kaca, 'your beauty has succeeded, since Devayānī is thus devoted to you, the devotee. Receive this magic of revival today, if you are not Indra in the form of Kaca, for no one other than a brahmin may return again alive from my stomach; therefore, take this magic formula. Since you have become my son, brought to life by me, so you must bring me to life, my son, when you have come out of my body. Keep this promise sanctioned by *dharma* when you have obtained the magic from me, your guru.' When Kaca the handsome priest had obtained the magic from his guru, he broke out of the right side of the brahmin's belly and came forth like the moon on full-moon night at the end of the bright half of the month. And when Kaca saw the pile of Vedic knowledge which was the fallen dead man, he caused him too to arise. Then, when Kaca had obtained the complete magic, he bowed to his guru and said, 'The guru is the giver of unsurpassed truth, the treasury of the four-fold riches of knowledge, worthy of respect. Those who do not respect him go to the bottomless evil worlds.'

When Kāvya Uśanas of great majesty saw the handsome Kaca whom he had swallowed when he was confused by wine, he realized that he had been deceived by drinking the wine so that he experienced a dreadful loss of consciousness. Then he became apprehensive about the drinking of wine, and he wished to do something for the welfare of priests; he arose in fury and declared: 'From this day forth, any brahmin who stupidly and in confusion drinks wine will be bereft of *dharma*, guilty of brahminicide, despised in this world and in the world beyond. Let all good priests who listen to their gurus, and all the gods, and all people heed this moral law that I have established in all the world to set a standard for the *dharma* of priests.' When the incomparable, majestic treasury of treasures of asceticism had said this, he summoned all the demons, whom fate had made stupid, and he said to them, 'I tell you, demons, you are childish, for Kaca, who has fulfilled himself, will live with me; now that he has obtained the valuable magic secret of resuscitation he is equal in might to Brahmā; he has become one with the godhead.'

Kaca spent a thousand years living with his guru, and then he received permission to leave, for he wished to go to the abode of the thirty-three gods. But when he had fulfilled his vow and had been dismissed by his guru and was setting out for the abode of the thirty-three gods, Devayānī said to him, 'Grandson of the sage Aṅgiras! You shine forth by virtue of your behaviour, your noble birth, your knowledge, your asceticism, and your self-control. Just as the famous sage Aṅgiras is to be honoured by my father, so is Bṛhaspati even more to be honoured and worshipped by me. Knowing this, you who are rich in ascetic power should understand what I say. As I devoted myself to you when you were performing your vow and under restraint, so you should be devoted to me, who am devoted to you, now that you have obtained the magic secret. Take my hand in the marriage ritual with the marriage hymns.'

Kaca answered, 'As I must worship and honour your blessed father, so you, with your faultless body, are even more to be worshipped by me. You are dearer to Śukra, the noble descendant of Bhṛgu, than his very life's breath; as you are the daughter of my guru, you are to be worshipped by me always according to *dharma*, good lady. Since Śukra, your father, is to be honoured constantly by me – for he is my guru – so are you, Devayānī, and you should not speak to me like this.' Devayānī said, 'You are the son of the guru

Bṛhaspati,[17] but you are not the son of my father. Therefore you are to be honoured and worshipped by me too, O best of twice-born ones.[18] From the time when you were killed again and again by the demons, you were pleased with me; you should remember that, Kaca, and know that my devotion is supreme in friendship and in passion. You who know *dharma* should not abandon a woman who is devoted to you and has not offended you.'

Kaca replied, 'Though you have performed a virtuous vow, you are asking me to engage in an improper act of union. Forgive me, fair lady with lovely brows; I respect you even more than I respect my guru. Wide-eyed, moon-faced, proud lady, I lived where you lived, in the belly of Kāvya. Therefore, by *dharma* you are my sister, fair one, and you should not talk to me in this way. There is no malice in me, good lady; I have lived here happily and I will go now; I beg you, wish me an auspicious journey and let me be remembered and spoken of without any obstacle to *dharma* in your heart. Propitiate my guru constantly and conscientiously.' 'If you refuse me,' said Devayānī, 'when I urge you in a matter conducive to desire, profit, and *dharma*,[19] your magic knowledge will not be successful.'

Kaca said, 'I am refusing you not because of any fault but rather because you are my guru's daughter. My guru gave me permission to depart; curse me as much as you like, but I speak the *dharma* of sages, Devayānī. You cursed me today because of desire and not because of *dharma*, for I do not deserve your curse; therefore your desire will never be granted; no

17. Devayānī and Kaca are in fact more closely related than she will admit, for Śukra is the son of Bhṛgu, who is, like Aṅgiras, a son of Prajāpati; thus Devayānī and Kaca have the same paternal great-grandfather.

18. Kaca is twice-born because he is a brahmin, but he is also twice-born because of his rebirth after the demons have killed him.

19. A reference to the three original goals of life.

sage's son will ever take your hand in marriage. Since you said to me, "Your magic knowledge will not bear fruit," it will be so, but the magic will bear fruit for him to whom I teach it.'

When Kaca, the best of the twice-born, had said this to Devayānī, he went quickly to the abode of the lord of the thirty-three gods. The gods, led by Indra, rejoiced when they saw him arrive; they honoured Bṛhaspati and said to Kaca, 'Since you have performed a most wonderful act for our welfare, your fame will never die, and you will enjoy a share of the sacrifice with us.'

The Purāṇic Myth: Bṛhaspati Tricks Śukra and Corrupts the Demons

The Purāṇa version of the myth employs the more traditional allocation of sexual roles, and the gods send a woman (the daughter of Indra) instead of a man (the son of Bṛhaspati) to seduce the demons and take the secret of resuscitation from them. Since the daughter of the guru of the demons is no longer necessary in this version, she is replaced by the mother of the guru of the demons, a figure vaguely foreshadowed in the *Ṛg Veda*;[20] it is then she, instead of Kaca, who is magically revived in a typical episode of beheading and restoration,[21] while Śukra is eaten and revived by Śiva just as he himself ate and revived Kaca (an episode to which he alludes).

The moral dilemma of the Epic (the daughter's poignant need to choose between father and lover, a conflict which reappears in the myth of Satī)[22] is here reversed when Indra kills Śukra's mother; and Śukra's daughter imperilled him, while Indra's saves him from Śukra. But Indra's sin (in which Viṣṇu participates) is then made to account for the incarnations of Viṣṇu, one of which – the Buddha-Jina avatar[23] –

20. See above, myth 24, p. 75.

21. Compare the restorations in myths 36, pp. 124–5, and 69, pp. 266–8, above, and the revival through an act of truth in myth 56, pp. 201–3, above.

22. See above, myth 67, pp. 250–51.

23. See above, myth 62, pp. 232–5.

is incorporated here in full. This time the heresy of the demons serves not as a mere technicality by which they are disqualified from participation in the power struggle, a lapse which robs them of their power, but as an actual philosophy of renunciation, whose content is taken into account to explain the demons' voluntary withdrawal from the battle scene. This apparently ideal solution cannot endure, however, for the fight cannot end (certainly not with the demons so sanctimoniously content), and the demon brahmin comes forth again to re-enlighten his congregation, to renew the conflict, and to re-activate chaos.

75. FROM THE *Padma Purāṇa*

At a time in the past when the triple world was safe in the sway of the great Indra . . . the sacrifice[24] deserted the demons and went to the gods. When the sacrifice had gone to the gods, the demons, sons of Diti, said to Kāvya, 'Our kingdom has been taken away by the bountiful Indra, and the sacrifice has gone to the gods. We are not able to stay here, and so we shall enter the subterranean watery hell.' When Kāvya heard this he said to them, soothing them with his words, for they were discouraged, 'Do not fear, demons. I will support you with my own energy. All the sacrificial formulas and herbs which exist on earth are within me, but only a part is with the gods. I will give all of this to you, for I have kept it for your sake.' But when the gods saw that the demons were supported by the wise Kāvya, they all took counsel together in order to compete with them. 'This Kāvya is taking all of this universe from us by force,' they said. 'Very well, let us go quickly before he deposes us. We will attack them by force, and we will cause the survivors to go to hell.' Then the gods attacked the demons furiously, and as the demons were being slaughtered they fled to Kāvya.

24. According to another version of this story, in the *Matsya Purāṇa*, it is Śukra himself who leaves the demons and goes over to the gods (as many demons defect), though he returns to the demons immediately.

When Kāvya saw that they had been quickly put to flight by the gods and were hard pressed by them, he drew them away from the gods to protect them, and when the gods saw Kāvya standing there they went away without hesitation. Then Kāvya thought deeply about what Brahmā had said,[25] and when he remembered what had happened before he said to them, 'The dwarf stole the entire triple world away from you in three steps; he bound Bali, killed Jambha, and slew Virocana. The gods slew the great demons in twelve battles; by many different methods the best of you have been killed until only a few of you remain, and so I do not think there should be a battle. I will devise a stratagem for you; wait until some time has elapsed. I will go to the great god Śiva in order to obtain a formula for victory, and when I have obtained irresistible spells from the god Śiva, the great lord, you will again wage war against the gods and then you will be victorious.'

The demons discussed this and Prahlāda, on their behalf, said to the gods, 'We have all laid down our weapons and are without our chariots, unarmed and clothed in bark garments. We are going to practise asceticism.' When the gods heard this speech of Prahlāda, uttered like truth, they all turned back and went away, relieved of their fever and rejoicing because the demons had laid down their arms. Kāvya said to the demons, 'Wait patiently for a little while, engaged in asceticism, for time will accomplish your ends. Wait for me, demons, in my father's hermitage.' When Kāvya had instructed the demons, he approached the great god and said, 'O god, I desire spells which Bṛhaspati does not have, for the

25. This may refer to one of the frequent instances in which Brahmā is forced to promise that a particularly powerful demon will obtain certain immunities, as Śukra is about to obtain from Śiva. The other text has a different reading: 'The brahmin Kāvya recalled what had happened before . . .'

defeat of the gods and the victory of the demons.' To this the god replied, 'Son of Bhṛgu, perform a vow inhaling thick smoke, head downwards, for a full thousand years, and then you will obtain the spells.' Śukra, the son of Bhṛgu, touched the two feet of the god in acceptance and said, 'So be it. I will perform the vow as you have instructed me, great lord.' When the sage Kāvya, the son of Bhṛgu, was thus instructed by the god of gods, he practised chastity for the welfare of the demons, in order to obtain the spells from the great lord.

But when Śukra had departed, the royal gods learned that this had been done as a mere stratagem, and so, happy to find this weak spot, all of the gods led by Bṛhaspati attacked the demons indignantly, wearing armour and bearing weapons. When the bands of demons saw that the gods had taken up their weapons again, they all leaped up quickly, terrified, and said, 'We have laid down our arms, for our preceptor has undertaken a vow. You gods granted us security, but now you have come here wishing to kill us. We bear no grudges, and we have all abandoned our weapons. We are clad in garments of bark and black antelope skin; we perform no rituals and are without possessions.' Then they said to one another, 'We cannot defeat the gods in battle in any way, so let us, without a fight, tell Kāvya's mother about this calamity and seek refuge with her until our guru returns. And then, when Śukra has returned, we will put on our armour and take up our weapons and fight.'

Then they went to Kāvya's mother for refuge, frightened, and she gave them shelter, saying, 'Do not fear, do not fear. Abandon your fear, demons, for there is nothing for you to fear while you are in my presence.' But even when the gods saw that the demons were under her protection, they attacked them violently, not considering their strengths and weaknesses. When she saw the demons being slaughtered by the gods, the goddess became angry and said, 'I will enchant the gods with sleep.' Gathering together all the requisites, she then spread a spell of sleep, and the goddess, who had great powers of yoga and asceticism, paralysed Indra and immobilized him. When the gods saw that Indra had been paralysed, stupefied, and placed in her power, they ran away in terror, and after the massed gods had gone, Viṣṇu said to Indra, 'Enter into me please, supreme god, and I will carry you.'

The Shatterer of Cities entered into Viṣṇu, and when the goddess saw that he was protected by Viṣṇu she became angry and said, 'I will burn you up by force, O bountiful one, together with Viṣṇu, even while all these creatures are looking. Let the power of my asceticism be seen.' Then the two gods, Indra and Viṣṇu, were overcome by fear, and Viṣṇu said to Indra, 'How can we both get free?' 'Kill her before she burns us both, O lord,' said Indra. 'I am particularly powerless; therefore you must kill her quickly.' But as Viṣṇu regarded her he realized the problem involved in killing a woman, and the lord thought of his discus, which came quickly to him. Viṣṇu acted in haste, rashly, for he was frightened, knowing the cruel act which the goddess wished to commit. Furious and terrified, he took up his discus and cut off her head.

When the lord Bhṛgu saw this terrible slaughter of a woman, he became angry, and he cursed Viṣṇu for killing his wife, saying, 'Since you who know *dharma* have slain a woman, who is not to be slain, therefore you will be born among men seven times.' And because of this curse, Viṣṇu is born among men here again and again for the sake of the welfare of the world when *dharma* is destroyed. After Bhṛgu had said this to Viṣṇu, he himself took the head and placed it upon the body and took her two hands and said, 'Goddess, Viṣṇu killed you and I revive you. If I know *dharma* fully and have also followed it fully, then by this truth, if I speak the truth, may you come to life.' He sprinkled her with cool water and said,

'Live!', and when he had said this the goddess came to life. All creatures saw her arise as if from sleep, and they cried, 'Bravo! Well done!' on all sides, for it was a great marvel to the gods looking on that the goddess was thus restored by Bhṛgu.

When Indra saw that Bhṛgu had calmly brought his wife back to life again, he could find no relief from his fear of Kāvya. Unable to sleep at night, Indra, the chastiser of Pāka, kept brooding, wishing to devise a treaty, and then he said to his daughter Jayantī, 'This Kāvya is practising a terrible vow in order that there should be no Indra. I am therefore seriously alarmed by that wise sage. My wide-eyed daughter, go and enchant Kāvya quickly and tirelessly with various services pleasant to the heart. Propitiate him so that the twice-born one will be pleased with you, my daughter. Go! You have been given to him. Make this effort for my sake.' Jayantī accepted her father's command and went where Kāvya was beginning to undertake his terrible asceticism. When the goddess saw Kāvya inhaling thick smoke, head down, suspended over the great pit of the sacrificial fire, exhausting himself, shunning any pillow like an enemy, weak in condition, she treated Kāvya as her father had told her to. With pleasant words and sweet speech she praised him; she massaged his limbs for long periods and presented him with balms soothing to the skin; she served him for many years with things suitable for one performing a vow.

When the awesome thousand-year vow of smoke was completed, Śiva became pleased and offered Kāvya a boon, saying, 'You alone have fulfilled this vow, and no one else. Therefore you alone will surpass all the gods in asceticism, intelligence, learning, self-control, and vitality. I will give all the knowledge that I have to you, O brahmin, delight of Bhṛgu, but you must not tell it to anyone. But what use is talk? You will be invincible.' After Bhava had given this boon to the son of Bhṛgu, he gave him lordship over creatures, lordship over wealth, and invincibility. When Kāvya had obtained these boons, the hair on his body stood on end with joy, and the seer spoke to the lord of gods, the blue and red lord, and he bowed humbly, joining his palms together, and prostrated himself before him.

Then the god vanished, and Kāvya said to Jayantī, 'Whose daughter are you, O well-endowed one? Who are you that have suffered when I suffered? Why do you rival me with your great asceticism? You have lovely hips and a fine complexion, and I am pleased that you have attended me with such devotion, attention, patience, and affection. What do you wish? What desire has arisen in you who have such excellent buttocks? I will grant it to you this very day, even if it should be very difficult to do.' When she heard this she said to him, 'By means of your ascetic power, O brahmin, you should know exactly what I wish to have done.' Then he said to her, seeing with his divine eye, 'Passionate lady with excellent hips, you wish to spend a hundred years with me, invisible to all creatures; you wish for our union, goddess dark as a blue lotus, lady of beautiful eyes, worthy of a boon. You may indeed choose this if these are your wishes, sweet-speaking one. So be it: let us go to my house, you fascinating creature.' And so Uśanas the son of Bhṛgu went home with Jayantī and lived with that goddess for a hundred years, invisible to all creatures because of his magic power of illusion, for he had performed a difficult vow.

The sons of Diti learned that Śukra had achieved his purpose, and they all rejoiced and went to his house to see him. But on arriving they did not see their guru nor find any trace of him, for he was enveloped in his magic power of illusion. Then they thought, 'Our guru is not coming today,' and they all went back to their own abodes, whence they had come. All the bands of gods then went to Bṛhaspati the son of

Aṅgiras and said, 'Go to the home of the demons and delude their army and put them quickly in your own power.' The wise one said to the gods, 'I will go there and do that,' and he went and put Prahlāda, the lord of the demons, in his power. He became Śukra and stayed there performing the office of household priest for a hundred years, until Uśanas returned.

When the demons saw Bṛhaspati in the assembly they said, 'This is one Uśanas, and here is a second one outside. This is most curious, and there will be a fierce conflict here. What will people say when this contradiction is revealed? And what will this guru of ours who stands in the assembly say?' As the demons were murmuring in this way, Kāvya arrived and saw Bṛhaspati sitting there in Kāvya's form. Then Kāvya became angry and said, 'Guru of the gods, why have you come here? You are deluding my pupils, as is your custom. The fools do not recognize me, for they have been thoroughly stupefied by your magic power of illusion. It is not right for you, a brahmin, to corrupt someone else's pupils. Go to the world of the gods and stay there, and you will be following your *dharma*. Your son, Kaca, came here to be my pupil when he wished to obtain the magic knowledge, and he was slain by the demon chiefs. It is not right for you to come here.'

When he heard this speech, Bṛhaspati smiled again and again. 'There are thieves on earth who carry off the possessions of others,' he said, 'but I have never seen this kind, that steal forms and bodies. Brahminicide arose formerly when Indra slew Vṛtra, and you covered it up with your heretical materialist doctrine.[26] I know you: you are Bṛhaspati, the preceptor of the gods, the son of Aṅgiras, and you have come

26. The most notorious heresy in ancient India was that of the Materialists, called Lokāyatikas here but often referred to as Bārhaspatyas, disciples of Bṛhaspati, to whom their doctrine was often attributed. In view of this, it is ironic that the true Bṛhaspati accuses Śukra of teaching the doctrine that he himself (Bṛhaspati) has invented.

here in my form. Let all of you demons see: this one has come here to delude you with the machinations devised by Viṣṇu. Therefore bind him in chains and throw him into the salt ocean.' '*That* one is the household priest of the gods who dwell in heaven,' replied Śukra. 'You demons who have been fooled by him will be ruined. Look at me – lord of demons, you have been fooled by this evil one. Why have you abandoned me and made another your household priest? This is the guru of the gods, Aṅgiras's son Bṛhaspati, who has certainly deceived you for the benefit of those who dwell in heaven. Abandon him, generous king, for he will carry victory to the side of your enemies.

'My lord, once long ago I set out because my pupils were in danger, and the great god Śambhu swallowed me while I was staying in the midst of the waters. I spent a hundred years in his stomach, and then I came out of his stomach through his penis and was thereafter called Śukra ['Seed']. Then the god said to me, offering me a boon, "Śukra, choose whatever boon you wish," and I chose a boon from the god of gods, the wielder of the Pināka bow: "Lord of gods, Śaṅkara, may the goals that I think of in my mind and any other thing that I wish for become real by your grace." "So be it," said the god, and he sent me to you. But meanwhile[27] this other one, Bṛhaspati, became your household priest. Lord of demons, king, I have told you the truth; heed it.'

Then Bṛhaspati said to Prahlāda, 'I do not recognize this one as a god or a demon or anyone else, O king. He has taken my form and come here in order to deceive you.' At this all the demons cried out, 'Bravo! Well done! Let the former one[28] be our household priest, whoever he really is. Do not let the

27. Śukra himself seems to be confusing the boon given by Śiva long ago (when Śiva swallowed him) with the one he has just obtained (when Śukra swallowed smoke).

28. Bṛhaspati, who had been there for the last hundred years.

other one who has just arrived perform any rituals for us. Let him go.' Then Kāvya cursed all the demon chiefs in fury, saying, 'Since you have abandoned me, therefore I will soon see all of you deprived of your prosperity, deprived of your very life's breath, miserable mendicants.[29] Very soon you will experience this terrible misfortune.' And when he had said this, Kāvya went away to an ascetic forest as he pleased.

When Śukra had gone, Bṛhaspati stayed there and protected the demons for a while. But when a long time had passed, the demons all came together and asked their 'guru', 'Grant us some sort of knowledge about the worthless circle of rebirth so that we may obtain release here by your favour, for you have kept your vow.' Then the guru of the gods, in the form of Kāvya, the demons' guru, replied, 'This is my own opinion, as I have explained to you before. Let everyone together seize the proper moment and become pure, and I will proclaim the knowledge to you, demons, and grant you release. This sacred scripture of the Vedas, as it is found in the *Ṛg*, *Yajur*, and *Sāma Vedas*, by the favour of fire gives nothing but misery to creatures that breathe here. The sacrifice and the oblation to the ancestors are performed by lowly people intent upon the goals of this world. The customs of Vaiṣṇavas and those practised by the followers of Rudra are evil *dharmas*, for they are generally performed by these people together with their wives and they involve taking life.[30]

'How could Rudra, the lord who is half woman,[31] find re-

29. The demons are to become Jains and Buddhists, who beg for their food.

30. To 'heretics', non-Hindus such as Jains, Buddhists, or Materialists, the presence of women in Hindu rituals would suggest unchastity, while the animal sacrifice would violate the Jain and Buddhist injunction against taking life. These and other arguments that follow are traditional 'heretic' criticisms of various Hindu sectarian practices.

31. A reference to the androgyne. See above, myth 68, p. 259.

lease, surrounded as he is by bands of ghosts and adorned by bones? . . . Lord of demons, how will people go to heaven by means of sexual intercourse? Where purification is obtained by means of dirt and ashes, what purification can there be? O demon, see how perverse this world is, which purifies the penis and anus which emit urine and faeces . . . Once, in the past, Soma carried off Tārā, the wife of Bṛhaspati, and Budha[32] was the son born in her; and yet the guru Bṛhaspati took her back again.[33] Ahalyā, the wife of the sage Gautama, was taken by Śakra himself;[34] see what kind of *dharma* this is. And other adultery like this is seen in the universe; where there is this sort of *dharma*, what can be considered the highest goal? Tell me that, O king of demons, tell me, and I will tell you more.'

When they heard their 'guru' rambling on in this way about the highest goal, they became eager for it and were freed from attachment to the ocean of existence. The demons said, 'Guru, as we stand here full of devotion consecrate us all so that, by your instruction, we will never again be deluded. We are quite free of attachment to the circle of rebirth which brings sorrow a thousandfold; lift us all up, guru, as if lifting us out of a well by dragging us by the hair. What god can we go to for refuge? O best of brahmins, noble one, reveal the divinity to us who have come to you. By remembering and fasting and meditating, by worship and offerings, one obtains final beatitude. We are free of attachment and will not be bound again by the cares and duties of family life.' When the

32. Budha is a king of the lunar dynasty, in no way related to Gautama the Buddha.

33. When Tārā, the wife of Bṛhaspati, was raped by Soma, she gave birth to a son by Soma, as she herself admitted, but was still restored to her husband Bṛhaspati. Again, it is ironic that the true Bṛhaspati, in disguise, tells this story to his own discredit, for a man of honour would have rejected such a wife, as Rāma rejected Sītā in similar circumstances (see above, myth 56, pp. 198–200).

34. See above, myth 28, pp. 94–6.

disguised 'guru' was thus addressed by those who were like bulls among the demons, he considered, 'How will I do what is to be done? How can I make them into evil ones who dwell in hell? A deception will place them beyond the pale of the Vedas and make them the subject of ridicule in the triple world.'

[He summons Viṣṇu, who appears as the great deluder twice, first naked (as a Jain) and then in red garments (a Buddhist), and makes the demons into Jains and Buddhists.][35]

Then Bṛhaspati went to the world of the gods and told those who dwell in heaven all that had been done to the demons. The gods then went to the Narmadā river and saw the demons there without Prahlāda,[36] and the king of the gods rejoiced and said to Namuci and all the other demons, 'Demon kings, formerly you held sovereignty over the triple world. How is it that you have now undertaken a vow which totally violates the Vedas – going naked, with bald heads, carrying begging-bowls, waving peacock fans?' The demons answered, 'We have abandoned our entire demon nature and have engaged in the *dharma* of sages. We preach all that increases *dharma* among all people. Enjoy the entire sovereignty over the triple world, Śakra, and go away.' The bountiful one agreed to this, and went back to the triple world. Thus all the supreme demons were fooled by the guru of the gods, and they went to the Narmadā river. But when Śukra enlightened them all, they awakened from their vow and once again they set their cruel hearts upon taking away the triple world . . .

35. See above, myth 62, pp. 232–5.
36. He alone, the virtuous demon, resisted corruption by Bṛhaspati.

Appendix A
ABBREVIATIONS

ASA *Association of Social Anthropologists*
ASS *Ānandāśrama Sanskrit Series*
BV *Bhāratīya Vidyā*, Bombay
Bib. Ind. *Bibliotheca Indica*
HJAS *Harvard Journal of Asiatic Studies*
HOS *Harvard Oriental Series*
IIJ *Indo-Iranian Journal*
JAOS *Journal of the American Oriental Society*
JGJRI *Journal of the Ganganatha Jha Research Institute*
JOIB *Journal of the Oriental Institute of Baroda*
JRAS *Journal of the Royal Asiatic Society*
JRASB *Journal of the Royal Asiatic Society of Bengal*
RHR *Revue de l'histoire des religions*
SBE *Sacred Books of the East*
SBH *Sacred Books of the Hindus*
TITLV *Tijdscrift voor Indische Taal-, Land-, en Volkenkunde*
WZKS&O *Wiener Zeitschrift zur Kunde des Süd- und Ostasiens*
ZDMG *Zeitschrift der Deutschen Morgenländischen Gesellschaft*

Appendix B

SELECTED BIBLIOGRAPHY

I. Dictionaries and Encyclopedias of Indian Mythology

Bhattacarji, Sukumari, *The Indian Theogony: A Comparative Study of Indian Mythology from the Vedas to the Purāṇas* (Cambridge, 1970).

Daniélou, Alain, *Hindu Polytheism* (London, 1964).

Dikshitar, V. R. R., *The Purāṇa Index*, 3 vols. (Madras, 1955).

Dowson, John, *A Classical Dictionary of Hindu Mythology and Religion*, 10th edn (London, 1961).

Hopkins, Edward Washburn, *Epic Mythology* (Strassburg, 1915, reprinted Wiesbaden, 1968).

Macdonell, Arthur Anthony, *Vedic Mythology* (Strassburg, 1897, reprinted Delhi, 1963).

Sörensen, S., *Index to the Names in the Mahābhārata* (London, 1904, reprinted Delhi, 1963).

II. Analyses and 'Retellings' of Collections of Indian Myths

Brown, W. Norman, 'Mythology of India', in *Mythologies of the Ancient World*, ed. S. N. Kramer (New York, 1961), pp. 275–330.

Coomaraswamy, Ananda K., and Nivedita, Sister, *Myths of the Hindus and Buddhists* (London, 1913, reprinted New York, 1967).

Dange, Sadashiv A., *Legends in the Mahābhārata* (New Delhi, 1969).

Fausbøll, Viggo, *Indian Mythology in Outline, According to the Mahābhārata* (London, 1903).

Gonda, Jan, *Viṣṇuism and Śivaism* (London, 1970).

Hariyappa, H. L., *Ṛgvedic Legends through the Ages* (Poona, 1953).

Keith, Arthur Berriedale, *Indian Mythology*: Vol. VI, Part I, of *The Mythology of All Races*, ed. L. H. Grey (Boston, 1917, reprinted, 1964).

Kennedy, Colonel Vans, *Researches into the Nature and Affinity of Ancient and Hindu Mythology* (London, 1831).

Moor, Edward, *The Hindu Pantheon* (London, 1810, reprinted Delhi, 1968).

Rao, T. A. Gopinatha, *Elements of Hindu Iconography*, 2 vols., 4 parts (Madras, 1916, reprinted Delhi, 1968).

Thomas, P., *Epics, Myths and Legends of India* (Bombay, 1958).

Wilkins, W. J., *Hindu Mythology, Vedic and Purāṇic* (London, 1882, reprinted London, 1973).

Zimmer, Heinrich, *Maya, der Indische Mythos* (Stuttgart, 1936).

Zimmer, Heinrich, *Myths and Symbols in Indian Art and Civilization* (New York, 1946, reprinted, paperback, New York, 1968).

III. Analyses of particular myth cycles

Śiva: Wendy Doniger O'Flaherty, *Asceticism and Eroticism in the Mythology of Śiva* (Oxford, 1973).

Viṣṇu: Jan Gonda, *Aspects of Early Viṣṇuism* (Utrecht, 1954, reprinted New Delhi, 1969).

Kṛṣṇa: Walter Ruben, *Kṛṣṇa: Konkordanz und Kommentar der Motive seines Heldenlebens* (Istanbul, 1944).

Gods and demons: Paul Hacker, *Prahlāda: Werden und Wandlungen einer Idealgestalt* (Wiesbaden, 1960).

Indo-European mythology: Georges Dumézil, *Les Dieux des Indo-Européens* (Paris, 1952); *Mitra-Varuṇa* (Paris, 1948).

Vedic mythology: Boris L. Ogibenin, *Structure d'un Mythe Védique: Le Mythe Cosmogonique dans le Ṛgveda* (The Hague, 1973).

IV. Editions and translations of Sanskrit texts

The reader should be forewarned that different editions and translations use different numbers to refer to chapters and verses of the same work, and some refer to the Sanskrit names of sub-sections rather than to any number at all. This bibliography lists the most common Sanskrit titles of sub-sections of large works, and the secondary references in the bibliographical notes are to the first edition cited for any particular work or (for all translated works) to the translation.

A. Ṛg Veda and Atharva Veda

Ṛg Veda with the commentary of Sāyaṇa, 6 vols. (London, 1890–92).

Translations: into German: Karl Friedrich Geldner, 3 vols., *HOS*, 33–5 (Cambridge, Massachusetts, 1951); into French: Louis Renou, *Études Védiques et Pāṇinéennes* (Paris, 1955–69); into English; Horace Hayman Wilson (London, 1866); R. T. H. Griffith (Benares, 1896).

Selection (and other translations): John Muir, *Original Sanskrit Texts*, 5 vols. (London 1872, reprinted Amsterdam, 1967).

Atharva Veda with the commentary of Sāyaṇa (Bombay, 1895).

Translations: Maurice Bloomfield, *SBE*, 42 (Oxford, 1897, reprinted Delhi, 1964); William Dwight Whitney, *HOS*, 7–8 (Cambridge, 1905).

B. Brāhmaṇas and Upaniṣads

Aitareya Brāhmaṇa with the commentary of Sāyaṇa, *Bib. Ind.* (Calcutta, 1896).

Translation: Arthur Berriedale Keith, *HOS*, 25 (Cambridge, 1920).

Bṛhaddevatā of Śaunaka, *HOS*, 5 (Cambridge, 1904).

Translation: Arthur Anthony Macdonell, *HOS*, 6 (Cambridge, 1904).

Gopatha Brāhmaṇa (Leiden, 1919).

Jaiminīya [*Talavakara*] *Brāhmaṇa*, Sarasvatī-vihara Series, 31 (Nagpur, 1954).

Translation; H. Oertel, *JAOS*, XVIII–XXVIII (1896–1906); (German) W. Caland (Amsterdam, 1919).

Kauṣītaki Brāhmaṇa (Wiesbaden, 1968).

Translation: A. B. Keith, *HOS*, 25 (Cambridge, 1920).

Maitrāyaṇī Saṃhitā, ed. L. von Schroeder (1881; Wiesbaden, 1970).

Nirukta of Yāska, edited, and partially translated, by Lakshman Sarup (Oxford, 1921).

Śatapatha Brāhmaṇa, Chowkhamba Sanskrit Series, 96 (Benares, 1964).
Translation: Julius Eggeling, *SBE*, 12, 26, 41, 43, 44 (Oxford, 1882, reprinted New Delhi, 1964).

Taittirīya Āraṇyaka with the commentary of Sāyaṇa, *Bib. Ind.* (Calcutta, 1872).

Taittirīya Brāhmaṇa with the commentary of Sāyaṇa, *Bib. Ind.* (Calcutta, 1859).

Taittirīya Saṃhitā with the commentary of Madhava, *Bib. Ind.* (Calcutta, 1860).
Translation: Arthur Berriedale Keith, *HOS*, 19 (Cambridge, 1914).

Tāṇḍya [*Pañcaviṃśa*] *Mahābrāhmaṇa* with the commentary of Sāyaṇa, *Bib. Ind.* (Calcutta, 1869–74).
Translation: W. Caland, *Bib. Ind.* (Calcutta, 1931).

Upaniṣads: *One Hundred and Eight Upanishads*, 4th edn (Bombay, 1913).
Translation: Robert Hume, *The Thirteen Principal Upanishads* (Oxford, 1921, reprinted Madras, 1958).

Vājasaneyi Saṃhitā (Berlin, 1952).

C. Epics

Mahābhārata, critical edition (Poona, 1933–69); *Mahābhārata* with the commentary of Nīlakaṇṭha (Bombay, 1862).
Translations: Pratap Chandra Roy, 11 vols., 2nd edn (Calcutta, 1927–32); Manmatha Nath Dutt, 7 vols. (Calcutta, 1895–1905); J. A. B. van Buitenen (Chicago, 1974–), Books 1–5.
Names of the books (Parvans): 1. Ādi; 2. Sabhā; 3. Vana (or Āraṇyaka); 4. Virāṭa; 5. Udyoga; 6. Bhīṣma; 7. Droṇa; 8. Karṇa; 9. Śalya; 10. Sauptika; 11. Strī; 12. Śānti; 13. Anuśāsana; 14. Āśvamedhika; 15. Āśramavāsika; 16. Mausala; 17. Mahāprasthānika; 18. Svargārohaṇa.

Rāmāyaṇa of Vālmīki (Baroda, 1960–75).
Translation: Hari Prasad Shastri, 3 vols. (London, 1962).
Names of the books (Kāṇḍas): 1. Bāla; 2. Āyodhyā; 3. Āraṇya; 4. Kiṣkindhā; 5. Sundara; 6. Yuddha; 7. Uttara.

The most famous 'translation' of the *Rāmāyaṇa* in India is the Hindi poem by Tulsī Dās: *The Holy Lake of the Acts of Rāma, an English Translation of Tulsī Dās's Rāmacaritamānasa*, by W. D. P. Hill (London, 1952, reprinted Bombay, 1971); another translation of Tulsī Dās's work is by S. N. Ghosal (Baroda, 1960). A very free 'translation' of Vālmīki's *Rāmāyaṇa* may be seen in Aubrey Menen's satire, *Rāma Retold* (London, 1954).

D. Purāṇas (cited by first word in bibliographical notes)

Agni Purāṇa, *ASS*, 41 (Poona, 1957).
  Translation: Manmatha Nath Dutt (Calcutta, 1901; reprinted Varanasi, 1967).

Bhāgavata Purāṇa with the commentary of Śrīdhara (Bombay, 1832).
  Translations: into English: J. M. Sanyal (Calcutta, 1930–34); Ganesh Vasudeo Tagare, in *Ancient Indian Tradition and Mythology*, ed. J. L. Shastri (Delhi, 1976); A. C. Bhaktivedanta Swami Prabhupāda (Los Angeles, 1972); into French: Eugène Burnouf, 5 vols. (Paris, 1840–98).

Bhaviṣya Purāṇa (Bombay, 1959).

Brahma Purāṇa (Calcutta, 1954).

Brahmāṇḍa Purāṇa (Delhi, 1973).

Brahmavaivarta Purāṇa, *ASS*, 102, 4 vols. (Poona, 1935).
  Translation: Rajendra Nath Sen, *SBH*, 24, 2 vols. (Allahabad 1919–22, reprinted New York, 1973).
  Names of the books (Khaṇḍas): 1. Brahma; 2. Prakṛti; 3. Gaṇapati; 4. Kṛṣṇajanma.

Bṛhaddharma Purāṇa, *Bib. Ind.* (Calcutta, 1888–97).
  Summarized by Rajendra Chandra Hazra in *Studies in the Upapurāṇas* (Calcutta, 1958 and 1963); Vol. I: *Saura and Vaiṣṇava Upapurāṇas*; Vol. II: *Śākta and Non-Sectarian Upapurāṇas*. Hazra also summarizes the *Bṛhannāradīya, Devī, Devībhāgavata, Kālikā, Kalki, Mahābhāgavata, Narasiṃha, Sāmba, Viṣṇudharma*, and *Viṣṇudharmottara Purāṇas*.

Bṛhannāradīya Purāṇa, *Bib. Ind.* (Calcutta, 1891).

Bṛhatsaṃhitā of Varāhamihira, *Bib. Ind.* (Calcutta, 1865).
  Translation: H. Kern, *JRAS*, IV–VII (1870–75).

Devī Purāṇa (Calcutta, 1896).
Devībhāgavata Purāṇa (Benares, 1960).
Translation: Swami Vijnanananda, *SBH*, 26 (Allahabad, 1921–3, reprinted New York, 1973).
Garuḍa Purāṇa (Benares, 1969).
Translation: Manmatha Nath Dutt (Calcutta, 1908, reprinted Delhi, 1968).
Detailed analysis: N. Gangadharan, *Garuḍa Purāṇa, A Study* (Varanasi, 1972).
Harivaṃśa (Poona, 1969); with commentary (Bombay, 1927).
Translations: into English: H. C. Das (Calcutta, 1897); M. N. Dutt (Calcutta, 1897); into French: Simon Alexandre Langlois (London, 1834–5).
Kālikā Purāṇa (Bombay, 1891).
Kalki Purāṇa (Calcutta, 1873).
Kumārasambhava of Kālidāsa (Bombay, 1955).
Translation: M. R. Kale (Bombay, 1923, reprinted Delhi, 1967).
Kūrma Purāṇa (Varanasi, 1972).
Translation: ed. A. S. Gupta (Varanasi, 1972).
Liṅga Purāṇa (Calcutta, 1812).
Translation: J. L. Shastri (Delhi, 1973).
Mahābhāgavata Purāṇa (Bombay, 1913).
Mārkaṇḍeya Purāṇa, with commentary (Bombay, 1890); *Bib. Ind.*, 29 (Calcutta, 1862).
Translation: Frederick Eden Pargiter, *Bib. Ind.*, 2 vols. (Calcutta, 1888–1904, reprinted Delhi, 1969).
Matsya Purāṇa, *ASS*, 54 (Poona, 1907).
Translation: a Taluqdar of Oudh, *SBH*, 17 (Allahabad, 1916–17, reprinted New York, 1973).
Detailed analyses: V. R. R. Dikshitar, *Matsya Purāṇa, A Study* (Madras, 1935); V. S. Agrawala, *Matsya Purāṇa, A Study* (Varanasi, 1963); S. G. Kantawala, *Cultural History from the Matsya Purāṇa* (Baroda, 1964).
Nārada Purāṇa, summarized by K. Damodaran Nambiar in *Purāṇa*, *XV*, 2 (July 1973), pp. 1–30.
Narasiṃha Purāṇa (Bombay, 1911).
Padma Purāṇa, *ASS*, 131 (Poona, 1893); *Padma Purāṇa* (Calcutta, 1958).

Names of the books (Khaṇḍas) of the *ASS* edition: 1. Ādi; 2. Bhumi; 3. Brahma; 4. Pātāla; 5. Sṛṣṭi; 6. Uttara. Calcutta edition: 1. Sṛṣṭi; 2. Bhumi; 3. Svarga; 4. Brahma; 5. Pātāla; 6. Uttara.

Raghuvaṃśa of Kālidāsa, edited and translated by Gopal Raghunath Nandargikar (Benares, 1971).

Sāmba Purāṇa (Bombay, 1942).

Analysis: Heinrich von Stietencron, *Indische Sonnenpriester* (Wiesbaden, 1966).

Saura Purāṇa (Calcutta, 1816).

Partially translated and analysed by Wilhelm Jahn, *Das Saurapurāṇam* (Strassburg, 1908).

Śiva Purāṇa (Benares, 1964). Names of the books (Saṃhitās): 1. Vidyeśvara; 2. Rudra (i. Sṛṣṭi Khaṇḍa; ii. Satī Khaṇḍa; iii. Pārvatī Khaṇḍa; iv. Kumāra Khaṇḍa; v. Yuddha Khaṇḍa); 3. Śatarudra; 4. Koṭirudra; 5. Umā; 6. Kailāsa; 7. Vāyavīya (i. Pūrva Bhāga; ii. Uttara Bhāga).

Translation: J. L. Shastri, in *Ancient Indian Tradition and Mythology*, I–IV (Delhi, 1970).

Śiva Purāṇa, with commentary. *Jñānasaṃhitā*, *Dharmasaṃhitā*, and *Vāyu Saṃhitā* (Bombay, 1884).

Skanda Purāṇa (Bombay, 1867).

Names of the books (Khaṇḍas): 1. Māheśvara (i. Kedāra; ii. Kaumārika; iii. Aruṇācalamāhātmya); 2. Vaiṣṇava (i. Veṅkaṭācalamāhātmya; ii. Puruṣottamakṣetramāhātmya; iii. Badarikāśramamāhātmya; iv. Kārtikamāsa; v. Mārgaśīrṣa; vi. Bhāgavata; vii. Vaiśākhamāsa; viii. Āyodhyā); 3. Brāhma (i. Setumāhātmya; ii. Dharmāraṇya; iii. Brāhmottara); 4. Kāśī; 5. Avanti (i. Avantikṣetra; ii. Avantisthacaturaśītiliṅga; iii. Revā); 6. Nāgara; 7. Prabhāsa (i. Prabhāsakṣetra; ii. Vastrāpathakṣetra; iii. Arbuda; iv. Dvārakā).

Skanda Purāṇa (Calcutta. 1959).

Skanda Purāṇa, Kedāra Khaṇḍa (Bombay, 1910).

Vāmana Purāṇa (Varanasi, 1968).

Translation: Anand Swarup Gupta (Varanasi, 1968).

Analysis: V. S. Agrawala, *Vāmana Purāṇa, A Study* (Benares, 1964).

Varāha Purāṇa, *Bib. Ind.*, 110 (Calcutta, 1893).

Vāyu Purāṇa (Bombay, 1897); *Bib. Ind.* (Calcutta, 1880); *ASS*, 49 (Poona, 1860).

Analysis: V. R. R. Dikshitar, *Some Aspects of the Vāyu Purāṇa* (Madras, 1933); D. R. Patil, *Cultural History from the Vāyu Purāṇa* (Poona, 1946).

Viṣṇu Purāṇa, with the commentary of Śrīdhara (Calcutta, 1972).

Translation: Horace Hayman Wilson, 3rd edn (London, 1840, reprinted Calcutta, 1961).

Viṣṇudharma Purāṇa. See Julius Eggeling, *India Office Catalogue*, VI, pp. 1308–9; MS. No. 3604.

Viṣṇudharmottara Purāṇa (Bombay, Veṅkaṭeśvara Steam Press, no date).

Appendix C.
BIBLIOGRAPHICAL NOTES

Notes to the Introduction

1. Cf. Xavier S. Thani Nayagam, *A Reference Guide to Tamil Studies* (Kuala Lumpur, 1966). See for example *The Śilappadikaram*, translated by V. R. Ramachandra Dikshitar (Madras, Oxford, 1939) or by Alain Daniélou (New York, 1962): R. Dessigane, P. Z. Pattabiramin, and Jean Filliozat, *La légende des jeux de Çiva a Madurai* (Pondichéry, 1960): *Les légendes Çivaites de Kāñcīpuram* (Pondichéry, 1964): R. Dessigane and P. Z. Pattabiramin, *La légende de Skanda selon le Kandapurāṇam Tamoul et l'iconographie* (Pondichéry, 1967): C. Jesudasan and Hepzibah Jesudasan, *A History of Tamil Literature* (Calcutta, 1961): V. Kanagasabhai, *The Great Twin Epics of Tamil* (Madras, 1956): George Uglow Pope, *Manimekalai* (Madras, 1911): William Taylor, *Oriental Historical Manuscripts* (Madras, 1835). Many Tamil myths may also be found in Wilber Theodore Elmore, *Dravidian Gods in Modern Hinduism* (Nebraska, 1915): Gustav Oppert, *On the Original Inhabitants of Bharatavarsha or India* (London, 1893): Henry Whitehead, *Village Gods of South India* (Oxford, 1921); Bartholomaeus Ziegenbalg, *Genealogy of the South Indian Gods* (Amsterdam, 1717, reprinted Madras, 1869).

2. The works of Verrier Elwin are the richest source of Indian tribal mythology. See particularly *Folk-Tales of Mahakoshal* (Oxford, 1944), *Myths of Middle India* (Oxford, 1949), and *Tribal Myths of Orissa* (Oxford, 1954). See also Lal Behari Day, *Folk-Tales of Bengal* (London, 1883); Christoph von Fürer-Haimendorf, *The Aboriginal Tribes of Hyderabad* (London, 1943 and 1948); Olivier Herrenschmidt, *Le Cycle de Lingal* (Paris, 1966); C. H. Tawney and N. M. Penzer, *The Ocean of Story*, 10 vols. (London, 1924–8); and R. C. Temple,

The Legends of the Punjab, 3 vols. (Bombay and London, 1884–1901).

3. J. N. Farquhar, *An Outline of the Religious Literature of India* (Oxford, 1920, reprinted Delhi, 1967); Jan Gonda, *Die Religionen Indiens*, Vol. II, *Der jüngere Hinduismus* (Stuttgart, 1963); translated into French, *L'Hindouisme récent* (Paris, 1965); Rajendra Chandra Hazra, *Studies in the Purāṇic Records on Hindu Rites and Customs* (University of Dacca, 1948); *Studies in the Upapurāṇas* (University of Calcutta, Vol. I, 1958, Vol. II, 1963); Willibald Kirfel, *Das Purāṇa Pañcalakṣaṇa* (Bonn, 1927); *Das Purāṇa vom Weltgebäude* (Bonn, 1954); Frederick Eden Pargiter, *Ancient Indian Historical Tradition* (Oxford, 1922, reprinted Delhi, 1962); *The Purāṇa Text of the Dynasties of the Kali Age* (Oxford, 1913, reprinted Varanasi, 1962); A. D. Pusalker, *Studies in the Epics and Purāṇas of India* (Bombay, 1955); Moriz Winternitz, *A History of Indian Literature*, Vol. I, Part 2, *Epics and Purāṇas*, translated by Mrs S. Ketkar (University of Calcutta, 1963).

4. *Aitareya Brāhmaṇa* 7.13–19; *Rāmāyaṇa* 1.61–2; *Bhāgavata Purāṇa* 9.7.

5. *Mahābhārata* 1.75–91; *Bhāgavata Purāṇa* 9.18–19; *Matsya Purāṇa* 24–42; *Padma Purāṇa* 2.72–84; *Viṣṇu Purāṇa* 4.9.

6. *Bhāgavata* 9.8; *Brahma* 8 and 78; *Brahmāṇḍa* 2. 3.46–53; *Bṛhaddharma* 2.52; *Bṛhannāradīya* 6–7; *Liṅga* 1.66; *Mahābhārata* 3.104; *Rāmāyaṇa* 1.38–44; *Śiva* 5.38; *Skanda, Kedāra Khaṇḍa* 29; *Vāyu* 2.26; *Viṣṇu* 4.4; *Viṣṇudharmottara* 1.18.

7. *Alambusā Jātaka* 523; *Nalinikā Jātaka* 526; *Mahābhārata* 3.110–13; *Rāmāyaṇa* 1.8–10; *Padma Purāṇa, Pātāla Khaṇḍa* 13; *Avadānakalpalatā* 65.

8. For recent discussions of the nature and meaning of mythology in general, see Mary Barnard, *The Mythmakers* (Athens, Ohio, 1966); Joseph Campbell, *The Masks of God*, 3 vols. (New York, 1959–64); Mary Douglas, *Purity and Danger* (London, 1966); *Natural Symbols* (London, 1970; Harmondsworth, 1973); Mircea Eliade, *Cosmos and History, The Myth of the Eternal Return* (New York, 1954); *The Sacred and the Profane* (New York, 1959); *Images and Symbols* (London, 1961); *The Two and the One* (London, 1965); *Myths, Dreams, and Mysteries* (London, 1968); *Myth and Reality* (London, 1964); G. S. Kirk, *Myth: Its Meaning and Functions in Ancient and Other Cultures* (Cambridge and Berkeley, 1970); John Middleton (ed.), *Myth and Cosmos, Readings*

in Mythology and Symbolism (New York, 1967); Henry A. Murray (ed.), *Myth and Mythmaking* (New York, 1960); Thomas A. Sebeok (ed.), *Myth, A Symposium* (Bloomington, Indiana, 1958); Alan W. Watts (ed.), *Patterns of Myth*, 3 vols. (New York, 1963). An introduction to the ritual view of mythology would include the writings of J. G. Frazer, *The Golden Bough*, 13 vols. (London, 1915); Jane Ellen Harrison, *Prolegomena to the Study of Greek Religion* (Cambridge, 1908); *Themis* (Cambridge, 1912); *Epilegomena* (Cambridge, 1921); *Mythology* (London, 1924); the last three titles reprinted New York 1962–3; and Lord Raglan, *The Hero* (London, 1936); *The Origins of Religion* (London, 1949). For the psychoanalytic approach to myth, see C. G. Jung, *Symbols of Transformation* (Princeton and London, 1967); *The Archetypes of the Collective Unconscious* (Zurich, 1954; reprinted in *Four Archetypes*, London, 1972, and *Essays on a Science of Mythology*, Princeton, 1969); Paul Radin, *The Trickster* (with commentary by C. G. Jung and C. Kerényi, London, 1956); Otto Rank, *The Myth of the Birth of the Hero* (New York, 1914; reprinted 1959). For the structuralist school see Edmund Leach (ed.), *The Structural Study of Myth and Totemism* (ASA Monograph 5, London, 1967); *Genesis as Myth and Other Essays* (London, 1969); Claude Lévi-Strauss, *Mythologiques* (*Introduction to a Science of Mythology*): I. *The Raw and the Cooked* (Paris, 1964; London, 1970); II. *From Honey to Ashes* (Paris, 1966; London, 1973); III. *L'Origine des manières de table* (Paris, 1968); Pierre Maranda (ed.), *Mythology* (Harmondsworth, 1972); Pierre and E. K. Köngäs Maranda (eds.), *Structural Analysis of Oral Tradition* (University of Pennsylvania, 1971); Vladimir Propp, *Morphology of the Folktale* (University of Texas, 1968).

9. Visual illustrations may serve to reanimate the myths by helping the reader to see the gods in their true Indian ambience. Representations of the myths in sculpture and painting may be found in many of the books cited in the bibliography (particularly the works of Keith, Moor, Rao, Wilkins, and Zimmer), as well as in the following: Shakti M. Gupta, *From Daityas to Devatas in Hindu Mythology* (Delhi, 1973); Veronica Ions, *Indian Mythology* (London, 1967); and J. Hackin (ed.), *Asiatic Mythology* (London, 1963), pp. 100–146.

10. Claude Lévi-Strauss, *Structural Anthropology* (New York, 1963), p. 210.

Notes to the Text

The exact Sanskrit source of each myth is given first, followed by a list of other versions of the myth in alphabetical order of four groups: Vedic, Brāhmaṇic, Epic (where these exist), and Purāṇic. Texts available in translation are preceded by *, and references to secondary versions are to translations. For the *Mahābhārata*, references are to the critical edition, followed by Roy's translation (in brackets). These lists are by no means exhaustive, but merely indicate a line for further research. For some myths, interpretations and discussions are listed after the Sanskrit sources; the reader should also bear in mind the usefulness of many translators' notes.

1. Incest: the Father Commits Incest with his Daughter

**Ṛg Veda* 10.61.5–7; 1.71.5; 1.71.8; 1.164.33.

Compare: **Ṛg Veda* 3.31.1; 10.61.7; **Atharva Veda* 10.10.16; **Aitareya Brāhmaṇa* 13.9–10; **Bṛhaddevatā* 4.110–11; *Maitrāyaṇī Saṃhitā* 4.2.12; *Taittirīya Saṃhitā* 3.4; 10.3; **Tāṇḍya Mahābrāhmaṇa* 8.2.10; **Bhāgavata* 3.13; *Brahmāṇḍa* 2.3.1; **Brahmavaivarta* 1.4, 4.31–5; *Kālikā* 1–3; *Mahābhāgavata* 21; **Mārkaṇḍeya* 50; **Matsya* 3–4; **Śiva* 2.2.2–4.

Discussions: Sadashiv A. Dange, 'Prajāpati and his Daughter', *Purāṇa*, V, 1 (January 1963), pp. 39–46; Friedrich Max Müller, *A History of Ancient Sanskrit Literature* (London, 1859), pp. 529 ff.; Muir, IV, 45 ff.; R. Panikkar, 'The Myth of Incest as a Symbol for Redemption in Vedic India' in R. J. Zwi Verblowsky and C. J. Bleeker (ed.), *Types of Redemption*, Studies in the History of Religion, vol. 18 (Leiden, 1970), pp. 130 ff.; O'Flaherty, *Asceticism and Eroticism in the Mythology of Śiva* (1973), pp. 114–23, 136–41. See also Edmund R. Leach, 'Genesis as Myth', in Edmund R. Leach, *Genesis as Myth and Other Essays* (London, 1969); Philip Spratt, *Hindu Culture and Personality, a Psycho-Analytic Study* (Bombay, 1966) pp. 105–12, 229, 260; A. K. Ramanujan, 'The Indian Oedipus' in Arabinda Podder (ed.), *Indian Literature* (Indian Institute of Advanced Studies, Simla, 1972), pp. 127–37.

2. Dismemberment: the Primeval Man is Sacrificed

**Ṛg Veda* 10.90.1–16.

Compare: **Ṛg Veda* 1.162–3; **Bṛhadāraṇyaka Upaniṣad* 1.4.11 ff.; **Manu* 1.8–12, 31–41; **Śatapatha Brāhmaṇa* 2.1.4.11; 14.4.2.23; *Taittirīya Brāhmaṇa* 3.12.9.2; **Taittirīya Saṃhitā* 4.3.10.1; 7.1.1.4; *Vājasaneyi Saṃhitā* 14.28 ff.; 31.1–16; **Bhāgavata* 2.5; **Brahmavaivarta* 1.5, 8.

Discussions: W. Norman Brown, 'The Sources and Nature of Puruṣa in the Puruṣasūkta', *JAOS*, LI (1931), pp. 108–18; Gonda (1963), I, 173 (with bibliography); (1969), pp. 25–8; W. Kirfel, 'Der Aśvamedha und der Puruṣamedha' in *Festschrift – W. Schubring* (Hamburg, 1951), pp. 39 ff.; Muir, I, 7–24; II, 454; IV, 3–62: V, 367; Paul Mus, 'Du nouveau sur Ṛg veda X.90', *Indological Studies in Honor of W. Norman Brown* (AOS 47), pp. 165–85; N. J. Shende, *The Puruṣa-sūkta in the Vedic Literature* (Poona, 1965).

3. Prajāpati Commits Incest and Rudra is Born

**Aitareya Brāhmaṇa* 3.33–4.

Compare: versions cited for myth 34 below.

Discussions: F. D. K. Bosch, *The Golden Germ* ('S-Gravenhage, 1960); Sylvain Lévi, *La Doctrine du sacrifice dans les Brāhmaṇas* (Paris, 1966); Herman Lommel, *Altbrahmanische Legenden* (Zurich, 1964); Bal Gangadhar Tilak, *Orion, or Researches into the Antiquity of the Vedas* (Poona, 1916); Jean Varenne, *Mythes et légendes extraits des Brāhmaṇa* (Paris, 1967). For astrological symbolism, see discussions for myth 34, below.

4. Prajāpati and his Sons Create, and Rudra is Born

**Kauṣītaki Brāhmaṇa* 6.1–2 (continued 6.3–9).

5. Oblation into Fire: Prajāpati Creates Agni and Sacrifices into him

**Śatapatha Brāhmaṇa* 2.2.4.1–8a.

Compare: **Śatapatha Brāhmaṇa* 2.5.1; 3.9.11; 10.4.2.2; 10.4.4.1;

Taittirīya Brāhmaṇa 1.1.10.1; 1.2.6.1; 1.6.2.1; 1.6.4.1.; 2.36.1; 2.7.9.1; 3.10.9.1; *Taittirīya Upaniṣad* 3.7–10; **Tāṇḍya Mahābrāhmaṇa* 6.7.19; 8.8.14. *Brahmāṇḍa* 1.2.12; **Brahmavaivarta* 1.4; 4.131; **Liṅga* 1.6; *Varāha* 18.

Discussion: O'Flaherty (1973), pp. 277–83.

6. Incest, Oblation, and Dismemberment: Brahmā Commits Incest

**Bṛhadāraṇyaka Upaniṣad* 1.4.1–6.

Compare: **Śatapatha Brāhmaṇa* 7.5.2.6; 14.4.2.1; **Taittirīya Āraṇyaka* 1.23.1–9; *Taittirīya Brāhmaṇa* 2.2.9.1 ff.

7. Brahmā and the Jealous Gods Create Evil Women

**Mahābhārata* 13.40.3–10 (Roy 13.50).

Compare: **Mahābhārata* 12.200.34–40 (Roy 12.207); **Liṅga* 2.6; **Mārkaṇḍeya* 46.1–35.

Discussion: Wendy Doniger O'Flaherty, 'The Origin of Heresy in Indian Mythology', *History of Religions*, 10, 4 (May 1971) pp. 271–333.

8. Brahmā Creates Death

**Mahābhārata* 12.248.13–21; 12.249.1–22; 12.250.1–37a, 41, and 1 line inserted after 12.250.19 (Roy 12.256–8).

Compare: (almost identical) **Mahābhārata* 7, appendix I, no. 8, lines 35–249 (Roy 7.52–5). Also: **Mahābhārata* 1.189.1–9 (Roy 1.199); 3, appendix 1, no. 16, lines 70–126 (Roy 3.141); 13.1.10–73; **Śatapatha Brāhmaṇa* 10.4.3.3–9; **Jaiminīya Brāhmaṇa* 2.69–70; *Brahma* 116.1–21; *Bṛhaddharma* 3.12.48–60; **Matsya* 3; *Skanda* 1.1.28. Śiva and Brahmā compete for power of death: **Mahābhārata* 12.122.14–29 (Roy 12.121); **Bhāgavata* 3.12; *Brahmāṇḍa* 2.3.9–10; **Kūrma* 1.10; **Liṅga* 1.6.10–22; 1.70.300–42; **Matsya* 4; *Saura* 23; 25; **Śiva* 2.1.15; 7.1.12–17; *Skanda* 7.2.9.5–17; *Varāha* 73; *Vāyu* 1.10. Śiva conquers Death: *Padma* 6.236; *Skanda* 1.1.32; 5.3.1 22; *Kedāra Khaṇḍa* 151; *Viṣṇudharmottara* 1.236. Cf. Rao, II, 1, 156–64.

Discussions: Sadashiv Ambadas Dange, *Legends in the Mahābhārata* (Delhi, 1969), pp. 306–10; J. Bruce Long, 'Death as a Necessity and a Gift in Hindu Mythology' in Frank E. Reynolds and Earle H. Waugh (eds.), *Religious Encounters with Death* (Pennsylvania State University Press, 1977), pp. 73–96; cf. Hopkins, pp. 189–202; O'Flaherty, 'The Origin of Heresy', pp. 303 ff.

9. Cosmic Creation: Brahmā Creates Good and Evil from his Body

**Viṣṇu Purāṇa* 1.5.26–48, 59–65.

Compare: **Śatapatha Brāhmaṇa* 6.1.1.1–15; 6.1.2.1–13; 11.1.6.1.–11; **Chāndogya Upaniṣad* 8.7–11; **Mahābhārata* 1.60; 12.160 (Roy 1.66; 12.167); **Bhāgavata* 2.5–6; 3.12; 3.20; *Brahma* 2; *Brahmāṇḍa* 1.2.8–9; **Brahmavaivarta* 1.5, 8; *Bṛhaddharma* 3.12.1–50; **Garuḍa* 4; *Kalki* 1.1.14–19; **Kūrma* 1.8; **Liṅga* 1.41; **Mārkaṇḍeya* 50–51; *Padma* 5.3; 5.6; 6.260; *Vāyu* 2.16; *Viṣṇudharma* 25.

Discussions; Muir, I, 24–106; 114–22; 155–8; O'Flaherty, 'The Origin of Heresy', pp. 287–306.

10. Nārada Curses the Sons of Dakṣa

Vāyu 65.121–9; 146–59; 161–2.

Compare: **Mahābhārata* 1.70 (Roy 1.75); **Bhāgavata* 6.5; *Brahma* 3; *Brahmāṇḍa* 2.3.2; **Garuḍa* 6; **Matsya* 5; 208; *Narasiṃha* 5; **Śiva* 2.2.13; **Viṣṇu* 1.15; 5.1; 5.15; *Viṣṇudharmottara* 1.110.

Discussion: O'Flaherty (1973), pp. 74–6.

11. Brahmā Curses Nārada

**Brahmavaivarta* 1.8.1–30a, 37–53, 62–8.

Compare: **Brahmavaivarta* 1.8–9, 13–21, 23–4; **Devībhāgavata* 6.26–9.

Discussion: Muir, IV, vi; O'Flaherty (1973), pp. 70–74; Philip Spratt, *Hindu Culture and Personality* (Bombay, 1966), pp. 105–12; 229; 260.

12. The Degradation of Brahmā: he Tries to Rape Anasūyā and is Cursed

Bhaviṣya 3.4.17.67–78.

Compare: **Mārkaṇḍeya* 16–17; *Padma* 5.17; 5.29; **Śiva* 2.5; *Skanda*

6.192–3; 7.1.165. Cf. also Rao, I, 1, 251–6 and Whitehead, p. 115. Discussion: O'Flaherty (1973), pp. 226–7.

13. Indra Beheads Dadhyañc, who Reveals Tvaṣṭṛ's Mead to the Aśvins

**Ṛg Veda* 1.117.22; **Śatapatha Brāhmaṇa* 14.1.1.18–24.

Compare: **Ṛg Veda* 4.18; **Jaiminīya Brāhmaṇa* 3.64; **Bhāgavata* 6.9–11; *Bhaviṣya* 1.19; **Bṛhaddevatā* 3.15–25; **Devībhāgavata* 1.5; 7.7. Indra vs. the Aśvins and Cyavana: **Mahābhārata* (Roy 1.3; 3.124–5; 12.343;13.161). The Aśvins replace Viṣṇu's horse-head: **Tāṇḍya Mahābrāhmaṇa* 7.5.6; **Śatapatha Brāhmaṇa* 4.1.5.18; 14.1.1.1–15; **Taittirīya Araṇyaka* 5.1.1–7; **Devībhāgavata* 1.5.

Discussions: A. K. Coomaraswamy, 'Sir Gawain and the Green Knight: Indra and Namuci', *Speculum* XIX (1944), pp. 104–25; Georges Dumézil, 'Mitra-Varuṇa, Indra, les Nāsatya', *Studia Linguistica*, I (Paris, 1947), 121–9; Muir, IV, 99–108, V, 77–139; H. Oertel, 'Indra in the Guise of a Woman', *JAOS*, XXVI (1904), pp. 176–90; 'Indra in the Guise of a Monkey Disturbs the Sacrifice', *JAOS*, XXVII (1905), pp. 192–6; O'Flaherty (1973), pp. 85–90. For Dadhyañc: F. D. K. Bosch, 'The God with the Horse's Head', in *Selected Studies in Indonesian Archaeology* (The Hague, 1961); R. H. van Gulik, *Hayagrīva* (Utrecht, 1935); P. C. Dumont, *L'Aśvamedha* (Paris, 1927); J. C. Heesterman, 'The Case of the Severed Head', *WZKS&O* (1967), pp. 22–43. For Viṣṇu as the horse, see Gonda (1963), 147–9, 167–71, and Rao, I, 1, 260–61.

14. Indra Makes a Weapon of Dadhyañc's Bones

**Ṛg Veda* 1.84.13–15; **Bṛhaddevatā* 3.22–4; Sāyaṇa's commentary on *Ṛg Veda* 1.84.13; 1.84.15.

Compare: **Mahābhārata* 3.100–101; 12.329 (Roy 12.343); Roy 9.51; **Bhāgavata* 6.10; *Brahma* 110; **Liṅga* 1.35–6; *Padma* 5.19;6.148.27 ff.; *Skanda* 1.1.16; 7.1.31–5; 7.1.65–6; 6.8.

Discussions: Friedrich Max Müller, *Contributions to the Science of Mythology* (London, 1897), pp. 743–72; Muir, V, 234–57; W. D. O'Flaherty, 'The Submarine Mare in the Mythology of Śiva', *JRAS* (1971), 1, pp. 19–23.

15. The Aśvins, Yama and Yamī, and Manu are Born

Yāska, *Nirukta*, 12.10 (commentary on *Ṛg Veda* 10.17.1–2).
Compare: *Kāṭhaka Brāhmaṇa* 2.30.1; **Śatapatha Brāhmaṇa* 1.1.4.14; *Taittirīya Brāhmaṇa* 1.1.4.4; 1.1.9.10; 3.2.5.9; **Tatttirīya Saṃhitā* 2.6.7.1; 6.5.6.1; 6.6.6.1; **Manu* 1.59–64, 79–80; **Devībhāgavata* 6.19–20.
Discussion: Muir, I, 38 ff.; 161–81, 186 ff.

16. Tvaṣṭṛ Begets Triśiras and Saraṇyū

**Bṛhaddevatā* of Śaunaka 6.162–3; 7.1–6.

17. Tvaṣṭṛ Gives his Daughter to Vivasvat

**Ṛg Veda* 10.17.1–2.
Discussion: Maurice Bloomfield, 'The Marriage of Saraṇyū', *JAOS*, XV (1893), pp. 173–88.

18. Yama Rejects Yamī

Ṛg Veda 10.10.1–14.
Compare: **Atharva Veda* 18.1.1–16; **Jaiminīya Brāhmaṇa* 1.53; *Mait. Sam.* 1.5.12; **Taittirīya Saṃhitā* 3.3.8; **Tāṇḍya Mahābrāhmaṇa* 11.10.21–2; *Narasiṃha* 13.
Discussion: K. Geldner, 'Yama und Yamī' in *Festgabe Albrecht Weber* (Leipzig, 1896), pp. 18–22; R. Goldman, 'Mortal Man and Immortal Woman: An Interpretation of Three Ākhyāna Hymns of the Ṛg Veda', *JOIB*, XVIII, 4 (June 1969), pp. 273–303; Ulrich Schneider, 'Yama und Yamī', *IIJ*, X (1967), pp. 1–32.

19. Yama Becomes King of the Dead

**Mārkaṇḍeya* 103.1, 3–40; 105.1–20.
Compare: **Mahābhārata* 1.60; *Bhaviṣya* 1.79; *Brahma* 6; 32; 89; *Brahmāṇḍa* 2.3.59–60; **Harivaṃśa* 1.9.1; **Mārkaṇḍeya* 77–80; **Matsya* 11; *Padma* 5.8; *Sāmba* 10–15; **Śiva* 5.35; *Dharmasaṃhitā* 11.53–66; *Skanda* 3.2.8; 3.2.13; 4.1.17; 5.1.53; 7.1.11–13; 7.1.146; *Varāha* 20; 26; *Vāyu* 2.3; 2.23; **Viṣṇu* 3.2; *Viṣṇudharmottara* 1.106.

Discussions: Georges Dumézil, *Mythe et épopée* (Paris, 1971), II, 243–99; Friedrich Max Müller, *Contributions*, II, 558–612; 810–17; Muir, V, 284–335; O'Flaherty, 'The Submarine Mare', pp. 15–17; Heinrich von Stietencron, *Gaṅgā und Yamunā* (Wiesbaden, 1972), pp. 70–79; Alex Wayman, 'Studies in Yama and Māra', *IIJ*, III, (1959), pp. 44–73 and 112–31.

20. Indra Beheads Triśiras

**Bṛhaddevatā* of Śaunaka 6.149–53.

Compare: **Śatapatha Brāhmaṇa* 3.8.3.11; **Taittirīya Saṃhitā* 2.5.1.

Discussion: Georges Dumézil, 'Deux Traits du Monstre Tricéphale Indo-Iranien', *RHR*, 120 (1939), pp. 5–20.

21. Trita Āptya and Indra Behead Triśiras

**Ṛg Veda* 10.8.8–9.

Compare: *Maitrāyaṇī Saṃhitā* 4.1.9; **Śatapatha Brāhmaṇa* 1.2.3; *Taittirīya Brāhmaṇa* 3.2.8.9–12; **Atharva Veda* 6.112–13.

Discussions: Maurice Bloomfield, 'Trita, the Scapegoat of the Gods', *American Journal of Philology*, 17 (1896), pp. 430–37; Georges Dumézil, *The Destiny of the Warrior* (Paris, 1969; translated by Alf Hiltebeitel, Chicago, 1970), pp. 12–28; K. Rönnow, *Trita Āptya* (*Uppsala*, 1927).

22. Saramā Drinks the Milk of the Paṇis

**Bṛhaddevatā* of Śaunaka 8.24–36a.

Compare: **Jaiminīya Brāhmaṇa* 2.438–40; *Kāṭhaka* 27.9; *Maitrāyaṇī Saṃhitā* 4.6.4; *Nirukta* of Yāska, 11.24–5; *Taittirīya Āraṇyaka* 1.10; *Taittirīya Brāhmaṇa* 2.5.8.10; *Vājasaneyi Saṃhitā* 33.59.

Discussions: H. L. Hariyappa, *Ṛg Vedic Legends through the Ages* (Poona, 1953), pp. 148–70; Boris Ogibenin, *Structure d'un mythe védique* (The Hague, 1973); J. Przyluski, 'Les Aśvin et la Grande Déesse', *HJAS*, I, 1 (1936), pp. 129–35; A. Venkatasubbi, 'On Indra's Winning of Cows and Waters', *ZDMG*, 115, 1 (1965), pp. 120–35.

23. Saramā Speaks with the Paṇis

**Ṛg Veda* 10.108.1–11.

Compare: **Ṛg Veda* 1.62.3; 1.72.8; 3.31.6; 4.16.8; 5.45.7–8; **Bhāgavata* 5.24.30; *Brahma* 131; *Varāha* 16.

Discussion: Theodor Aufrecht, 'Saramā's Botschaft', *ZDMG*, XIII (1859), pp. 493–9; Maurice Bloomfield, 'The Two Dogs of Yama', *JAOS*, XV (1893), pp. 163–72.

24. Indra Slays Vṛtra and Releases the Waters

**Ṛg Veda* 1.32.1–15.

Compare: **Ṛg Veda* 10.124.1–9.

Discussions: Émile Benveniste et Louis Renou, *Vṛtra et Verethraghna* (Paris, 1934); W. Norman Brown, 'The Ṛgvedic Equivalent for Hell', *JAOS*, LXI (1941), pp. 76–80; 'The Creation Myth of the Ṛg Veda', *JAOS*, LXII (1942), pp. 85–98; 'Theories of Creation in the Ṛg Veda', *JAOS*, LXXXV, 1 (1965), pp. 23–34; A. K. Coomaraswamy, 'Angel and Titan', *JAOS*, LV (1935), pp. 373–419; Heinrich Lüders, 'Der Vṛtrakampf als vedischer Weltschöpfungsmythos', in *Varuṇa* (Göttingen, 1951–9), pp. 183 ff.

25. Indra Slays Triśiras and Vṛtra

**Mahābhārata* 5.9.3–52; 5.10.1–46a; 5.13.8b–13, 14b–18; plus 2 lines inserted after 5.9.29, 12 after 5.9.39, 5 after 5.9.45, 4 after 5.9.52, 2 after 5.10.31, 5.10.32, 5.10.34 and 5.10.42 (Roy 5.9–17).

Compare: **Ṛg Veda* 7.14.13; 10.131.4–5; **Aitareya Brāhmaṇa* 3.20–21; 15.2; **Jaiminīya Brāhmaṇa* 1.97; 2.153–7; 2.180; *Maitrāyaṇī Saṃhitā* 2.4.3; 3.6.3; 4.6.5; 4.7.4; **Śatapatha Brāhmaṇa* 1.6.3.8; 1.6.4.18–20; 2.6.1.5; 7.5.3; 12.7.1.1–13; *Taittirīya Brāhmaṇa* 1.7.8; 4.3.4; 7.69; **Taittirīya Saṃhitā* 2.5.2–3; **Mahābhārata* 12.329 (Roy 12.343); **Devībhāgavata* 6.1–7; *Padma* 2.23–4; *Skanda* 5.2.35; *Viṣṇudharmottara* 1.24.

Discussions: Maurice Bloomfield, 'The Story of Indra and Namuci', *JAOS*, XV (1893), pp. 143–63; W. Norman Brown, 'Indra's Infancy according to Ṛg Veda IV. 18', in *Dr Siddheshwar Varma Presentation Volume* (Hoshiapur, 1950); Léon Feer, 'Vṛitra et Namoutchi dans le Mahābhārata', *RHR* 14 (1886), pp. 291–307; Gonda, *Aspects*, pp. 28–55; E. W. Hopkins, *Epic Mythology*, pp.

130–32; Walter Ruben, 'Indra's fight against Vṛtra in the Mahābhārata', in *S. K. Belvalkar Felicitation Volume* (Banaras, 1957), pp. 113–23.

26. Indra Slays Vṛtra and is Afflicted by the Fury of Brahminicide

**Mahābhārata* 12.272.28–31, 273.1–58, 60 (Roy 12.282).

Compare: **Mahābhārata* 9.42 (Roy 9.43) and 12.270.13 (Roy 12.274); *Vājasaneyi Saṃhitā* 5.7; **Jaiminīya Brāhmaṇa* 2.134; **Bhāgavata* 2.13.10–17; 6.9–13; *Brahma* 96; **Brahmavaivarta* 4.47–50; *Mahābhāgavata* 60–63; **Mārkaṇḍeya* 5; **Rāmāyaṇa* 1.23; 7.84–6; *Skanda* 1.1.15–17; 3.1.11; 3.2.19; 4.2.81; 5.3.118; 6.269. For the related motif of Śiva's brahminicide see below, myth 35, and *Brahma* 40; **Kūrma* 2.30–31; **Matsya* 72; 183; *Padma* 5.24; **Śiva* 3.8–9; *Jñānasaṃhitā* 49.65–80; *Skanda* 5.1.2.1–65.

Discussions: Georges Dumézil, *The Destiny of the Warrior* (Chicago, 1970); O'Flaherty (1973), pp. 123–6 and 283–6; 'The Origin of Heresy', pp. 299 ff.

27. Indra Destroys the Embryo in the Belly of Diti

**Rāmāyaṇa* 1.45.1–22; 1.46.1–9.

Compare: Sāyaṇa on *Ṛg Veda* 1.114.6; 8.28.5 (trans. Muir, IV, 305); **Bṛhaddevatā* 4.47–56; **Śatapatha Brāhmaṇa* 3.2.1.27–8; **Taittirīya Saṃhitā* 6.1.3.4–8; **Agni* 19; **Bhāgavata* 3.14.–17; 6.18; *Brahma* 3; 124.; *Brahmāṇḍa* 2.3.5; **Harivaṃśa* 1.3; **Matsya* 7; 146; *Padma* 2.25; 5.7; **Vāmana* 45–6; **Viṣṇu* 1.22; *Viṣṇudharmottara* 1.127.

Discussion: Muir, V, 147–54.

28. Indra Seduces Ahalyā and is Castrated by Gautama

**Rāmāyaṇa* 1.47.15–32; 1.48.1–10.

Compare: **Rāmāyaṇa* 7.30; **Mahābhārata* 12.329.14 (Roy 12.343); *Śatapatha Brāhmaṇa* 3.3.4.18; 5.2.3.8; 5.2.4.8; 12.7.1.10–12; *Brahma* 87; **Brahmavaivarta* 4.47, 61; *Padma* 1.56.15–33; 5.51; *Śiva, Dharmasaṃhitā* 11; *Skanda* 5.3.136–8; 6.207–8; *Viṣṇudharmottara* 1.128.

Discussions: Kumārila Bhaṭṭa, cited by F. Max Müller, *History of*

Ancient Sanskrit Literature, pp. 529 ff.; Edward Washburn Hopkins, 'Indra as a God of Fertility', *JAOS*, XXXVI (1916), pp. 242–68.

29. Agni Flees from the Gods and Hides in the Waters

**Ṛg Veda* 10.51.1–9.

Compare: **Ṛg Veda* 1.65, with Sāyaṇa's commentary; **Kauṣītaki Brāhmaṇa* 1.2; **Śatapatha Brāhmaṇa* 1.2.3; 2.2.3.2–5; 2.3.4.1–2; 6.2.1.1–9; 6.3.1.31–2; 7.3.2.14–15; *Taittirīya Brāhmaṇa* 1.1.3.9; **Taittirīya Saṃhitā* 1.5.1; 2.6.6.1; *Brahma* 98.

Discussions: F. D. K. Bosch, *The Golden Germ: An Introduction to Indian Symbolism* (The Hague, 1960); Jean Filliozat, *The Classical Doctrine of Indian Medicine* (Delhi, 1964; Paris, 1949), pp. 46–67; Willibald Kirfel, *Die fünf Elemente insbesondere Wasser und Feuer* (Walldorf-Hessen, 1951); Claude Lévi-Strauss, *The Raw and the Cooked* (London, 1970; Paris, 1964), pp. 188–98; F. Max Müller, *Contributions*, II, 780–813; Muir, IV, 199–223; O'Flaherty (1973), pp. 90–110.

30. Agni Hides in the Waters and is Distributed

**Bṛhaddevatā* 7.61–4; 7.73–80.

31. Agni Hides in the Waters and Curses the Fish

**Taittirīya Saṃhitā* 2.6.6.1–2, 4–5.

Compare: **Śatapatha Brāhmaṇa* 1.2.3.1; 1.3.3.13–16; 6.1.1.1–5; 9.1.2.21–2; **Taittirīya Saṃhitā* 6.28.4–5.

32. Agni Curses the Frogs and is Distributed

**Mahābhārata* 13.84.19b–47, plus 2 lines inserted after 13.84.35a (Roy 13.85).

Compare: **Mahābhārata* (Roy) 5.13–17.

33. Agni Seduces the Sages' Wives and Begets Skanda

**Mahābhārata* 3.213.3–52; 214.1–37; 215.1–23; 216.1–15; plus 4 lines interpolated after 3.213.31, 4 before 3.215.1, 2 after 3.215.15 and 1 after 3.215.18 (Roy 3.222–30).

Compare: **Śatapatha Brāhmaṇa* 2.1.1.4–5; 2.1.2.4–9; 4.4.2.9; 6.1.1.1–5; 6.1.3.7–8; *Taittirīya Brāhmaṇa* 1.1.3.8; **Taittirīya Saṃhitā* 5.5.4.1: 6.5.8.1–2; *Brahma* 128; *Brahmāṇḍa* 2.3.10; **Brahmavaivarta* 4.131; **Śiva* 2.4.2; *Dharmasaṃhitā* 11.28–35; *Skanda* 1.1.27.44–102; 1.2.29; 5.1.34.60–66; 5.3.22; *Varāha* 25.

Discussions: For astrological symbolism, cf. bibliography for myths 3 and 34, and see also M. Raja Rao, 'The Astronomical Background to Śiva', *BV* (Bombay), XIII, pp. 158–68; B. Ia Volchok, 'Towards an Interpretation of Proto-Indian Pictures', *Journal of Tamil Studies*, II, 1 (May 1970), pp. 29–53; and Volchok, 'Protoindiiskie paralleli k mifu o Skande', *Proto-Indica* (Akademiia Nauk, SSSR, 1972), pp. 305–12; similarly, Asko Parpola, 'Reconstructing the Harappan Hinduism', in *K.A. Nilakanta Sastri Felicitation Volume* (Madras, 1971), pp. 335–44, and *Cycle and Turning Point: Outlines of Harappan Astronomy and Ideology* (Scandinavian Institute of Asian Studies, 1975). Cf. also O'Flaherty (1973), pp. 93–107, and Heinrich von Stietencron, *Gaṅgā und Yamunā* (Wiesbaden, 1972), pp. 48–60.

34. Rudra Punishes Prajāpati and Distributes the Seed

**Śatapatha Brāhmaṇa* 1.7.4.1–8.

Compare: Rudra is born and weeps: **Kauṣītaki Brāhmaṇa* 6.1–14; *Maitrāyaṇī Saṃhitā* 4.2.12; **Śatapatha Brāhmāṇa* 2.1.2.6–10; 6.1.3.7–19; 9.1.1.1–2, 6–14; **Agni* 18; 20; *Brahma* 32–9; **Bhāgavata* 3.12; *Kālikā* 1–5; **Kurma* 1.10; **Mārkaṇḍeya* 52; *Narasiṃha* 3–4; *Saura* 23; *Varāha* 2; 33; 73; *Vāyu* 1.25, 27; **Viṣṇu* 1.7–8. Śiva beheads Brahmā: *Bhaviṣya* 1.22; 3.4.13; *Brahma* 135.1–25; **Kūrma* 2.31; **Matsya* 183; *Nārada* 2.29; *Padma* 5.14; **Śiva* 1.4–9; 3.8–9; *Dharmasaṃhitā* 4.9–10; *Jñānasaṃhitā* 49.65–80; *Skanda* 2.3.2; 3.1.24; 3.40; 4.1.31; 5.1.2–3; 5.3.184; **Vāmana* 2–3; *Varāha* 97. Cf. Śiva threatens Brahmā at Satī's wedding: **Mahābhārata* 13.85; *Brahma* 72; *Saura* 59; **Śiva* 2.2.19–20; 2.3.49; *Jñānasaṃhitā* 18.62–8; *Skanda* 1.1.26; 6.77; **Vāmana* 27.

Discussions: Heinrich Meinhard, *Beiträge zur Kenntnis des Śivaismus nach den Purāṇa's* (Thesis, Bonn, 1928), pp. 10–15; Muir, IV, 299–393; O'Flaherty (1973), pp. 114–17, 121–7. For astrological symbolism, see myth 3 above and: G. R. Kaye, *Hindu Astronomy*, Memoirs of the Archaeological Survey of India, No. 18 (Calcutta, 1924), pp. 1–134; Willibald Kirfel, *Symbolik des Hinduismus und des Jinismus* (Stuttgart, 1959), pp. 59–69; Bal Gangadhar Tilak, *Orion* (Poona, 1916); David Pingree, 'Representations of the Planets in Indian Astrology', *IIJ*, VIII (1965), pp. 249–67.

35. Śiva Destroys Dakṣa's Sacrifice and Distributes Fever

**Mahābhārata* 12.274.2–58. Cf. the expanded interpolation given as appendix I, no. 28, 212 lines, and appendix II, no. 1, 46 lines (Roy 12.283).

Compare: **Atharva Veda* 1.24; 5.22.13; *Brahma* 34; 39–40; 109; **Matsya* 72; *Skanda* 5.1.29; *Vāyu* 1.10.

Discussion: O'Flaherty (1973), pp. 283–6.

36. Śiva Destroys Dakṣa's Sacrifice and Restores it

Varāha 33.4–15, 25–34.

Compare: **Aitareya Brāhmaṇa* 6.5; 13.9–10; *Gopatha Brāhmaṇa* 2.1.2–4; **Kauṣītaki Brāhmaṇa* 6.13; *Maitrāyanī Saṃhitā* 4.2.12; **Śatapatha Brāhmaṇa* 1.7.4.1; 3.2.4.18; 3.5.1.13–23; 6.2.2.6; **Tāṇḍya Mahābrāhmaṇa* 7.9.16; 8.2.10; **Taittirīya Saṃhitā* 2.6.8.3; **Rāmāyaṇa* 1.66; **Mahābhārata* 7.202; 10.18 (Roy 7.201; 10.17); 12.274 (Roy 12.285); 12.343; 13.76 (Roy 13.77); 13.160–61. *Brahmāṇḍa* 1.2.12; **Bhāgavata* 4.2–7; 10.88; **Brahmavaivarta* 4.38; *Bṛhaddharma* 2.33–41; **Devībhāgavata* 7.30; *Kālikā* 8–11; 15–17; **Kūrma* 1.14; **Liṅga* 1.35–6; 99–100; *Mahābhāgavata* 4–10; **Mārkaṇḍeya* 49; **Matsya* 13; 72; *Padma* 5.5; *Saura* 7; **Śiva* 2.2.2–4; 2.2.26–43; 5.16–20; 6.1.18–23; *Skanda* 1.1.1–5; 1.1.38; 3.1.23; 4.287–9; 5.2.9; 5.2.82; 7.1.103; 7.1.199; 7.2.9.42; *Kedāra Khaṇḍa* 103–6; **Vāmana* 2.4–6; *Varāha* 21; 33; *Vāyu* 1.30; **Viṣṇu* 1.8; *Viṣṇudharmottara* 1.107, 110, 234–5.

Discussions: See bibliographies cited under myth 13 above. See also J. Bruce Long, 'Śiva and Dionysos, Visions of Terror and Bliss', *Numen*, XVIII (1971), pp. 180–209; Thomas Mann, *The Transposed Heads, A Legend of India* (New York, 1941); Meinhard, *Beiträge*, pp. 35–8; Muir, IV, 200 ff. and 372 ff.; O'Flaherty, 'The Origin of Heresy', pp. 315–18; O'Flaherty (1973), pp. 128–30; Rao, II, 1, 174–88, 295–309; Heinrich von Stietencron, 'Bhairava', *ZDMG*, Supplementa 1, Teil 3 (1969), pp. 863–71.

37. The Epic Myth of the Destruction of the Triple City of the Demons

**Mahābhārata* 8.24.3–44, 52–124, plus 5 lines after 8.24.30, 2 after 8.24.34, 3 after 8.24.67, 9 after 8.24.69, 2 after 8.24.74a, 3 after 8.24.75, 2 after 8.24.83a, 1 after 8.24.114 and then appendix 1, no. 4, 21 lines (Roy 8.33–4).

Compare: **Atharva Veda* 5.28.9; **Aitareya Brāhmaṇa* 1.23; **Kauṣītaki Brāhmaṇa* 8.8; **Śatapatha Brāhmaṇa* 3.4.4.3–27; **Taittirīya Saṃhitā* 6.2.3; *Vājasaneyi Saṃhitā* 5.8; **Mahābhārata* 7.172 (Roy 7.202); 12.283 (Roy 12.295); 13.145; **Harivaṃśa* A.1(43); **Liṅga* 1.71–2; **Matsya* 125–40; 187–8; *Padma* 1.14–15; *Saura* 34–5; **Śiva* 2.5.1–10; *Skanda* 5.1.43; 5.3.28; 7.1.45.

Discussions: Gonda, *Aspects*, pp. 35–6; B. Mukhopadhyaya, 'The Tripura Episode in Sanskrit Literature', *JGJRI*, VIII, 4 (1951), pp. 371–95; Muir, II, 378–82, IV, 203 ff.; O'Flaherty, 'The Origin of Heresy', pp. 306–8; Rao, II, 1, 164–71.

38. Śiva Castrates Himself

Śiva Purāṇa, Dharmasaṃhitā 49.23b–46, 74–86.

Compare: *Dharmasaṃhitā* 10.1–23; **Mahābhārata* 10.17; **Kūrma* 2.37; *Skanda* 6.1.50–52; *Vāyu* 1.10.

Discussions: O'Flaherty (1973), pp. 130–36; Philip Spratt, *Hindu Culture and Personality*, pp. 105–12.

39. The Pine Forest Sages Castrate Śiva

Brahmāṇḍa 1.2.27.1–64a, 91b–97, 101–23.

Compare: **Devībhāgavata* 7.39; 12.9; **Kūrma* 2.37; **Liṅga* 1.29; 1.31; *Padma* 5.17; *Sāmba* 16–17; *Saura* 69; **Śiva* 4.12; 4.25–7;

Dharmasaṃhitā 10.79.215; *Jñānasaṃhitā* 42.1–51; *Skanda* 1.1.6; 3.3.26–7; 5.1.51; 5.2.8; 5.2.11; 5.3.38; 5.17.75–84; 6.1; 6.32; 6.258–9; 7.1.187; 7.2.94–142; 7.3.39; **Vāmana* 6.60–93; S. 21–2. For the related myth of the flame *liṅga*, compare: *Brahma* 135; *Brahmāṇḍa* 1.2.26; **Liṅga* 1.17; **Śiva* 1.5–8; *Skanda* 1.3.1.1–2; 1.3.2.10–16; 3.1.14; 5.1.49; 7.3.34; *Vāyu* 1.55. See also Rao, II, 1, 73–112.

Discussions: F. D. K. Bosch, 'Het Lingga-Heiligdom van Dinaja', *TITLV*, LXIV (1924), pp. 227–91; Wilhelm Jahn, 'Die Legende vom Devadāruvana', *ZDMG*, LXIX (1915), pp. 529–57; LXX (1916), pp. 301–20; LXXI (1917), pp. 167–208; Herman Kulke, *Cidambaramāhātmya* (Wiesbaden, 1970), pp. 46–94; O'Flaherty (1973), pp. 172–204; O'Flaherty, 'The Origin of Heresy', pp. 323–9; Rao, II, 1,113–14; 235–6, 276–7, 304–7; cf. also C. D. Daly, *Hindu-Mythologie und Kastrationskomplex, eine psychoanalytische Studie* (Vienna, 1927; reprinted from *Imago*, XIII, 1927).

40. Bhṛgu Curses Śiva to be Worshipped as a Liṅga

Padma (Ānandāśrama edition) 6.282.8–22a, 23b–52, 85–93. Additional verses from the Calcutta edition (6.255.31–2, 37–42a, 50) and replacements for *ASS* verses 6.282.25, 32.

Compare: **Bhāgavata* 4.2; 10.89; *Padma* 1.13.244–7; *Skanda* 5.3.81.

Discussion: O'Flaherty (1973), pp. 302–10; O'Flaherty, 'The Origin of Heresy', pp. 314–22.

41. Śiva Destroys Kāma and Revives him

Saura 53.21–65a, 69–73; 54.1–8, 16–22.

Compare: **Rāmāyaṇa* 1.23, 36; *Bhaviṣya* 3.4.14; *Brahma* 34–8; 71–2; *Brahmāṇḍa* 3.4.11; 3.4.30; **Brahmavaivarta* 4. 38–45; *Bṛhaddharma* 2.53; **Devībhāgavata* 7.31; *Kālikā* 1–13; 42–6; **Kumārasambhava* 1–8; **Liṅga* 1.101–3; *Mahābhāgavata* 12; 14–15; 20–28; **Matsya* 148; 154; *Padma* 5.40; **Śiva* 2.2.2–20; 2.3.1–54; *Jñānasaṃhitā* 9–18; *Skanda* 1.1.20–27; 1.2.22–6; 2.7.8; 5.1.34; 5.2.13; 5.3.150; 7.1.200; 7.3.40; *Kedāra Khaṇḍa* 120; **Vāmana* 6; 25; 31; *Varāha* 22.

Discussion: O'Flaherty (1973), pp. 141–71; Rao, II, 1, 147–9, 337–50.

42. Śiva Engenders the Submarine Mare

**Śiva* 2.3.20.2–23. In this text, the story is told by Brahmā; I have changed it to the more usual third-person narrative.

Compare: **Ṛg Veda* 1.163.1–2; *Gopatha Brāhmaṇa* 1.2.18–21; **Taittirīya Saṃhitā* 5.5.10.6; 7.5.25.2; **Mahābhārata* 1.169–71 (Roy 1.181–2); 9.50 (Roy 9.51); *Brahma* 110; 113; 116; *Brahmāṇḍa* 2.3.50–56; **Harivaṃśa* 35–6; *Kālikā* 44; *Mahābhāgavata* 22–3; **Matsya* 154.251–2; 175–6; *Padma* 5.18; 6.148; *Dharmasaṃhitā* 11.28–35; *Skanda* 1.1.9.90; 1.1.17; 1.2.24; 6.174; 7.1.29; 7.1.32–3; *Varāha* 147; *Viṣṇudharmottara* 1.32.

Discussion: See bibliography for myths 13 and 14 above; also Georges Dumézil, *Le Problème des Centaures* (Paris, 1929).

43. Śiva Engenders Skanda

**Śiva* 2.4.1.44–63; 2.4.2.1–73. In the text, Brahmā narrates the story; I have changed it to third-person narrative.

Compare: **Rāmāyaṇa* 1.36–7; **Mahābhārata* 3.213–16 (see above, myth 33); 9.43–5 (Roy 9.44–6); 13.83–5 (Roy 13.84–6); *Brahma* 34–7; 71–2; 81–2; 128; *Brahmāṇḍa* 2.3.10; **Brahmavaivarta* 3.1–2, 8–9, 14–17; 4.46; *Bṛhaddharma* 2.53; *Kālikā* 42–6; *Kumārasambhava* 9–11; **Liṅga* 1.103–5; *Mahābhāgavata* 29–34; **Matsya* 146; 158; *Padma* 5.40–41; *Saura* 60–62; **Śiva* 2.3.14–16; 2.4.1–2; *Jñānasaṃhitā* 19.7–15; *Skanda* 1.1.20–27; 1.2.29; 2.7.9; 3.3.13–14; 3.3.29; 5.1.45; 5.2.6; 5.2.20; 5.3.11; 6.70–71; 6.245–6; 6.261; **Vāmana* 28; 31; *Varāha* 25; *Vāyu* 2.11.6–40; *Viṣṇudharmottara* 1.228–9.

Discussions: Prithivi Kumar Agrawala, 'Skanda in the Purāṇas and Classical Literature', *Purāṇa*, VII, 1 (January 1966), pp. 135–88; Muir, IV, 349–55; O'Flaherty (1973), pp. 90–111; 261–77; 293–313; Philip Spratt, *Hindu Culture and Personality*, pp. 338–42.

44. Śiva Engenders Andhaka

Śiva, Dharmasaṃhitā 4.4–26.

Compare: **Mahābhārata* 13.127 (Roy 13.140); **Śiva Purāṇa* 2.5.42.15–22.

45. Śiva Kills and Transfigures Andhaka

**Kūrma* 1.15.121–5, 168, 184, 187, 201–5, 210–12, 218.

Compare: **Harivaṃśa* 2.86–7; *Kālikā* 87; **Liṅga* 1.93; **Matsya* 179; 252; *Padma* 5.43; *Saura* 29; **Śiva* 2.5.42, 44–6; *Dharmasaṃhitā* 4.4–208; *Skanda* 5.1.38; 5.2.51; 5.3.45–9; 6.149–51; 6.228–9; 7.2.9; **Vāmana* 9–10; 33–7; 41–4; *Varāha* 27; 90; *Viṣṇudharmottara* 1.53; 1.226.

Discussion: O'Flaherty (1973), pp. 190–92; Rao, I, 2, 379–83; II, 1, 192–4.

46. The Sage Maṅkaṇaka Dances for Śiva

**Vāmana* S.17.2–23.

Compare: **Mahābhārata* 3.81; 9.37 (Roy 3.83; 9.38). **Kūrma* 1.5; 2.34; *Padma* 1.27; 5.18; 5.1.2–3; 5.1.49; 5.2.2; 7.1.270; **Vāmana* 36; *Skanda* 6.40.27–52; 7.1.270.1–46.

Discussions: O'Flaherty (1973), pp. 245–7; also W. D. O'Flaherty, 'The Symbolism of Ashes in the Mythology of Śiva', *Purāṇa*, XIII, 1 (January 1971), pp. 26–35; Rao, II, 1, 223–70, 322–3.

47. Viṣṇu Takes Three Strides

**Ṛg Veda* 1.154.1–6.

Compare: There are several other references to the three strides, but this is the only Ṛg Vedic hymn addressed to Viṣṇu alone.

Discussions: Jan Gonda, *Aspects of Early Viṣṇuism* (Utrecht, 1954), pp. 55–72 and 145–6; F. B. J. Kuiper, 'The Three Strides of Viṣṇu', in *Indological Studies in Honour of W. Norman Brown* (1962), pp. 137–51; Muir, IV, 63–97 and 121–56; Gaya Charan Tripathi, *Der Ursprung und die Entwicklung der Vāmana-legende in der Indischen Literatur* (Wiesbaden, 1968).

48. Viṣṇu Becomes a Dwarf

**Śatapatha Brāhmaṇa* 1.2.5.1–9a.

Compare: **Aitareya Brāhmaṇa* 6.15; **Śatapatha Brāhmaṇa* 1.9.3.8–12; *Maitrāyaṇī Saṃhitā* 3.8.3; *Taittirīya Brāhmaṇa* 3.2.9.7.

Discussions: Paul Hacker, *Prahlāda: Werden und Wandlungen einer Idealgestalt* (Wiesbaden, 1960), pp. 33–60; Adalbert Kuhn, *Ueber Entwicklungsstufen der Mythenbildung* (Berlin, 1874), pp. 128 ff.

49. Viṣṇu Becomes a Dwarf to Trick the Demon Bali

Vāyu 2.36.74–86.

Compare: **Mahābhārata* 3.270; 3.313; 12.343; **Rāmāyaṇa* 1.29; **Agni* 4.5–11; 49; **Bhāgavata* 1.3; 2.7; 8.15–23; *Brahma* 73; 180; 213; *Brahmāṇḍa* 2.3.72–3; *Bṛhaddharma* 2.45–7; *Bṛhannāradīya* 10–11; **Harivaṃśa* 31; A.1 (42B), lines 1–3071; **Kūrma* 1.16; *Mahābhāgavata* 65; **Mārkaṇḍeya* 4; **Matsya* 48; 161; 231–3; 244–6; *Nārada* 2.10–11; *Padma* 5.13; 5.25; 5.73; 6.239–40; 6.257; 6.267; *Skanda* 1.1.18–19; 5.1.63; 7.1.114; 7.2.14–19; 7.4.19; **Vāmana* S.2, S.6–10; 47–51, 62–7; *Viṣṇudharma* 75–7; *Viṣṇudharmottara* 1.55; 1.126.

Discussions: B. N. Sharma, 'Vāmana and Viṣṇu', *Purāṇa*, VIII, 2 (July 1966), pp. 246–58; entire *Purāṇa* issue (January 1970); Heinrich von Stietencron, *Gaṅgā und Yamunā* (Wiesbaden, 1972), pp. 60–69; Rao, I, 1, 161–80.

50. The Fish Saves Manu from the Flood

**Śatapatha Brāhmaṇa* 1.8.1.1–6.

Compare: **Mahābhārata* 3.185 (Roy 3.186); **Bhāgavata* 8.24.

Discussions: Adam Hohenberger, *Die Indische Flutsage und das Matsyapurāṇa* (Leipzig, 1930); Willibald Kirfel, *Symbolik des Hinduismus und des Jainismus* (Stuttgart, 1959), pp. 29 ff.; Muir, I, 181–220; Suryakanta, *The Flood Legend in Sanskrit Literature* (Delhi, 1950).

51. Viṣṇu Becomes a Fish to Save Manu from the Universal Dissolution

**Matsya* 1.11–34; 2.1–19.

Compare: **Mahābhārata* 12.300 (Roy 12.313); **Agni* 2; **Bhāgavata* 1.3; 2.7; 8.24; **Garuḍa* 1; *Kālikā* 33–4; *Mahābhāgavata* 12.340, 348; **Matsya* 164–5; *Padma* 5.4; 5.73; 6.230; 6.257–8; *Skanda* 2.2.3; 5.3.3; *Viṣṇudharmottara* 1.75–6.

52. Prajāpati Becomes a Boar to Create the Earth

**Taittirīya Saṃhitā* 7.1.5.1.

Compare: **Ṛg Veda* 1.61.7; 8.77.10; **Śatapatha Brāhmaṇa* 7.5.1.5;

14.1.2.11; *Taittirīya Brāhmaṇa* 1.1.3.5; **Taittirīya Saṃhitā* 6.2.4.2.
Discussion: Muir, I, 52 ff.; IV, 39 ff., 67 ff.

53. Prajāpati Becomes a Boar to Save the Earth

**Śatapatha Brāhmaṇa* 14.1.2.11a.
Discussion: Gonda, *Aspects of Early Viṣṇuism*, pp. 129–45.

54. Viṣṇu Becomes Incarnate as the Boar to Save the Earth

**Viṣṇu* 1.4.3–11, 25–9, 45–9.
Compare: **Mahābhārata* 3.141; 12.202; 12.339–40; **Agni* 4; **Bhāgavata* 3.13–19; *Brahma* 79; 180; 213; *Brahmāṇḍa* 1.1.5; 2.3.72; **Devībhāgavata* 8.2; **Garuḍa* 1.142; **Harivaṃśa* 31; A.1(42), 1–660; *Kālikā* 25–6; 30–37; **Kūrma* 1.6; **Liṅga* 1.94; **Mārkaṇḍeya* 4: **Matsya* 247–8; *Padma* 5.3; 5.13; 5.73; 6.237; 6.257; *Skanda* 2.1.36; 5.1.52; *Varāha* 113–15; *Viṣṇudharmottara* 1.3.
Discussion: V. S. Agrawala, 'Varāha, An Interpretation', *Purāṇa*, V, 2 (July 1962), pp. 199–236; Gonda, *Aspects*, pp. 28–55; Rao, I, 1, 128–45.

55. Śiva Chastises the Boar

Kālikā 30.7.42; 31.1–3, 18–71, 82–93, 134–53.
Compare: **Bhāgavata* 10.59; **Harivaṃśa* 55; 120; *Kālikā* 36–41; **Liṅga* 1.95–6; **Śiva* 3.11; 3.22–3; *Skanda* 5.1.66; **Viṣṇu* 5.29.
Discussions: Paul Hacker, *Prahlāda*, pp. 24–33, 119–21, 174–86, 194–202; Meinhard, pp. 37 ff.; O'Flaherty (1973), pp. 282–3; Rao, II, 1, 172–4.

56. Rāma Rejects Sītā and is Enlightened by the Gods

**Rāmāyaṇa* 6.103.1–25; 6.104.1–27; 6.105.1–12, 25–6; 6.106.1–20.
Compare: **Rāmāyaṇa* 7.42–9, 95–8; **Mahābhārata* 3.291 (Roy 3.289); **Agni* 11; **Bhāgavata* 9.10–11; **Devībhāgavata* 3.30, 4.8, 9.11; **Kūrma* 2.33; *Nārada* 2.75; *Padma* 4.56–9, 67; *Skanda* 3.1.22; *Viṣṇudharmottara* 1.221. Also *Raghuvaṃśa* 14.31–71 and Tulsī Dās (Hill trans.), pp. 310–11 and 421–3.

Discussion: For the *Rāmāyaṇa* in general: H. Jacobi, *Das Rāmāyaṇa* (Bonn, 1893); C. V. Vaidya, *The Riddle of the Rāmāyaṇa* (Bombay and London, 1906); Moriz Winternitz, *History of Indian Literature*, Vol. I, Part 2, *Epics and Purāṇas* (trans. Mrs S. Ketkar, University of Calcutta, 1963), esp. pp. 417–55. For this particular myth, see E. W. Burlingame, 'The Act of Truth', *JRAS* (1917), pp. 429–67; W. Norman Brown, 'The Basis for the Hindu Act of Truth', *Review of Religion*, V (1940), pp. 36–45; 'The Metaphysics of the Truth Act', *Mélanges d'Indianisme à la mémoire de L. Renou* (Paris, 1968), pp. 171–8; J. J. Meyer, *Isoldes Gottesurteil* (Berlin, 1914).

57. Kṛṣṇa and Balarāma are Conceived by Devakī and Transferred to Other Mothers

**Harivaṃśa* 47.1–57; 48.1–37a.

Compare: **Agni* 12: **Bhāgavata* 10.1–4; *Brahmāṇḍa* 2.3.71.200–41; **Brahmavaivarta* 4.1–7; *Bṛhaddharma* 3.16; **Devībhāgavata* 4.18–23; **Liṅga* 1.69; *Padma* 6.245; **Viṣṇu* 5.1–3.

Discussions: Daniel H. H. Ingalls, 'The Harivaṃśa as a Mahākāvya', in *Mélanges d'Indianisme à la mémoire de L. Renou* (Paris, 1968), pp. 381–94; A. B. Keith, 'The Child Kṛṣṇa', *JRAS* (1908), pp. 169–75; D. D. Kosambi, *Myth and Reality* (Bombay, 1962), pp. 12–41; Rao, I, 1, 195–212; Charlotte Vaudeville, 'Aspects du mythe de Kṛṣṇa Gopāla dans l'Inde ancienne', in *Mélanges . . . L. Renou*, pp. 727–62.

58. Kṛṣṇa Kills the Ogress Pūtanā

**Bhāgavata* 10.6.1–20, 30–44.

Compare: **Agni* 12; *Brahma* 184; **Brahmavaivarta* 4.10; **Harivaṃśa* 50; *Mahābhāgavata* 49–53; *Padma* 6.245; **Viṣṇu* 5.5.

Discussions: V. S. Agrawala, 'A Note on Pūtanā and Yaśodā', *Purāṇa*, III, 1 and 2 (July 1960), pp. 279–81; William Archer, *The Loves of Krishna in Indian Painting and Poetry* (London, 1957); Jean Herbert, 'Śakaṭa and Pūtanā', *Purāṇa*, III, 1 and 2 (July 1960), pp. 268–78; Gonda, *Aspects*, pp. 154–63; Willibald Kirfel, 'Kṛṣṇa's Jugendgeschichte in den Purāṇas', *Festgabe Hermann Jacobi* (Bonn, 1926), pp. 298–316; Muir, IV, 182–99; 243–60; M. S. Randhawa,

Kangra Paintings of the Bhāgavata Purāṇa (Delhi, 1960); Walter Ruben, *Kṛṣṇa: Konkordanz und Kommentar der Motive seines Heldenlebens* (Istanbul, 1944); Milton Singer (ed.), *Krishna: Myths, Rites, and Attitudes* (Honolulu, 1966), esp. 'The Social Teaching of the *Bhāgavata Purāṇa*', by Thomas J. Hopkins, pp. 3–22, and 'On the Archaism of the *Bhāgavata Purāṇa*', by J. A. B. van Buitenen, pp. 23–40.

59. Kṛṣṇa's Mother Looks Inside his Mouth

**Bhāgavata* 10.8.21–45.

Compare: **Brahmavaivarta* 4.13; *Padma* 3.13; 4.69; *Skanda* 2.6.3; 3.1.27; **Viṣṇu* 5.6. Also **Mahābhārata* 3.186–7.

60. Kṛṣṇa Subdues the Serpent Kāliya

**Bhāgavata* 10.17.2–12; 10.15.47–52; 10.16.4–34, 51–67.

Compare: *Brahma* 185; **Brahmavaivarta* 4.19; *Bṛhaddharma* 3.17; **Harivaṃśa* 55–6; **Viṣṇu* 5.7. For Garuḍa and the snakes, cf. the myth told in **Śatapatha Brāhmaṇa* 3.1.13–16; 3.2.4.1–6; 3.6.2.2; **Taittirīya Saṃhitā* 6.1.6; **Mahābhārata* 1.16.25 (Roy 1.17–36) and retold in *Brahma* 90; 100; 159; **Devībhāgavata* 2.12; *Nīlamata Purāṇa* (ed. Ved Kumari, Srinagar, 1968); *Padma* 5.6, 44; *Skanda* 3.1.38; 4.1.50; 5.3.72; *Kedāra Khaṇḍa* 167.

Discussion: Dange, *Legends*, pp. 1–153; Rao, I, 1, 212–13.

61. Kṛṣṇa Steals the Clothes of the Girls of the Village

**Bhāgavata* 10.22.1–28.

Compare: **Brahmavaivarta* 1.27; *Bṛhaddharma* 3.17.

62. Viṣṇu Becomes the Buddha to Delude the Demons

**Viṣṇu* 3.17.9–10, 35–45; 3.18.1–33.

Compare: **Agni* 16; **Bhāgavata* 2.7; 10.40; 11.4; **Devībhāgavata* 10.5.13; **Garuḍa* 1.32; **Liṅga* 1.71; *Nīlamata Purāṇa* 684–90; *Saura* 34; **Śiva* 2.5.3–6; *Jñānasaṃhitā* 21.3–24; *Skanda* 4.1.43–58; *Viṣṇudharma* 25.

Discussions: O'Flaherty, 'Origin of Heresy', pp. 308–13; Rao, I, 1, 216–21; S. N. Roy, 'Date of the *Viṣṇu Purāṇa* chapters on Māyāmoha', *Purāṇa*, VII, 2 (July 1965), pp. 276–87; Adalbert J. Gail, 'Buddha als Avatāra Viṣṇu's im Spiegel der Purāṇas', *ZDMG*, Supplementa 1, Vorträge, Teil 3 (1969), pp. 917–23.

63. Viṣṇu Becomes Incarnate as Kalkin to End the Kali Age

**Viṣṇu* 4.24.25–29.

Compare: **Mahābhārata* 3.188.86–93; 3.189.1–7 (Roy 3.189–90); **Agni* 16; **Bhāgavata* 12.2.16–23; *Bhaviṣya* 3.1.2–7; 3.3.4; 3.4.25–6; *Brahma* 213; *Brahmāṇḍa* 2.3.73.104–24; **Brahmavaivarta* 2.7; *Bṛhaddharma* 3.19; *Devī* 6; **Harivaṃśa* 31; *Kalki* 1.1–4; 2.6–7; 3.1–2, 14–19; **Liṅga* 1.40; **Matsya* 47; 248–63; *Narasiṃha* 54; *Saura* 4; *Skanda* 7.4.1; *Vāyu* 2.37.390 ff.; **Viṣṇu* 5.7; 6.1–2; *Viṣṇudharmottara* 1.74.

Discussion: Emil Abegg, *Der Messiasglauben in Indien und Iran* (Berlin, 1925), pp. 39 ff., 71 ff.; Cornelia D. Church, 'The Purāṇic Myths of the Four Yugas', *Purāṇa*, XIII, 2 (July 1971), pp. 151–9; and *Purāṇa* XVI, 1 (January 1974), pp. 5–25; Mircea Eliade, *Mephistopheles and the Androgyne* (New York, 1965), pp. 125–59; Ronald M. Huntington, 'Avataras and Yugas: An Essay in Purāṇic Cosmology', *Purāṇa*, VI, 1 (January 1964), pp. 7–39; Muir, I, 43–9 and 122–55; David Pocock, 'The Anthropology of Time Reckoning', in *Contributions to Indian Sociology*, 7 (1964), pp. 18–29 (reprinted in *Myth and Cosmos*, ed. John Middleton, New York, 1967, pp. 303–14); O'Flaherty, 'The Origin of Heresy', pp. 329–33; Rao, I, 1, 221–3.

64. Devī and the Buffalo Demon are Born

Skanda 3.1.6.8–42.

Compare: **Jaiminīya Brāhmaṇa* 2.115; *Maitrāyaṇī Saṃhitā* 3.8.5; **Śatapatha Brāhmaṇa* 3.5.1.13–36; **Taittirīya Saṃhitā* 6.2.7; *Devī* 1–20; **Liṅga* 1.106; *Skanda* 5.2.55; 6.119–22; **Vāmana* 18; *Varāha* 28; *Kālikā* 62.136–57.

Discussions: C. D. Daly, pp. 17–60; Philip Spratt, pp. 193–9, 225–91, 346–50; Rao, I, 2, 327–44, 355–72.

65. Devī Entices the Buffalo Demon

Skanda 1.3.1.10.1–69.
Compare: **Brahmavaivarta* 2.16–20; **Liṅga* 1.97; *Padma* 6.3–19; 6.98–107; **Śiva* 2.5.22 ff.; 2.5.40–41; 2.5.59; 7.1.24; *Dharmasaṃhitā* 4.68–9; *Vāyu* 1.69.
Discussion: Rao, I, 2, 345–54.

66. Devī Slays the Buffalo Demon

**Mārkaṇḍeya* 80.21–44.
Compare: **Devībhāgavata* 5.2–18; *Padma* 5.30; *Skanda* 1.3.1.10–12; 1.3.2.19–21; 3.1.6–7; 4.2.68; 6.119–22; 7.1.83; 7.3.36; *Kedāra Khaṇḍa* 201; **Vāmana* 19–21; 32; *Varāha* 92–5; *Viṣṇudharmottara* 1.233.
Discussion: V. S. Agrawal, *The Glorification of the Great Goddess* (Varanasi, 1963); D. D. Kosambi, *Myth and Reality* (Bombay, 1962), pp. 1–11 and 82–110.

67. The Corpse of Satī is Dismembered

**Devībhāgavata* 7.30.27–37, 40–50.
Compare: **Brahmavaivarta* 4.42–3; *Bṛhaddharma* 2.40; *Kālikā* 17–18; *Mahābhāgavata* 11–12; *Skanda, Kedāra Khaṇḍa* 162.
Discussion: O'Flaherty (1973), pp. 298–300; D. C. Sircar, 'The Śākta Pīṭhas', *JRASB Letters*, XIV, 1 (1948), pp. 1–108; Heinrich Zimmer, *The King and the Corpse* (New York, 1960), pp. 239–316.

68. Kālī Obtains a Golden Skin and Śiva Slays the Demon Āḍi in her Form

Skanda 1.2.27.58–73a, 74–84; 1.2.28.1–14; 1.2.29.1–69a, 72b–81.
Compare: **Devībhāgavata* 5.23; *Kālikā* 47; **Mārkaṇḍeya* 85.37–41; **Matsya* 139; 154–7; *Padma* 5.41; **Śiva* 7.1.25–7; *Dharmasaṃhitā* 10.28.215; *Skanda* 1.2.27–30; 5.2.18; **Vāmana* 28. For other quarrels between Śiva and Pārvatī: *Brahma* 38; *Mahābhāgavata* 23; *Saura* 54; **Śiva* 7.24; *Skanda* 1.1.34–5; 1.3.1.3; 1.3.2.18; 5.1.18–19; 5.2.18; 7.1.68. For Nandin as Śailādi, see **Kūrma* 2.41; **Liṅga* 1.42–5.
Discussion: O'Flaherty (1973), pp. 186–90 and 224–36.

69. Devī Persuades Śiva to Let her Create a Son, Gaṇeśa

Bṛhaddharma 2.60.1–4, 7–97, 106b–8.

Compare: **Agni* 71; *Bhaviṣya* 1.28; **Brahmavaivarta* 2.39; 3.8–13, 18, 20, 24; *Brahmāṇḍa* 2.3.41–2; 3.4.27; *Devī* 111–15; **Harivaṃśa* 1.1; **Matsya* 154.502–41; **Liṅga* 1.104–5; *Mahābhāgavata* 35; *Padma* 5.40; 5.61–3; **Śiva* 2.4.13–20; *Skanda* 1.1.10; 1.2.27; 3.2.12; 3.2.20; 6.214; 7.1.167; 7.3.32.3–23; **Vāmana* 28.64–75; *Varāha* 23. For the related myth of the slaying of the elephant demon, cf.: *Brahmāṇḍa* 4.27.98–101; **Matsya* 55; **Śiva* 2.5.57; *Skanda* 4.2.68.

Discussion: A. K. Coomaraswamy, 'Gaṇeśa', *Bulletin of the Boston Museum of Fine Arts*, XXVI (April 1928); Alain Daniélou, 'The Meaning of Gaṇapati', *Adyar Library Bulletin* (1954), pp. 107 ff.; Alice Getty, *Gaṇeśa: A Monograph on the Elephant-faced God* (Oxford, 1936); O'Flaherty (1973), pp. 210–24 and 261–77; Louis Renou, 'Note sur les origines Védiques de Ganesh', *Journal Asiatique*, 229 (1937), pp. 271 ff.; Juan Roger Rivière, 'The Problem of Gaṇeśa in the Purāṇas', *Purāṇa*, IV, 1 (February 1960), pp. 92–102; Moriz Winternitz, 'Gaṇeśa in the Mahābhārata' *JRAS* (1898), pp. 380 ff. Cf. also Edmund Leach, 'Pulleyar and the Lord Buddha: An Example of Syncretism', *Psychoanalysis and the Psychoanalytic Review* (Summer 1962), pp. 81–102; Rao, I, 1, 35–67; II, 1, 114, 150–56; Philip Spratt, *Hindu Culture and Personality*, pp. 124–7, 350–51.

70. Gods and Demons are Created and the Battle Begins

**Śatapatha Brāhmaṇa* 11.1.6.6–11.

Compare: **Chāndogya Upaniṣad* 8.7–12; **Maitrāyaṇi Upaniṣad* 7.9; **Śatapatha Brāhmaṇa* 1.2.2.6; 1.4.1.35; 1.7.2.22; 5.1.1.1; 5.5.5.1; 9.5.1.12–15; *Taittirīya Brāhmaṇa* 1.4.11; 2.3.8.1–3; **Mahābhārata* 3.92.6–10; 12.160.26; 12.221; *Vāyu* 2.16.29–35; *Viṣṇudharma* 25.

Discussion: Mircea Eliade, *Mephistopheles and the Androgyne*, pp. 78–124; Sylvain Lévi, *La Doctrine du sacrifice dans les Brāhmaṇas* (Paris, 1966), pp. 12–62; Muir, I, 23 ff.; O'Flaherty, 'The Origin of Heresy', pp. 294–6.

71. The Gods Trick the Demons into Leaving the Sacrifice

**Śatapatha Brāhmaṇa* 9.5.1.12–17, 26–7.

Compare: **Aitareya Brāhmaṇa* 3.45; **Śatapatha* 5.1.1.1; 6.6.2.11; 6.6.3.2; 11.5.1.12; *Taittirīya Brāhmaṇa* 3.2.9.6; **Taittirīya Saṃhitā* 2.5.1; **Tāṇḍya Mahābrāhmaṇa* 8.6.5; 8.9.15.

Discussion: O'Flaherty, 'The Origin of Heresy', pp. 306 ff.

72. The Gods and Demons Churn the Ocean to Obtain Ambrosia

**Mahābhārata* 1.15.5–13; 1.16.1–40, 1.17.1–30, plus 7 lines after 1.61.35 followed by 3 occurring after 1.61.32; 3 after 1.16.36, 3 after 1.16.40 and 3 after 1.17.7 (Roy 1.17–20).

Compare: **Aitareya Brāhmaṇa* 1.27; **Śatapatha Brāhmaṇa* 3.2.4.1–6; 3.9.3.18–21; **Mahābhārata* 5.100.1–13; **Rāmāyaṇa* 1.45; **Agni* 3; **Bhāgavata* 8.6–12; *Brahma* 106; *Brahmāṇḍa* 1.2.25; 3.4.9–10; **Garuḍa* 1; **Harivaṃśa* 3.30; **Matsya* 249–51; *Padma* 3.8–10; 5.4; 5.14: *Skanda* 1.1.8–13; 5.1.44; 5.2.14; 6.210; 7.1.18; 7.1.258; *Vāyu* 1.54; **Viṣṇu* 1.9; *Viṣṇudharmottara* 1.40–43.

Discussions: V. M. Bedekar, 'The Legend of the Churning of the Ocean in the Epics and Purāṇas', *Purāṇa*, IX, 1 (February 1967), pp. 7–61; Sadashiv A. Dange, *Legends*, pp. 239–80; Georges Dumézil, *Le Festin d'Immortalité* (Paris, 1924); Franklin Edgerton, 'The Fountain of Youth', *JAOS*, XXVI, 1 (1905), pp. 1–67; Gonda, *Aspects*, pp. 126–8; J. Bruce Long, 'Life out of Death: A Structural Analysis of the Myth of the Churning of the Ocean of Milk', in Bardwell Smith (ed.), *Hinduism: New Essays in the History of Religion* (Leiden, 1975): O'Flaherty (1973), pp. 277–9: Klaus Rüping, *Amṛtamanthana und Kūrma Avatāra* (Wiesbaden, 1970).

73. Indra Tricks Śuṣṇa into Giving up the Ambrosia

Kāṭhaka Saṃhitā 37.14a.

Compare: **Ṛg Veda* 1.121.10; 4.26–7; 10.123.6; **Aitareya Brāhmaṇa* 1.27; 3.25–8; **Śatapatha Brāhmaṇa* 1.7.1.1; 3.2.4.1; 3.9.4.10; 10.1.3.1–7; 10.1.4.1; 10.4.3.1–10; 11.1.2.12; 11.2.3.6; *Taittirīya*

Brāhmaṇa 6.1.6.5; **Taittirīya Saṃhitā* 2.3.2.1; **Tāṇḍya Mahābrāhmaṇa* 8.4.1; *Brahma* 133.

Discussions: M. Bloomfield, 'The Legend of Soma and the Eagle', *JAOS*, XVI (1894), pp. 1–24; Jarl Charpentier, *Die Suparṇasage* (Uppsala-Leipzig, 1920); Sadashiv A. Dange, *Legends*, pp. 67–91; Adalbert Kuhn, *Die Herabkunft des Feuers und des Göttertranks* (Gütersloh, 1886), pp. 52–61, 123–31, 218–23: Muir, IV, 54 ff.: V, 262 ff.: O'Flaherty (1973), p. 277 ff.: Ulrich Schneider, *Der Somaraub des Manu* (Wiesbaden, 1971). See also the myths of Garuḍa and Kadrū, myth 60 above.

74. The Gods Send Kaca, the Son of Bṛhaspati, to Learn the Secret of Revival from Śukra

**Mahābhārata* 1.71.5–58; 1.72.1–23, plus 4 after 1.71.31, 2 after 1.71.33 (Roy 1.76–7).

Compare: **Jaiminīya Brāhmaṇa* 1.125–7; **Taittirīya Saṃhitā* 2.5.1; 6.3.7.4; **Bhāgavata* 9.18; *Brahma* 52–6: 95; **Matsya* 25–6; *Padma* 6.18; **Śiva* 2.5.47–50; *Skanda* 2.2.3; 3.15; 4.1.16; 6.1.149; 7.1.31.1; 7.1.48; 7.3.15; **Vāmana* 36; 43; **Viṣṇu* 9.24–5.

Discussions: Dange, *Legends*, pp. 155–237; Georges Dumézil, *Mythe et épopée*, II, pp. 133–238; *The Destiny of the Warrior*, pp. 19–28; O'Flaherty (1973), pp. 190, 279–82; Philip Spratt, *Hindu Culture and Personality*, pp. 129, 338–42.

75. Bṛhaspati Tricks Śukra and Corrupts the Demons

Padma (Ānandāśrama) 5.13.201a, 203–322, 332–3, 336–47, 411–12, 416–21.

Compare: **Atharva Veda* 8.10.22; **Maitrāyaṇi Upaniṣad* 7.9–10; **Taittirīya Saṃhitā* 6.4.10; **Tāṇḍya Mahābrāhmaṇa* 7.5.20; **Mahābhārata* 12.271; **Bhāgavata* 8.10, 15; *Brahmāṇḍa* 2.3.72–3; **Devībhāgavata* 4.10–15; **Matsya* 47; *Padma* 5.13; *Skanda* 1.1.14; *Vāyu* 2.30.76–100; 2.35–6; **Viṣṇu* 4.9.1–22. Bhṛgu curses Viṣṇu; **Rāmāyaṇa* 7.51: *Padma* 5.4.

Discussions: Robert P. Goldman, 'Myth as Literature in Ancient India: the Saga of Śukrācārya; *Mahfil*, VII, 3 and 4 (Fall–Winter 1971), pp. 45–62; Muir, IV, 151–5; V, 272–83; O'Flaherty, 'The Origin of Heresy', pp. 313–15; Hanns-Peter Schmidt, *Bṛhaspati und Indra* (Wiesbaden, 1968); V. S. Sukthankar, 'The Bhṛgus and the Bhārata', *Annals of the Bhandarkar Oriental Research Institute*, 18, pp. 1–76; reprinted in the memorial edition, I (Bombay 1944), pp. 278–337. Cf. also Robert P. Goldman, 'Myth and Metamyth: A Critical Study of the Evolution and Manipulation of the Bhārgava Corpus in the *Mahābhārata*' (Ph.D. dissertation, University of Pennsylvania, May 1971).

Appendix D

GLOSSARY AND INDEX OF PROPER NAMES

(N.B. Many of the etymologies are conjectural.)

Āḍi, a demon, perhaps originally in the form of an aquatic bird; sometimes regarded as an incarnation of Vasiṣṭha: pp. 251–61.

Āditya, a name of the sun. The Ādityas, sons of Aditi ('infinity') and Kaśyapa, are solar gods who shine forth at doomsday. Various lists of their names are given, but important Ādityas are Mitra, Aryaman, Bhaga, Varuṇa, Aṃśu, Indra, Dakṣa, and Vivasvat. Originally eight, they are later enumerated as twelve: pp. 30, 39, 91, 106, 179, 185.

Agastya, 'mountain-thrower' – so called because he subdued the Vindhyas – a great sage; the star Canopus: p. 199.

Agni, god of fire. Among his many forms are the brothers Vaiśvānara (the digestive fire within all men), Gṛhapati (the household fire), Yaviṣṭha ('the youngest', fire when it has just been produced from the wood), Pāvaka ('the purifier', particularly the fire of lightning), Sahaḥsuta ('son of strength'), and Saucīka ('needle-sharp'): pp. 98–115, and *passim*.

Agnihotra, the oblation offered into fire: p. 33.

Ahalyā, 'unploughable', adulterous wife of Gautama: pp. 92, 94–6, 299.

Airāvata, 'born of the milky ocean', the white elephant, Indra's mount: pp. 54, 103, 111, 114, 242, 266–9, 277.

Amarāvatī, 'place of the immortals', the city of the gods: pp. 240, 266.

Ambikā, 'Little Mother', a euphemistic epithet of Kālī: p. 148.

Anakadundubhi, a name of Vasudeva: p. 217.

Ananta, 'infinite', the serpent upon which Viṣṇu sleeps: pp. 153, 190, 221, 275.

Anasūyā, 'free from envy', name of the wife of Atri: pp. 53–5, 149.

Andhaka, 'blind', a demon: pp. 168–74, 238, 242, 256.

Aṅgiras, a great sage, mediator between gods and men (cf. Greek *angelos*): pp. 26, 30, 51, 74, 86, 107–9, 119, 133, 147, 282–8, 296–7.

Araṇi, 'turning round', a fire-stick; name of a sage: p. 51.

Arbuda, 'the swelling', name of a sacred Śaiva mountain in the west of India: pp. 260–61.

Arthaśāstra, the earliest extant Indian textbook of political science, attributed to Kauṭilya, the minister of Candragupta Maurya: p. 272.

Aruṇācala, 'tawny mountain': pp. 244–6.

Arundhatī, the wife of Vasiṣṭha, personified form of the Morning Star. She alone of the Pleiades remains the model of conjugal chastity: pp. 110, 112, 167.

aśvattha, 'under which horses stand', the sacred fig tree, *Ficus religiosa*: p. 103.

Aśvins, 'horsemen', the Dioscuroi, horse-gods, twin sons of the sun and a mare. The physicians of the gods: pp. 39, 56–61, 66–70, 118–19, 202.

Atharvan, a priest in charge of the worship of fire and Soma: pp. 56–8, 133.

Atri, 'devourer', a great sage, a son of Brahmā, author of many Vedic hymns, husband of Anasūyā: pp. 51, 54, 147, 195.

Ayāsyas, 'agile ones', descendants of Aṅgiras: p. 74.

Baka, 'the crane', a demon killed by Kṛṣṇa: p. 256.

Bala, nickname of Balarāma, 'he who delights in power', elder brother of Kṛṣṇa: p. 224.

Bali, 'offering', a demon, son of Virocana, conquered by Viṣṇu as the dwarf: pp. 82, 178–9, 240–41.

Balarāma, elder brother of Kṛṣṇa: pp. 205, 209, 211, 218–20, 223–5.

Bhadrakālī, 'gracious Kālī', an epithet of Durgā: pp. 229, 251.

Bhaga, 'dispensing wealth', an Āditya, brother of the dawn: pp. 116–17, 124–5, 143, 253.

Bharadvāja, 'bearing swift flight' or 'sky-lark', one of the seven sages: p. 195.

Bharata, a brother of Rāma, son of the wicked Kaikeyī but devoted to Rāma: p. 200.

Bhava, 'existence', a form of Rudra: pp. 31, 122–4, 129–30, 135, 141, etc.

Bhoja, a country (or the inhabitants thereof) near the Vindhya mountains: pp. 206–7.

Bhṛgu, a great sage, son of the first Manu, one of the seven sages. Father of Śukra: pp. 30, 51, 149–54, 284–8, 292–5, etc.

Brahmā, the creator: pp. 25–55, and *passim*.

Bṛhaspati, 'lord of sacred speech', originally an epithet of Indra, then an independent deity, the preceptor of the gods. The planet Jupiter: pp. 30, 72, 74, 86, 118, 126, 178, 268, 281–300.

Buddha, 'the enlightened': pp. 175, 231–5, 289, 300.

Caitraratha, a grove of Kubera cultivated by Citraratha ('of bright chariot'), king of the Gandharvas: p. 112.

Cākṣusa, see Manu.

Candramas, the moon. Incarnate as a god and as a sage, son of Atri and Anasūyā: p. 55.

Cāraṇas, 'wanderers', celestial strolling players: pp. 95–6, 208, 226.

Citra, 'bright-coloured' or 'variegated', the name of an elephant: p. 111.

Dadhyañc, 'sprinkling curdled milk', son of an Atharvan priest: pp. 56–60, 94, 101, 118, 133.

Dakṣa, 'dextrous', son of Brahmā, one of the seven sages, father of Satī, Rohiṇī, and other wives of the gods: pp. 46–53, 105–9, 118–25, 137–8, 211, 250–51, 262, etc.

Dark Blue, see Nīla.

Daśaratha, 'possessing ten chariots', father of Rāma: pp. 95, 202–4.

Dasra, 'accomplishing wonderful deeds', an epithet of one or both of the Aśvins: pp. 61, 69.

Dattātreya, a sage, son of Atri and Anasūyā, regarded as an incarnation of Viṣṇu: p. 55.

Devakī, mother of Kṛṣṇa, daughter of Devaka: pp. 205–13, 230.

Devayānī, 'leading to the gods', daughter of Śukra: pp. 20, 282–9.

Devī, the Goddess, the essential form of whom Durgā, Pārvatī, Umā, Gaurī, etc. are manifestations: pp. 238–69, and *passim*.

Dhanañjaya, 'wealth-conquering', name of a serpent demon in the *Mahābhārata*: p. 132.

Dhanvantari, 'moving in a curve', the physician of the gods: p. 277.

dharma, the social order, the ideal order of the world, social law; the way things should be: pp. 48, 143 (incarnate).

Dharmaketu, 'having justice for his banner', an epithet of the Buddha: p. 145.

Dhenuka, 'full of cows', a place of pilgrimage: p. 41.

Dhṛtarāṣṭra, 'whose empire is firm', name of a serpent king also called Airāvata: p. 132.

Digvāsas, 'clothed in the sky', i.e. naked: p. 145.

Diti, mother of the demons called Daityas, wife of Kaśyapa. Counterpart of Aditi: pp. 91–4, 239, 290, 295.

Doomsday clouds, sometimes enumerated as two (Balāhaka, ['the crane'], and Saṃvarta or Saṃvartaka ['destroying']), sometimes, as seven (the original two plus Bhīmanāda ['frightening roar'], Droṇa ['the bucket'], Caṇḍa ['fierce'], Vidyutpatāka ['having lightning for its banner'], and Śoṇa ['blood-red']: pp. 132, 138, 145, 183–4.

Door of the Ganges, see Gaṅgādvāra.

Durgā, 'difficult of access', an epithet of Devī in her fierce aspect: pp. 241, 247.

Durvāsas, 'badly clad' or 'naked', an irascible sage, an incarnation of Śiva: pp. 55, 156, 250.

Gandharvas, celestial musicians. The *Ṛg Veda* knows only one Gandharva, the father of Yama and Yamī, who guards the Soma and gives it to the gods, and presides over marriages. The post-Vedic class of Gandharvas have similar qualities and are the husbands of the celestial nymphs (Apsarases) who dance in Indra's court: pp. 45, 47, 52–3, 63, 82–4, etc.

Gaṇeśa, 'lord of hosts', the elephant-headed son of Śiva: pp. 54, 165, 168–9, 255–8, 261–9.

Gaṅgādvāra, 'door of the Ganges', a town situated where the Ganges enters the plains: p. 120.

Ganges (Gaṅgā), a holy river: pp. 20, 41, 54, 120, 131, 153, 160–61, 167–8, 182.

Garuḍa, 'the devourer', son of Kaśyapa and Vinatā, enemy of serpents. Identified with fire and the sun. The bird on whom Viṣṇu rides. Garuḍī is the female bird: pp. 54, 105, 110–12, 191, 221–8, 232, 251–61.

Gaurī, 'the golden one', a name of Pārvatī: pp. 104, 152, 169–71, 242–5, 255–61.

Gautama, a sage: pp. 94–6, 143, 147, 195, 244.

Gāyatrī, 'song', a Vedic metre of three lines of eight syllables, personified as the wife of Brahmā and mother of the four Vedas. Sometimes personified as a bird: p. 177.

Ghora, 'horrible', a son of the boar incarnation of Viṣṇu: pp. 189–97.

Govinda, 'cow-finder', a name of Kṛṣṇa: pp. 154, 191–2, 218, 223, 230.

Grandfather, an epithet of Brahmā or Prajāpati: pp. 36–8, 41–2, 51, 88–90, etc.

Guha, 'reared in a secret place', a name of Skanda: pp. 110, 114, 165.

Guhyakas, 'hidden ones', a class of demi-gods who, like the Yakṣas, are the servants of Kubera: pp. 70, 119.

guṇas, the three 'strands' or qualities of which all matter is composed in various proportions, interwoven like the strands of a rope: *sattva* (goodness or light), *rajas* (dust, passion or activity) and *tamas* (darkness, inertia or heaviness): pp. 43–5, 50, 145, 148, 150, 154, 186, 227.

Hanūmat, 'having large jaws', name of a monkey who helped Rāma win back Sītā by leaping over the ocean and setting fire to Laṅkā: pp. 198, 201.

Hara, 'the remover', a name of Śiva: pp. 133–4, 165, and *passim*.

Hari, a name of Viṣṇu. Also the name of a demon, son of Tāraka: p. 128 (the demon), and *passim*.

Haryaśvas, 'possessing bay horses', name of the sons of Dakṣa: p. 47.

Heramba, 'the buffalo', a name of Gaṇeśa: p. 268.

Himālaya, 'abode of snow', a great mount or range, father of Pārvatī: pp. 41, 95, 105, 111, 119, 131, 142, 167–8, 254–5, 260.

Hiraṇyakaśipu, 'having golden garments', name of a great demon, twin brother of Hiraṇyākṣa and father of Prahlāda, killed by Viṣṇu as the Man-lion: pp. 170, 207–8.

Hiraṇyākṣa, 'golden-eye', name of a great demon killed by Viṣṇu in his boar incarnation. Also called Hiraṇyanetra or Hiraṇyalocana: pp. 170–72.

Hotṛ, the priest who offers the oblation: pp. 98, 100.

Hrāda, 'the roar', name of a serpent demon, son of Hiraṇyakaśipu: p. 232.

Hṛṣīkeśa, 'lord of the senses', an epithet of Viṣṇu: p. 182.

Indra, king of the gods, son of Aditi and Kaśyapa: pp. 56–97, and *passim.*

Jagatī, 'moving', a Vedic metre of four lines of twelve syllables: p. 177.

Jaimini, a celebrated sage and philosopher: pp. 262, 269.

Jamadagni, 'fire-eating', a sage descended from Bhṛgu: p. 195.

Jambha, 'jaws' or 'eye-tooth', a demon killed by Viṣṇu: p. 291.

Janaka, 'begetting', a king of Videha, father of Sītā: pp. 198–204.

Jātavedas, 'knowing all who are born', an epithet of Agni: p. 98.

Jayantī, 'conquering', a daughter of Indra: pp. 294–5.

Jyeṣṭhā, 'the eldest', the goddess of misfortune: p. 277.

Ka, 'Who?', an epithet of Brahmā: pp. 139–40.

Kaca, 'hair', son of Bṛhaspati: pp. 281–9, 296.

Kadamba, a tree, *Nauclea cadamba,* with orange-coloured fragrant blossoms: p. 223.

Kadrū, 'tawny', a daughter of Dakṣa, wife of Kaśyapa, mother of the Nāga serpents: p. 222.

Kailāsa, a mountain in the Himālaya range, the paradise of Śiva: pp. 119, 151, 154, 162, 244.

Kākutstha, 'descendant of Kakutstha' ['standing on a hump', so named because in a battle he stood on the hump of Indra who had been changed into a bull], an epithet of Rāma: p. 202.

Kālanemi, 'rim of the wheel of time', name of a demon killed by Kṛṣṇa: pp. 207–8.

Kālapṛṣṭha, 'black-backed', a serpent: p. 132.

Kālī, 'the black goddess': pp. 104, 114, 159, 205–10, 213, 251–9.

Kali Age, the last and worst of the four ages; the present age: pp. 43, 49, 145, 235–7.

Kalinda, a mountain on which the river Yamunā rises: pp. 70, 222–3, 229.

Kāliya, 'black', a snake inhabiting the Yamunā river, subdued by Kṛṣṇa: pp. 207, 221–8.

Kalkin, 'impure' or 'sinful', the last incarnation of Viṣṇu in the Kali Age: pp. 175, 235–7.

kalpa, an aeon, a day of Brahmā, one thousand ages, a period of four thousand, three hundred and twenty million years as mortals count them: pp. 39, 43–6, 49, 53, 59, 140, 145, 186.

Kāma, 'desire', Eros, god of desire: pp. 54, 154–62, 242, 262.

Kamalākṣa, 'lotus-eyes', a son of Tāraka: pp. 127–37.

Kaṃsa, 'brass', the wicked king of the Bhojas, cousin of Devakī, enemy of Kṛṣṇa. Identified with the demon Kālanemi: pp. 206–15.

Kanaka, 'gold', son of the earth and Viṣṇu in his boar incarnation: pp. 189–97.

Karkoṭaka, 'sugar-cane', name of one of the principal serpents of the subterranean hell: p. 132.

Kārttikeya, 'son of the Kṛttikās', a name of Skanda: pp. 49, 114, 269.

kāśa, a grass, *Saccharum spontaneum*, used for mats and roofs: p. 100.

Kaśyapa, sometimes Kāśyapa, 'tortoise' a great sage, husband of Aditi, Diti, and twelve other daughters of Dakṣa. One of the seven sages; pp. 48, 91–2, 147, 170, 173, 195, 222, 269.

Kātyāyanī, an epithet of Durgā: p. 229.

Kauśikī, 'daughter of a sheath', a name of Durgā; also a river in Bihar: pp. 41, 210, 259.

Kaustubha, a fabulous jewel obtained from the churning of the ocean and placed on the breast of Viṣṇu: p. 277.

Kāvya, 'endowed with the qualities of a seer or poet', a name of Śukra: pp. 281–300.

Keśava, 'long-haired', an epithet of Viṣṇu: pp. 182, 218.

Keśin, 'long-haired', the name of a demon; in the *Ṛg Veda*, Keśin is the name of an unorthodox sage who drinks poison with Rudra; elsewhere, he is a demon in the form of a horse, killed by Kṛṣṇa: p. 106.

Kinnaras, 'What?-men', demi-gods with the heads of horses and bodies of men, or the reverse. Also called Kiṃpuruṣas or Aśvamukhas ('horse-heads'): pp. 107, 275.

Kratu, a son of Brahmā, one of the seven sages; also a personification of the sacrifice: pp. 51, 123–5, 145, 147.

Krauñca, 'the curlew', a mountain in the Himālaya range, situated in the east, on the north of Assam: p. 111.

Kṛṣṇa, 'the dark one', an avatar of Viṣṇu: pp. 14, 49–50, 52, 154, 175, 177, 181, 203–31, 240.

Kṛta Age, also called Satya Age ('the age of truth'), the first and best of the four ages; the golden age: pp. 13, 43, 49, 131, 142, 145, 149, 183, 236–7.

Kṛttikās, 'the cutters' or 'the razors', the wives of the Seven Sages, the Pleiades (sometimes represented as a razor), mothers of Skanda: pp. 49, 104–15, 141, 167–8, 187, 205, 230.

Kṣatriyas, nobles or warriors, the second of the four classes: p. 28.

Kubera, lord of wealth, guardian of the north, overlord of the Yakṣas: pp. 69–70, 119, 132, 240–41.

Kumāra, 'the youth', a name of Skanda: pp. 110–14, 269.

Kurus, a country beyond the most northern range of the Himālaya, a country of everlasting happiness, sometimes identified as the ancient home of the Aryans: pp. 58, 67, 69.

kuśa grass, *Poa cynosuroides*, a grass with long pointed stalks, used in certain religious ceremonies: pp. 92, 95, 100, 147, 173, 222.

Kusumāmodinī, 'fragrant with blossoms', a mountain goddess: pp. 255–8.

Lakṣmaṇa, 'endowed with lucky signs', younger brother and companion of Rāma: p. 200.

Lakṣmī, 'good fortune', wife of Viṣṇu: pp. 153, 162–3, 203, 215, 241.

Laṅkā, the island capital of Rāvaṇa, later identified with Ceylon: p. 198.

liṅga, the sacred phallus of Śiva: pp. 26, 54, 137–54, 195, 201–2, 250–51, 257, 262.

Lokapālas, 'world-protectors', the four guardians of the quarters (Yama in the south, Indra in the east, Kubera in the north, Varuṇa in the west); sometimes enumerated as eight (the first four, plus Agni in the south-east, Vāyu in the north-west, Soma in the north-east, and Sūrya in the south-west): pp. 62, 70, 132, 184, 202, 247.

Madana, 'the maddener', a name of Kāma: pp. 157–9.
Mādhava, 'descendant of Madhu' or 'vernal', a name of Kṛṣṇa: pp. 156, 179, 192.
Madhu, 'spring', a demon killed by Viṣṇu (not the same person as the Madhu who is an ancestor of Kṛṣṇa): pp. 183, 212, 222.
Mahiṣa, 'buffalo', a demon: pp. 238–49.
Maithilī, 'princess of Mithilā', an epithet of Sītā. Mithilā was the capital of Videha, the modern Tirhut: pp. 198–204.
Malaya, a mountain range on the west of Malabar, the western Ghāts: p. 181.
Mānasa, 'spiritual', a sacred mountain and sacred lake on mount Kailāsa, to which wild geese migrate every year during the breeding season: pp. 105–6, 190–91.
Mandara, 'dense', a mountain: pp. 81, 105, 131, 149, 169, 172, 274–9.
Māṇḍavya, a sage whom Dharma cursed to be born of a Śūdra woman; Māṇḍavya retaliated by cursing Dharma to be born of a Śūdra woman, and so Dharma was born as Vidura: p. 143.
Maṅkaṇaka, a sage: pp. 173–4.
Manu, progenitor of the human race, who are called human (*mānava*) after him. There are said to have been fourteen Manus, one in each great age (*manvantara*), of whom the most famous are Manu Svāyambhūva (son of Śatarūpā and Svayambhū, the self-created Prajāpati), the first Manu; Manu Revanta ('brilliant'), son of Vivasvat and the mare Saṃjñā, the fifth Manu; Manu Cākṣusa ('perceptible by the eye'), son of Tvaṣṭṛ, the sixth Manu; Manu Vaivasvata (son of Vivasvat and Saṃjñā), the seventh Manu and progenitor of the present race of mankind; Manu Sāvarṇi ('of the same kind' or 'son of the look alike', i.e. the son of Vivasvat and the Shadow), eighth Manu and first of the future Manus: pp. 25, 30, 47, 50, 53, 60, 62, 65–7, 70, 75, 98, 149–50, 179–84.
Marīci, 'shining mote', one of the seven sages, father of Kaśyapa: pp. 51, 91–2, 147.
Mārkaṇḍeya, a great sage who floated on the cosmic waters after the

dissolution of the universe until he was swallowed by Viṣṇu, in whose body he saw the universe: pp. 184, 218.

Mārtāṇḍa, 'born of a lifeless egg', an epithet of the sun, so-called either because the sun is 'the bird in the sky' and a bird is 'born of an (apparently) lifeless egg', or because when the sun was dwelling in the womb of his mother, Aditi, she performed such severe asceticism that her husband, Kaśyapa, feared that the egg in her womb would be destroyed: pp. 66, 69.

Maruts, 'flashing', storm-gods, also called Māruts or Rudras, martial deities who form the entourage of Indra or of Rudra. The seven Maruts are named Wind-speed, Wind-force, Wind-destroyer, Wind-circle, Wind-flame, Wind-seed, and Wind-disc (Vāyuvega, Vāyubala, Vāyuhā, Vāyumaṇḍala, Vāyujvāla, Vāyuretas, and Vāyucakra): pp. 30–31, 63, 80, 91–4, 96, 117, 123, 129, 156, 173, 205, 267.

Maya, 'the maker', architect of the demons (not to be confused with Māyā, magic illusion, a power of god or an aspect of the Goddess): pp. 36, 126–8.

Meru, the golden mountain, *axis mundi*: pp. 41, 111, 119, 155–7, 190, 206, 247, 274.

Mitra, 'the friend', a god regarded as the worldly counterpart of the spiritual Varuṇa; later, a sage, son of Vaśiṣṭha: pp. 63, 98.

Mohinī, 'the enchantress', a form of Viṣṇu: pp. 277–8.

Nahuṣa, 'neighbour', a king, father of Yayāti, who usurped Indra's throne and ruled heaven until he touched with his foot the sage Agastya, who cursed him to become a serpent: pp. 132, 143.

Namuci, 'not releasing [the heavenly waters; that is, a demon of drought]'. A demon slain by Indra and the Aśvins; later, slain by Indra alone with a weapon of foam at twilight, a story then told of Indra and Vṛtra: pp. 179, 300.

Nanda, 'joy', a cow-herd (*gopa*), head of the village of Gokula, who adopted Kṛṣṇa: pp. 209–17, 224–30.

Nandana, 'gladdening', Indra's garden paradise: p. 242.

Nandin, 'the happy one', an attendant of Śiva, his door-keeper, or his bull: pp. 120–21, 151–2, 157, 172, 254–62, 266–9.

Nara, 'the man', the primeval Man associated with Nārāyaṇa: pp. 278–9.

Nārada, 'bringing to man' (?), a son of Brahmā, messenger between gods and men; a meddlesome sage: pp. 46–53, 119, 166, 207.

Nārāyaṇa, 'the son of Man', or 'son of the waters', a name of Viṣṇu (compare the etymology offered in myth 54, pp. 186–8): pp. 136, 171, 186–91, 202, 226, 240, 274–9.

Narmadā, 'pleasure-giving', name of a river, the modern Nerbudda: pp. 184, 233, 300.

Nāsatya, 'helpful' (traditionally derived from '*nāsa*', the nose, because of the birth of the Aśvins from the nose of the mare), an epithet of one or both of the Aśvins: pp. 61, 69.

Navagvas, 'going by nine' or 'nine-fold', name of a mythical family said to have aided Indra in battle: p. 74.

Nīla, 'dark blue', a mountain immediately north of the central division: p. 187.

Nīpa, 'low', the *Nauclea cadamba*, a tree with orange-coloured, fragrant blossoms: p. 229.

Padmavatī, 'the lotus-bearer', a name of Śrī or Lakṣmī, wife of Viṣṇu: p. 268.

Pāka, 'childish' or 'naïve', a demon slain by Indra; pp. 72, 78, 80, 85–6, 294.

Pāñcāla, 'of the five tribes', a Yakṣa, son of Kubera: p. 259.

Paṇis, 'misers', a race of demons or of native inhabitants of India, enemies of the invading Aryans, who fought them for the treasure that they guarded: pp. 71–4, 76, 176, 214, 238.

Parvata, 'mountain', a sage, companion of Nārada: p. 119.

Pārvatī, 'daughter of the mountain', daughter of Himālaya, wife of Śiva: pp. 62, 119, 152, 163, 168–73, 205, 238, 251, 256, 261–9.

Paśupati, 'lord of cattle', an epithet of Rudra-Śiva: pp. 29, 77, 80, 117, 119–20, 125, 136, 148.

The Pillar (Sthāṇu), an epithet of Śiva in his chaste aspect, see Sthāṇu.

Pināka, the name of Śiva's bow: pp. 111, 122, 124, 133–4, 170, 256–7, 297.

Piśācas, 'flesh-eaters', a class of demons: pp. 45, 47, 110, 119, 142, 279.

Pleiades, see Kṛttikās.

Pracetas, 'mindful', an ancient sage, father of Dakṣa Prācetasa: pp. 48, 51.

Prahlāda, 'joyful excitement', a demon, a son of Hiraṇyakaśipu and worshipper of Viṣṇu, who appeared in the form of a Man-lion to defend Prahlāda from the abuse of his father: pp. 170, 179, 246–7, 291, 296–7, 300–301.

Prajāpati, 'lord of creatures', an epithet of Brahmā or of any of a class of primeval creators: pp. 25–55, and *passim*.

Prakṛti, Nature, composed of the three strands or *guṇas*: pp. 148, 261.

Pulaha, one of the Seven Sages: pp. 51, 147.

Pulastya, 'having smooth hair', one of the Seven Sages: pp. 51, 147.

Puruṣa, 'the Man', the primeval male; according to Sāṅkhya philosophy, the Puruṣa is inert spirit that conjoins with Prakṛti, Nature, to produce the universe: pp. 27, 34, 148, 150, 223, 226.

Pūṣan, 'nourisher', a solar deity, keeper of herds and bringer of prosperity: pp. 116–18, 124–5.

Pūtanā, 'stinking', a demoness regarded as causing certain diseases in children; she tries to kill Kṛṣṇa and is killed by him; also regarded as one of the Mothers who attends Skanda: pp. 214–18, 242.

Rāgas and Rāgiṇīs, 'emotions', the particular musical formulas out of which classical Indian music is composed; usually there are said to be six or twenty-six Rāgas married to six or thirty-six Rāgiṇīs: p. 49.

Rāghava, 'descendant of Raghu', a name of Rāma: pp. 200–204.

Raghu, 'fleet', son of Kakutstha, grandfather of Daśaratha: p. 204.

Rāhu, 'the seizer', name of a demon who is supposed to seize the sun and moon and thus cause eclipses: p. 278

rajas, 'passion', the second of the three *guṇas* or strands, see *guṇas*.

Rākṣasas, 'to be guarded against', a class of demons: pp. 45, 47, 84, 107, 110, 119, 139, 142, 152, 199–203, 215.

Rāma, 'charming', a king, son of Daśaratha and a descendant of Raghu, regarded as an incarnation of Viṣṇu. Also (no relation to Rāma son of Daśaratha) Rāma is a nickname of Balarāma, elder brother of Kṛṣṇa: pp. 95, 197–204, 299.

Ramaṇaka, 'delightful', name of an island: p. 228.

Rambhā, 'plantain', a nymph: p. 173.

Rati, 'loveplay' or sexual pleasure, the wife of Kāma: pp. 156–9.

Rāvaṇa, 'screaming', a demon: pp. 198–204.

Revanta, 'brilliant', a son of Vivasvat and Saṃjñā, the fifth Manu: pp. 69–70.

Rohiṇī, 'red', or 'a red cow', a constellation, wife of the moon; also (no relation to the constellation) the wife of Vasudeva, mother of Balarāma: pp. 30, 205–11.

Ṛtadhāman, 'whose abode is truth', a name of Viṣṇu: p. 202.

Rudra, 'howler' or 'ruddy one', the Vedic antecedent of Śiva, a malevolent god associated with wildness and danger. He is the god of tempests and father and ruler of the Rudras and Maruts: pp. 116–174, and *passim*.

Rudras, the hosts of Rudra, originally enumerated as eight (Bhava, Śarva, Paśupati, Ugra, Mahādeva, Rudra, Iśāna, and Aśani [existence, he who has arrows, lord of cattle, dread, great god, howler, ruler, and thunderbolt]), later as eleven (Mahan, Mahātman, Matiman, Bhīṣaṇa, Bhayaṃkara, Ṛtudhvaja, Ūrdhvakeśa, Piṅgalākṣa, Ruci, Śuci, and Rudra [great, noble, wise, terrifying, frightening, he who has the seasons as his banner, he whose hair stands up, tawny-eyed, brightness, purity, and howler]). They are sometimes identified with and sometimes distinguished from the Maruts: pp. 39, 50–51, 185, 202.

Śabalāśvas, 'possessing piebald horses', sons of Dakṣa: p. 48.

Śacī, 'powerful help', wife of Indra: pp. 78, 94, 156, 240.

Sādhyas, 'to be attained', a group of twelve celestial beings who inhabit the region between sun and earth. Nara and Nārāyaṇa are listed among the Sādhyas: pp. 27–8, 202.

Śailādi, 'son of Śilāda' or 'son of a rock', a name of Nandin: pp. 157, 260–61.

Śāka, 'vegetable', name of an island, the sixth of the seven great continents, called after the teak tree growing there: p. 69.

śakti, 'power', particularly the active power of a deity personified as his wife. The word may also designate a spear or sword: pp. 69, 113, 139, 162, 166, 238, 243, 250.

Śakra, 'powerful', an epithet of Indra: pp. 77–90, 106–115, etc.

Sāma Veda, the Vedic book of verses intended to be chanted: pp. 28, 133, 186, 298.

Śambara, a demon thrown down a mountain and slain by Indra: p. 179.

Śambhu, 'granting welfare', an epithet of Śiva: pp. 38, 54, 124, 139, 157, 160–68, etc.

śamī, 'toil', a tree (*Prosopis spicigera*) possessing a hard wood supposed to contain fire; it was used to kindle the sacred fire: pp. 103, 235.

Saṃjñā, 'sign' or 'name', daughter of Tvaṣṭṛ and wife of the sun: pp. 65–70.

Saṃkarṣaṇa, 'he who draws or ploughs', a name of Balarāma: pp. 209, 211, 218.

Saṃvarta, 'rolling up' or 'destroying', a name of a sage descended from Aṅgiras: p. 147.

Saṃvartaka, 'destroying', name of one of the doomsday clouds or fires: p. 132.

Śanaiścara, 'moving slowly', a name of the planet Saturn: pp. 67, 265.

Sanaka, Sananda, Sanātana, and Sanatkumāra ('the ancient', 'joyous', 'eternal', and 'eternally a youth'), the four mind-born sons of Brahmā: pp. 50, 186–7.

Śaṅkara, 'giver of peace', a name of Śiva: pp. 166, 263, etc.

Sāṅkhya, an ancient Indian philosophy which divides the universe into inert *puruṣa* and active *prakṛti*, the latter divided into the three *guṇas* or strands: pp. 129, 148, 221.

śapharī, a fish, either a bright little fish found in shallow water (*Cyprinus saphore*) or a large carp that preys on other fish: p. 182.

Saptasārasvata, the sacred place on the river Sarasvatī where seven rivers meet: p. 174.

śarabha, a fabulous animal said to inhabit the snowy mountains and to be an incarnation of Śiva: pp. 193–7.

Saramā, 'the fleet one', a female dog, mother of the four-eyed brindled dogs of Yama: pp. 62, 71–7, 176, 214, 238.

Saraṇyū, 'nimble', daughter of Tvaṣṭṛ, later called Saṃjñā, q.v.: pp. 60–62, 65–70.

Sarasvatī, 'flowing', the river that, with the Ganges, replaced the Sindhu as the most holy river of India. Also the goddess of speech, wife of Brahmā: pp. 131, 174, 268.

Śarva, 'possessing arrows', a name of Rudra: pp. 69, 136, 139, 252–4.

Śaryaṇāvat, 'reedy', a lake: pp. 58–9.

Ṣaṣṭhī, 'the sixth', a divine mother regarded as a form of Durgā and supposed to protect children; worshipped on the sixth day after delivery, when the chief danger for a mother and child is considered to be over: p. 49.

Śatarūpā, 'having a hundred forms', name of the daughter and wife of Brahmā and the mother of Manu Svāyambhuva; sometimes regarded as the daughter and wife of Manu Svāyambhuva: p. 50.

Satī, 'the good woman', daughter of Dakṣa, wife of Śiva: pp. 14, 105, 119, 123, 249–51, 289.

sattva, 'goodness', first of the three strands or *guṇas*. See *guṇas*.

Sātvatas, a tribe in which Kṛṣṇa was born: pp. 206, 215, 221.

Satyavatī, 'truthful', name of a servant of the Goddess, a woman said to have become the Kauśikī river, in Bihar: p. 244.

Satya Age, 'the age of truth', a name of the first or Kṛta Age: pp. 43, 49.

Saubhari, a great sage who, in his old age, married the fifty daughters of king Māndhātṛ and begat one hundred and fifty sons upon them: p. 222.

Sāvarṇi, see Manu.

Savitṛ, 'the vivifier', a form of the sun, one of the Ādityas: p. 118.

Sāvitrī, 'descended from the sun', a name of a daughter of the sun, wife of Brahmā: p. 49.

Self-created (Svayambhū), an epithet of Brahmā: pp. 46, 50, 54, 88, 148–9, 202, 208.

Seven Sages, mind-born sons of Brahmā, themselves Prajāpatis or primeval creators, forming the constellation Ursa Major; they are married to the Kṛttikās or Pleiades. The names of the seven varied in different ages, but among the most famous are Gautama, Bharadvāja, Viśvāmitra, Jamadagni, Vasiṣṭha, Kaśyapa, Atri, Marīci, Aṅgiras, Pulaha, Kratu, Pulastya, Bhṛgu, and Dakṣa: pp. 511, 04–5, 131, 141–9, 167–8, 195.

Siddhas, 'perfected', a class of semi-divine beings of great purity and perfection and said to possess the eight supernatural faculties (*siddhis*: the ability to become infinitely small, light, great, etc.): pp. 95, 102, 119, 123, 136, 173, 186, 208, 226.

Śilāda, 'eating ears of corn' or 'rock-giver', name of a man, father of Nandin in his reincarnation: pp. 260–61.

Sindhu, 'the river', probably the Indus river in the Punjab: p. 131.

Sītā, 'the furrow', daughter of Janaka, wife of Rāma: pp. 197–204, 299.

Śiva, 'auspicious', god of ascetics, of the *liṅga*, and of cosmic destruction: pp. 116–74, and *passim*.

Śivā, 'auspicious woman', wife of Aṅgiras (pp. 109–10); also a name of the Goddess (pp. 164–5, 251).

Skanda, the six-headed son of Śiva, also known as Guha, Kārttikeya, Kumāra, etc.: pp. 14, 69, 97, 104–15, 159–68, 205–6, 214, 261.

Smara, 'memory', an epithet of Kāma: pp. 159, 192.

Soma, the ambrosial offering to the gods, by which they sustain their immortality; also a name of the moon, in which the ambrosia is stored; and sometimes incarnate as a god: pp. 48, 70, 108, etc.

Śrī, 'prosperity', a wife of Viṣṇu: pp. 114, 150, 154, 215, 276–7.

Śrīvatsa, 'favourite of Śrī', a distinctive twist of hair upon the chest of Viṣṇu: pp. 145, 224.

Sthāṇu, 'the pillar', an epithet of Śiva in his chaste aspect: pp. 37–9, 129, 134–7.

strands, see *guṇas*.

Sudarśana, 'beautiful to see', a name of the discus of Viṣṇu: pp. 279–80.

Sugrīva, 'having a fine neck', a monkey king who, with his army of monkeys headed by Hanūmat, assisted Rāma in conquering Rāvaṇa: p. 198.

Sukeśa, 'having beautiful hair', name of a sage: p. 147.

Śukra, 'bright' (also 'seed'), name of the guru of the demons, son of Bhṛgu, regarded as the planet Venus: pp. 20, 126, 281–300.

Sumbha and Nisumbha (sometimes Śumbha and Niśumbha), a pair of demons, brothers, grandsons of Prahlāda, slain by the Goddess: pp. 210, 241–2, 259.

Suparṇa, 'having beautiful feathers', an epithet of Garuḍa: pp. 222, 228.

Supārśva, 'having beautiful sides', name of a sage: p. 239.

Śuṣṇa, 'hisser' or 'scorcher', a demon of drought killed by Indra: pp. 280–81.

Suvṛtta, 'well-rounded', the name of one of the three sons of Viṣṇu in his boar avatar: pp. 189–97.

Svāhā, 'hail', the exclamation made in offering the oblation to the gods; also the name of the oblation itself or the oblation personified as the wife of Agni: pp. 33, 99, 105, 109–12.

Svayambhū, 'self-created', an epithet of Brahmā. See 'self-created'.

tamas, 'darkness', the third of the three strands. See *guṇas*.

Tapatī, 'heating', a daughter of the sun: p. 67.

Tārā, 'star', the wife of Bṛhaspati, stolen by Soma and restored to Bṛhaspati after a great battle: p. 299.

Tāraka, 'saving', a demon slain by Indra and Skanda: pp. 126–7, 136, 154–6, 163, 259.

Tārakākṣa or Tārākṣa, 'star-eyed', a demon, son of Tāraka: pp. 127–37.

Tārkṣya, a mythical being, originally a horse, later a bird identified with Garuḍa, or (in the *Bhāgavata Purāṇa*) called the father of Garuḍa: p. 222.

Triple Peak (Trikūṭa), Rāvaṇa's mountain stronghold on the island of Laṅkā: p. 191.

Triśiras, 'three-headed', a demon killed by Indra: pp. 60, 70–71, 76–80, 84, 86, 91, 282.

Triṣṭubh, a metre of four lines of eleven syllables each: p. 177.

Trita Āptya, 'the third one of the water', a Vedic deity associated with the Maruts and Indra, said to have fought with Vṛtra and to reside in the most remote regions of the world: p. 71.

Tvaṣṭṛ, 'architect', the artisan of the gods, maker of divine implements: pp. 56–71, 75, 77–81, 91, 126.

Uccaiḥśravas, 'long-eared' or 'neighing loudly', the horse of Indra, prototype and king of horses: pp. 222, 243, 276–7.

Umā, said to be derived from the exclamation, 'U! Mā! [Oh! Don't]' uttered by her mother when Umā began to practise asceticism; Umā is the daughter of Himālaya and Menā; the wife of Śiva: pp. 120, 129, 155, 159, 192, 257–9.

Upabarhaṇa, 'the pillow', a Gandharva regarded as an incarnation of Nārada: pp. 52–3.

Uśanas, 'intense', a name of Śukra: pp. 282–300.

Vaikuṇṭha, 'related to what is not blunt', a name of Viṣṇu and of Viṣṇu's heaven: p. 192.

Vaiśrāvana, 'widely famed', a name of Kubera: p. 119.

Vaiśvānara, 'relating to all men', a name of Agni, particularly of the digestive fire: pp. 30, 99.

Varuṇa, 'all-enveloping', a Vedic god regarded as hating falsehood, and inflicting diseases, especially dropsy, upon sinners; later, he is the god of the waters and guardian of the western quarter: pp. 30, 63, 70, 84, 97–9, 107, 132, 230, 240.

vaṣaṭ, an exclamation uttered by the Hotṛ at the end of the sacrificial verse, when the oblation is cast into the fire: pp. 99, 133.

Vāsava, 'of the Vasus [q.v.]', a name of Indra: pp. 80–85, etc.

Vasiṣṭha or Vaśiṣṭha, 'most excellent' or 'most wealthy', one of the seven sages, husband of Arundhatī, owner of the wishing-cow; pp. 51, 108, 147, 195.

Vāstoṣpati, 'house-protector', name of a deity who presides over the foundation of a house, identified with Rudra: p. 26.

Vasus, a group of eight gods, whose chief was originally Indra, then became Viṣṇu: the eight original Vasus were the deities of day, water, the moon, the pole star, wind, fire, dawn, and light; later, the Aśvins, Ādityas, Rudra, Viṣṇu, Śiva, and Kubera were regarded as Vasus. When the Vasu Dyaus (Sky) stole the magic wishing-cow of Vasiṣṭha, Vasiṣṭha cursed them all to be reborn on earth, the sons of the sage Śāntanu and the river Gaṅgā: pp. 39, 50, 119, 143, 185, 202, 241.

Vāsudeva, 'son of Vasudeva', a name of Kṛṣṇa: pp. 55, 150, 154, 182, 184, 191–2, 236.

Vasudeva, 'lord of wealth', father of Kṛṣṇa, a descendant of Yadu of the lunar dynasty (and hence called Yādava): pp. 206–14.

Vāsuki, one of the great serpent kings: pp. 131, 275.

Vāyu, the wind and its deity: pp. 28, 31, 93, 185, 241.

Vibhīṣaṇa, 'terrifying', a brother of Rāvaṇa who left Laṅkā to join Rāma and was installed upon the throne of Laṅkā by Rāma after the death of Rāvaṇa: pp. 198–200.

Videha, a country (the modern Tirhut) whose capital was Mithilā and whose king was Janaka, father of Sītā: pp. 198–204.

Vidyādharas, 'possessing spells', supernatural beings dwelling in the Himālaya and possessed of magic powers: p. 119.

Vidyunmālin, 'garlanded with lightning', name of a demon, son of Tāraka or of Vipracitti: pp. 127–37, 240.

Vinatā, 'bent' or 'hunch-backed', a wife of Kaśyapa, daughter of Dakṣa, mother of Garuḍa and the race of birds in some texts, wife of Garuḍa in the *Bhāgavata Purāṇa*: p. 222.

Vindhyas, a low range of hills separating North India from the Deccan: pp. 131, 199, 210, 259.

Vipracitti, 'sagacious', name of a demon, father of Vidyunmālin and Rāhu: p. 240.

Vīrabhadra, 'gracious to heroes', a son or incarnation of Śiva, fierce and hideous: p. 251.

Virāj, 'ruling afar', the first-born of Brahmā, a primeval creator: p. 27.

Vīraka, 'little hero', a name of Nandin: pp. 242, 254–61.

Vīraṇa, 'heroic', a primeval creator, father of Asiknī, the wife of Dakṣa: pp. 47–8.

Virocana, 'illuminating', a demon, son of Prahlāda and father of Bali: pp. 179, 207, 291.

Viśākha, 'branched' or 'forked', a name of Skanda, or of a son of Skanda; or a demon, regarded as a form of Skanda, dangerous to children: p. 115.

Viṣṇu, 'the pervader', originally a solar god, then the supreme god: pp. 174–237, and *passim*.

Viśvakarman, 'all-maker', originally a name of Prajāpati, then of Tvaṣṭṛ: pp. 50, 59, 66–9, 127, 131, 185.

Viśvāmitra, 'friend of all', a great sage originally born as a Kṣatriya; vying with Vasiṣṭha for the wishing-cow, he became a brahmin: pp. 113, 147, 195.

Viśvanātha, 'lord of the universe', a name of Śiva and of his great shrine in Benares: p. 261.

Viśvāvasu, 'beneficent to all', a Gandharva: p. 119.

Vivasvat, 'shining forth', 'brilliant', a name of the sun: pp. 47, 60–61, 65–70.

Vṛndāvana, 'forest of the chorus of women', a grove near Kṛṣṇa's village in the district of Mathurā: p. 223.

Vṛṣaparvan, 'strong-jointed', name of a demon: p. 211.

Vṛṣṇis, 'manly', a tribe of Yādavas from whom Kṛṣṇa was descended: p. 211.

Vṛtra, 'restrainer', a great demon slain by Indra: pp. 22, 56–8, 74–91, 104, 118–19, 122, 126, 216, 221, 281, 296.

Yājñavalkya, a great sage to whom the sun revealed the *White Yajur Veda*: p. 34.

Yajur Veda, the Veda arranged for use in the sacrifice: pp. 28, 133.

Yakṣas, a class of semi-divine beings, attendants of Kubera, generally benevolent but sometimes responsible for demonic possession: pp 45, 47, 84, 107, 119, 123, 139, 207, 259.

Yama, 'twin', or 'curb' or 'bridle', king of the dead, sovereign over hell and the south, the first man, son of Vivasvat and Saraṇyū-Saṃjñā: pp. 37, 40, 60–70, 97–101, 132, 157, 172, 208, 240–43.

Yamī, twin sister of Yama: pp. 60–66.

Yamunā, a river (now called the Jumna), sometimes identified with Yamī and regarded as the daughter of the sun. It rises in the Himālaya and flows for 860 miles to join the Ganges at Allahabad: pp. 65–6, 70, 222–9.

Yaśodā, 'conferring fame', wife of the cow-herd Nanda, foster-mother of Kṛṣṇa: pp. 205–25.

Yayāti, a king of the lunar race, son of Nahuṣa; he married Devayānī, daughter of Śukra, and Śarmiṣṭhā, daughter of Vṛṣaparvan: p. 20.

yoni, 'womb' or 'source', particularly the sacred image of the organ of generation of the Goddess, worshipped together with the *liṅga*: pp. 26, 151, 250–51, 262.

Yuga, an age of the world; there are four: the first (Kṛta Yuga or Satya Yuga) is the best, the golden age, and the last (Kali Yuga), in which we live, is the worst: pp. 13, 43, 49, 131, 145, 178.

READ MORE IN PENGUIN

In every corner of the world, on every subject under the sun, Penguin represents quality and variety – the very best in publishing today.

For complete information about books available from Penguin – including Puffins, Penguin Classics and Arkana – and how to order them, write to us at the appropriate address below. Please note that for copyright reasons the selection of books varies from country to country.

In the United Kingdom: Please write to *Dept. JC, Penguin Books Ltd, FREEPOST, West Drayton, Middlesex UB7 OBR*

If you have any difficulty in obtaining a title, please send your order with the correct money, plus ten per cent for postage and packaging, to *PO Box No. 11, West Drayton, Middlesex UB7 OBR*

In the United States: Please write to *Penguin USA Inc., 375 Hudson Street, New York, NY 10014*

In Canada: Please write to *Penguin Books Canada Ltd, 10 Alcorn Avenue, Suite 300, Toronto, Ontario M4V 3B2*

In Australia: Please write to *Penguin Books Australia Ltd, 487 Maroondah Highway, Ringwood, Victoria 3134*

In New Zealand: Please write to *Penguin Books (NZ) Ltd,182–190 Wairau Road, Private Bag, Takapuna, Auckland 9*

In India: Please write to *Penguin Books India Pvt Ltd, 706 Eros Apartments, 56 Nehru Place, New Delhi 110 019*

In the Netherlands: Please write to *Penguin Books Netherlands B.V., Keizersgracht 231 NL–1016 DV Amsterdam*

In Germany: Please write to *Penguin Books Deutschland GmbH, Friedrichstrasse 10–12, W–6000 Frankfurt/Main 1*

In Spain: Please write to *Penguin Books S. A., C. San Bernardo 117–6° E–28015 Madrid*

In Italy: Please write to *Penguin Italia s.r.l., Via Felice Casati 20, I–20124 Milano*

In France: Please write to *Penguin France S. A., 17 rue Lejeune, F–31000 Toulouse*

In Japan: Please write to *Penguin Books Japan, Ishikiribashi Building, 2–5–4, Suido, Bunkyo-ku, Tokyo 112*

In Greece: Please write to *Penguin Hellas Ltd, Dimocritou 3, GR–106 71 Athens*

In South Africa: Please write to *Longman Penguin Southern Africa (Pty) Ltd, Private Bag X08, Bertsham 2013*

READ MORE IN PENGUIN

A CHOICE OF CLASSICS

The Brothers Karamazov Fyodor Dostoyevsky

A drama of parricide and intense family rivalry, *The Brothers Karamazov* is Dostoyevsky's acknowledged masterpiece. It tells the story of the murder of a depraved landowner and the ensuing investigation and trial.

Selections from the Carmina Burana
A verse translation by David Parlett

The famous songs from the *Carmina Burana* (made into an oratorio by Carl Orff) tell of lecherous monks and corrupt clerics, drinkers and gamblers, and the fleeting pleasures of youth.

Fear and Trembling Søren Kierkegaard

A profound meditation on the nature of faith and submission to God's will, which examines with startling originality the story of Abraham and Isaac.

Selected Prose Charles Lamb

Lamb's famous essays (under the strange pseudonym of Elia) on anything and everything have long been celebrated for their apparently innocent charm. This major new edition allows readers to discover the darker and more interesting aspects of Lamb.

The Picture of Dorian Gray Oscar Wilde

Wilde's superb and macabre novel, one of his supreme works, is reprinted here with a masterly Introduction and valuable Notes by Peter Ackroyd.

Frankenstein Mary Shelley

In recounting this chilling tragedy Mary Shelley demonstrates both the corruption of an innocent creature by an immoral society and the dangers of playing God with science.

READ MORE IN PENGUIN

A CHOICE OF CLASSICS

Evelina Frances Burney

Subtitled *The History of a Young Lady's Entrance into the World*, the novel records in letters its young heroine's encounters with society, both high and low, in London and at fashionable watering places. It is acutely observant of the social laws regarding power, authority and authorship, which the author herself partly had to subvert.

The Republic Plato

The best-known of Plato's dialogues, *The Republic* is also one of the supreme masterpieces of Western philosophy, whose influence cannot be overestimated.

Brigitta and Other Tales Adalbert Stifter

Each of these four stories is set in a recognizable world depicted with measured realism. But once the reader has learned to look beneath the calm, apparently seamless surface of the narrative, and, in Stifter's words, 'to see with the heart', strange tensions are revealed.

The Poems of Exile Ovid

Exiled from Rome for his scandalous erotic verse and a mysterious (probably political) misdemeanour, Ovid spent his declining years in the remote Black Sea port of Tunis, trying to use poetry to win a reprieve.

The Birth of Tragedy Friedrich Nietzsche

Dedicated to Richard Wagner, *The Birth of Tragedy* created a furore on its first publication in 1871; it has since become one of the seminal books of European culture.

Madame Bovary Gustave Flaubert

With *Madame Bovary* Flaubert established the realistic novel in France while his central character of Emma Bovary, the bored wife of a provincial doctor, remains one of the great creations of modern literature.

READ MORE IN PENGUIN

A CHOICE OF CLASSICS

Basho	**The Narrow Road to the Deep North**
	On Love and Barley
Cao Xueqin	**The Story of the Stone** also known as **The Dream of The Red Chamber** (in five volumes)
Confucius	**The Analects**
Khayyam	**The Ruba'iyat of Omar Khayyam**
Lao Tzu	**Tao Te Ching**
Li Po/Tu Fu	**Li Po and Tu Fu**
Sei Shonagon	**The Pillow Book of Sei Shonagon**
Wang Wei	**Poems**
Yuan Qu and Others	**The Songs of the South**

ANTHOLOGIES AND ANONYMOUS WORKS

The Bhagavad Gita
Buddhist Scriptures
The Dhammapada
Hindu Myths
The Koran
The Laws of Manu
New Songs from a Jade Terrace
The Rig Veda
Speaking of Siva
Tales from the Thousand and One Nights
The Upanishads